33 DEGREES

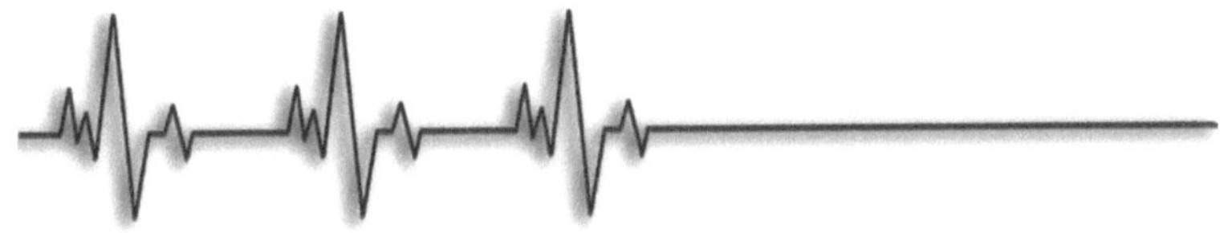

MICKY O'BRADY

Published by Snowy Wings Publishing
PO Box 1035, Turner, OR 97392

Paperback ISBN: 978-1-958051-18-4
eBook ISBN: 978-1-958051-17-7

Chapter One

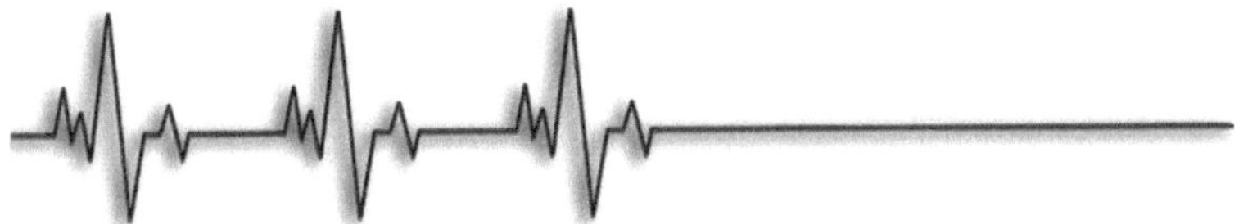

Frozen

Cold winter air bites into my skin like a thousand hungry mosquitos out for a quick lunch. How anything can be alive out here I really don't know.

Sniffing once, I wrap my arms tighter around my body, keeping my gloved hands balled to fists in an attempt to preserve as much body heat as I can. I've always loved this place in the summer, but I hate it during winter. I'm a California girl. I don't do cold long-term.

Maybe I should have stayed in Los Angeles, no matter what.

Maybe I should've put on my big girl panties and faced the music.

Maybe I shouldn't have run.

"It's not running, sweetie. You need time. Anybody would. And Grandpa needs your help."

Right, Mom.

I'm not buying her pretense. This isn't for Grampie, this is for me. A time-out. Psych-rehab.

Or as my dad said, a time to pull myself together.

I huff once. Yeah, sure. Like distance is going to heal the wound inside my soul, the one the knife tore in there with a single quick flick that changed my life forever.

I kick a little rock unlucky enough to wind up in front of my black boots. With a little plopping sound, it sinks into the river flowing by this little nature trail somewhere in the outskirts of Kampton, Oregon. *Northern* Oregon, to be specific. Even colder.

A couple of birds mind the interruption from my movement and flutter up, their croaking and complaining disrupting the near-total silence.

"Whatever," I mutter under my breath. Little puffy clouds form in front of my face. It's *that* cold. "You shut up. It's freezing, so thank me for keeping you moving."

As if they'd understood, the birds settle into a couple of trees down the trail but still keep a suspicious eye on me.

I remember coming here as a kid. I loved it. Staying with Grammie and Grampie was always the highlight of my summer, and back then, even the couple of times I came here in winter it was fun. Building snowmen, sledding downhill in the snow, warming up with gallons of hot cocoa later…

A small smile plays over my face. Hot chocolate. Those

were the good days. Before Grammie died five years ago, and before Grampie got so weak he needed more and more supervision—which for now is my job, at least until I get ordered back home. Until then, it's independent study and taking care of Grampie. That's the deal my parents struck.

"I want you out of here, Gwen. This needs to blow over."

Well, thank you, Dad. Maybe it'll blow over for you and the company, but it won't for me.

It never will.

In fifteen days, it will be the six-month anniversary of the day I was kidnapped.

Of the day Sarah died.

Of the day I don't remember.

No matter how hard I try to fill the gaping holes with images, all I get is—

Fear. White, hot, blinding fear so consuming it overtakes every fiber of my being, every cell, every thought, every breath. I don't see the blood, but I feel its warmth on my palms. Death. I will die here, no doubt about it. I can't breathe, I can't—

I suck in a sharp breath. No. Not going there. It'll only end up with me rocking in a corner somewhere, and the last thing I need is more meds.

I sigh and sit on the trunk of a broken tree with a view of the river and the tiny bridge crossing over it. The more of those flashbacks I get, the happier I should be I don't remember much. A little part of me wonders though what is worse, remembering everything or next to nothing.

I rest my chin on my hands, keeping my knees close together. I'll have to listen to the advice I gave the birds and keep moving, or I'm going to be a block of ice in no time. My ears are frozen already—I'm not quite used yet to having a short bob in the winter. The mop of brown locks always kept me warm, while the newer and shorter do… not really.

For a tiny moment, I allow myself to close my eyes, sit still, and listen to nature.

Serenity. Peace.

A few leftover leaves rustle in the wind, breaking the typical almost-buffered silence that hangs over a forest when the snow lies more than a couple of inches thick. The Kampton County River rumbles quietly, gurgling where it flows against the pillars of the bridge to my left. It really helps against the headaches, I gotta say.

Somewhere, a couple of birds fly up, complaining yet again, but I don't open my eyes. My mind takes me back to life when it was still normal, and when I wasn't either a victim or an enabler, or both. When my best friend was still alive.

The birds get more excited. A whole flock flies up, looking for a new place. Maybe there's a predator close by or something. I don't speak nature very well, I'm more of a city kid.

Without warning, something loud splashes into the water not far away from me.

I pop my eyes open barely in time to see a head full of short, black hair vanish under water together with a second splash.

"Whoa!" I'm up in no time. "Dude! Are you crazy? Shit!" That water is freezing! Who jumps in like that? Where are we, like, in a camp in Siberia?

My gaze stays glued to the spot the black hair vanished, a sick feeling in the pit of my stomach. Where is that guy? You fall in, you come right back up, unless…

… unless the freezing water made him lose consciousness.

Oh, crap.

I run closer to where he went in, but nothing. No bubbles, no body floating under the surface, and sure as heck nobody coming up for air anywhere downstream from below the bridge.

I groan.

Crap.

My coat is off before my decision is made.

Please no, please no. There can't be somebody drowning right in front of me, that's not happening.

Not another death on my watch. *Please.*

As quickly as I can without slipping and falling on the icy rocks that line the riverbed, I cross the distance to the spot where he went under.

I take a deep breath. This is going to suck.

Majorly.

One, two—

Three!

I throw myself forward into the river like I did a million times when I was a kid.

But that was summer, and now it's winter.

The freezing water is merciless. I'm soaked in less than a second, the icy pricks of water at its highest density penetrating my skin, numbing me in an instant. Holy shit, it's worse than freezing!

I scream out silently, the cold sucking all energy out of me like a vacuum.

Still no sign of the guy.

So, I do what I have to.

I take a deep breath and lower my head under water, bending my upper body by ninety degrees to make this a quick face-forward dive, using my hands to pull me down farther, feeling for something human below me. It's too murky here, I can't see much besides the occasional ray of light breaking through.

My heart's beating like crazy, maybe because it's trying to keep my body supplied with oxygen, or maybe because if I don't find this guy, he's going to drown.

How long has it been? Thirty seconds? Forty? People survive forty seconds, right?

It's been ten for me, and I can't feel my hands. Or my face.

Frantically, I push deeper and search. The river is about fifteen feet deep here. I know because that's the only reasons the adults allow the kids to jump off the bridge here in the summer. No risk for head injuries.

My lungs burn and scream for oxygen. Crap, I can't hold my breath any longer, I—

There.

Something cold, boney—an arm. I've got an arm! I grab it and pull, but nothing happens. I pull again. Nothing.

Shoot, how heavy can one person be? I give it one more yank, but the burning in my lungs demands attention first. I've gotta get air.

After the quickest turn-around of my life I shoot up and break through the surface, gasping for air, barely holding myself afloat with my clothing completely soaked and my muscles rigid from the cold.

"Help!" I croak, and again louder. "Help! Somebody is in here! Help!" Chances of people hearing me are slim. That's why I came here. Because in the winter, it's a great quiet spot.

Another lungful of air, another dive down. At least this time I know where he is.

There's the arm.

I pull.

Still nothing.

F-ing crap, what—

Okay, think, Gwen. *Think!*

Maybe he's trapped somewhere. Okay. Dive down deeper, come on, come on, stupid weak lead-legs, move!

I glide my hands down his arm to his chest, following a thick coat down to jeans, and legs to feet—feet tied together with rope.

What the—

Despite the freezing cold my heart skips a beat.

Rope?

I give it a pull, but it won't budge, it's tied to something seriously heavy. That's when I remember: *two* splashes. First the… *heavy thing*, then the person.

Something cramps inside my stomach. Is this an attempted suicide or… a murder?

Oh god, do I hope he's not dead already.

Neither of us has much more time, if the gagging in my throat is any indication.

For one teeny-tiny moment, I wonder what if… what if I

let go. Stopped trying to swim. Didn't rise to the surface. How long would it take for the cold to take over? How long until my vision dimmed, my heart slowed down and stop—

Screw yourself, Gwendolyn! Nobody else dies on my watch, including myself.

As fast as I can in this icy water, I pull out my pocketknife, Grampie's gift for my seventeenth birthday last August. *Every girl needs to have a pocketknife*, he said, and right he was.

Despite my frozen, stiff fingers, I get it flipped open without amputating a finger or dropping it. Like a crazy person I slice it against the rope. *Please cut through, please cut through!* I didn't come here to see somebody die, and I if I have to go up for air again… he will.

I'm *this* close to throwing up under water.

Like a maniac, I cut, not caring if I get skin. I can't see much, and who cares. As long as he survives, it'll heal.

The moment the rope comes apart, the angels start singing. Seriously.

Freed of its weight, the body begins to float up.

Thank whomever for small favors.

Pushing off the ground, I grab whatever I can of him and propel the both of us through the water until we break through, me gagging, coughing and spurting, him way too quiet.

I was too late.

I'm holding a dead body in my arms.

Again.

Then, suddenly: a gasp, a choke, and a violent cough that lets him slip in my grip, numb fingers and all. A hoarse laugh bursts through my lips.

"Y-you're a-alive. H-holy hell, y-you're alive!" The weight falling off my shoulders equals the one I just cut off the guy's legs.

He's alive!

As quickly as I can, I drag him through the water and toward the shore, kicking my legs like crazy now that the added weight of another person is dragging me down. I keep the guy's back pressed to my chest, my right arm wrapped around him in an improvised rescue hold, using only one hand to stroke.

The moment I feel uneven ground under my feet is the most wonderful in my life so far.

Pulling him out is more a scrambling and slipping until we're both out of the water, lying on our backs in the snow, the water still lapping at our feet, like an angry monster robbed of its prey.

The guy coughs with a wheeze when he's breathing in, but at least he's moving now.

It's the first time I get a look at him, and right away, familiarity tugs at my core with all its might. The boy's not much older than me, maybe a year or two, and I've seen him before.

Oh hell yeah, I've seen him before.

The cage I so carefully constructed around my soul rips open wide and releases an army of butterflies. No matter the dirt and debris in his hair, no matter the water ruining all styling, I'd always recognize that black hair and pale face with the longest lashes I've ever seen in a boy.

Always.

The boy coughs again and curls into a ball on his side.

"Hey." I suppress my shaking and extend a careful hand, only hesitating the slightest before I place it on his shoulder. "Are you o-okay? Sh-should I c-call an ambulance?"

That's when his eyes fly open, dark brown irises set into wide white orbs staring at me as if they'd seen a ghost. "Oh, shit." His voice is nothing more than a croak, and a pitiful one at that. His elbows give in under him twice as he tries to push himself up to sitting. No wonder, the poor thing is shaking from head to toe, shivers racking his body like crazy.

"Y-you got me out." His teeth chatter worse than mine. He looks miserable.

"Yeah, c-couldn't really let you drown, you know?" Lame joke. I rub my hands together. Geez, I'm frozen solid. "S-so, uh, that thing on your legs—"

"N-none of your concern." It's the first time he seems more alive than dead.

"Excuse me?"

"None of your concern. You sh-should've just left me, I had it all worked out, I—" He stops himself and works a hand through his hair, bringing it back wet and dirty, staring at it as if only now he realized what just happened.

Somewhere in the distance sirens howl, accompanied by honking horns.

Sirens. Loud. Lights, so many lights, all flashing blue-and-red.

"You're safe now." A blanket gets wrapped around my body. "Just one poke—there you go."

A needle burrows into my skin—

Geez—

I blink twice as he gets up, trembling and shivering so much he slips and barely catches himself before falling right down again. Guess I'm not the only one whose frozen body doesn't quite comply with its owner's wishes. He stuffs his fingers into the inside pocket of his jacket and pulls out a wet cell phone—which he throws to the ground and stomps on, digging his heel in to smash it into complete obliteration.

"Whoa! Shit! Your phone, you—" I'm up as quickly as I can in my popsicle-state, arms wrapped around my body. Why did I have to drop the coat that far away?

He drives his heel down onto his poor unsuspecting phone once again, then throws me a quick look.

"Leave."

That's all he says before he turns around and walks away, posture frozen stiff and rigid, not looking back once, a piece of rope dragging from his left foot behind him.

"But—" I reach out my right hand as if I wanted to stop him.

But what?

Why did he jump?

Why did he smash his cellphone?

He's crazy. That much is for sure.

Crazy and suicidal.

The sirens get louder, coming from around the corner close to the little bridge. Should somebody have heard my screams? Well, thanks for lending me a hand, buddy.

I should maybe wait and—

The boy's black hair is the last thing I see of him as he

vanishes behind a tree.

I sprint to my coat as fast as I can and pick it up.

"Wait!" I call after the boy, but when I look for him again, he is gone.

Chapter Two

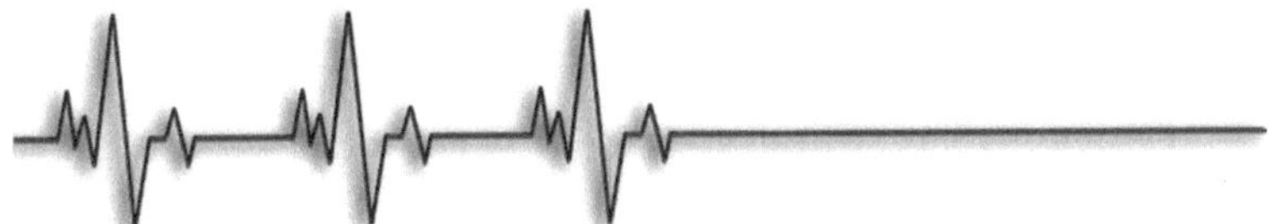

Thawing

My way back home is short but takes forever. Luckily for me, Grampie's house is close to the woods, a fact that gave me nightmares as a child, but is invaluable right now.

I'm frozen solid by the time I finally unlock the front door with shaking hands. The blissful warmth of central heating combined with a fireplace in Grampie's living room surrounds me, unfreezing me one pore at a time.

And boy, does unfreezing hurt.

"Gwen?" Grampie's voice comes from the living room. "Are you back?"

I slide out of my squeaking wet boots and drop my coat right where I stand. "B-back," I stutter-shout into the hallway, teeth still not quite unclenched yet.

"Would you mind helping me please?" Some shuffling sounds come with that question. That would be Grampie trying to get from the couch to the chair at the window.

I sigh. "Sure." Would've preferred taking a shower first and avoid questions, but life has taught me well. We don't always get what we want, said the heir to a multi-billion-dollar company.

I force my wet, frozen socks off my feet and tiptoe into the living room. The tile floor is usually too cold for me to walk on barefooted, but right now feels like I'm walking over coals.

The moment I open the door and Grampie sees me, his mouth drops open and the little bit of delicate balance he still has left wobbles. "Gwennie, what—" He looks me up and down, but there's no way I can look as bad as his shocked features imply. I mean, I've been wet before.

"Nothing, Grampie." I get a good grip on the forearm not holding a cane to support him. The moment my hands touch him he jerks.

"You're ice cold." I get a disapproving glance down his nose. "Don't tell me that bull, Gwendolyn. What happened?" He gives me another once-over and despite still feeling mainly frozen and somewhat shocked from what happened, a grin spreads over my face. Grampie is cool. Always was. His mind is still sharp as a tack, only his almost ninety-year-old body is slowly refusing to work, and it pisses him off. Majorly.

"The river happened, Grampie." I lead him toward the chair and help him settle down. "I'll tell you all about it when I'm showered and warmed up, okay?"

He looks at me suspiciously. "Don't you think for a moment I'll forget about it, young lady, because I won't. Now go and get yourself warmed up. I intend for you to be at my funeral, not me at yours." He points his cane at the door. Grampie is about the only one allowed to mention anything death-related when I'm around, and that would be because there are only two people in our family who wouldn't mind if death claimed them. One of them is Grampie.

The other is me.

Alas, today was not the day. "Aye, captain," I respond with a mock salute and walk off, leaving little wet footprints on the wonderfully warm tile floor on my way out.

Once I've showered and towel dried my choppy bob, I dress in all the layers of sweat-wear I can find. It'll take about a year until I stop shivering, maybe two, but to speed it up I make a tea for Grampie and myself before I go back to the living room.

Grampie sits in his favorite chair by the window, balancing a brown wooden box on his lap. It's beautiful with intricate ornaments carved into the lid. I think it used to be Grammie's. When I come in, Grampie gives the sturdy lock an annoyed flick with his fingers and sets the box aside onto the table next to the window. Careful not to spill, I set the tray down next to it before I fall into the other cushy chair. Best view in the house. The backyard is more part of the forest than a true backyard. Always loved it. It held a ginormous swing set for me when I was little.

I pour us some Earl Grey. Milk and sugar for Grampie, black for me. The moment I set the tea pot down, I remember

I should've brought my pills. Dang it. Funny how a little jump into freezing waters can preoccupy someone's mind. Guess the pills will have to wait until later. Oh, whatever. "So, something weird happened." I push the filled cup over to him.

Grampie raises an eyebrow. "You don't say?" He takes his mug with shaking fingers rivaling the guy's when he tried to fumble his cell out of his pocket.

Crazy.

Suicidal.

I sigh.

"Well… I was at the river, down where the bridge is, and… somebody went in."

That gets Grampie's attention. "Define 'went in'. Jumped, was pushed, or fell?" All three have happened at the bridge before, not all three during winter though. He takes a sip of his tea, eyes watching every twitch of my facial muscles.

"Good question. I don't know. I heard two splashes and saw him go under, so…" I shrug. "So, when he didn't come back up, I went in and got him out."

Grampie's face splits into a wide, open smile. "That's my girl." He pats my leg closest to him. "That summer as a lifeguard sure paid off, didn't it?"

I chuckle once. The summer I played lifeguard I only did it because Chuck Willemsen was going to be there too. Never gave me the time of the day that idiot, but at least I learned something.

I wrap my fingers around the blissfully warm cup of tea. "Kind of. It wasn't that freezing then though." Quite the opposite, and not just because Chuck was a good-lookin' guy.

"So, what was somebody doing at the river, or, more specifically, in it? I doubt somebody accidentally slid and went over the railing, Gwen. Suicide attempt? It wouldn't be the first on that bridge." He raises one eyebrow.

And that's where it gets complicated. Accident? No. Murder attempt, including concrete boots? Well, he didn't seem afraid someone was coming after him, only mad that I got him out.

Mad. And disappointed.

Yep. Suicide attempt. A shiver runs down my spine. Something in his eyes… it went beyond desperation. A sadness so profound it turns life into a burden.

It's a look I only know too well: I see it in the mirror. Every day.

And that's the reason I decide to protect him. "Don't know, Grampie. We didn't have time to talk." True dat.

Grampie's forehead scrunches up. "Huh." He harrumphs. "Do you know who it was?"

Of course, I do. I would recognize him anywhere, and anyhow. Wet. Dry. In the dark. Upside down. "Yeah." I don't know many kids in this town, after all I was only here for a couple of weeks once or twice a year, and even that was ages ago. It's just that this particular boy… He stuck out.

He and his twin brother, they both did.

With their close-to identical looks featuring black and always carefully tousled hair, a couple of freckles over their noses, and bodies shaped by sports even when they were still kids, Kai and Cole Harrison always stuck out.

And I noticed.

When I went to the river to swim, they were there.

When I went to the ice cream parlor, they were there.

When I went shopping, they were there.

I would go as far and say that the twins were the only kids in Kampton I kind of knew, despite never talking to them. Doesn't mean I hadn't made up a whole dream-world in my head—all about Kai.

It started harmless back in sixth grade when Kai bumped into me at the ice cream parlor. It was nothing, really, but in my mind, it became everything. In my mind, the mini-run-in took on a life of its own and played out completely different: we talked. We became friends. I wasn't the girl with the overprotective dad anymore, I was like everybody else. Free to go where I wanted to, free to do what came to mind. And the only thing that came to my mind was Kai.

From there on every visit to Kampton was about him. Would I see him? Where? What about him would provide fuel for more of my daydreams? And those dreams, they went the whole mile. They held hands with him. They kissed him. They even—

Yeah. I know. Pathetic.

Anyway. I focus back on Grampie. "It was one of the twins. K—"

"Kai then." Grampie nods. "If you think it was one of the twins, then it must have been Kai, because—"

Realization strikes and my eyes pop open wide. "Holy cow! Because Cole—" Because Cole got injured even worse in the accident that made the news for several days.

Grampie sighs. "Because Cole is still in a coma, and by

now, the doctors think he will never come out. Not after months in it already."

I bite my lower lip and stare down into the cup of tea I'm clinging to. The twins were in a car accident a month before… a month before Sarah and my kidnapping happened. I only know about it because Grampie is friends with the twin's grandma, Dora, and he told me as soon as he heard, mainly to hide a lecture in it and to keep me from ever drunk driving or riding with a drunken driver. Apparently, the twins were on their way to the next town over, Kai driving and Cole riding shotgun when they got hit head-on by a nineteen-year-old student home from college—a nineteen-year-old *drunk* student home from college.

The force of the impact killed the nineteen-year-old and injured Kai and Cole severely enough to spend several days in the intensive care unit. Kai eventually recovered, but Cole never woke up from his coma.

The pieces fall into place with a bang.

Holy shit.

That's why he tied himself to a block of concrete, because his brother will never wake up again. How guilty must he feel if he can't take it anymore? How alone? How desperate?

Desperate.

That's what he looked like when he stomped on his phone. Desperate.

Desperate for death?

A year ago, I would've declared him crazy. Now I know better.

Grampie pats my leg again. "Gwennie, this is just an old

man thinking, but are you sure he didn't try to kill himself? He's been through a lot." *As have you*, adds the look in his eyes.

Like a fish on dry land, I open and close my mouth, but before Grampie can pressure me for more, his iPad chimes. "Hm. Your father."

Oh, joy. Just what I needed.

Grampie swipes over the screen. "Rob."

"Hey, Dad." I can't see his face, but I know that tone of voice. Stressed, worried—about the company, of course. "Is Gwendolyn there?" Straight to the point, that's my dad.

Grampie rolls his eyes. "Thanks for asking how I'm doing, Rob. Fine, would be the answer. But yes, Gwendolyn is here, where else would she be?" He throws me a challenging glance and hands me the iPad.

Where else would I be—because Dad has set clear parameters for my time with Grampie, such as *stay within the city limits, or better, don't even leave the house. The press is everywhere.*

I take the pad. "Hey, Dad." My dad sits at his desk in his downtown Los Angeles office, his back to the wall with all the framed certificates and achievement plaques on it. The Wall of Fame.

"Honey. How are you doing?"

What a harmless question, yet it's loaded. "Fine, Dad."

Dad nods absentmindedly. "Good, good. Taking your meds? Your mom wanted me to ask." He adds a hesitant smile.

Right. My *mom* wanted to know. Rather my dad, before I ruin his life's work completely. "Yes."

Awkward silence hovers. We used to be good, my dad and

I. Never as good as me and my mom, but we used to be good. That all stopped on July 31st. Well, a couple of days later. When the press found out the details I don't remember.

My dad clears his throat. "Just… just thought of you and figured I'd call. I mean… you're doing well, right? Distance doing you good?"

Distance doing you good? As in: am I sane enough he can release me back into normality without damaging the company even more?

I bite down on the inside of my cheek until it bleeds.

"Gwen?"

"Uh-huh." Heard him.

"So… is it? The distance, I mean? You're taking it easy, and—"

Taking it easy? "No, Dad, I'm not taking it easy! Sarah died, Dad! Sarah is dead and I still can't even remember it! So no, I'm not *taking it easy*." The pad drops down onto my lap with the image of my dad facing the rustic wooden ceiling.

I can't remember a thing about my best friend's last moments.

I don't know how it happened.

I don't know who said what, what led to what, or how Sarah ended up dead.

I. Don't. Know.

And every day, it's killing me more.

Taking it easy.

Screw my dad. Seriously.

How can one *take it easy* after a kidnapping and a—

"Honey, no, that's not what I meant, I—"

Grampie takes the pad off my lap. "Rob? She's doing well. Give her some space, and stop calling her every day, for heaven's sake. Once she feels better, you'll be the first to know."

So he can call a press conference and start damage control. And to think that for a moment there it looked like my kidnapping was actually good for business.

"*MediSync Connect: Heir found alive! Recovered with company's own tools!*"

"*MSC: The development, the kidnapping, the rescue.*"

"*A life of dedication saved his daughter: MSC's CEO Rob O'Karran in an exclusive interview.*"

Yup. That was really good press. The stock market went crazy for those couple of days—well, until it tanked to previously unknown depths, when the yellow press began to spin its web of lies:

"*MSC-Murder: The Party-Girl's fault.*"

"*Need for Speed: Party drugs found in both MSC-girls.*"

"*MSC: CEO's daughter has done drugs before.*"

That's what I hated the most: The lies to boost the sales.

Granted, Mom protected me from most and I didn't read much, but those lies are the reason why I'm here now. Out of the public eye.

Also granted, those headlines hurt MSC. Badly.

But they hurt me even more.

They implied it wasn't a kidnapping. They implied we came willingly.

They implied it was me who went wild, got us drugs, and got Sarah into it.

Liars. Victim-shaming at its best.

We didn't do anything. That was all *him*.

Guess a drugged girl makes for an easier kidnapping victim.

Consider *that*, yellow press.

I chew on my cheek until it's raw. I still have headaches. Lots. After I woke up, I had a goose egg the size of a tennis ball on my head. He knocked me out. Just like Sarah. But at least I survived.

Yeah.

Lucky me.

My dad sighs through the speaker. "I just—"

"I know. Gwen is doing well, but you can't expect her to heal when all you do is bring everything up again, can you? So, trust in your old dad and your daughter. We're doing fine. Tell those shareholders of yours they can kiss my—"

"Dad!"

"Well, what? I know what you're up to, Rob, and I ain't liking it, so pull yourself together." Grampie growls. Funny, same words Dad used for me—only Grampie has my back.

"But anyway, give my best to Michelle, will ya?"

"Will do, Dad. Bye."

My dad hangs up and Grampie lays the iPad down next to his cup of tea. "He means well, Gwennie."

I pick up my cup and wrap my fingers around it. Any increase in temperature I can get to chase away the chill that has me. "Yeah, he means well." Mostly for his company.

I rub my warmed palm over my eyes. Everything feels so foggy these days, and I can't get rid of it. Like my mind truly had stepped off the grid and decided to do its own thing, consequences be damned.

"But anyway." Grampie takes a sip of his tea. "Back to that Harrison-boy. I meant what I said. I'm worried about him. I know Dora is."

Kai's Grandma. Since Grammie died, she's been in more and more of Grampie's stories, and I can't say I fault him. Grammie and him… they were wonderful together. He misses her. He needs company.

"Maybe you should check up on him. It can't be easy for him in a town small as this one with all the gossip."

I hear the implication of what he doesn't say. Just like it was for me in small, cozy Costa Azul, California.

State-wide news. TV. Newspaper. Web. Our pictures were everywhere, not that I had a single look at them after the initial yellow-press debacle. Still thanking my mom for keeping me sheltered.

I hide my face behind another sip of tea. "I'll check up on him tomorrow, Grampie. He seemed fine." Kind of. In the sense of being alive and not dead. "I'm sure it was just something stupid, like boys do all the time."

Grampie takes another slurping sip of tea himself, measuring my reaction carefully, that old hawk. "You check on him, Gwennie. From what Dora is telling me, Kai has barely spoken to anybody over the last months. He might need a new friend."

A new friend.

You should have left me, he said after I pulled him out.

I didn't.

Nobody dies on my watch.

Never again.

Chapter Three

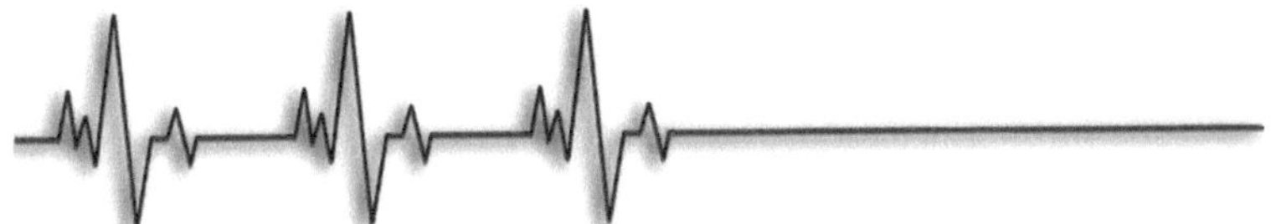

All Official

I know where the Harrison twins live. Well, where *Kai* lives. It's one of the houses on the way to the ice cream parlor not too far from Grammie's and Grampie's house, and the only one that has a blue door and blue-framed windows. In the summer, the Harrison's house looks like hippies live there, wildflowers blooming everywhere in the rather chaotic front yard, each window decorated with a planter overflowing with many more flowers.

Even now that everything is barren and snow-covered it hasn't lost its charm. Warm light shines through the windows into the oh-so-typical cloudiness for winter in Oregon. *Northern* Oregon.

A couple of steps before I'm up their porch, I pick up on classical music coming from the inside. It's some piece I used to know how to play on the piano, but probably have forgotten by now.

Happens when you don't practice for six months.

I step up to the door and straighten up before I push the button on the right of it. The bell's musical chime adds an odd dissonance to the string quartet streaming from their stereo. Five seconds later, quick steps come closer over what must be hardwood floors.

The door opens.

Kai.

That's the Kai I remember from my summers in Kampton. Tall. Handsome.

Alive.

His black hair is carefully styled into chaos, swiped a little bit into his face to give him more of an emo look, emphasizing his large, dark eyes. All those years I never got close enough to actually see much of the freckles over the back of his nose—if you don't count yesterday, that is.

I take a small step back so I don't have to crane my neck.

A good head taller than me, the Harrison twins were always kids I looked up to, literally and figuratively. They were so confident and exuberant, basically owning this town... At least until the accident.

I know how that feels.

Kai narrows his eyes as he tries to piece together where he's seen this weird girl in front of his door before. A little sting shoots through my chest that he doesn't recognize me from years of summers here, but then, why would he? Him and Cole, they're something special. I was just a visitor. And since my only distinguishing feature—my wavy, brown, butt-long hair—is gone, he has nothing to even remotely remember me by. I'm run-of-the-mill tall, not quite curvy, not quite skinny, and equipped with absolutely nothing worth mentioning. Well, besides freckles just like Kai's.

Finally, he tilts his head to the left. "You're the girl who pulled me out." His voice has lost the croaking it had yesterday, and instead is soft and deep, like a singer's voice. "I know you."

Unease twists my stomach into knots. News doesn't travel that far. He doesn't know about the kidnapping. Nobody here does, but for a moment the fear is there—the fear that he *knows-*knows. That he'll look at me like all the others, with this mix of pity and wariness, as if—

A sharp spike of pain, the image of a knife pressed against my throat, a hand so rough, that when I touch it—

Ow. A headache pierces my temple.

That—

That was new. A memory? I rarely have flashbacks this real, thanks to a PTSD'ed and scared-shitless mind. When I'm ready, my mind is going to bring it back to me, Mom says. But knowing that Sarah is dead, that she died because of who I am, can I ever be ready? I'm definitely not ready right here, right now. Hell of an inconvenient timing. I shudder, the memory of cold steel against my skin—

"Or maybe I'm wrong." Kai tilts his head. Then, a small

smile tugs on the corners of his lips. "But I don't think I am. I think I know you from—"

"Uhh, yes." I lift one shaking hand to my throat and massage it. I don't want to hear what he might've read about me. "Yes. No. I mean, yes, I'm the girl who pulled you out." Get a grip, Gwen. "But I don't think you know me, I'm not from here."

I'm suddenly not sure what else to say. Maybe I should've thought about that before I came over, but all the one-liners I had in mind seem so stupid now that I'm actually standing in front of Kai.

How are you? Hope you didn't catch a cold.

Yeah. Not so smooth.

Instead, I take off my glove and hold out my hand. "Gwen O'Karran."

Out of reflex he takes it, his warm palm fitting into my colder one even better than the glove. "O'Karran?" he repeats with the same question to it as everybody in this town would.

The O'Karran, it means. *The* O'Karran, as in Mayor O'Karran, as in Doug O'Karran, as in Rob O'Karran?

"Yup," I say, wishing I had a less famous last name. I don't mind Grampie's contribution to it, but Uncle Doug's and my dad's I do, mainly because they like rubbing their success into my face.

Five years my father's senior, uncle Doug had already built up a multi-billion-dollar enterprise before I was even old enough to understand what any of those words meant. Apparently, that's something one can do as a really good lawyer with a talent for business in solar energy and recyclable materials.

My dad, determined to at least reach his older brother's success if not surpass it, went into medical technology, designing tools like robots for assisting during surgeries, or anesthesia machines that kept patients alive during said surgeries. Being an O'Karran, he apparently also had the lucky gene and made the Forbes index of Billionaires the year I turned three, beating his brother's listing in the same magazine by a year.

Now Kampton, Oregon, has an O'Karran elementary school thanks to Grampie, a Doug O'Karran library thanks to Uncle Doug, and a Rob O'Karran football arena thanks to my dad.

All that's missing is a freakin' O'Karran graveyard.

I suppress a chuckle. That could be my contribution to the O'Karran legacy. Thirty percent of my dad's stocks are mine since I turned seventeen a few months ago, and after all, something will have to be done with that money. A graveyard would be more than fitting.

One day, Gwendolyn. One day.

Kai squeezes my hand once. "Kai Harrison."

I know, I want to say, but don't. Too stalker-ish.

He lets go of my hand and stuffs his into his pockets.

Neither of us says a word.

And it quickly becomes awkward.

I clear my throat. "Uhh, about yesterday—"

"It was nothing." Kai shrugs. "Forget about it. An experiment. Nothing worth mentioning."

My mouth drops open. "An experiment? Are you kidding

me?" What about throwing yourself into a river with a freakin' block of cement tied to your feet is an *experiment?*

He frowns and glides a hand through his hair. "Seriously, it's nothing. I, uhh, appreciate you checking in on me, but it's absolutely nothing to be worried about, and—"

"Kai," somebody calls from the inside of the house, "who is it? Get them inside, honey, all that freezing air is coming in."

He tries to hide it, but I see the widening of his eyes, the twitch of his jaw, and how his hand stops its movement for the tiniest second before he drops it to the doorknob.

"Got it, Mom," he calls over his shoulder, but instead of asking me in, he steps out onto the porch and closes the door behind him. A whiff of cookies accompanies him, as if I interrupted him baking.

"Look, I appreciate it, but… let's just forget about it, okay? You're not from here, and… When did you say you go back home?"

Wow.

When do I go back home? What a subtle way of asking when am I out of his hair. I take another step closer to him, bringing me a few inches from being chest to chest. I've got to crane my neck, but I don't care. Anger shoots through my veins, the same anger I have a harder and harder time to keep in check ever since the day six months ago that took my best friend along with my memory. "Listen, buddy. I don't know what stunt you pulled or what's up with that, but I know I jumped in to get you out of that freezing water. Obviously, you don't want your mom to know, and I get it, but—"

He harrumphs. "I don't care if my mom—"

I hold up my index finger. "*But,* at least don't try to get rid of me the minute after I saved your life!" I glare at him, hands on my hips, chin lifted up high out of necessity more than spunk. Kai's tall, dang it.

A muscle in his jaw twitches, and for the shortest of seconds I think I'm getting through to him, but no.

"Okay then." He shrugs again, this time without looking at me. "*Thank you* for saving me. And have a nice trip home."

And with that, he slides back through the gap in the door and closes it right into my face.

Chapter Four

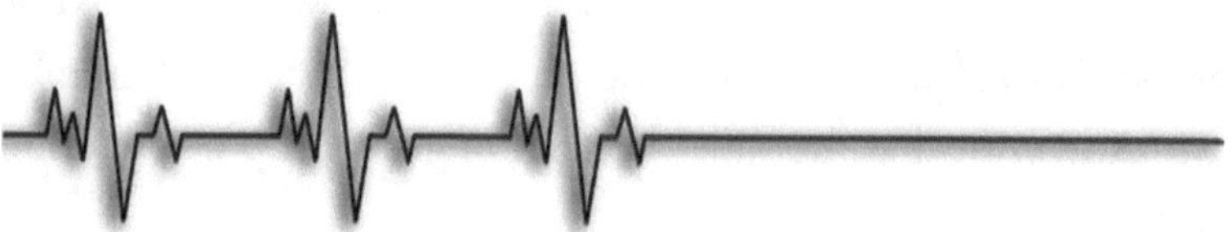

Power Surge

I'm mad.

I'm steaming, flipping, madly mad—so mad that I'm sure little smokey clouds puff out of my ears every couple of seconds.

Seriously? I pull him out and check in on him, and he basically tells me to leave? I mean, granted, it appears he didn't *want* to be pulled out, hence the weight tied to his feet, but he also didn't want his mom to know.

"You don't care if your mom knows, yeah right," I quote him under my breath. Of course he cares! He was terrified she'd find out. It was written all over his face!

Yeah, not exactly fun when people know your deepest fears.

She's a trouble-maker, that Gwendolyn. Of course, she's the one who got Sarah into this.

I shake my head to clear it. Screw them. I didn't. I don't do this crap anymore.

My foot gets stuck in a heap of snow. Gah! This is not my weather. At all.

I pull it out and shake off the white powder. Kai sure as hell doesn't want his mom to know, because I bet—

I stop dead.

Aww, dang.

"Because I bet he's going to try it again," I breathe, little puffy clouds coming from my mouth, courtesy of my warm breath versus the freezing sub-zero degrees.

I groan.

How could I not see it when I was there? Must be that fog clogging my brain for good. I should've confronted him right away, threatened to get him hospitalized or what else they do with suicidal teens. But no, I was too busy being annoyed by his lack of proper thankfulness.

"Grrr," I growl to myself as I do a one-eighty-turn. "Grr, grr, grrr." Well, yes, d'uh. Of course I'm going back. What am I supposed to do? That boy tried to kill himself yesterday and didn't tell anybody why he came home drenched and frozen solid, and now I'm thinking he wants to do it again. Can't really let him succeed.

Something heavy lies on top of me. Solid. Warm. Wet.

Can't breathe. Too heavy.

The stench of iron hangs in the air, making me nauseous.

Can't breathe.

Can't—

A sharp spike of headache shoots straight into my brain. Crap. Holy freakin' moly, today my memory is out to punish me. Nothing for months and then... then *this*. The meds should've— I took them, didn't I? Pretty sure.

I bend over and support my weight on my knees, gasping for air: A knife to my throat, blood, all-consuming fear. If that's what remembering is like, maybe I agree with my mom. Maybe I should give my brain all the time in the world. Like, forever.

I shake my head, although it doesn't do anything to clear the headache. Quite the opposite.

I deserve it.

Like an old woman, I straighten up one vertebra at a time. It's true, I deserve it. Sarah's dead. I'm not. Her pain dying was worse than mine having a single, three-second flashback.

Man up, Gwen.

I suck in a desperate big breath and stomp on through the knee-high snow. Back to matters at hand. I'm gonna give that Kai a piece of my mind about his plans. Plus, he's not going to kick me out again. Maybe when he opens the door, I'll put a foot in, the classic foot-in-the-door move, or I'll just barge through. I can force my way in, right? Pretend I'm cold?

My mind runs through scenario after scenario of how to get to Kai and how to start the conversation, and this time with hopefully a better result than the last. I went through enough counseling sessions myself. I should be able to at least throw some of the crap I had to listen to back at him.

Tell me about your feelings.

Let it all out, honey.

If I do it right, maybe he doesn't even need to be hospitalized. I can help him.

By the time I'm back at Kai's house, my feet are frozen into ice blocks inside my boots, courtesy of my pair of favorite warmer boots recovering from an impromptu swimming session the day before.

I ring the doorbell like a couple of minutes ago, but this time the music gets turned down and softer steps approach the door. Not Kai.

It's his mom.

I hope my face doesn't show any of the oh-shit-moment I'm just experiencing, because for this scenario I didn't come up with a pre-planned script.

"Hi there," Mrs. Harrison says, a friendly smile on her face. It's obvious where Kai has his freckles from. While his mom's hair is lighter and curlier, her skin is as fair as Kai's, decorated with the same freckles that give her a cute mischievous look, despite her age.

"Uhh, hi." I wave a quick greeting. "Uhh, I was wondering if Kai was in?"

Mrs. Harrison's smile falters. "Sorry, honey, he just left. I wish I could tell you where to, but these days I'm not privy to that kind of information anymore." Her face falls, a flicker of sadness mixed with anger crossing it, gone as fast as it came. "I guess I'll add it onto his tab. What's one more thing to be in trouble for, right?" She sighs, and I feel like the biggest idiot for coming here thinking I could fix Kai with my second-hand psych gibber gabber. I don't have a clue how much this family has been through—how much Kai has been through.

"Oh, okay." I look down on my shoes. What do I do next? I was expecting Kai here, not facing his mom. I should tell her he tried to drown himself yesterday, right? It's his mom, she needs to know.

On the other hand… Seems like he's in trouble already. Doesn't take a huge leap of faith to know said trouble is going to be even bigger when I drop that bit of news to his mom.

And what if I misinterpreted the situation? I'm the one who knows what it feels like to be judged without all the facts, which I kind of have been doing to him as well, if we're being honest. Also, I know what it feels like to be dragged into a maelstrom of well-meant chaos that makes everything worse, rather than better.

Pity surges, the kind that comes from experience: I don't want Kai to die, but I also don't want his life to go up in smoke even more than it already has.

Which is why I make an executive decision: I'll wait telling his mom. For now. I'm not *that* stupid. I find Kai, I talk to him, I get somewhere—we're good. None of these things happen— I'll tell his mom. My second-hand psych gibber gabber might not be treatment level, but maybe it's better than nothing. Better than the never-ending questions, the meds, the *everything* only worsening the wounds.

I lift and drop my shoulders and nod. "Okay. I'll… I'll try again later. Thank you." I give Kai's mom a short smile and turn around, walking down the steps.

"Oh, honey," Mrs. Harrison calls after me, "why don't you

come back tomorrow? He could really use some good company these days, you know?"

It sounds much sadder than it should.

I turn and give her a thumbs up. "I'll be back!" Either to keep an eye on him, or to tell on him. Choice is Kai's, so to speak.

The door closes behind me and the second after the music swells up again, streaming out all the way to the sidewalk. I swear and stop right behind their fence to blow a raspberry.

That plan worked out well. Go back, talk to Kai. Right. He must've left basically the second I was gone, which is impressive, since it takes me almost ten minutes to get bundled up enough to survive this weather.

Huh.

Somehow that thought makes my stomach go sour: I go and check up on him, and he leaves the minute after me, not telling his mom where he went.

My gaze drops to the ground.

My small, size eight footprints leave to the right and come back the same way… and to the left bigger, wider prints lead away from the Harrison's house.

It's not like I was Sherlock Holmes or something, but following tracks in the snow is neither hard nor an exclusive idea of mine.

So, I do it.

Speeding up my usual shuffle-walk through the snow, I stay hyper-focused on the trail on the ground,_learning the width of Kai's steps and subconsciously adjusting mine to it. He's nowhere to be seen in front of me, but this is a residential neighborhood with lots of bends in the street. He could easily be behind the next one.

Only he isn't—and neither is he behind the next, or the one thereafter.

By now, I'm jogging along his tracks, and I can't help it. I have this feeling that I need to catch up with him as quickly as possible. I'm probably crazy, because, come on, who tries to kill himself two days in a row, but at the same time, I can't get myself to drop that thought. All alarms are going off inside my head, ringing like crazy and forcing me to keep up my speed despite my heart hammering at an unhealthy rhythm already. Maybe I should've told his mom and let the real adults handle it. Hand off the responsibility, forget about him. I'm good at running from unpleasant thoughts, as I've learned over the last six months.

Which is why I'm not running away from Kai, but toward him. I ball my hands to fists. Maybe it's easier when it's somebody else's problem rather than my own, but this time I'm stronger.

Kai's tracks lead me out of the neighborhood and away from the town. Just like our house, theirs is close to the outskirts, which means mountains, forests and wide fields are within walking distance. This still counts as the city limit, right? It better, or my dad is going to throw a fit if he ever finds out.

As soon as I'm out in the open and crossing through a couple of trees surrounding Kampton like a belt, I see him: a lone figure stomping through the snow, maybe four hundred yards in front of me, heading right to the small, rather newly built railyard that always keeps a couple of train cars stored.

Okay, phew. At least he isn't trying to kill himself this time. Maybe he wanted to clear his head, and that's it.

I speed up my walk. "Kai!" I yell with no visible sign from him that he heard me.

Instead, he keeps walking toward the rail yard…

… and that's when I have my moment of clarity.

The power lines.

Oh no, please. He isn't going to get himself electrocuted. He is *not.*

"Shit." I curse and start to run, no—to sprint. "Kai!"

Still no reaction. By now, he's at the railyard and walking straight toward one of the train cars, one of the cigar-shaped ones that usually holds liquids, I think.

Horror spreads through me. This can't be real. He can't be climbing up there. My legs pump like I was running the Olympics, and my heart is about to give out, but mostly because I'm scared to death—scared to death Kai will kill himself in front of me, and that there's nothing I can do about it. That I'll be helpless as I was before, only more stupid, because this time I should have seen disaster coming.

He's two-thirds up the ladder attached to the side of the wagon, and I still have a freakin' fifty yards to go. "Kai, stop! Wait!" Wait with what—wait to kill yourself? *Stupid,* I curse at myself, but it's not as if my choice of words mattered.

Step by step, Kai climbs up the ladder, gaze glued to the power line above it. At the last rung he pauses for a second, then pulls himself up onto the roof of the railcar. He stays in a crouch, both hands firmly planted against the rusty metal underneath him.

After an eternity, I finally reach the car and slow down. "Kai." I keep my voice soft. I really don't want to scare him. "Don't."

The only sign he hears me is the tension in his shoulders.

I keep walking until my hands wrap around the ladder. "Kai. Come down. Please."

Still no response, if you don't count a choked, chopped breath.

I place my foot on the first rung. "I'm coming up."

Second rung.

"Stay down." His voice is so low, I have a hard time hearing him.

Still, I freeze on the spot. "Kai—"

"Go away," he says, head kept down, body still as stiff as the moment before.

But at least he isn't standing up and touching that transmission line.

I shake my head, although he can't see it. "Only if you come with me."

He huffs drily. "If you want to ride in the ambulance with me."

The ambulance? More like the hearse. I swallow dry. He *can't* be touching that power line.

"Please come down. We can talk about it—"

"I don't think so." There it is again, the desperation.

I creep another two steps up. I need to change my approach. "Come down. You might release an electric arc up there, and I really would like to not be caught by that." Electricity scares me. Just by being up there a spark could kill him.

Or me.

That thought brings goosebumps to run down my spine. Goosebumps I don't want to know the reason for. I close my eyes for one second, then shake my head to clear the funk. Not going to happen. Snap out of it.

Kai's shoulders heave up and down. "You've got a phone?"

"Uhh, yeah?" I stretch the words. Only two more steps and I'd be high enough to—

"Use it."

That's all the warning I get before he straightens his legs—and before I react without thinking. With a speed I didn't know I had in me, I shoot up the last part of the ladder and grab Kai from behind. Since he's still higher up than me with my feet firmly planted on the second-to-last rung, I only reach up to his waist, but it's enough.

In the bearhug of my life, I grab fabric, possibly some skin, and push myself and Kai backward off the rung with all the power I have.

Kai's arms fly forward, caught in the momentum of the unexpected change of direction, before gravity does its job and hurls both of us down toward the ground.

For a second, we're weightless.

Then we hit the frozen dirt with a force so brutal, it drives the air out of my lungs and pain through my entire spine, yet I won't let go. One arm is trapped under Kai's back, my body pressed into his, and I keep holding on to him as if my life depended on it—only it's his that does.

For a moment, I think he's going to fight me, to push me

away and climb back up, but after a small eternity, all tension leaves his body.

It takes me a good five seconds to realize the light shakes I feel are not an aftershock of the fall but are coming from Kai.

Kai is crying.

Without thinking, I reach my free arm over his body for his other shoulder and pull him in. As if we had done this a million times, his face finds the crook of my shoulder. He curls his body into mine, still shaking. Sobbing breaths leave puffy little clouds to rise up to the sky.

He snakes one arm around me, digging his fingers into my coat as if I could anchor him to life.

We're lying on the cold, hard ground, bodies hurting, and, for at least one of us, soul bleeding.

But we don't move.

Neither of us does.

Chapter Five

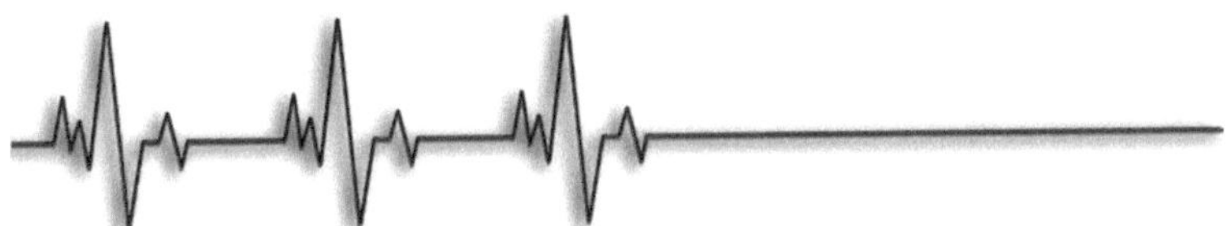

Trust

It might take us five minutes, five hours, or five days to get up, I wouldn't know. And it doesn't matter. The only thing that does is that over time Kai's sobbing becomes less desperate, the grip on my coat less forceful, and his breathing less wheezy.

Eventually, he sits up, the back of his hand wiping away tears. He works himself up to standing like an old man and extends a hand to me. "Come on."

He helps me up and we brush off our behinds from the snow. Thank whomever for water resistant clothing, or we'd both be soaked through by now.

Surprisingly, it's not as awkward as it could be. I mean, guy tries to kill himself—twice—and cries on strange girl's shoulder.

There's definitely potential for awkwardness, can't deny that. But maybe we've passed that point already, or maybe we had passed it already when I followed him here. Kai looks more relaxed now after I kept him from turning himself into human barbeque than he did back at his house.

He holds on to my hand and leads me over to one of the railroad cars. This one's a boxcar, a regular rectangular one with sliding doors, not a tank car.

I don't show it, but I'm ready to jump him at a moment's notice if he starts climbing again.

Instead, he searches for a lever, pulls it, and uses his whole bodyweight to move the screeching metal door a couple of feet. Once the door is open, he wordlessly lifts himself into the empty wagon. One hand pats the dirty wooden floor next to him, and I get the hint.

Not quite as quickly or gracefully as Kai, I pull myself up, having to jump quite a bit higher to make it in. Once up, I settle down next to him, my feet dangling just like his. We're so close, my thigh is pressed into his.

The proximity makes it burn.

Neither of us speaks as we look out into the cold. The snow comes down heavier now and collects on the tips of our shoes. The view of fields covered in undisturbed, pristine white together with the silence of falling snow might be the definition of peaceful. Definitely much more peaceful than trying to keep Kai from killing himself.

He sighs once, and it carries the weight of the world. "I was ready to do it, you know? I would have touched the power line." A hint of resignation colors his deep voice. And sadness. The same sadness hanging over him like a dark, rainy cloud.

I shoot a short glance at him, but Kai still stares straight ahead into the snowy landscape lying behind this tiny rail yard. It's probably easier for him to talk that way.

And we do need to talk. I can't let this go and carry on as if nothing happened. Like I said, I get somewhere with him, cool, I don't, I tell his mom.

I clear my throat. "So… why are you trying to kill yourself?" I could list a couple of potential reasons, guilt and loss being on top of the list and the ones I only know far too well, but I want to hear it from him. If we want to fix this, we need to start at that.

Acceptance is the first step, Gwendolyn.

Ugh. Thank you, shrink.

Kai blows a puff of air through his nose, rubbing his un-gloved hands together before stuffing them between his thighs. "You're going to call me crazy."

I give a sarcastic chuckle. He's talking to the gal who can't remember anything of the night that changed her life. The gal who went through about a million counseling sessions and made her shrink rich. The gal on a million different meds to help her cope and remember, none of them working. And mainly the gal who's learned one thing over the last months, namely that judgement is a weapon best not used. "I won't." For many reasons. "Look, you know I'm not even from here. You have nothing to lose. As you said, I'll be gone eventually, and with me your secrets, right?" I don't know any of his friends, and I won't be ruining his reputation, if that's what he's worried about—although honestly, after just trying to kill himself twice, a reputation shouldn't matter. "I want to help you, or I wouldn't be here."

I pause for a second. Proceed with caution, Gwen. "Why did you try to kill yourself?"

"I wasn't." This time the answer comes without missing a beat. "I was trying to stop my heart."

Huh? Twisting at the hip I face him. "Well, that'll usually get the job done."

Kai sighs another weight-of-the-world-sigh. "Yes. Kind of. But only temporarily. Hopefully. To avoid brain damage, you know?" He pulls his hands out from between his thighs and blows on them, warming them up. His gloves must still be up on the other wagon, taken off so the electricity wouldn't even have the negligible resistance of Thinsulate fabric to go through.

I realize I'm still staring at him. Shaking my head once does nothing to clear the confusion. "What are you trying to say?" Like, a timed suicide? On-off? Get a taste of it and be done? I don't think it works that way.

He blows into his hands again. "I don't know how much you know from your grandpa, but I have a brother, Cole." His body tenses up.

I decide to go with the truth. "I know. I spent a couple of summers here. I remember you guys." And that's not stalker-ish. Nu-uh.

Kai looks at me with an expression that holds something I can't quite interpret, and it carries a faint upwards tug of his lips. "I know. I said I recognized you. You're the summer girl, the one that only came during summer break, with the long curly hair and the frog on her bathing suit."

I blush. "The stupid frog? Dang, you saw that?"

For the first time since I met him for real Kai grins—a true, face-splitting grin with dimples in his cheeks and sparkles in his eyes.

And it's mesmerizing. Absolutely beautiful. It turns him into a completely different person than the one I pulled out the water, or off the wagon. "Sure did." He wiggles an eyebrow and my face is on fire.

"Oh, uhh, well, I was young." That awful bathing suit lasted exactly one season—that awful bathing suit I will surely find a picture of next time I go home, so that I can frame it. Just to remember it, of course.

He keeps his eyes glued to mine. "But you were the only girl our age who dared to jump off the bridge."

My jaw drops. Forcing myself to jump took quite the mental prep talk, but Kai did it. So did Cole. And I didn't like sitting it out. "You remember that?"

Kai stares at me for an eternal second, then clears his throat and drops his gaze down to his shoes. "Of course I do. Memorable occasion."

My face is so hot I must be glowing like a light bulb. I clear my throat. "Uhh, so, anyway… Cole?"

Yeah, that makes him lose his smile. Well done, Gwen.

"Cole," Kai starts again. "We were in an accident, about seven months ago. Some drunk driver rammed his truck into our Volvo. The driver died on impact. And so did we."

They *what?*

"You died?" I gasp. They *both died?* Holy shit, I didn't know that! I knew it was a bad accident, but I didn't know they both died! Death must've been on a roll last Summer.

"We died. When the medics came, neither of us had a heartbeat. Eventually, they got us back. We were both beaten up pretty badly, and Cole is still in a coma from it." At the end his voice breaks a little.

Without thinking, I take the hand closest to me and hold it. "From what I know I don't think it's your fault." I'm sure I'm not the first person to tell him that, and maybe that's exactly what Kai is thinking, because he stays quiet.

For a very long time.

I know how that feels as well.

Finally, after minutes that seem like forever, he closes his eyes. "That's not it," he whispers. "Not even close."

It's not? Survivor guilt maybe? His brother is down, and Kai himself isn't? I could write a book about that. "Okay. Tell me more." No judgement. It's exactly what my therapist does when she wants me to open up.

He clamps his hand down on mine, but I don't think he notices. "I haven't told anybody," he whispers so low, it barely carries over the ambient sounds.

"Told them what?"

He sucks in his lower lip and bites it, keeping his eyes closed tight. "The last things I remember are the lights of the truck and a deafening noise. No pain, no nothing—just noise, then *boom*, everything was gone. No, not gone, but… different. All colors were faded, washed out like in an old photograph. It was dead quiet, and while I was still there, in the car, I also wasn't. Something was there, calling me, calling Cole, and we followed it." He swallows heavily, and suddenly I feel the cold so much more than a moment before.

"It's so confusing to remember. Everything felt right in that moment. There were voices, people, but not like the people we know, more like... shadows. I... I only have little bits and pieces left and it all feels so far away, but..."

He opens his eyes and looks straight into mine, vulnerability shining from every pore.

"Something was there, Gwen. Something took Cole and led him away from me just before the shadows threw me back into reality and I woke up, pain everywhere, sirens around me." He swallows hard. "And as crazy as that might sound, I think that's why Cole is in a coma, trapped there."

Absentmindedly, he smooths his thumb over the back of my hand. "All I'm doing is trying to get him back."

Chapter Six

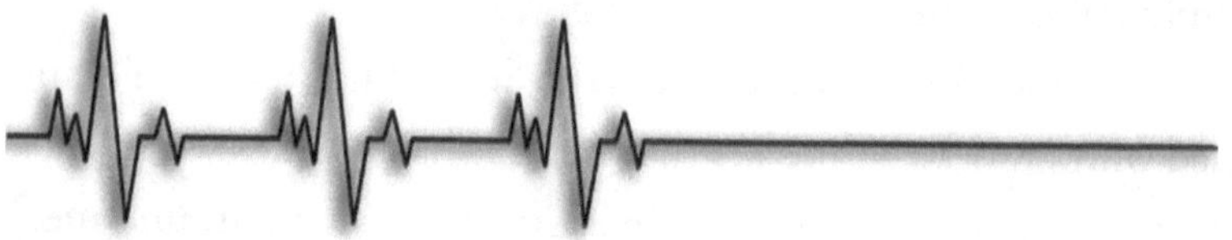

Theory

His gaze isn't wavering. Not at all.

He means it. He truly means it.

"You… want to get Cole back from… where, exactly?" I must have not gotten that right. He's suggesting there is… what, an afterlife?

"From the afterlife," Kai answers, completely calm.

"The afterlife." There is no afterlife. The dead are gone, and all we can do is keep them in our hearts and minds and make sure we don't lose ourselves to the grief. End quote. Thank you again, shrink.

He nods once. "See, from what I remember and from what I've come up with, there must be *something* after death. That wasn't a dream. I'm a fairly boring guy when it comes to imagination and dreams. No way my mind could have made that up. It was *real.* I was there, and so was Cole. Only the… *spirits*, or whatever, kicked me out and kept Cole back."

"But he isn't dead." A coma doesn't equal death. "And neither are you."

"But we both *were* dead, Gwen! They pulled us out of the car, both in traumatic cardiac arrest—believe me, I've read our reports. They poured IV fluid into us and did CPR, bringing both of our bodies back, only Cole's mind never woke up. It never made it out of the afterlife."

I use my second hand to cover his. When this became natural, I don't know. "So, you think Cole's… soul, spirit, essence, whatever, is trapped in the afterlife, while yours escaped?" My eyes are wide like saucers. "And that's why you said you were trying to get your heart to stop. You wanted to go back to that place—"

"—and get Cole. If I need to die to get there, then so be it."

That's not possible. It doesn't work this way.

You have to live with that, Gwen. You have to let it go and make the past a part of who you are now.

A small smile plays around Kai's lips as he shrugs. "Told you it sounds crazy. That's why I haven't told anybody."

Crazy? Yeah. A soul trapped in the afterlife. His story should make me check him for head injuries, yet I don't. Instead, I look at him, so completely serious, convinced that what he's saying is true.

Part of me envies him.

I bite my tongue, waiting for the pain to ground me before my eyes tear up.

Kai looks down at our entwined hands, his voice soft when he speaks. "I would've made it. Only I didn't expect you to show up and stop me from dying. Twice."

He would've made it. Quote-unquote *best* euphemism for suicide I've ever heard. "Sorry." I shrug. "Although, not really, you know?"

"I had it all figured out." He continues without taking his eyes off our hands. "The water was supposed to cool me down, so that I'd survive a couple of minutes dead. My brain should've tolerated it. And here at the train yard, I was hoping the electricity would short-circuit my heart and get me into V-fib, that should also be easy to shock back into rhythm." He chuckles drily. "As you can see, I did my research."

I work on a swallow. Not creepy at all. "Yeah, I can tell." Only, I think he's missing a couple of important points, like… "So, who would have pulled you out if not me?" If I hadn't been there, he would've drowned, just as planned.

"The Firefighter EMTs of course. I called 911 exactly two minutes before I jumped. With an approximate response time of five minutes that should have left me enough time under water to die, but not too much to not be brought back."

A shiver runs down my spine, and it has nothing to do with the cold, but everything with the clinical detachment he describes his planned suicide with. "Wow," I breathe, "just wow."

He shrugs again, this time a bit embarrassed. "That's why I stomped the phone. Bye-bye, iPhone and brand-new, cheap

SIM-card imported from Mexico. It's just that I called the ambulance from it so that they could track me and find me under water. And now that I was out—"

"You didn't want them to find you and ask what you were doing or keep you from doing it again."

"Correct. Hence the no-name attached SIM from Mexico."

That explains a lot, although it still doesn't make it better. If I've learned one thing over the last six months, it's that life is too short to waste it, no matter if you feel you deserve to live or not. I know it's complicated, but to a degree throwing your life away is disrespectful to the ones who didn't have a choice. Whom the choice was taken from. I've been working hard on internalizing that idea whenever I feel like giving up.

I swallow hard. "Kai... Come on, you can't pseudo-kill yourself. Seriously, you can't, no matter if you want it to be short-term or not. So much stuff can go wrong, and then you're dead-dead, and..." I really don't want to go there. "And that's not cool at all. Like, the power lines?" I nod toward the transmission lines high above us. "Those things burn like crazy and turn you into a crisp, rather than just stopping your heart."

His eyes widen, and that's all I need. "Obviously, you didn't do your research on that," I remark drily, causing him to chuckle. I like that sound, it's like a deep rumble somewhere inside his chest and so much better than the sadness that colors most of his words.

"No, not as much as I should have. I was kind of under pressure after you spoiled my first plan and showed up at my house the next day with my mom about to catch on."

Oops. So, had he succeeded today, it would indirectly have been my fault he went here.

I would have driven him to do this.

He would have been the second person I killed just by being me.

"It wasn't your fault, Gwennie." My mom's hand glides over my head. "Nobody could've known you were going to be targeted. Or that Sarah was in danger with you."

Something breaks inside of me, something fragile. I turn sideways, pulling the leg closest to him up and tuck it under my other thigh, knee resting on his upper leg. And despite Kai being Kai, one of the awesome Harrison twins, and despite us holding hands, my body and mind only peripherally notice all of this.

My main focus is on a way more important matter. "No more, Kai. No more. You have to promise me you won't try this again. Please. I know we're basically strangers, but we've also been through stuff that should mean something." I take a deep breath. "I promise you I won't tell anybody, but only if you promise me you won't attempt another pseudo-suicide."

My eyes bore into his darker ones until they're all I see.

He sweeps his thumb back and forth across the back of my hand, like it's no big deal he's touching me—but it is. It's shooting sparks straight from the back of my hand to the inside of my heart. His lips curve up in a faint, sad smile. "What would you do, Gwen? If you had a chance to see somebody you loved. To talk to them. To maybe get them back. I can't leave Cole behind, Gwen. I just can't."

I want to scream at him that he *can* and that he *must*, that he has no business in trying to kill himself on a whim, a theory—but I don't. His story tugs on a heart string cramping ever since the day that took Sarah from me.

I never got to tell her I'm sorry. I never got to apologize.

But I also never expected to, and I'm slowly starting to come to terms with that: to live with the fact that I can't remember exactly what happened. To live with the bits and pieces of a drugged memory haunting me for eternity. And most of all to live with the guilt that if I wasn't who I am, we wouldn't have gotten into this mess.

But… what if?

What if Kai was right, and there is an afterlife?

I could apologize.

I could see her one last time.

All the tiny hairs on my body rise to attention. It's crazy, but—

The movement of Kai's thumb develops magical powers on the back of my hand. Like, for reals. His touch unties a knot inside my soul and opens it up. I fall into those dark brown eyes in front of me until my head spins and the pain inside my heart goes numb.

Until I have an idea.

A crazy idea.

Maybe death is an invitation to start living.

Or maybe it's the one and only chance I have.

If we play it right… What if…?

I blink twice. "I… I might have an idea."

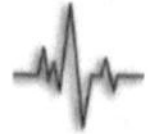

By the time we've made it back through the snow into our neighborhood it's pretty much dark outside.

Kai never let go of my hand.

Not when he helped me down from the train car.

Not when we walked back.

Not now, when we arrive at Grampie's two-story pseudo-villa with its two garages and another smaller building in the back, my father's workplace when in Kampton.

Kai stops me with a tug to my hand just before we walk into the cone of the streetlight close to our house.

"Hey." He traces down each of my gloved fingers with his free hand. "Thank you for not letting me get burned to a crisp," he says quietly. "That would have sucked." A small smile plays around his lips.

"Yeah." No doubt about it. "It totally would have." For so many reasons, like permanently dead Kai. Me causing his death.

I probably wouldn't have found out, but still. Knowing my luck, it might just end up on some kind of plus-minus-list of cosmic balance, screwing me up for the future.

And as it is, I'm already deep down the negative slope.

I look up at Kai. The harsh streetlight throws shadows across his face, giving him more of a five o'clock shadow from his stubble. I need him to keep his word. "Remember. You promised to not do anything stupid, Kai. No trying to kill yourself. You *promised*." He promised—because I promised I'd help him.

Now, I didn't give any specifics. I don't *have* any specifics. Yet. I have a vague idea, and it's still a long shot. Which is why I'd like a second opinion first, so to speak. But if there is a chance Kai is right—and he is convinced he is—don't I have to take it too? Don't I have to at least try to make amends and apologize to Sarah? To say good-bye, no matter if it was my fault or not?

I suck in my lower lip.

It was my fault. I was the one who wanted to go to that party. I was the one who dragged her along. You can't kidnap and kill somebody who isn't there.

Kai flashes a grin. "I promise. If I break it, you're allowed to kill me, okay?" He sticks out his tongue at me.

Laughing once, I use my free hand to punch him into the shoulder. "I'll pick you up tomorrow then. You better be there."

"I will," he says. "Thank you." He pulls me into a hug so tight his breath warms the side of my neck. "Thank you," he whispers again. He clings to me like to a lifeline, and I know he's going to be safe.

For now.

Chapter Seven

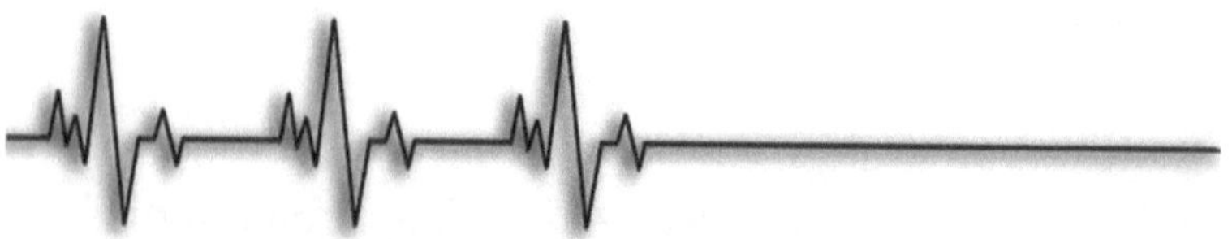

Clairvoyance

"Hey, Grampie? Say, whatever happened to Aunt Calista?" I place the spoon in his right hand and push the plate closer to him. Minimizes spilling. We've learned the hard way.

Grampie frowns at his plate, although I doubt it's because of my choice of dinner. No, I'm sure it's because of his very deeply rooted dislike for his baby sister.

"That old hag?" He stabs his spoon into the shepherd's Pie as if it were a knife. Note to self: definitely no more knives for Grampie. He huffs. "Probably the same as always, lying to people for money."

I barely suppress an eye roll. "I doubt she'd phrase it that way." I sit across from Grampie and take a sip of water together with my pills. "She's a medium, not a crook."

"Same difference," he grumps.

Calista is the black sheep of the O'Karran clan, the only one who didn't make it to fame and fortune, and the only one none of them like to be associated with. I can totally understand why Grampie has trouble with his sister though. If there ever were siblings more different than Grampie and Calista, I haven't met them yet. Straight arrow and former mayor versus former wild child, then medium. Laws and regulations versus spirits and tarot cards.

I take a bite of my shepherd's pie and chew carefully. Somewhere in there I hid several whole cloves of garlic, Grampie's favorite. "So, she's still in that pink house down the street from city hall?" I only saw her a couple of times in my life, and most of those times without Grammie and Grampie knowing about it, and that was at her home, not her... uhh, office.

Grampie throws a suspicious glance at me over the rim of his plate. "Yes. And why for heaven's sake would you ask?"

Now here comes the truth. Kind of. "Because I think Kai might benefit from seeing her." And me too.

If Aunt Calista knows what she's talking about, at least.

A puffy pink cloud of hope rises inside my chest, but I force it back down. Everything about my idea screams crazy. Oh, and risky. I'd be an idiot clinging to hope.

That gets Grampie's attention. "So, you spoke to him?" Grampie leans back into his chair.

I spoke to him and pulled him off a train car.

"Yup."

"Okay then." He nods. "Good plan."

I cock my head. "Good plan? And that's coming from you?" Anything that involves his sister is a nail in Grampie's proverbial coffin.

Now it's his turn to shrug. "Good plan, yes. See, I read the newspaper. It must've been a slow news day, because it said there was a call to 911 from a Mexican phone number by a man about to throw himself off the River bridge on the day you pulled Kai out of the water. Only they searched for two hours, never found anybody and couldn't trace the call, chalking it up to a prank. Ergo, something tells me there is more to the story than meets the eye." He watches my reaction like a hawk.

"Dang you, Grampie." I whistle through my teeth. "Nicely done, Sherlock."

"So, what is it that you're not telling me?"

I wouldn't even know where to start.

What happened between Kai and me today… it's personal. I promised I'd keep his secret—making it mine in the process.

I can't very well tell Grampie about my true reason to visit Calista though. What am I supposed to say? Oh, just checking if there really is an afterlife, because you know, reasons?

Yeah… nope. I'd be on twice the meds I'm on already in less time than it takes to say 'but', and rightfully so. My idea is a crazy one, but then, I am my father's daughter. Technology and medicine run in my blood, no matter if I want that or not.

So, I play it simple, meaning, I give him a reply that sounds believable. "I think he might benefit from somebody telling him Cole is fine and not mad at him. If I can get Calista to tell him all is well, he might get closure." *Closure.* The buzz-word of the season.

Grampie's freakin' light grey eyes stay on me, waiting for me to give myself away, like I used to when I was younger and insisted I didn't take the candy, while I totally did. Three seconds of Grampie's hard stare and I usually spilled the beans quicker than a piñata its candy filling.

"Closure," he says. "For him… or for you?"

A boy, tousled blond hair, maybe nineteen, twenty. A cute smile, with dimples. A scar under his eye, like it was busted open once. My stomach tightens with a little tingling and the slightest bit of butterflies as he dances across the floor toward me.

A pain like lightning slices through my head. I wince once. Ouch. That… that felt weird. Off. Not right at all. I don't know that boy. Or wait, where was that? Dang, could that have been the party—

"Gwen?"

I swallow hard. "M-mainly for him." I shake off the image of the blond boy. Nothing but my desperate brain trying to fill the voids.

"Okay." Grampie nods. "Go and see that old witch. But be careful. You've had your share of worries over the last year, Gwen." He pauses. "And we don't want to mess with things we don't understand."

And just like that, his focus is back on his shepherd's pie, as if this last sentence wasn't the most mind-blowing thing Grampie ever said to me.

We don't want to mess with things we don't understand.
What things?
I push my plate away.
My appetite is gone.

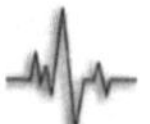

"Good morning." Kai opens the door, and what a difference. Compared to yesterday, he's *vibrant* today. Dressed in tight blue jeans and a black, not-quite-buttoned-to-the-top dress shirt, he rocks the cool dude look. Especially with his black emo-hair swept across his forehead.

Best of all though is the look he gives me.

Like he was waiting for me.

Like he was happy to see me.

Something stirs deep down inside my chest, and before I know it, I'm grinning back at him like an idiot. Dammit, something about that guy makes me happy, despite the sad circumstances of our introduction. Well, no: happy circumstances. He survived, after all.

Speaking of. "Still alive, I can see." I nod at his very well-built frame.

The grin widens. "Had something to look forward to." He winks at me, and I think I'm flying. Summer dreams coming true right here and now.

"So, I'm curious to meet your aunt." Kai grabs his black coat from a hook close to the door. He slides into it and ignores the scarf and hat over on the next hook, like it wasn't windy or snowing at all. "You trust her? I mean, that she truly is a psychic, medium, or whatever you call it?" He locks the door behind him and leads the way. "And don't get me wrong, it's just that until seven months ago, I would've dismissed it all as bull. Afterlife, psychics, the whole thing."

Yeah, I get it. I'm a skeptic anyway, I had to hogtie the part of me about to enroll in medical school in order to even *entertain* the idea of consulting a psychic to get information about life after death. Again, for emphasis: *a psychic. Life after death.* "No worries. Same here before I met you, but…" I shrug. "Calista has a pretty good reputation around mediums. I Yelp-ed her."

Kai bursts out laughing. "You checked your aunt's street cred online? Nice!" He buries his hands deep inside his pockets instead of taking my hand, like yesterday.

I frown. "Well, yeah. You wanna check your sources, right?" I'm not going to lead us to a crook. We do this right, or we don't do it at all. "But still, I can't guarantee anything. From what my grandfather says, she's off her rocker."

Kai chuckles. "We'll see. I didn't even know our town's very own psychic was your aunt."

"She's not the most liked member of my family. They made her take 'O'Karran' off the store front."

Kai grins again, with full-blown dimples. Gosh, it would've been such a pity had he killed himself.

"Well, given their standards, I'm surprised they don't have you in Harvard yet, on track to become your dad's VP or something."

My heart plummets as I trip over my feet, barely catching

my stumble. Lightning fast, Kai shoots out his hand and grabs me by the elbow. "Whoopsie. Slippery when wet."

It takes all the willpower I have to smile back at him.

"Harvard, Gwendolyn." My dad's finger hammers onto the admission papers. "You will go, like we—"

"Rob." Mom's hand on Dad's forearm calms the hammering. "It's been only a couple of weeks. And we don't even know if—"

Dad tears his arm out from under hers. "Irrelevant. A minor inconvenience. Gwendolyn will enroll. Period."

Well, obviously I didn't, and at one point Dad let it go.

Three years of pre-med nighttime college classes, most likely all for naught. Granted, it was Dad's dream, not mine, but he set me on track for success all these years ago, and as much as I wanted to make him proud I… I couldn't do it.

After July 31st, school wasn't so important anymore.

Living wasn't so important anymore either.

Maybe that's why I feel so drawn to Kai. Two lives, screwed up by death.

After a short pause, Kai bumps his shoulder into mine. "So… you think it's legit? Afterlife?" He shoots me a careful glance.

"Well, I'm thinking your experience is worth checking out and cross referencing. Enter my aunt. We'll take it from there." We'll see if there is a chance we could get Cole back. Or if I could see Sarah. Apologize.

"You want to try a séance?" He gives me a careful look from under his lashes.

"Actually, no."

"No?"

"Nope. Thought about it, but from what I read, it can be faked." D'uh, of course it can. Crystal ball, incense, some mumbo-jumbo, and there we go. "If she offers a séance, her credibility is gone. If she seems reasonable—for a medium I mean—I'd like to hear what she has to say about the afterlife." Given the fact that she claims to have been there. Call it scientific curiosity, logical reasoning, careful research, but I need something to cling to besides Kai's story if I'm even considering to set my plan into action.

"And then?" His voice is soft. Careful. Because the real question he's asking is how he can get there, into the afterlife.

And like I said, I have an idea.

I've got my resources and I've got a plan. A good one. I think. Crazy, but good. One I'll only implement once I'm certain Kai's afterlife is not what it very well could be: the last twitches of a brain deprived of oxygen, some kind of Mother Nature's way to soften the impending death.

I sigh. "Told you. I might have an idea." All I need now is the verification that this is viable. *Viable.* Ironic.

Kai nods. "Okay."

Ta-daaah! Knighted. Right there. Kai trusts me.

He trusts me with his story, and... with his life. With his brother's life.

No pressure at all.

Luckily for me, he drops the topic and we walk silently next to each other until we reach Calista's Psychic Studio, or, the only pink house in this whole county.

I rest my hand on the doorknob. Here we go. Twisting it to the left, I enter, the warmth and smell of incense assaulting me with my first step into Aunt Calista's reception area.

Huh, look at that. Maybe she's an O'Karran all right, despite the odd choice for a profession. Not that I've ever been to a psychic before, but I didn't expect a storefront with crystal balls, tarot cards, voodoo dolls, and dozens of books all neatly stacked behind a modern register.

Our arrival is announced by a bell mounted above the door. Not a second after it falls shut, the beaded curtain separating the storefront from the back of her office jingles as Aunt Calista walks through. She's dressed the part of a psychic in wide, flowing robes in all the colors of the rainbow.

"Good morning, how can I—" Her gaze falls on me, the gears inside her head working until they click in place, visibly so. Her face splits into a big smile. "Gwendolyn O'Karran!" She opens her arms wide and crushes me into a hug that doesn't leave much room to breathe.

"My, it's been years! You've grown so much!" Aunt Calista lets me catch a breath of air but keeps me close, both hands resting on my shoulders while she gives me the once-over. "And I love your hair! Used to have it that short when I was young—granted, the sixties were all about pixie cuts, but—"

That's the exact moment she sees Kai. It's obvious by the way her eyes widen and the pupils in her light grey eyes dilate. Her and Grampie don't share much in terms of looks, but the eyes are the same.

I clear my throat. "Uh, hi Auntie, I— I brought m... Kai." My cheeks heat up. Gosh, embarrassing.

I brought Kai.

Well, duh, obviously, although that's not why I'm blushing. It's because the embarrassing part is that I wanted to label him.

And I have no right to.

Dang it.

Aunt Calista lets go of me and pulls Kai down into an equally chest-crushing hug. Gotta say though, he handles himself well. Only a slightly amused and confused expression drifts across his face as he hugs her back.

It makes him pretty darn charming, by the way.

"So, uh, Calista, I know I haven't been by for a while, but—"

She waves a hand, keeping the other one on Kai's forearm like for support. She's in her eighties, after all. Why she's still working, I have no clue. "Never worry, child. I know how your gramps is, and I know the last months haven't been easy for you." She closes her eyes. "And the worst…" She frowns once. "Ah, well, anyway. I know why you're here, so—"

"You do?" I'm sorry if I sound so surprised, but to be honest, I'm still a bit wary of her skills. Well, of the whole afterlife story, to be honest. I believe Kai believes what he saw is real. And even if the afterlife itself is not real, his sensation of having been there is. I'm willing to explore that story some more and give it a chance, but that doesn't mean I'm not a skeptic at heart.

A desperate skeptic, but still a skeptic.

Calista throws an irritated glance at me. "Of course I do. That's my job, sweetie. Anyway, let's go and sit, these old bones aren't quite so willing to work for me anymore." She leads the way through the same beaded curtain as when she entered the room but ignores the velvet-covered room to the right, instead leading us down a short hallway into a comfortable little office with a desk on one side, and a couch, coffee table and thick leather chair on the other.

Kai raises an eyebrow, and so do I. This here looks completely normal. No psychic stuff, no nothing.

Calista points to the couch. "Have a seat. I'll get you some water. The news I have for you needs *something*, and you're too young for what I'd usually have in mind."

Kai loses most of his color. I cringe inwardly. Well, I was the one bringing up Calista as a possible source of knowledge… gotta take 'em as they come.

Calista gets the water before she lets herself fall into the heavy leather chair. Across from her, Kai and I take a seat on the couch, and because it's an older model, just like its owner, it has seen better days. Despite sitting a polite distance apart, we slide together when the middle part of the couch's seat gives.

My aunt smiles to herself. "Good," she murmurs under her breath. I think.

Kai folds his hands in his lap. "So, Ms. O'Karran—"

"Call me Calista, sweetheart." The smile Kai gets is part grandmotherly, part sad, and it makes me a tad nervous, I gotta say. Why again did I think asking a medium about the afterlife was a good idea?

"Okay, thank you, Calista." Kai tries out the new name. "Well, here's my problem. My brother—"

My aunt sighs. "I know, honey. I know."

He tilts his head sideways. "You do?"

Another sigh, this time deeper. "I do. The real question though is, how much do *you* want to know?"

And just like this the atmosphere has changed, shifted from careful anticipation to dreaded suspense.

"Everything," Kai says without a hint of hesitation. "Everything."

Something passes between my aunt and Kai, something that makes him swallow hard.

I lay out my trap. "Maybe with the help of a séance—"

"I don't offer traditional séances."

Advantage Calista. I cock my head. "You don't?"

"I don't. It's nonsense. Fake."

Kai and I exchange a look. 40-Love Calista. She passed my credibility-test. "What do you do then?"

She sighs. "I take the customer's information, connect to the Realm, and then look for information on their loved ones."

Oo-kay. I take it back. The bonus points I gave Calista a mere twenty seconds ago just blew up in smoke. "You connect to the Realm."

"Yes."

"Just like that." I snap my fingers, and Calista rolls her eyes with a heavy sigh.

"No, Gwendolyn. Not *just like that*. Don't be like your gramps. Keep an open mind." Calista slides her palms over her flowing dress, evening out the wrinkles. With the sun shining in from the window on our left, her white long hair pulled back into a simple ponytail glows bright white, like a beacon in the dark. "You know, most people take me for a crazy psychic, or a crook, as if I was cheating people out of their money for the hope of a last word from or to their loved ones—your grandpa included." She gives me a chastising look and folds her hands in her lap, like Kai. "You need to understand where I'm coming from. When I was very young, I was also very stupid. I thought I was invincible, living life to the fullest, which included drugs. Ah, you know, those were the times. Of course, it came as it must and I overdosed. My brother—your gramps—found me and somehow brought me back, but the time I was dead… it changed me."

Kai and I exchange another, slightly less skeptical glance, as Calista takes a sip of her water. "It sounds cliché, I'm well aware of that. Truth is that I expected absolutely nothing from life after death. I'm not religious, never was. To me, being dead equaled being gone, and that was it. But when I died, there was so much more. Dying showed me what lies beyond. It connected me to the Realm."

The Realm. There's that word again.

"The Realm?" Kai asks. Like pulled up by a string he sits up straighter and leans forward. "The afterlife?"

Aunt Calista nods. "Yes. The spirits prefer calling it the Realm, so that's what I'm calling it. Well, as you can imagine, everybody including myself initially attributed my experience to the drugs, or to a brain deprived of oxygen."

Look at that. Exactly my thinking.

Calista shrugs. "The more I talked about it, the more people distanced themselves from me. Even I couldn't come to terms with what I'd seen. It seemed so real, and at the same time completely different from all my drug-induced highs. The experience didn't let me go though. It haunted me, and I felt… a *pull* to go back. Like part of me was still there, keeping the connection, you know? I remember, the first time I reconnected with the Realm… one night I was meditating when the world around me slowed down." Her eyes focus on something behind us only she can see. "The colors went first. It wasn't quite black and white, but everything was washed out, like—"

"In an old photograph," Kai whispers, gaze glued to Calista's lips.

"And then the sound went, and the voices started."

"Yes," Kai breathes.

Holy shit.

I turn my head from Kai to Calista and back. They had the same experience—that can't be coincidence. Then… I mean, does it mean it's true? There's an afterlife?

A spike of anticipation and hope shoots through me and takes root inside my heart. Maybe Sarah isn't lost to me after all. Not completely, at least.

"So, you did see it?" Calista leans her head to the side, the hint of a proud smile on her lips.

"I did." The pulse in Kai's neck beats at an unhealthy pace. "But I made it out, and Cole… Cole didn't." He pushes his chin up high. "So, how do you do what you do, if it's no séance?"

"No traditional séance, correct. Like I said, I connect to the Realm. As crazy as it sounds, but I have friends there who can find or get information about your loved ones and pass your message on to them. It takes time, sometimes days, before I'm successful. Sometimes we can't find them at all or they don't want to be found, which happens in about thirty percent of cases."

Kai swallows. "You're a messenger service to the afterlife."

Calista chuckles once. "You could say so, yes."

For a moment, Kai is silent. Then, he shakes his head and looks my aunt straight in the eye. "That's not enough. I want to get him back. I need to enter the Realm and bring him back."

There it is, his heart laid open in front of my aunt.

Aunt Calista's smile turns sad. "The only way to the afterlife is death, sweetheart. And even that isn't a guarantee. There are multiple layers in the Realm. Older souls buried under layers and layers of younger souls. It's not easy to find someone if they don't want to be found. Or if they don't expect you." A silent sigh. "There are also rules. The dead are dead, and that cannot be changed. They cannot be resurrected."

"But Cole isn't dead." Kai's fingers ball into a fist, knuckles turning white.

"No, he isn't. But it doesn't make a difference at this point. His spirit has been in the Realm for too long, Kai. His soul can't leave the afterlife anymore, even if he wanted to. I'm afraid there's nothing you can do. Cole is lost to you until the day you die."

Chapter Eight

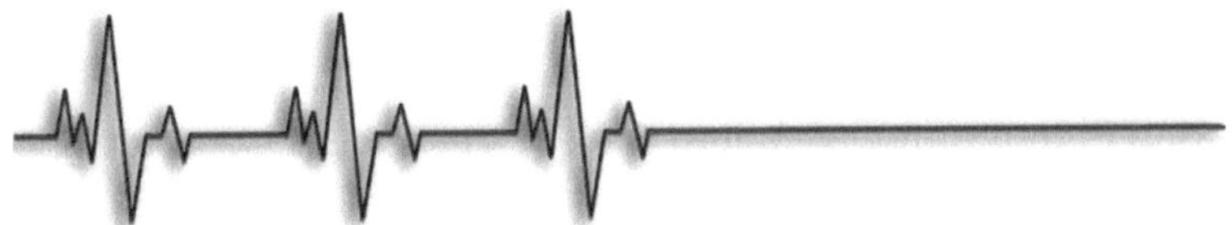

Maybe Too Crazy

I let go of the curtain in Aunt Calista's backroom office.

Kai's been out in the backyard for over fifteen minutes now, his back to the house, hands stuffed into his pockets, and so much tension in his shoulders I can very well imagine what he must feel like. The guilt as heavy as on day one. Heart ripped apart once more.

Calista did that when she took away his hope.

I let go of the curtain and turn toward my aunt. "Was that really necessary? You could've at least tried to soften the blow."

Calista folds her hands in her lap, her light eyes on me ever since I got up to check on Kai. "Sometimes the band-aid has to be ripped off, Gwen. I'm not like the other mediums. I don't prey on people's hopes with fake promises and made-up stories. Kai wants to get his brother back, and it's not going to happen."

I throw my hands in the air. "Why not? Seriously! People wake up from a coma all the—"

"Intent alone doesn't get you out of the Realm once you've been in for a certain period of time." She shakes her head. "It works for a couple of minutes to hours after you arrive there, maybe after days. But not after weeks. Months." She shakes her head. "Honey, at that point, only a soul can buy another one out."

My jaw drops to the floor. "Only a soul— What the hell? An eye for an eye? A soul for a soul? That's crazy—"

"It's the law of nature. Of balance. Only an exchange of souls could—*could*—free Cole. But it's complicated. That soul would need to enter with the intent of freeing Cole's, and it would only work *if* his body was still receptive and *if* he wanted to leave. If not, the sacrifice would be for naught."

My aunt is completely calm with her explanation. Discussing the weather would be the same to her. Me, I'm disappointed. Mostly at myself. What did I think this visit would bring? Some kind of blessing? A user's guide of how to visit the afterlife, or how to bring back a comatose soul? Like, yeah, sure, it's all totally legit, entering the afterlife is a breeze, go right ahead. *Saying Goodbye To Your Dead Friend, For Dummies.*

I let my head hang. "Law of nature, got it." I'm not sure what to believe anymore. Two days ago I would've declared myself crazy for entertaining the idea of an afterlife, even more so for considering crossing over. But now there's a lot I can get behind. Calista's story lines up with Kai's. There's *something* after death, alright. If I am to believe Calista, it's a Realm with its own rules.

But if I wanted her thumbs up for entering said Realm, I'm not getting it.

What did I expect?

I huff to myself. There goes my plan. Won't risk Kai's life if there's nothing to gain for him from the risk. Mine… whatever. But I can't very well do it alone.

A pang of guilt shoots through me, a loss of something I didn't have any right to in the first place. Nobody gets to talk to the dead, why should it be different for me and Sarah? What a stupid, idiotic idea to believe and let my hopes take root.

Calista works herself out of her chair with quite the effort. She lays one hand on my shoulder. "Gwen, I know it's a difficult concept, but it doesn't mean it isn't true." She pauses. "That's how I found out before anybody knew. That's why I called your gramps. Because I knew. About Sarah and—"

An iron fist buries itself into my intestines, twists them into knots and tears them apart. A small puff of air escapes me as always when I hear someone say her name without preparing myself for it. The pain and guilt are still the same as on the first day.

Because if it wasn't for me, she'd still be alive.

Calista squeezes my shoulder once more. "And I knew about Niparko."

The small puff of air turns into a wheezy breath. Gone is the disappointment, replaced by ice-cold fear and the non-existing memory of a day in my life I want to remember more than anything else, yet don't dare to think about. Horror surges, coupled to nausea. "Niparko," I whisper, "that's his name?" I never asked my mom who *he* was. His name was in all the newspapers I didn't read, in all the news reports on TV I didn't see, in all the conversations I wasn't part of. In this case, forgetting was a blessing. Knowing his name would've turned the faceless shadow in my mind into a person, and I wouldn't have known how to handle that. A shadow is menacing. A person is haunting.

"Yes, that's his name." The pressure of her hand on my shoulder never wavers. "And you should know he's still dangerous. Still out for money for—"

A harsh laugh breaks free. "Well, tough luck, he ain't getting any! What the heck is wrong with him—with you?" I glare at her. "He killed Sarah! He almost killed me! He deserves to rot in jail—"

Bright white neon lights, a hard gurney, curtains to all sides. Machines are beeping, loud noises come from everywhere.

"Hold still, sweetie. I need to wash that off of you. Hold still," a female voice says. Somebody's hand is holding my shoulder down.

I'm naked besides a sheet covering my lower half. "Nghh." I grunt and swat away the hand pushing me down into the bed.

"Sweetie, no, hold still, I—"

I push myself up onto my elbows, but the moment I look down my naked body I freeze: blood. Blood everywhere. On my chest, my breasts. My stomach. My arms. Blood everywhere. Blood, blood, blood. A vortex of vertigo pulls me under and I open my mouth and scream, scream, SCREAM, until there's no voice left.

I take a small stumbling step forward.

Nauseous.

I drop my hands to cover my stomach, heart racing, skipping every other beat. That... that can't have been a flashback. That stuff I just saw, that... that never happened. I was unconscious from drugs *he* forced into me, and when I woke up, I was in the ICU. I would know about being covered in that much blood; somebody would've told me. An image right out of a nightmare conjured up by a mind slowly losing its marbles. None of my injuries could've bled that much. Even if it had been Sarah's, I mean, how would I have gotten it all over me? Did I hold her when he stabbed her? If I did, how could I have forgotten that? How—

They would've told me if that had happened.

There was no blood.

There was no blood.

There was no—

Nauseous. So nauseous. I want to throw up, and that makes me angry.

It's all Calista's fault. How dare she think she can talk to me about this after everything I've been through? How dare she pretend she understands? How dare she mention Sarah, and how dare she speak her name in the same sentence as her murderer's?

I pull free of her grip. "Coming here was a mistake. Thanks for nothing," I hiss.

With three quick strides, I'm back at the couch and grab our coats. I hope I have my pills in here. My head's killing me—

and no wonder.

A sad smile plays around my aunt's lips. "You're so much like Owen. Full of doubt."

I roll my eyes. "Don't talk bad about Grampie. He has more common sense than you." Than either of us, or I wouldn't even have entertained the idea of using Calista as quote-unquote source and second opinion.

Calista chuckles. "Tell him I said hi. Even better, tell him Laura says hi."

I freeze, hand on the doorknob. "Aww, come on. Don't do that to him." Grammie has been dead for five years, and Grampie still hasn't gotten over her. Maybe he never will.

Calista hands me my beanie from the floor. Didn't even notice it drop out of my coat's pocket. "I know he doesn't believe. But if he ever wonders... Tell him the key is taped to the inside of the medicine cabinet. The only place he'd never voluntarily look into."

She winks at me before her face creases with worry as she turns back to the window and Kai's lone figure out in the backyard. "And then watch over that boy, Gwen. Before he too is dead."

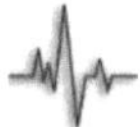

"Hey."

I don't think Kai heard me come closer, despite the snow crunching under my soles. A small pile of white fluffy flakes has collected on his shoulders and hair, and from experience I know it takes a while for that to happen. First it melts from body heat, and only when the surfaces have cooled down enough, will snow actually start collecting. Winter one-oh-one for California city kids.

Kai must be freezing.

I brush the snow off and drape his coat over his shoulders. "Let's go." I take him by the elbow in a gentle grasp. "This didn't go so well. I'm sorry I brought you here. I don't know, maybe she's crazy after all."

Kai looks like he's seen a ghost. The face that showed the most amazing dimples and was so… hopeful about an hour ago is now pale. Hollow.

Lost.

"I don't know what to make of it," Kai whispers into the snowy silence. "I want to call her a crook and liar, but…" He pauses, kicking at a heap of snow with the tip of his booted foot. "But she *knew*. She knew exactly what I've seen, and how could that be if she hadn't crossed herself? How could we both have had the same experience, if there wasn't some truth to it? I really don't know what to believe anymore."

I hook my arm into his. Exactly my problem. All our visit here did is show me what a crazy idea I was entertaining for a moment there. "Me neither. I… I wish she had given us more." More to convince me my plan was worth setting in motion. "Sounds like my grandpa is right, and she's off her rocker." And me following a close second.

Kai looks down at me on his side, a faint smile working on the corners of his lips. "So am I. Because I still want to bring him back."

"But I don't think we can." No matter for what reason, that soul-for-a-soul crap, or the sheer laws of nature.

"Maybe not." It's a soft whisper that tears through the backyard louder than a scream.

I lean against Kai's arm, trying to comfort him. For a moment we stand in silence, leaned into each other and lost in thought. The whole scene is so calm and serene, it's in stark contrast to the chaos inside my mind—to the hope that had surged high and then dropped low, to the possibility of a reunion, albeit a short one.

I wish I could remember more. It's a dishonor to her life to have forgotten her last moments. Her death. But there's nothing but bits and pieces, and mostly the ones I don't want: The sensation of complete helplessness. Fear.

"You look hot, girl." The boy takes my hand, and I let him. "Want something to drink?" I throw a glance at Sarah, who shakes her head. We're both behaving tonight. The blond boy still hands me a bottle of beer. "Cheers." He winks at me and tips his head back to take a long swig from his drink.

Whoa.

I squeeze my eyes shut. Dang. Where did that come from? Today my mind's on a roll, I—

Kai blows out a puff of air, resolve hardening his voice when he speaks. "But even if your aunt is right and I can't bring him back, I still need to try. What kind of brother would I be if I gave up on him without trying? And if Calista is right and his soul is stuck in the afterlife, then I want to say goodbye to Cole.

I still want to apologize. In person."

It takes me a moment to catch up to the conversation we just had. My gaze flies up to him. "In person—"

"And I don't mean in a séance or any of that crap, but I need to see that Cole is all right, for a lack of a better term. In person."

Meaning, he still wants to enter the afterlife. I tilt my head and look up at him. "That would still mean having to kill yourself."

"She didn't say *getting there* was impossible. She said *getting him back* was."

I roll my eyes. "Picking and choosing?"

A small chuckle leaves his throat. "Yeah? Why not? It's not as if this isn't crazy enough to begin with, so I'm choosing to believe in what she said about getting to the afterlife. If she can do it, so can I." He looks down at me. "You said you had a plan, and I need your help, Gwen."

The desperation on his face, mixed with longing and trust, damn, it nearly kills me. Pun intended. "Kai—"

"You brought me here, to your aunt. So that means you must've believed in some part of my story. Or in the afterlife."

"Yes, but—" But I thought my plan would help him do something good, bring back Cole. I grunt to myself. I wanted to play the hero, the one who saves the day and helps reunite the brothers. Sure, I would've benefitted as well, but mostly I liked the idea of making up for what I did. I got one soul into the afterlife. It would've been nice to help free another.

And it would've helped mine to apologize to Sarah. To talk to her.

None of it is going to happen. To be blunt, I won't help stop Kai's heart if the gain isn't even close to worth the risk.

And it's not.

My plan is off, and disappointment swamps me.

I let myself hope, and that was a mistake.

"But nothing has changed, Gwen." He turns toward me, gripping my upper arms with both hands. "I'm still convinced what I saw is the real deal. I'm still convinced I can get there. What I can do once I see him…" He shrugs. "I don't know. But I still need to try."

Maybe Calista isn't that much off her rocker. *Watch that boy, before he too is dead.* A groan leaves my throat. "Kai—"

"He's my brother, Gwen. My *twin* brother." He tilts his head to the left, giving me a long look. "You're an only child, aren't you?"

"Yes." But I doubt it makes a difference. I can imagine very well what he must feel like. Losing Sarah… it tore a hole into my chest. She was as much a part of me as any sibling I could ever have had.

Kai squeezes my arms. "Then let's go." He lets go of me and slides both arms through the openings of his coat.

"Go where?"

A small smile as he flips up the collar. "To meet Cole. It's about time I introduce you to my brother."

Chapter Nine

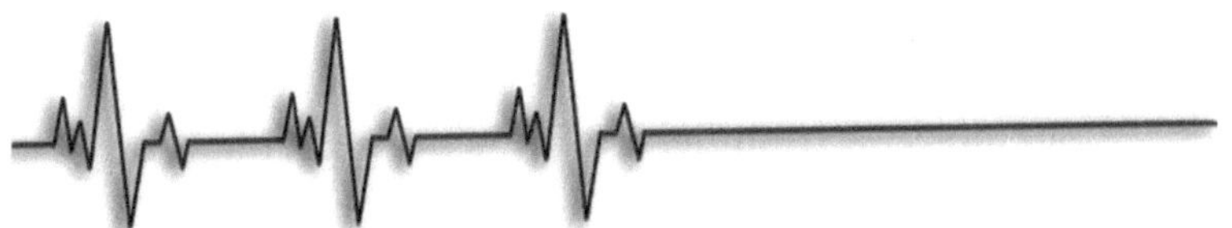

Cole

The Silverlake care facility isn't quite in the center of town, but also not too far out either. On the other hand, this is a small town, so... anyway. The building Kai is guiding me to has two-stories and a red-shingled roof. Many of the comfy-looking bow windows on either floor have their curtains drawn back, allowing for a nice view into the perfectly manicured front yard. A walkway leads from the street through said yard to the entrance doors. One smaller way goes off to the left, and another one to the right, both curving through areas with bushes, trees and a couple of benches on either side.

"Cole's been here for the last five months," Kai says as we walk up toward the front door. "Ever since the doctors said there was nothing they could do to wake him up." He opens the door for me. "The insurance wouldn't keep him in the hospital anymore, so we transferred him to Silverlake."

He leads me past a reception desk I would rather expect in a hotel lobby than in a care facility, but my frame of reference is limited.

"Hey, Susan." Kai greets the middle-aged woman behind the desk. "How's it going?"

Susan looks up from her work, a smile spreading over her face when she sees Kai. "All's well. Thank you, Kai. I was starting to miss you. It's been a couple of days."

He shrugs. "Busy. You know how it is."

Busy trying to kill himself, but Susan obviously is unaware of that small, but crucial piece of information.

"I know, tell me about it. Bringing a visitor today?" She waves a small 'hi' to me which I return.

"Yup. Gotta cheer the man up a little." Kai grins back at her, only it doesn't reach his eyes.

"You go right ahead." Susan presses a button, and the glass doors at the end of the lobby open. "Say hi from me," she adds with another wave before she focuses on her work again and Kai leads me down the hallway to the left.

Our steps echo on the squeaky-clean linoleum floors. Every couple of yards, there's a door either on the left or the right, all numbered, some of them decorated with a wreath or something else. It feels odd in here. Not quite as serene as in a hospital, but not quite as normal as in a hotel. Plus, the smell of antiseptic makes this too obviously not a hotel, but a medical place.

Kai stops in front of a door at the end of the hallway, room twenty-three. He knocks twice before he enters, holding the door open for me before he closes it behind him.

"Hey, old man," Kai calls into the room. "I'm back to visit." This time it's him who takes me by the elbow and guides me closer to the bed in the middle of the sparsely decorated room—the bed with a boy in it, a boy who could be Kai if not for a few crucial differences.

I knew they were identical twins. I spent enough summers obsessing over them to know they looked the same to most people, if their hairstyles hadn't set them apart. To me, their mannerisms differed, making it easy to pick out Kai between the two of them, but yes, Kai and Cole come from the same mold.

But their similarities are not why I stop dead in my tracks staring at Cole.

It's the differences that bring goosebumps to my skin, and when I say *differences* I'm not talking about the tube attached to a hole in his throat, or the monitors around him. I'm talking about the small distinctions, so subtle, yet so obvious. Where Kai's face is red from the cold, Cole's is pale and missing all color. He looks like he's asleep, yet it's clear he isn't. Nobody sleeps that... calmly. Somebody covered him with a blanket, but left the arms out, giving him the impression of being draped in this position. His eyes are mostly closed but with a little bit of a gap between the lids, showing the white, as if he was deeply asleep.

Cole looks so much like a ghost of Kai, it hurts.

Kai pulls two chairs from the small table next to the window on the left and lines them up next to Cole's bed. "I brought a new friend. Gwen, meet Cole. Cole, meet Gwen."

"Hey, Cole," I say softly, sitting down in the chair Kai offers me. "I used to see you at the river during summer."

Kai smiles at me, maybe because of the memory or because I'm talking to his brother—his *comatose* brother. "She's the frog bathing suit, Cole," he says, as if that would explain everything.

I stick out my tongue at him and get a chuckle in return.

Kai leans forward in his chair and gently punches his brother in the shoulder. "So, I tried what we talked about. It didn't work. Gwen kind of screwed that up for me. Twice." The wink he gives me lessens the sting of his words, but it's a sad wink. A wink that says he wouldn't have minded succeeding.

"I don't want you dead." I frown at Kai, and a wistful smile crosses his face.

"And Cole'd be the first to agree with that." He leans back into his chair, gaze aimlessly wandering around the room, skipping from heart monitor to the ventilator pumping air into Cole's lungs, and back. "We might look alike, but Cole was always the more reasonable of us. Me, I'm the butt-headed one."

He reaches to his left and takes a framed picture from Cole's nightstand. "That's us about a month before the accident. Cole and I finished our first triathlon. Dad was so proud." He hands me the picture.

Their dad stands in the middle between his two boys, and even if he hadn't pointed it out it would've been obvious. Mr. Harrison is beaming, one arm around Kai on his right and Cole on his left. Both of the boys are sweaty in their racing tops, Kai's hair wet against his forehead, Cole's more spiky mess much less tousled than even now. Both of them are alive, vibrant, full of energy and ready to take on the world, powered by their success and by each other.

And somehow, I envy them.

My dad never looks at me this way. Success is expected and nothing is rewarded. Failure, on the other hand, is punished, but success… is taken for granted.

I blink twice to get the moisture out of my eyes. Right here, right now, is not the time for self-pity.

As I take a closer look at the picture, more and more details pop into view. The light in Kai's eyes is now so much more dimmed, even when he seems fine. The muscles Cole had before he became comatose and didn't move for seven months. How Kai's and Cole's hands are hooked into the other one's behind their dad's back, like they were linked together, no matter what.

It reminds me of Sarah and me—Sarah, my only true friend and confidante.

Sarah yanks on my sleeve. "Let's go. I wanna go home."

I pull my arm away. "I don't." Dad annoyed the hell out of me. No way I'm going back into that cave of misery for at least another hour. I point over my shoulder. "He's cute."

Sarah looks over toward the bar in this huge living room. "Blondie is getting you another beer?"

Yes, he is. No biggie. I shrug. "We can get a cab."

She grins. "Are we being responsible?"

"We are being seventeen, Sarah." I don't think I'm being irresponsible. Flirting is allowed. A beer is allowed, or two, as long as I'm not driving. And Blondie is cute. Older than us by a few

years. Not quite dressed for a party, but something in his eyes speaks to me. Something that looks for more in life, or maybe I'm just being girlie. "We'll leave after that next beer, okay?"

Inch by inch I lower my hands, letting the picture sink into my lap. I blink hard. Again.

That… My mind must've made that up. I don't remember anything like that happening—

When was that supposed to have been? *A* party? No, I'd remember somebody getting me beer. *The* party from *that* day? Nu-uh. I didn't drink that night. Sarah didn't drink either. We both promised after—

Point is, we both promised. And had they found alcohol in my blood, Mom would've chewed me out like there was no tomorrow. She'd—

"It makes it worse, doesn't it?" Kai asks quietly. "Seeing him how he was, and what he's like now? How can I not try to fix it, no matter the cost?"

I clear my throat, maybe it'll clear my mind as well. "Uhh, yes. Worse." A cold chill runs down my spine. Where the heck did that come from? What's my mind trying to tell me? All that crap my subconscious came up with over the last days, it all must've been triggered by talking about death and Sarah. A desperate attempt to fill the void. None of it is real.

Somewhere in the depth of my mind a little voice whispers, *but what if it is?*

I ignore it.

Because it isn't.

Kai takes the frame from me and returns it to its proper

place on the nightstand next to one of Cole arm in arm with a pretty blonde girl, both grinning ear to ear. I can all but see the little comic-book hearts rising above their heads.

Kai scoots around on his chair until he's facing me. "I don't want to die, you know? I really don't want to." His eyes seem even darker now, bottomless and filled with sorrow. He leans forward to support his weight with his arms on his knees. "But if there's any chance I can see him one more time… I've got to take it. I have to, no matter if I can bring him back or not."

I look at Kai, I look at Cole.

Cole, trapped in a world we don't understand.

Kai, so loyal to his brother he's willing to risk it all.

A lump forms inside my throat.

Nothing about Cole being in the Realm is his fault. Can't say the same about me and Sarah.

I swallow dry.

Kai's gaze never wavers from mine. "I just wanted you to see why I need to do this. Why I have to do something so crazy. I'm a butthead, but I'm not an idiot."

Just a brother desperate enough for the ultimate sacrifice.

But not an idiot.

Something cracks open inside of me. "No," I whisper, "you're not." Neither of us is. We're two people left behind trying to deal with the cards handed to us.

I gently tug on Kai's sleeve. "So, you would still want to see him, even if you can't get him out?" Just to clarify I understand him correctly.

He looks over to his brother, answering without any hesitation. "I want to see him *and* try to get him out. No idea how, like, do I grab his soul and run, or what do I do? But yeah, if that doesn't work, I want to at least see him one last time. Say goodbye. I'd give anything for that."

Even his life.

But… so would I.

Those glimpses of whatever-they-were, memory, or made-up figments of a mind going crazy, they scare me. *Everything* about them scares me. I have a gaping hole in my memory and no bridge to cross it.

Unless I talk to Sarah, my best friend. My *dead* best friend.

Am I officially crazy yet? Thinking about entering the afterlife?

Let's be honest, I've been teetering at the edge of the abyss since July 31st. How much worse can it be taking a step over it? To be fair, I should probably take Calista's statement and my common sense for what it's worth and run with it. The outcome doesn't always justify the means. The benefit-risk ratio is too high, as one of my pre-med instructors would say.

And she'd be right, yet absolutely wrong.

To me, the risk isn't dying. The risk is living without knowing what happened. Without apologizing. If I died—

My heart stumbles once. If I stayed in the afterlife, it wouldn't be the worst to happen to me, simply because the worst already *has* happened to me.

Kai lowers his lashes in a slow blink, desperation in every single word he speaks next. "I need this," he whispers. "I need Cole."

Whatever cracked with his earlier words bursts open into a full-blown chasm. *Need.* Such a strong word. Such an accurate description. I don't think I knew seeing Sarah was what I needed to begin to understand, to begin to heal, but Kai is right. I need to see her, just like he needs to see Cole.

And for that we need each other.

Call me an egoistic, selfish bitch, but who am I to deny him a chance to see his brother when all I want is to talk to Sarah?

And I can't do it alone.

Nausea roils inside my stomach, warning me to take the next step.

I ignore it.

"Then I'd say… we're going in. Hell be damned." I throw in a cocky grin before he can see the fear in my eyes, or the desperation.

Kai sucks in a surprised breath, the only sound disturbing the near-perfect silence in this hospital room. "You'd help me?" His voice is full of hope, and I feel like the biggest fake.

I should tell him that helping him will help me.

I should tell him I will visit the Realm too.

I should tell him what happened on July 31st.

But I don't.

It's one step too close to being *that* girl, the one everybody thinks I am now. *The crazy one*, and I'm too selfish to ruin what I have with Kai.

I lift and drop my shoulders. "I think we should give everybody a chance." Him. Cole. Myself. I chew on the inside of my cheek. "But we're doing it my way." Nobody touches a live wire on my watch.

Kai's eyebrows shoot up even farther. "Your way?"

I nod. "My way. I told you I have an idea. A rough one. It needs a day or two." At least. A day should be enough to figure out the rough outline, then maybe another to get it set into motion.

His gaze meets and holds mine, dark brown on light grey. There's a spark in his eyes, the one I used to see during the summers I spent here. The one visible from across the river. Heck, from across town.

Now that spark lights up something inside my soul, something thought dead and gone. I'm more anchored than I've been in months. More focused. My shrink would say more of a danger to myself, but then, neither of us knows what truly happened on July 31st.

But we're going to find out.

Just like at the train yard, Kai takes my hand. He weaves his fingers in between mine, a move so intimate like we'd been doing this for eons. My heart stutters from his touch and falters when he moves his thumb across the back of my hand. Our gazes lock, and time skids to a halt. The room around me melts away until nothing else exists but Kai. Kai's dark brown eyes in front of me. Kai's hand in mine. Kai's touch on my skin. I'm in deep, and I know it—I always knew that given the chance, this ridiculous school-girl crush could turn into a teenage-obsession.

Without breaking eye-contact, Kai reaches for Cole's hand and lays it onto my lap.

He doesn't need to say it.

My free hand covers Cole's larger one, only to have Kai's fingers close over mine. "Thank you, Gwen. From both of us."

I soak up Kai's touch, every spark it brings, and save it for eternity.

And I try not think about what I'm going to do to him.

Chapter Ten

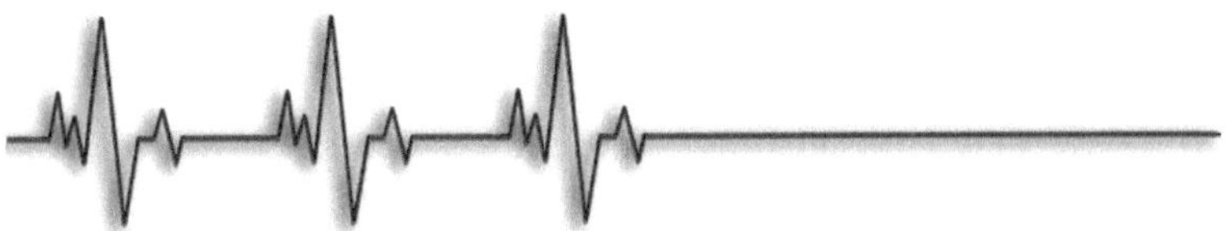

First Steps

"**Y**our mother called an hour ago." Grampie lets himself sink into his favorite chair at the window, inch by inch, and most of his body weight supported by his cane. "Her regular check-in if you're taking your meds, how you're doing. The usual." He winks at me as his frail body melts into the cushions.

I groan. Geez, is there no rest for the wicked? They sent me here for peace and quiet, and having my parents check in 24/7 doesn't quite qualify as that.

"Told her you're doing just fine, and you've already looked into late applications for med school." He lifts his palms in a what-can-you-do gesture, and he's right. What can you do? We both know that's what Dad is going to ask her. Grampie's white lie probably saved me from another annoying FaceTime call.

True to their professions, my parents have a different outlook on life. Like, one-eighty degrees different. My mom, being a pediatrician, always puts health first. She's the one who gave me all my meds, who tailored everything to my needs, and who spent hours with me, searching for my memory and processing what little I found. My dad on the other hand, being an extremely successful businessman with a superiority complex, prefers a more practical approach: all that PTSD, all those meds—all nonsense. Throw yourself back into work. It'll take your mind off, you'll be fine. An O'Karran doesn't get derailed. An O'Karran copes.

Said the man who never had to cope with anything besides the stock market tanking, courtesy of his only daughter.

"Thanks, Grampie." I fall into my chair next to his in front of the window. "Here, to not make a liar out of you." I pop the lid off the orange pill box my mom gave me. "One horse pill coming right up. Whether it helps or not."

Grampie gives me a suspicious glance from below his lashes. "You don't think they help?"

"Meh. They sure don't do much against the headaches. Or the brain fog. But at least I dream less." That's a plus, where I'm coming from.

"Have you tried not taking them?"

"Have you met my mom?"

He chuckles. "What she doesn't know can't hurt her. Maybe you should give it a try. Give your mind a chance to fix itself." He taps a finger against his temple.

"It's kinda what I've been trying with the meds."

"And how's that been working for you?" Grampie wedges his cane between the armrest and the wooden box he played with the other day.

I sigh. "Not so well." And I think I forgot to take this one yesterday. Busy day, prevented suicide of a certain Harrison twin and all.

"See? Give Mother Nature a chance, Gwen. More often than not she knows what she's doing." He winks at me. "And now hurry up with that cake. My blood sugar is dropping."

Well, we can fix that. I cast one more look at the pink pill in my hand, and then stuff it into my pocket. I'll think about it. "Cake coming right up." I grab a plate with marble cake on it and hand it to Grampie. His eyes light up. Marble cake is his favorite.

For a while we eat in silence. In front of Grampie's large bow window a couple of birds fight for the best place at the feeder I put there on the first day I arrived. Grammie used to have it out every year. She even fed the squirrels.

"Hey, Grampie?" I wipe some crumbs off my shirt. "Do you mind if I'm gone for another couple of hours later on?" I know he won't, but I don't want to assume. Plus, I'm not just here for myself, I'm also here to support him. He doesn't need half as much help as he makes our family and his usual caretaker believe, but that's just Grampie. He likes an ace up his sleeve.

Grampie tilts his head to the left, a curious look on his face, mouth still full with cake. "Am I to assume it has to do with that Harrison boy?" A few crumbs fly from his mouth, coming to lie on his shirt like little sprinkles.

Damn that old-age wisdom or whatever. I wipe my mouth with my napkin, but that thing won't do anything to wipe off the stupid blush warming my cheeks.

"Uh, yeah, kind of. Well, actually, completely." Wow. Now that was idiotic even by my standards. My face warms up by another couple of degrees, probably making me glow in the dark or something.

Grampie giggles like only ancient grandfathers can. "Gwen, my dear. Go. Have fun. He's quite a handsome boy, just like your Grampie was back in his day." He winks at me. "Have fun but be responsible." Of course, he had to add that last part. That's a typical Grampie remark. Ex-mayor. Responsibility runs in his blood.

Not so much in mine apparently, or I wouldn't be about to do what I'm planning to do.

"Thanks, Grampie." I grin at him. "I'll be back at dinner."

"You better." A mischievous grin tugs on the corners of his mouth. "Otherwise, I might eat all the dessert myself."

And with that he focuses back on his marble cake, all important things being said.

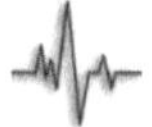

An hour later, I catch Kai a moment before he rings the doorbell. "Grampie is napping," I whisper while grabbing my thick coat, complete with scarf around the collar and gloves in its pockets. "Good to see you." I smile up at him. Seeing Kai warms me up on the inside like I'd swallowed part of the sun.

Taking a breath of the scent I think might be his typical Kai-scent makes me want to bury my nose close to his neck and inhale. It's something warm, with a little bit of spice and a lot of Kai.

He smiles back at me, and those dimples… Grampie said it right. He is one handsome boy. "Same here."

We both hesitate for a moment, which makes the following hug completely awkward and stiff, not like the last times we hugged, and not at all as easy-going like when he held my hand in the train car, or when he cried in my arms.

Huh. Maybe we're just not good at hugging when we're normal, and not all emotional.

Or… maybe we need more practice. Yup. That must be it. More practice, please, because practice makes perfect.

I clear my throat, distracting from what most likely is a healthy red on my cheeks, and slide my arms into the coat while directing Kai out and around the house to the left. "So, I don't know how much you know about my family and all this." I gesture to Grampie's mansion. "My dad founded his company here, in Kampton." When he was really young, like, in high school. Which is why he made me work on college credits in my uhh, *spare time*. Yay for paternal pressure and expectations.

Dad was so obsessed he used Grampie's tool shed in their old house's backyard and transformed it into his tinker-place, coming up with all kinds of ideas during that time. After he'd become successful and built Grampie and Grammie this new villa a few years before I was born, he made it a point to include another tinker-place, only this time a more advanced one.

Kai follows my lead around the side of the house and

toward the backyard. Since we don't have any neighbors behind us or to the side, the tree line isn't far behind our property line—which is still quite the distance. When Dad bought this, he called it *the park*, for its size.

"Your dad's in engineering, right?" Kai asks, little clouds of air rising from his mouth. "Your uncle is the lawyer-slash-environmentalist?"

"Yup," I nod. "My dad's the engineer. The *medical* engineer." I stomp my feet twice on the rug under the small awning of my dad's tinker-place. "And that's the point."

I press my thumb into the indentation next to the lock until a small click and a green light indicate my print was accepted. That's the thing with O'Karran genes. They get you into everything.

I open the door wide for Kai. "Ta-daaah!"

He steps through, the movement triggering the ceiling lights and bathing my dad's so-called *office away from home* into bright white light.

Kai stops dead in his tracks. "Wow!"

Well, can't fault him for being impressed. What looks like a moderately sized guest house on the outside is anything but on the inside. Working tables line the walls of this large, rectangular room, most of them filled with some kind of electronic stuff. I don't recognize it all, I'm not that much into engineering, but there on one of the shelves I recognize the needle-less diabetes pump, for example. It's still an earlier model, twice the size of what ended up going into production, and already replaced by a better model Dad came up with a while ago.

More toward the left stands an earlier version of his iCare Robot, designed to facilitate medical care in rural areas with a shortage of doctors. Besides being remotely accessible, the iCare can complete tasks, like change settings on machines or listen to a patient's heart, all while the physician is logged in from remote somewhere. That one is still being used all around the world, especially because it generates its own uplink to the satellite system to transfer the data.

Tons of other stuff is clattered around the room, some old and clearly from the beginning of his career, some newer, and from when Dad visited Grampie a couple of months ago.

I shrug. "What can I say. My dad likes to build stuff."

"No kidding." Kai whistles through his teeth. "How does your dad... I mean, this is *tons*. How does he come up with all of that? Does he even have time to do anything besides work?" He picks up some kind of contraption I don't recognize and turns it in his hands.

I lock the door behind me to keep the cold out and the warm in. I spent almost four hours in here, making sure I had what I needed and that it was working, and only after the central heating kicked in was it actually bearable in here.

"Well, I don't know about sleep, and I can tell you he doesn't have much time for anything else than work." Or anybody else, Mom and me included. A dry chuckle leaves my throat. "Heck, if it hadn't been for me, he wouldn't even have met my mom."

That earns me a questioning look. "Huh?"

Okay, true, that sounded confusing. "I found my dad a wife. Well, four-months-old me did, to be clear." I give him excited jazz hands. If it hadn't been for me, Dad still would be single. "My mom was my pediatrician, and my dad a single dad. Enter beautiful little me, check-up visits, instant love, *boom*, married." And I've never once missed my biological mom. As far as I know, she's barely nineteen years older than me, in Hawaii, teaching surfing and enjoying life. Well, so am I.

Correction: so *was* I, until six months ago.

Kai throws me a glance that warms me down to the toes. "I can totally see that." I swear his cheeks turn reddish as he bends down and checks out something else my dad built, and me... Let's just say that school-girl crush just cranked it up to mega proportions.

Deep breaths. Easy there, Gwennie-girl. Just take it down a notch.

I clear my throat. "That was my only contribution to the family so far. Don't ask me how he's doing any of this. I didn't inherit that part of his genes."

Kai walks around the room, taking his time to check out the devices scattered everywhere. "What's this?" He points to a large, odd-looking gadget.

"Medical printer. Need a new skull bone? New ear? This one will do the trick." My dad was the first to bring something at this level of sophistication on the market and it became one of his greatest success stories, at least until the police used his GeneTracer to find Sarah and me on July 31st.

The modern version of police dogs, it says in the marketing material, I think.

Kai brushes his fingers over a small, contorted piece of metal with a pink bow on it: the pancake-machine my dad built me when I was six. When we were still like peanut butter and jelly. Before the company was more important than me. Before my mom became my number one confidante, because Dad… Dad couldn't be bothered finding time for me.

Oh, well. I stick my tongue out at myself when Kai isn't watching. I have enough self-pity about recent events, no need to add fuel to the fire by thinking about the good old pancake-filled days.

Leaving Kai to do his explorations, I cross through the room to the corner in the far right, take my coat off and drape it over a chair next to the device I want to show Kai.

This is the piece of technology I had in mind. Well, in combo with another one, but still. My gaze follows Kai around the room, how he stretches to look at something, twisting his body to get another angle at it. He keeps his hands folded behind his back as if to make sure he doesn't accidentally touch anything, and it gives him a very scholarly expression.

Until he bends down low to check my dad's biomechanical arm implant.

That's when scholarly goes out the window and something else enters, something that suddenly makes it very, very warm in here.

Those jeans. They fit him perfectly. Something warm, tingly, and completely inappropriate for what we're going to discuss in a minute or two coils low in my stomach. Ignoring it is next level, because, gee, it is quite warm in here. I use my hand to fan some air to cool my flushed face. He does have a nice butt.

"Gwen?"

"Huh?"

Kai straightens back up, an upwards curve to his lips and amused twinkle in his eyes. "Are you staring at my butt?"

I squeak and jerk back, caught red-handed. "St-staring? At your—"

He points behind him, now grinning ear to ear. "Whatever that thing is, it has a mirror."

I groan and close my eyes, covering them with the palms of my hands. "No. Nope. Not staring. Definitely not at your butt. Just…" I keep my eyes squeezed shut and take one hand off my face to wave it at him. "Just keep looking at things and ignore me." Excuse me while I invent a machine to make him forget what he just saw.

Kai chuckles, but thankfully drops the topic. Eventually he has finished his rounds, and, to his credit, he pretends like those uber-awkward thirty seconds didn't happen. I appreciate it.

He shakes his head in amazement. "I mean, I knew your dad was a genius, but seeing all this stuff…" He gestures to all four sides of the room. "Quite the inventor."

"That he is, which brings me to this little baby here." I tap the plastic cover in front of me, hoping by now my cheeks are back to normal.

"This?" Kai asks, giving the odd gurney-length tube a critical once-over. "What is it?"

I sigh. "Well, this is our ticket to die." Okay, that sounded worse than intended. "I mean, to die without damaging our brains." This thing here is what I meant when I said I had a plan. "We can't leave anything to chance. If we want this to succeed, we have to plan for every eventuality. We have to be ready—no, more than ready. Death… death is bigger than us, and if we don't watch it… we're gonna lose this one." I swallow hard. Death has millions of years of experience. We have none. This better be airtight, or we're going to regret it.

"I see your point." Kai nods. "So, what does it do?" He glides one hand over the man-sized capsule's smooth white plastic cover I opened up and slid half-way down earlier today. Kai bends forward to look inside, then, after a questioning look at me sticks his hand in, feeling around.

"Squishy," he says, sounding surprised when his hand sinks into the cool blue material covering every square inch of the capsule's internal lining.

"Has to be." Or else this thing wouldn't work. "This is one of my dad's first models of the CryoTherm. He developed it to induce medical hypothermia—to drop the body's temperature."

Kai raises an eyebrow. "Meaning?"

"Meaning, it basically does what you intended to do when you threw yourself into the river. It lowers your body temperature, which slows down your metabolism, which protects your brain from damage."

Kai whistles. "Nice. So, you think we cool me down until I die? Doesn't that take forever if you don't drown or deprive yourself of oxygen at the same time?"

I cringe. I might be on board for many reasons, one or two being my personal egoistical ones and not just Kai's, but it's not to get somebody to die, especially not Kai.

Yet it's the nature of the beast and what we need.

"Yes, you're right. Freezing to death would take a while.

So, we're using this." I point to the small, carry-on luggage-sized pack next to the table.

"An AED?"

I raise an eyebrow. "You know AEDs?"

"CPR certified." He shoves his hands down his pockets and shrugs.

All right then. Makes my life easier—or rather, my survival. "Close. Once I take it out of its carrying case you'll see it's not an AED, but a defibrillator. The same principle, but you're calling the shots, quite literally, not the machine." The newer models of the CryoTherm have an integrated AED, but this one doesn't. "We use it to shock our hearts into fibrillation when the body is cooled down to thirty-three degrees Celsius, and then use it again to get our hearts re-started into a normal, blood-pumping rhythm as we warm up." Everybody who has watched any kind of medical TV show knows how that works. It doesn't take my pre-med classes to get that part.

Kai cocks his head to the side. "*Our* hearts?"

Oops. Hadn't really gotten to that part yet. "I want to see the Realm too." Not to be too dramatic, but the rest of my life depends on it. My sanity.

"No way." He shakes his head, emojified-hair falling into his face. "This is dangerous enough doing it once. We've already established I'm an idiot with a tendency for self-harm. You, on the other hand, have so much more to lose, Gwen. You're not getting into that thing."

"So much more to lose?" I blink twice. I don't have *anything* to lose. Nothing. But then, Kai doesn't know that. His lips are pressed into a tight line and his eyes shine with determination to keep me out of this. As much as I appreciate a protective streak in a guy, and as much as it makes my heart all soft and mushy, this goes the way I want it. Period.

I lift my chin up high. "We're *both* going to do it. First you, then me. You go first, because, well, this is your thing, and because I'm the one who knows the tech. Then I go after you, and you handle the tech." I hold his gaze across the CryoTherm.

"Gwen—"

I shake my head. "No, Kai. We do this, it's under my terms and conditions." I hope he doesn't see the slight shake of my hands before I stuff them down my pockets. I just officially announced I want to stop my heart.

Must be a new high on the crazy-scale.

Kai pinches his lips together and runs a hand through his hair to no avail. It falls straight back down his forehead into his usual wind-swept emo-style.

"Why?" he asks, never taking his eyes off me.

Without losing a beat I tell him my excuse. "Because I'm curious." My shrink would have the time of her life with that answer.

Curious to die?

And why don't you tell him, Gwendolyn? Sarah was your best friend. You have to come to terms with it.

Stupid shrink.

"I don't like it." Kai purses his lips. "Not one single bit. You'd never have gotten the idea if it wasn't for me. I don't want to be the one shocking you with that thing. For all intents and purposes, I already killed my brother, that's bad enough."

I flinch like slapped. Let's not talk about that, because it's *my* belt that carries a true notch.

He bends over the capsule and supports his upper body with his hands on the rim. "I really don't like it. No way in hell you're going in." His eyes spit black fire. "It's way too dangerous."

Shaking off the funk his words induced, I put my hands on my hips. "Oh really? Said the guy who tried to kill himself twice and who wants me to help him die? Hypocrite much?"

Kai grimaces. "Touché. But come on, Gwen. We both know this isn't normal. Normal people don't talk about the afterlife, or if they do, not how to get there and come back." He works a hand through his hair. "Seriously. It's too risky. Me… I don't mind. If something goes wrong, I mean." The apple in his throat moves up and down twice. "I drove that car. I… I need to at least try to get him back. Or apologize."

He *doesn't mind* if something goes wrong.

Something cramps up inside my chest.

Neither do I.

We're both guilty, carrying that guilt until it kills us. Maybe even literally.

And we both need to apologize.

He reaches over and lays his hand onto my shoulder. "You have no reason to die, Gwen. Then don't."

I shove his hand off me and serve him the next part of my excuse. "I've been drilled for med school all my life." Not a lie. "Chalk it up to researching, to firsthand experience. I *am* doing this, or neither of us is."

Part of me wants to go ahead and tell him—tell the little bit of what I remember. I want him to understand, and, crazy as it is, because his opinion shouldn't matter, I want his approval. But telling him what happened *that* night would also mean to tell him my worst fear: That Sarah blames me for her death.

Like I said: No party, no kidnapping. No rich girl, no ransom money.

I look into the eyes of the boy who hasn't judged me the slightest, the boy who doesn't care my dad is rich. I want to sink into those eyes and get lost in them.

I never want them to look at me like the others do, with pity, or like I'm crazy.

Taking a step closer to the capsule I pinch the bridge of my nose. "Kai, do you think I like the idea of shocking you into cardiac arrest? It gives me the creeps, seriously. I mean, I have a good baseline understanding of what we need to do, but I'm no doctor." Nor am I ever going to be one. Dad's dream for me is gone, dissolved in PTSD. I take a deep breath in. "If we do this, we both do this. It's only fair."

Kai's hands clamp around the rim of the capsule, the muscles in his jaw twitching. Then he lets go of it and slams his palm down. He pushes himself off and takes a couple of steps away from the capsule. "Fine. Fine. I guess I can't be a hypocrite doing it myself but not letting you take a turn, but—" He spins on his heel toward me, one finger pointed right at my chest. "I go first. If something goes wrong, it's me. Not you." The last two words are spoken so softly, they melt all argumentation I still had in me.

And it melts my heart right with it.

"Okay," I whisper. That's what I wanted anyway.

"Okay," he repeats firmer, a small smile playing around his lips. "So, now that that's settled, what do we do next?"

"Now we find a new home for this baby." I tap the CryoTherm's lid.

We need secrecy to kill ourselves and secrecy to keep us alive.

That, and a whole big portion of good, old-fashioned luck.

Chapter Eleven

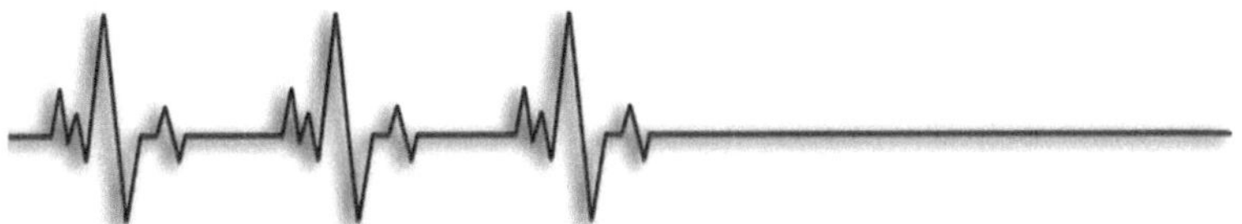

Old Train Yard

"And you're sure this is abandoned-abandoned?" It must be the umpteenth time I ask Kai the same question.

"Yes," he says without missing a beat. "Abandoned-abandoned. Ever since like eighty percent of it burned down and they built the new train yard maybe twenty years ago. This was too far off the new tracks up to the town, and remodeling or keeping it intact was too expensive."

Hence, they left this formerly large, red brick stone building in the middle of nowhere to itself. Twenty years of exposure to the elements haven't done the remainder of the walls or roofing any favors. All the gaps and holes and a rather added spooky feel to it.

"In the summer it's actually quite beautiful here," Kai says while ducking under a beam laying across what must have been a huge floor-to-ceiling window once. "In winter it's still beautiful, just harder to maneuver. Freezing cold, slippery from all the ice and snow that makes it through the broken ceiling, and not necessarily a fun place." He holds out his hand and helps me over some debris piled up on the floor behind the window we just climbed through.

Slippery sounds right, especially since the layer of snow doesn't make it any easier.

The whole thing has a very industrial feel to it, which makes sense, of course, but combined with the age of the building, it looks odd. The outside reminds me of images of the Colosseum in Rome, with empty arches framed by broken bricks. That part looks totally wild-romantic, and I see why Kai says it's beautiful here in the summer. The inside of the building is completely at odds with the outside though. It's nothing but steel beams. Steel beams, pipes, and cables, all tangled, mangled, and in all states of disorder and disarray and blocking my view into the building.

Oh, and debris. Did I mention debris?

"If you think we can use this place, I'll drive the truck to the back. That's where Cole and I usually park and tailgate in the summer. The hole in the wall is bigger. Should fit the freezer." Kai climbs ahead over a beam leading to a metal plate obstructing the way, like part of the ceiling had given up and crashed down. I mentally add climbing-when-cold to my list of never-do-agains. The temperature doesn't improve my coordination at all.

"So far, I think it's not very practical." I gasp pulling myself up the man-high obstacle, only to struggle not sliding down again. "Couldn't we have taken the easy way in?"

Kai jumps back down to the ground in a smooth and easy move despite the height. Aww, crap. I'm about to embarrass myself and—

"Nope." He holds both arms up at me, like he was waiting. Waiting for me.

For a short moment I hesitate. I *could* make it down alone, not that it's going to be graceful. But here's Kai, arms wide open, and waiting for me.

No-brainer.

Leaning forward until he gets a hold of me and supports my weight from under my arms. I drop my hands onto his shoulders as Kai lowers me down, technically keeping me much closer to his body than necessary, not that I mind it.

My gaze sinks into his, and my insides tighten when he pulls me closer, lowering me to the ground one slow inch at a time. For a wonderful moment, our faces align. The warmth of his breath glides past my cheek, while the rest of my body is pressed into his. A dark fire comes to life in his eyes, a spark that lights me up just the same. My feet meet the ground, but he doesn't let go. A charged silence hovers, loaded with implications.

I'm so close, I feel every breath he takes. Kai digs his fingers into the fabric of my jacket, but just when I think I know what's going to happen next, he lets go of me and steps aside, clearing his throat. "Well, you had to see it from this entrance. Plus, I needed to show you the switch anyway." He avoids my gaze, and I suppress a sigh.

In a movie, that would've been a kiss.

But the fact that we're about to kill each other… yeah, not a romance movie, that's for sure. A freaky horror-show, maybe.

Deciding to drop it, I move next to him. "What switch?"

"The power switch. This thing is officially off the grid, but not if you know how to override the block."

"And you do?" I raise a skeptic eyebrow. "Why?"

His grin turns mischievous. "Because Cole and I more or less own this place. My dad's an inspector for the city. Part of his job is to keep an eye on this thing here, which is why we know about it and how to get here. Most people have completely forgotten about it. It's been too long, and it looks way crappier from the outside than it does in here." He gestures up to the ceiling, and only now do I realize he is right.

What I thought was nothing but broken-down beams and building materials looks so much better now that we've crossed the obstacles blocking the entrance.

It's not a ginormous building, maybe enough for three or four train cars in a row and with five or six tracks next to each other, but still. Arched beams separate the tracks from another, like an ancient train station, only with a bit more chaos to it. It's quiet, serene, and somehow… beautiful.

Kai steps next to me. "During summer, grass and wildflowers grow everywhere. All the brown twigs you see going up the beams? Those are some kind of vines. That's all green then." He pauses. "Ideal for picnics and stuff. In the summer… in the summer I'll take you." I could swear his cheeks take on a reddish hue just before he works a hand through his hair and quickly takes a couple of steps forward.

My heart does a weird fluttering thing inside my chest as the first genuine smile in a long time appears on my face. "I… I'd like that."

Kai turns, his gaze snapping to mine. His chest rises sharply before he nods once. "Then it's a plan." He clears his throat, then points at the floor in front of us. "Careful here," he says without looking at me and jumps down into a trench in the ground that swallows him whole. "This is what our dad showed us. Up until a couple of years ago, there was still machinery here, and when they removed it they forgot about the power. Or maybe they left it on purpose, who knows." Something metal screeches before there's a click and a soft hum. "Cole brought string lights once, when he took Claire out for a date." He holds his hand up, holding a rolled-up cord with lightbulbs dangling from it. "Ta-daaah!"

I laugh out loud, and it feels great. "String lights! Wow. This place must've looked beautiful with them." Dystopian chic, but romantic for sure.

Kai focuses on rolling up some of the cord that escaped. "Assume so. Obviously, he didn't take me when he went on that date." He lifts and drops his shoulders.

I don't know what comes over me, but I say the first thing popping into my mind. "You didn't take your girlfriend here?" The moment the words leave my mouth, I want to take them back. Or rewind time. One of the two. Way to go being a weirdo, Gwen.

For the length of one tiny second, Kai stops his movement

before he gives the string lights another tug. "That was never an option." He swallows then bends down and out of sight, tucking the string lights back to where they were before.

That was never an option? What does that mean? He doesn't have a girlfriend, or didn't at the time? He couldn't come here, like, Cole called dibs?

Really fantastic job, Gwen. Stupid questions deserve unhelpful answers.

Awkward silence stretches, and while I'm scrambling to come up with something less embarrassing to smooth things over, Kai beats me to it.

"But if you'd like, I can hang them up for you. It's a bit morbid to make everything look pretty and then kill ourselves, but you know…?" He straightens up, grinning at me. "Morbid is kind of our middle name at this point."

I snort, then slap a hand over my mouth. "Sorry." So, Gwen, how's that whole less-embarrassing-thing working out for you?

Kai chuckles, climbing out of the work trench. We aren't quite close enough to touch, but close enough for his body heat and scent to engulf me. I should probably step back. I'm crowding him. But… I don't know if I could, even if I wanted to. Kai is like a magnet, drawing me in. Has been, ever since I saw him for the first time. The laws of nature must work differently around him, I'm sure of that. Humans don't work like magnets. Only, Kai does, defying nature.

And he isn't moving either.

For the longest seconds of my life, we look each other in the eye, and it's not even awkward. His grin disappears, as something heavier charges the air around us. Kai sucks in his lower lip and chews on it, making me wonder, like, *really* wonder, if this is when he's going to kiss me. Because, I mean, he offered to hang up the string lights. Was that code? Does it mean anything? This is *so* where he should kiss me.

Alas, he doesn't.

He lowers his thick lashes, and when he opens his eyes again, he sighs. A sad smile plays around his lips. "Power's on, so…" He raises and drops his shoulders once, the smile shriveling up and dying, pun intended. "I guess… I guess we can set up the freezer."

And—*squeeze*—the tight feeling in my chest is back. I blink as I swallow hard. "S-sure. Let's do it." I step back, creating not only physical, but also emotional distance. I can't be distracted by my feelings for Kai. I'm already projecting way more confidence than I actually feel. Talking about our plan back in my dad's tinker place, driving here and looking at the old train yard—all of that was easy, because it was only talk and no action. Now though, now we're taking the first true step toward setting our plan in motion.

We're setting up the CryoTherm.

We're prepping for a death without consequences.

Boy, does that sound wrong.

Kai leads me through the train yard toward the back, and he was right. The opening here is bigger, albeit hidden by way more vines. In the summer it must be a wall of green, making it impossible to find if one doesn't know what they're looking for.

Kai goes to get the truck, then drives it around and backs

it through the curtain of evergreen-vines into the building, carefully avoiding all obstacles. I'm glad their family has a truck, because my Beetle won't do it. I also can't use Dad's old truck in the garage for no good reason, and there's no way we can set our plan into action at home. Not when Grampie or the cleaning lady could walk in at any time. Not when this thing pulls so much power it requires a high-voltage line. Last time Dad worked on it at home, it caused a power-outage for the whole block. Kai found us the perfect spot, abandoned, secret, and with enough electricity to move worlds.

We set up shop in one of the corners close to the hidden truck entrance, snow under our feet and vines above our heads. Sliding the CryoTherm off the bed of the truck is way easier than getting it on there, although it comes with wheels that fold in, just like a gurney for an ambulance. That doesn't make it any lighter though.

Once we find the perfect spot close to one of the arches appearing like they could've been the connection between platforms nine and nine-and-three-quarters, both of us take a step back.

The CryoTherm looks eerily beautiful in this light: a sleek, blueish outer hull, a bright blue interior, a large, black control panel at the head and a blue oxygen tank mounted on the outside behind it. The way the light falls in through the partially broken roof it illuminates just the top part, a spotlight onto where tomorrow first Kai and then me will be lying.

Waiting for our death.

Waiting for our loved ones.

I swear I hear Kai swallow next to me. I reach for his hand

without looking at him. "What… How do you think it's going to be? Tunnel, light, angels singing?" Not that I believe in that, but who knows? I might come out a changed person.

If I come out. *If* there is anything besides death.

Kai entwines his fingers with mine. He sighs and flicks some lint off his thick woolen sweater with his other hand. How that man can survive without a coat is one big question mark for me. "Dunno. Like I said, for me, it was more of a transition than anything else. Your aunt said that too."

True. They had the same description.

"On the other hand… well, I've done some quote-unquote research before I decided to get Cole out. All inconclusive. Out-of-body experience, tunnel, nothing at all… Some wake up in what looks like the real world, only their dead friends are there. So, yeah." He sighs again. "I'm expecting either nothing and all of this is made up by dying brains, or I'm hoping for the movie version, with something that looks close to our world."

A smile plays on my lips. Movie version. But, yes, I've got to agree. "Would also be nice if the souls looked like people."

"Yeah, right? Makes it easier to find Cole."

And Sarah.

Kai sighs for a third time, heavier. Never letting go of my hand, he bends down and picks up the CryoTherm's plug, shoving it into a dirty outlet that hasn't been used in over twenty years.

With a faint hum and spooky blue glow, the CryoTherm comes to life.

All of a sudden this becomes real.

Kai places his free hand on the softly vibrating capsule, a

reverent look on his face. The freezer's blue reflects in his eyes. "Tomorrow, Cole," he whispers, the weight of the world on his shoulders.

Tomorrow.

Tomorrow is a good day to die.

Chapter Twelve

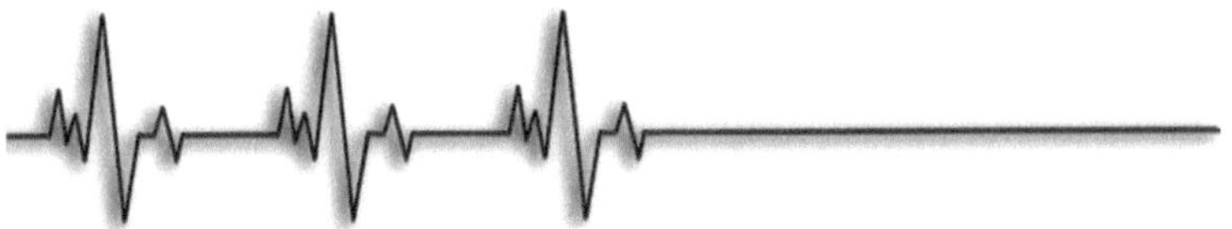

Second Thoughts

I don't get much sleep that night.

First, my brain's as foggy as an afternoon in London. Maybe a bit less than on my worst days, but still. Seems to be my new normal, at least there's no change whether I take the meds or not. Grr. I hate that fogginess. For the last six months, my thinking machine has been reduced to half its power, it feels. As if it had decided to abandon me after what I put it through on that fateful day.

Alas, I'm not one to give up. So, I get out of bed at like midnight, splash water into my face, take some painkillers for the headache, and do this the O'Karran way: power through. Aww. Daddy would be so proud.

Second, I do my research. *Again.* There's a reason why I passed pre-med at sixteen. I'm good.

Well, I used to be good.

And right now, my abilities are limited, thanks to my mom's strict no-internet-no-smartphone-no-nothing-rule to keep my PTSD under control. Was quite the fight to at least leave a couple of web-based apps on my phone, and she couldn't really keep me off PubMed, the source for all research articles. Not as a physician herself.

Anyway, I do my research just to make sure, and it makes me nervous.

Like Kai said, there isn't much out there to support our theories. Most of it is pseudo-scientific stuff I don't even want to take seriously. Tunnel, white light, god-like figure, etc. It sounds good, but… I don't know.

I really don't.

Maybe they're all right, and maybe the skeptics are wrong.

I want them to be wrong.

I scroll through paper after paper, article after article, grasping at anything that could help us tomorrow. I know how to induce hypothermia. I know what should happen during our procedure—how the brain will not have any activity once the heart stops and flatline all electric activity about twenty seconds after the heart stopped beating. How cooling down to thirty-three degrees Celsius will prevent the cells from being oxygen deprived, keeping them alive. How careful rewarming will keep the toxins out, and the brain intact.

I know all of it.

But still it feels like I've bitten off too much to chew.

Eventually, I go to bed again, but toss and turn, unable to find a good position to fall asleep in. Nothing works. Neither my body nor my mind find much of a rest, no matter what I do. Instead, my thoughts drift to the train yard and the CryoTherm, to Kai's determination to pull through with our foray into the unknown, and the love that shines in his eyes whenever he mentions Cole.

Tomorrow, both of us will cross a personal threshold and neither of us should be proud about it.

Funny thing is, thinking something could go wrong with Kai freaks me out.

Thinking something could go wrong with me isn't even on my list of worries.

Meeting Sarah is.

What does she remember that I don't? How mad will she be? Will she be able to forgive me for dragging her to the party neither of us would've gone to under normal circumstances?

"Mom, please. Please, please, please! I've been studying every night for the last month, I just want to have one night off. Please!"

Mom looks at me with that sad look she always carries when she thinks Dad works me too hard. "Honey—"

I know what she's going to say: Dad made a decision, and I'm staying home. So, I don't let her say it.

"Just this once. I'll be back at eleven. At ten." I don't care. I'd even be back at nine, as long as it means I can do the exact opposite of what Dad wants. For once I want to be free, for once I want to do what other teens my age do.

I want to be one of them, not Gwen O'Karran, a billionaire's daughter and almost-med student.

My mom swipes a strand of hair out of my face. "Gwennie... You know Dad doesn't like you at parties."

Unspoken addition to that statement: since the last time Sarah's mom dropped you off drunk. I got in quite a bit of trouble there, enough to keep me off anything stronger than water.

I close my eyes to keep the tears in, defeated. "But Dad doesn't have to know." It's enough if I know I won this round. "I won't drink, Mom. I promise."

My mom sighs. "Honey..." Another sigh. "Where is the party?"

My eyes fly open, hope in my heart. "At Chris Wellington's place."

"Well, then say hi to Chris from me. His next check-up is overdue." She winks at me and pats my back. "Off. And hush-hush. I won't tell your dad."

I fall around her neck and squish her. My mom's awesome.

Kind of ironic I begged to go to the party that ultimately killed Sarah and came close to killing me. If I hadn't gone, Sarah wouldn't have gone. And without me there, no kidnapping. What were our lives worth to him? They never told me the sum he asked for. Did he kill Sarah because her family had less money than mine and keeping her alive didn't pay off?

A cold shudder runs down my back.

I hope he rots behind bars for what he did. I hope Sarah haunts him every night and makes his life hell. One day, I'm going to visit him in prison. I'm going to visit him and look the man in the eye who thought kidnapping me would make him rich, who thought money was worth killing Sarah.

And I'll spit in his face.

I ball my hands into fists.

No matter how traumatic, what wouldn't I give to remember. It's a dishonor to Sarah and her last hours on Earth. The police asked me over and over how he got us, how my car ended up at the shack where… where *it* happened. The only answer I could give is that I don't know.

No, I can't say how he got me to stop my car.

No, I can't say whether it was at gunpoint.

No, I don't know why there were no signs of struggle inside the car—but I assume there was a gun. I wouldn't stop like that and hand over my car. There must've been a gun. Something.

I press a hand against my temple. We went to the party. I wake up in the ER on my way to be transferred to the ICU. That's it. Damn those neurons for deleting everything in-between. I hate my brain for that, I—

I can only hope Sarah can fill in the blanks. And that she'll accept my apology, if I even find her. How do you find people in the afterlife? Ask? Probably not Google. Maybe Kai's theory holds, and it's like in the movies, and Cole and Sarah are waiting for us.

Kai. My lips curl up on one side. Sarah would get a kick out of me spending time with him. The summer before Grammie died, when we were twelve or so, she came up here with me for two weeks when her parents were on a business trip to France. Needless to say we had a blast shadowing the Harrison twins' activities. A summer of swimming and eating ice cream? Fantastic in and by itself. A summer of swimming, eating ice cream, and watching Kai and Cole? Endlessly better.

She's the frog bathing suit, Kai said to Cole.

Even alone and in the darkness I blush. I never caught him even as much as glancing over in our direction. If I had, Sarah and I would have had even longer nights talking and dreaming about the twins, imagining stories of how we'd get to know them, dividing them up between us as if they were a boy band and we had our pick.

Sarah had a thing for Cole, the more roguish one with his spiky hair and bad boy attitude.

Me, I always liked the other brother, the quieter one. I always liked Kai best.

And tomorrow I'm going to stop his heart.

I blow out a harsh breath of air and hold it mid-way. Stop it, Gwendolyn! Yes, I'm going to stop his heart, but I'm going to restart it. Is it without risks? No, not at all. But it's less risky than Kai drowning or electrocuting himself, and that's a good thing. *I'm helping him stay safe.* I'm helping him stay safe and find closure, so that he can live on. I'm *helping* him.

Not difficult to recognize the hypocrisy here: When I pulled Kai out of the river or off the train car, I was so happy he didn't die. Relieved. Imagining another person had died on my watch was twisting the knife in my heart by another ninety degrees.

And now? Now I'm going to freakin' *help him die.*

If I feel guilty about Sarah's death, how do I imagine I'll feel if something goes wrong with Kai?

Frustrated, I slam my hands down into my blanket. In the dark of the night all our planning seems so ridiculous. Ruthless. Crazy. Idiotic. There aren't nearly enough adverbs to describe the magnitude of stupidity that must have possessed us.

But it's controlled, another voice whispers inside my head, *we've planned for everything, and if there is a chance Kai and Calista are right…*

Then we have to take it.

Then *I* have to take it.

And while common sense says to let it go and forget this crazy plan, I can't.

Risking my life is worth the potential gain. And Kai's life—

No. Don't think about it.

Everything will be fine.

I pull the pillow out from under my head, press it onto my face and scream into it.

It's going to be fine.

It's. Going. To. Be. Fine.

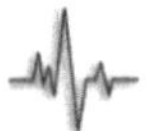

I must have fallen asleep at one point, since all of a sudden, it's six o'clock and time to get up. I feel like I got hit by a truck. One glance into the mirror confirms that assessment. I also look like I was hit by a truck.

Great.

It takes me a good ten minutes longer than normal to get ready, and when I finally make it downstairs, Grampie is already in the kitchen, reading the newspaper on his iPad.

Grampie is a pretty good techie, considering his age.

"Gwendolyn, my sunshine." He cringes a second after he

says it and gives me a wordless once over that I ignore while I make breakfast. Maybe fate wants to warn me it's not my day today or something, since I burn myself on the toaster when prepping the bagels, then knock over the salt and only barely catch it before it spills all over the table.

Grampie raises an eyebrow. "What has your knickers in a twist this morning? Is it that Harrison boy?" He gets his typical grandfatherly mischievous expression in his face he always has when he knows I'm doing something my dad wouldn't approve of—meaning, basically anything besides breathing, or maybe even that.

I hand him the cream cheese. "Yes, it's the Harrison boy, Grampie. You can call him Kai, you know?"

Grampie giggles. "Kai. So, what's up with Kai, my dear?"

I'm sure he doesn't really want to know. "Well—"

Grampie's iPad chimes. "Early bird, your mother." He hands me his pad. "Take it in the living room. Your mother is too cheerful for me at this time."

I take the iPad and swipe the screen. "'Morning, Mom."

After a short feedback noise my mother's voice comes through the speaker. "Gwennie, honey. Good morning to you, too." She takes a sip from her cup. Coffee, milk, and about a pound of sugar. She's in her white coat, meaning, at work. Must be a research day, or else she wouldn't wear it.

"Just calling to say hi." She wiggles her fingers at me. "How's Grampie?"

I close the living room door behind me and curl up in my favorite seat. "Fine. He can do better than he lets on, you know?"

My mom smiles. "I know. But I'm sure he appreciates your help." The way she says it, I know she also means it the other way around. Thanks to Grampie's offer, I get some distance from the press at home.

She puts her cup down and rests her chin on her hand. I know the next question before she's made up her mind which one to ask. "How's your memory, honey?"

I let my head fall back against the chair's headrest. Good question. "Dunno. About the same. Bits and pieces." Plus a couple of new bits and pieces that don't make sense. I blink twice, staring at the ceiling.

Out of the corner of my eye I see my mom nod. "How are you handling it? Do you need more meds?"

Thank whomever for my mom being a pediatrician. Seriously. I wouldn't have survived the first couple of days after the kidnapping otherwise. The psychiatrist couldn't get me in for two weeks, so Mom took over, even though it's slightly unethical to treat your family members. Not forbidden, just discouraged. But had she not helped me, I don't know what would've happened. I'm eternally grateful. Whatever she gave me, I was blissfully numb. Of course, it backfired with a vengeance once the meds wore off, but still. Wouldn't have survived without them, period. And without my daily dose of sanity, my life would've sucked even more. Now, since I moved to Grampie, is the first time I've not religiously taken them every single day.

"I can send the prescription to the pharmacy next to the bakery, if you need more." Mom raises an eyebrow to emphasize her point.

"No, thanks, Mom. I'm fine, I have enough." Especially since I keep forgetting them. "But… can I ask you something?"

"Sure, honey, anytime. What's going on?" She adjusts the stethoscope around her neck.

I pause. "Mom? You've… you've seen people die, right?" I swallow hard into the silence on the other end.

"Yes. Why do you ask?" Suddenly, she's dead serious, pun again intended.

I shrug. "Dunno. Is it… peaceful? In general, I mean?" Not when you're stabbed to death, like Sarah. I don't need to remember to know that much. But… I've seen Grammie succumb to cancer. That wasn't peaceful either.

My mom's brows pull into a V. "What's going on, Gwendolyn? Are you sure you're feeling well? Where's that coming from? Honey, be honest, if you need more meds—"

"No, really." Bad idea, Gwen, bad idea! "I don't need more meds, I'm fine, I just… dunno. Was curious." Because, you know, I'm going to die later today, and I'm freakin' scared.

A muscle twitches in Mom's jaw. She doesn't buy my answer. She doesn't like it either, I can tell. "Gwen, why don't we—"

Her phone rings with the same tone she's used since the two of us recorded it when I was in second grade and we had nothing better to do than goofing around that Sunday afternoon. *"I like to eat my beans, beans, beans,"* seven-year-old me belts out to some kind of melody vaguely reminding me of something by Lady Gaga, *"hear the noise they're making in my Jeans, Jeans, Jeans!"* I cringe. My vocal abilities definitely rank lower than I thought at that time.

She frowns. "Honey, I—"

"It's fine." I wave a hand in front of the pad's camera. "Pick up. Patients need you." And I'm more than happy about it.

She reaches for her phone. "Okay. But promise me, call me if you're not feeling well, okay? I'm here for you."

"I know." Au contraire to Dad.

"Love you."

"Love you too. Bye."

Last thing I see is Mom picking up her cell, luckily interrupting prima donna-me at *whenever I eat corn—*', and then she's hung up on me.

I blow out a big puff of air. Not cool, Gwen. Not cool. My mom's radar is super-sensitive. Last thing I need is more parental supervision. Or any, for that matter. If Dad knew I was leaving the house and—gasp—maybe even the city limits, he'd be furious.

After another deep breath or two, I join Grampie in the kitchen. "Mom says hi." Doesn't matter she didn't say it, she always means it.

"Huh," Grampie answers in-between chews. "Thank you, but please don't think your Grampie is getting senile. Harrison boy?"

I freeze.

For a moment, I think he knows.

For a moment, I have all but forgotten our conversation from before the phone call. I stare at Grampie wide-eyed, until he chuckles.

"Girl, don't look at me like that. I don't mind if you're out for some fun. Just do me a favor, stay close to home and behave, will ya?" He winks at me.

With an effort equal to moving a mountain, I get my features under control again.

Behave.

"Of course," I lie straight into his face. "Always."

Chapter Thirteen

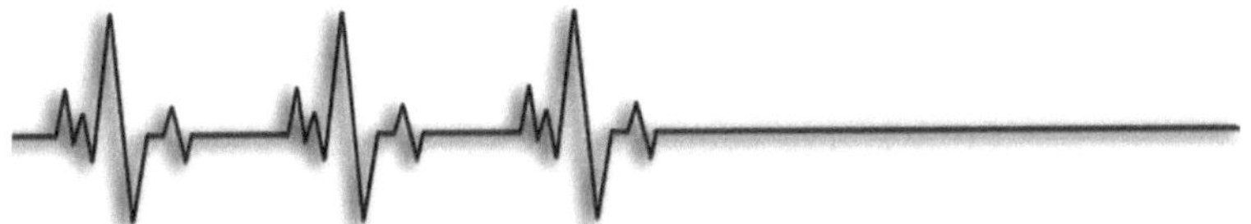

Going In

It's exactly eight o'clock when Kai's truck rumbles up the driveway. Before he has a chance to turn off the engine, I'm out the door, wrapped in an extra layer of clothing against the chill annoying me since the morning, which has nothing to do with today's temperatures. My bag dangles over my shoulder, hitting me in the leg when I stride up to meet him.

He opens the door for me from the inside and I hoist myself up and in.

"Morning, Gwen." The tight smile he gives me does nothing to distract from the paleness of his face.

"Hey." I would bet a substantial amount of money my smile isn't any more relaxed than his.

"Rough night?" He turns out of our driveway, gripping the steering wheel so tightly his knuckles turn white.

"Kind of." Like, totally. "No surprise." I strap myself in, locking the seatbelt into its buckle. "What about you?" Not that one look at him wouldn't answer that question.

He sighs, shoulders heaving up and down, knuckles turning even whiter. "Same. Spent the better half of the night writing a letter to my parents, in case… in case something goes wrong, you know?" He keeps his eyes straight on the road. "I felt like I owed them that much for what I'm about to do… Plus, I didn't want anybody to think this is something you did to me. I'm doing this out of my own free will, and for something I believe in." He blinks rapidly.

Turning left, he drives us out of Grampie's neighborhood and onto the small dirt road that eventually leads to the abandoned train yard in another couple of miles.

"I figured my parents shouldn't have to lose another son and not have closure." He swallows hard.

Closure.

There it is again, the magic word.

"It's going to be fine." When exactly I became the voice of reassurance I don't know. I adjust the heater vents, trying to suck up as much heat as I can, but still I keep shivering.

"I know." This time Kai looks at me, and for the second our eyes connect, I want to cancel this whole thing.

Screw closure. Screw the afterlife. Screw all of it—for both of us.

But then he smiles at me with that spark of hope in his eyes, the hope that depends on me doing this right, getting him to the afterlife to find his brother, and then to bring him back. And man, snuffing out that hope… I can't do it. Neither for him, nor for myself.

We're doing this.

I won't let Kai down. Or Sarah. Or… myself.

We spend most of the ten-minute trip in silence. Like yesterday, Kai backs the truck through the curtain of vines into the part of the building hiding our CryoTherm. From the moment he turns off the engine, the tension in the air is palpable, thick as fog and heavy as rain.

We don't talk as we get out of the truck, and we don't talk as we go through the same set-ups as yesterday. I pop a quick Motrin. Can't be all foggy and headachy, not today, of all days.

Kai plugs in the CryoTherm, then I make sure the settings are right. He checks the defibrillator's batteries and replacement batteries, while I make sure it works well. He hooks the BVM, the self-inflating bag for the rescue breaths, up to the O2 while I make sure the flow is set right.

If either of them gives out on us…

Well, that's not going to happen.

Fifteen minutes later, everything is ready to go. The blue light from the CryoTherm illuminates the dusky corner of the building like an alien spaceship had made its way down here through the big gaps and holes in the old building's ceiling.

We both stare at it.

"I guess that's it then," Kai says in a low voice. "Showtime." He shrugs out of his coat and throws it over the opened flap of his pick-up truck, then grabs the hem of his sweater and pulls it over his head, leaving him only in a tight black undershirt.

And two seconds later, that's gone as well.

I can't help but stare.

It's not like I hadn't seen him before—I did, every summer at the river, but I never truly saw him: the wide shoulders, the narrow waist, the six pack.

He kicks off his boots, tears off his socks in a quick motion and grimaces when he sets his feet down into the snow. "Oh shit, this is going to be cold, ugh."

My gaze follows his hands up to his belt. It only takes a second to undo it before the buttons pop open with one quick movement of his fingers.

At this point my mouth is dry.

I should look away, but I can't.

Watching Kai undress in front of me is surreal. It's strangely personal, yet completely clinical—a necessity on our way to meet death at his doorstep.

"Holy cow." Kai slides his jeans down and steps out of them, wearing nothing more than black boxer briefs. "Freezing. Already. Shit." He hops from one bare foot onto the other, rubbing his hands over his upper arms.

I shake my head quickly, forcing myself back into reality.

Inducing hypothermia.

Right.

I open the CryoTherm's lid a little more. "I know it's cold, but—"

"I know, I know. It's going to get much worse. I know." There it is again, that soft smile, so sad and yet utterly adorable.

He climbs into the chamber and stretches his legs out all the way down into the depth of the blueish glow. "Definitely squishy. Comfy though, if it weren't so cold." He winks at me, but it lacks his usual confidence.

I'm next to him like he was a patient in a strange bed and I'm taking care of him. With one hand, I take the EKG electrodes off the panel behind him, with the other one I stick them to his chest. Goosebumps break out where my fingers touch him.

I suck in my lower lip.

Get a grip, Gwen. It's because I'm warmer. That'll do it.

Next, I hand him the nasal cannula for some extra oxygen, then take the electrodes for the brain activity and attach them to his temples. Once they're attached, I press a button on the display on my right.

"You don't have to do anything. The CryoGel will cool you down to thirty-three degrees Celsius. The gel molds around your body, and don't worry, the lid only closes up to your lower ribs, so I have access to shock you." With the press of a button, the lid slides up, covering Kai's body from the feet up to a good three inches above the belly button.

"Once we reach thirty-five degrees, you'll feel a slight stinging sensation all over your body. That's the neurotoxin making sure you won't start shivering from cold, which would generate more warmth instead of cooling you down." That's what made my dad's invention so ingenious. The machine that does it all: oozing a neurotoxin through the gel that reaches the skin within seconds and numbs the body to the cold within milliseconds.

I try to swallow, but my mouth is too dry. "Then, either your heart will start fibrillating on its own, or I'll shock you once you reach thirty-three degrees. You'll be barely conscious at that point, if at all." For whatever reason, my voice sounds strong and confident. Like I know what I'm doing. Maybe that's why Dad thought I'd be good in medicine. Maybe I'm good under pressure.

Kai's gaze is trained on me, waiting.

"I'll give you four minutes, Kai. Not a second more, okay? You have four minutes." Then I'm going to shock him, no matter what. I wanted to max at three minutes, but Kai insisted he needed four.

His Adam's apple moves up and down twice. "Okay then." His gaze is glued straight to the heigh ceiling. "Let's do this."

I ask him once more, because I owe it to myself. "Are you sure? We can take this down, bring it back, and nobody will be the wiser. We don't have to do this, Kai. After I press enter, we're setting it in motion." And the longer he stays in there, the harder it will be to bring him back, no matter how far down the path we are. Every procedure has its risks, and so does this one. My stomach twists into a figure eight. I exhale roughly and hurry to get the words out before I overthink them. "I get why you need to do this." And I know why I need to be the next one entering the Realm. "But that doesn't change I'm scared shitless that something will go wrong, Kai. That I will cool you down, stop your heart, and that you won't come back. I'm scared." I pulled Kai out of the river, thinking nobody was going to die on my watch, and now… Yeah. Now everything has changed.

He closes his eyes for a moment before he turns his head and looks at me. "I'm scared too," he whispers, "beyond belief. But I have to find Cole. I need to say good-bye myself. I have to apologize. I owe it to him." He pulls his left hand out of the CryoGel and holds it out for me. It's already cold as ice when my fingers entwine with his.

"The letter I wrote to my parents, it's under my frog on the shelf," he whispers. "No matter what happens, thank you, Gwen. Thank you for everything. And… if something goes wrong… I won't be mad at you. I wanted this. If it goes wrong, I'll be with my brother."

It takes all the willpower I have not to tear up. "Okay," I whisper, my right finger hovering over the button until Kai nods at me. "Enter."

A split second later, the blueish glow around Kai increases in intensity as the machine's hum becomes deeper, more vibrant. Kai's eyes widen. "Oh man, that's fast." The pulse in his neck speeds up, fingers squeezing around mine. "Don't let go." He clenches his teeth. "Please."

I wrap my second hand around his. "I won't. I'm here. I'm right here, and I'm watching over you. It's all going to be well. I'm here." Again and again, I repeat the same sentences, smoothing my thumb over his freezing hands, my eyes either fixed on him or the display behind his head. With every tenth of a centigrade he drops in temperature his breathing picks up a little bit.

At thirty-five point five degrees, his eyes lose focus and start darting left and right, but I never stop talking to him.

Even without looking at the display I can tell the exact moment when he reaches the critical thirty-five degrees, because he takes a sharp breath in and then relaxes visibly, lips pulled up in the faintest smile. The brain-activity squiggly lines even out some more. Must be the numbing taking away the pain.

At thirty-four degrees, Kai's fingers loosen in mine, but I refuse to let go. His breathing is irregular, his eyes wide, pupils dilated and skin white like a ghost's. I check over my shoulder to make sure I have the defibrillator close by.

For the first time since we met, I can look at Kai all I want to, although it comes with a surge of guilt for what I'm about to do. Still… the little bit of stubble in his handsome face, the long eyelashes that make me only the slightest bit envious, the bushy dark eyebrows that give him such a strong, determined look… No wonder I fell for him when I was barely old enough to know what that meant.

Another five minutes later, we hit the thirty-three point five degrees, and then the thirty-three.

And yet his heart is still beating. Slower, more irregular, but beating.

I place a soft kiss on his knuckles before laying his hand down into the gel. "Just one moment, okay?" It feels right to talk to him, although I doubt he can hear me. His brain is cooled down already, just as we planned it.

I hang the defibrillator on the two hooks at the side of the pod and press the charge button. A high-pitched whine fills the silence, hurting in my ears and hurting in my heart. The two paddles way heavily in my hands.

If I chicken out now, all this was for nothing.

I rub the cold metal electrodes together to spread the gel between them. "Good luck," I whisper, then press them hard into Kai's chest, careful not to touch any part of his body with mine.

Then I press the button that will stop his heart.

A zapping sound, like a whip cracking, a short, violent twitch of Kai's upper body—and then nothing.

Nothing besides the EKG showing a fine, irregular and squiggly line.

I drop the paddles back into their holder, placing my hand on his frozen chest.

Nothing.

I just stopped Kai's heart.

Chapter Fourteen

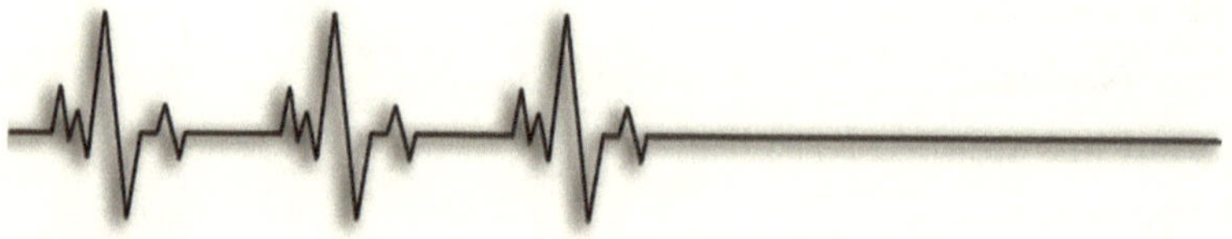

Coming Back

Four minutes are an eternity.

Four minutes are torture.

I stare at Kai as if he'd miraculously wake up on his own, but no, of course not. He lies there, unmoving, glassy eyes fixed onto the ceiling, cold chest still and without a sign of life.

Without a sign of life.

Kai's irregular squiggly line keeps flickering over the heart monitor, his brain activity on the other display is non-existent.

Not panicking has never been more difficult.

I want to rip out that defibrillator and shock him back.

That's thirty seconds into it.

My breathing turns raspy as my throat closes off. The

inside of my cheek is chewed raw already.

One minute.

I recheck the defibrillator. Batteries are working, it's ready to charge. I take Kai's icy hand, sliding my fingers in-between his.

Two minutes.

Snow falls through the holes in the ceiling, collecting on top of the CryoTherm and on Kai. Gently I wipe flake after flake away from his face, but the ones I miss, they don't melt very fast.

Because he is just as frozen as them.

Three minutes.

My heart rate should be enough for the two of us. I'm close to dizzy at this point. Kai has been dead for three minutes.

Three freaking minutes, and I can't stand it anymore.

I can't stand looking at him like this. Still. Unmoving. Without everything that makes Kai, Kai.

Gently I cup his cheek with my palm. His face is cold, so, so cold. The years I dreamed about touching him, I didn't expect it to be like this. I swallow down the burn inside my throat. Swiping my thumb over his cold face I whisper, "I want you back." I wouldn't dare to touch him like this or saying those words under normal circumstances, but alas, these are not. With one last caress for his cheek, I take my hand away.

Three minutes and thirty seconds.

My heart beats up in my throat, but my throat is so dry it turns my breathing raspy.

A sharp pulse of pain slices through my head, like a knife to the brain.

"One more beer?" He takes my empty bottle.

"Naah, I'm good. Thank you." If I have more, Mom will smell it on my breath. Been there, done that.

He raises a playful eyebrow. "I've got a better idea then. Wait." With a quick, playful gesture he brushes his finger along my jawline before he takes off into the crowd of people around us.

Sarah squeaks the moment he's out of earshot. "Gwen! Oh my gawd, he's totally into you!"

I hiccup. "I'm not imagining it, right?"

Her smile turns into a face-splitting grin. "Nope. Totally not."

As fast as it came, the image is gone. I gasp and suck in a painful breath of air. Holy whatever—

Three minutes forty-five seconds.

Focus.

I shake my head, make sure the oxygen for the self-inflating ventilation bag is on, take out the paddles, and press my thumb onto the charge button. I don't really hear the whining sound disturbing the silence; I *feel* it tear through my soul.

Four minutes.

Game time.

I hit the "Emergency Rewarm" button with my right fist. A split second after a *thud* breaks the silence, the CryoTherm's gel turns from blueish to reddish as it changes from cooling to heating.

"Kai!" I yell, while jamming the paddles onto his chest. "Come back!" I fire the paddles, their zapping and whipping sound shooting through the air and the surge through his body like lightning, and—

Nothing.

No heartbeat.

Only the squiggly line. V-fib. Still.

"Shit." I stare at the line a second too long before I understand what it means. Before the panic sets in.

What do I do?

Right. Reload, reload, reload.

I press the button again. "Faster, faster, come on, you stupid thing." I curse at the whining defibrillator. Why does recharging take so much longer than when I tested it?

The second it's reloaded I fire.

Nothing.

No heartbeat, no flatline, no nothing. Kai's body is still cold, not moving, and in V-fib.

I hit the reload button with my palm and the force of a sledgehammer, for a split second afraid I broke it.

"Come on, come on. Kai, don't do this to me. Come *on!*" Recharge, you stupid defib, recharge! I'm towering over Kai and there's nothing on my mind but him—that he is dead because of me. I push that thought away, no time for it now.

The whine stops. I fire. Kai twitches.

The EKG flatlines.

Fate, thank you.

I drop the paddles and start CPR. All I want to do is curl up and cry, but I don't. A flatline is good, in the grand scheme of things. A flatline means there's a chance.

My gaze flies over the display as I push down hard on Kai's chest, flexible ribs bending under the pressure of my bodyweight. Counting the number of compressions in my head is much harder than it should be. Once I hit thirty, I reach for the BVM, but knock it off its hook with my shaking hand.

My heart about stops into cardiac arrest. "Crap," I curse. No time to lose. I jump off the little step and fish the BVM out from under the CryoTherm, using my leg. Ten seconds lost. Can't let that get to me.

One rescue breath, two. Resume compressions.

Thirty-three point five degrees.

I keep on pumping, lungs burning already.

Thirty-four degrees.

I stop, panting heavily, checking his pulse with shaking fingers. Nothing.

More CPR, more desperate pushing, more frantic counting, keeping the compressions and rescue breaths at a frequency that will get oxygen to his brain.

Thirty-five degrees—and suddenly a gasp.

I jerk my hands off his chest like I was the one shocked.

A breath.

Another one.

And another one.

More freakin' breaths, one after the other, more and more regular, each and every one of them a blessing in itself. I can't stop my hands from shaking.

Thirty-five point five degrees.

The EEG looks almost as spiky as before.

Kai starts to focus. His lips are moving, but no sound's coming out.

Thirty-six degrees.

Kai turns his head in super slo-mo, gaze finding me and locking with mine.

His lips turn up the slightest bit, and never have I seen a more beautiful smile.

"I saw him." His whisper is hoarse. "I saw him."

He saw him.

A relieved choking sound breaks from my throat and echoes through the train yard. It worked. He saw Cole. It worked!

I close my eyes, letting go of a slow and stuttering breath. My heart cramps in my chest, squeezed by the conflicting emotions assaulting it from either side. Kai is alive. Talking. Our plan worked. That's what I've been hoping for. What I wasn't *prepared* for was the sheer panic flooding me during every single moment of the process. The fear that came with the thought of losing him. The sensation of helplessness.

"Hey." Kai sounds hoarse. He pulls one hand out of the gel cushion. "What's—"

"You were gone." My voice shakes. "You were gone for six minutes, Kai."

"But I'm here now." His eyes are still heavily hooded. "I'm back, Gwen."

I hear him, but that doesn't mean I understand him.

I almost lost him.

No. I almost *killed* him.

He must've read that on my face, because he covers my hand on his chest with his, flattening it right over his heart. "I'm here."

His breastbone is still red from where I did CPR, but right

under his skin, so much warmer than before… right under his skin, the reassuring beat of his heart bounces against my palm from below, one double-sound at a time.

Du-dun.

Du-dun.

Du-dun.

He's alive.

The tension of the last minutes oozes out of me, replaced by a relief of a magnitude I never thought possible. A wave of dizziness assaults me. I almost lost him. I almost killed Kai. For real.

A dart of fear shoots through my veins: in a short while I'll be lying there, cold as ice, my heart stopped. How hard will it be for Kai to get me back from the dead?

And what if he doesn't?

Pressure builds in my chest, the kind that isn't relieved by crying, only by the knowledge that if I stayed in the Realm… I wouldn't mind too much.

Kai sneaks his hand up to the back of my head, digging into my short hair, effectively chasing away all thoughts of whats and ifs. "Hey." He lowers me down until my forehead rests against his. His breath caresses over my cheek, a soft reminder of what could've gone wrong.

We stay like this for an eternity, our foreheads connected, our hands together above his beating heart, and the fingers of his other hand digging into my hair. We stay like this until the CryoTherm beeps, announcing a core temperature of 36.6 Celsius, and Kai lets go of another shuddering breath.

"Gwen?" His warm breath so close to my mouth is torture and pleasure at the same time. "Thank you."

Chapter Fifteen

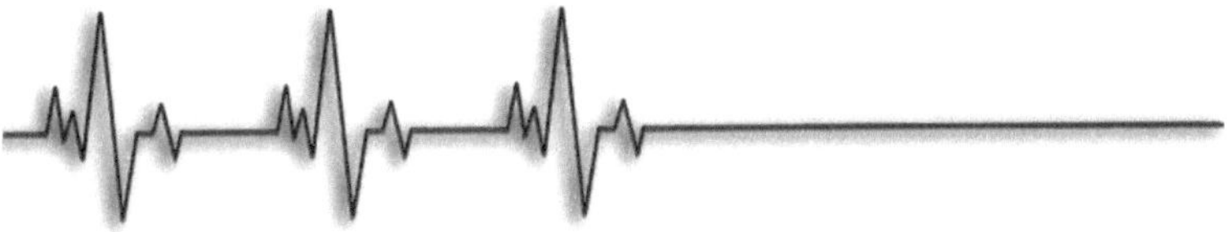

Thawing, Again

"**H**oly cow, I don't think I'm ever going to be warm again," Kai mutters. His hands are all but shoved into the vent integrated into the dashboard of his truck. The heat is set to max, and that includes the heated seats. After five minutes of running the engine, it's already pretty cozy in here, but it probably depends on the point of view.

I bend down, pick up my bag from the floor and take out a thermos. "Try this." I pour some of the hot, steaming liquid into the cup that came with the thermos and hand it to Kai.

"Hot chocolate?" His eyes light up like a kid's on Christmas day. "You brought hot chocolate?"

My cheeks warm up. "Thought you might like it." I would

know, because that's what he always ordered in the cafe, when it was too cold for ice cream. Kai's obsession with hot chocolate made me an addict myself, choosing hot chocolate whenever it was on the menu, as if somehow it could bring me closer to him. It's what teenage girls do.

I watch him take a sip and close his eyes as he savors the warmth and flavor. "Good stuff. You might have saved my life in the freezer, but you're saving my soul right now. Not much is more life-affirming than hot chocolate." He lets his head fall against the head rest; eyes closed. "Warming up. Feels good."

This is as lively as I've seen him since he woke up again. First, I thought it was because of the aftereffects of hypothermia, or because I basically assaulted him with my pent-up worry and grief, but when he climbed out of the CryoTherm, dressed himself and then jogged around the empty train yard to warm up, something was off.

I nudge his side with my elbow. "Tell me what happened." Obviously, something did. I slide out of both boots and pull my legs up on the passenger seat, criss-cross-applesauce.

Kai takes another sip and sighs, turning the cup in his hands and staring into it. "I really saw Cole. No doubt about it."

My heart skips a nervous beat. So, he meant what he said when he woke up from… death. "Tell me everything." I lean forward, clinging to his every word. If he saw Cole, then I could see—

"I saw him, but—"

"*But* what?" Dang. I figured there was a reason for his lack of exuberant joy that this actually worked.

"*But* I couldn't reach him." He turns the cup some more, warming his hands on it. "First, it was just like the car accident. I remember hearing you talk to me, and that's actually the last thing that faded away. Before that I couldn't see, I couldn't quite think anymore. Then the colors went, bleaching out like last time. Your voice came from far away, and then it was gone—then I was gone, and back in the Realm, only... Only it looked different this time. More real." He takes a sip of hot chocolate.

My gaze stays glued to him. "What then?" He was in there for over four minutes. *Something* must have happened during that time.

"I wondered how to find him. Hadn't really thought about that, you know? So, I started calling out his name, and then I saw him, in the distance, like behind a wall of fog so thick I thought I couldn't keep track of him. I started to run, but like in a bad dream I wouldn't get there, as if that fog was keeping me back, and whenever I thought I would soon have caught up with him, the fog got thicker, and—" His voice cracks and he closes his eyes. "And then I was back here."

Dang. Over four minutes of chasing his brother, and then nothing. "At least you saw him." It's not what he wants to hear, I know that. Beyond frustrating.

Kai looks up from his cup, eyes filled with sorrow, voice barely a whisper. "He looked happy, Gwen. Happy. Not desperate to get back, not in pain. *Happy.* Maybe... maybe it's where he's supposed to be. Maybe I'm hunting a ghost, just to make myself feel better."

I pull my knees up to my chest and wrap my arms around

them. Cole looked happy… that's good, right? Isn't that what we want? That our loved ones are happy in the afterlife? "Did he see you?" I know the answer from the way his face drops before he says it.

"No. He never saw me." Sadness radiates off him coupled with a tinge of disappointment and a sorrow that wasn't there before, at least not to that degree. He gave it all, literally, to get in contact with his brother, and then this. Maybe we should have prepped more for failure.

Another thought takes root, one I don't want to give voice, but have to. I bite down on my lip. "I'm sorry to ask this, but… Are you sure this was the Realm and not something your O2-deprived brain came up with? How do you know it was real?" I don't know what I want to hear. *Pic or it didn't happen* is obviously *not* going to happen. I can't expect any proof whether his experience was real other than what he says, but boy, do I want it to be real. With all my might, because let's be honest, I only have two options: Buy into the idea of an afterlife and contacting it, or not. And as it is, the only experts—and I'm using that term loosely—the only experts telling me it's real are Kai and Calista.

The seconds tick by while Kai stares into the cup of hot chocolate, ever so slowly turning it in his hands. "It was real," he says eventually, his voice firm. "It started the same as when we both died during the accident. Heck, Gwen, your aunt described it the same. It was real." His jaw is set in a hard line.

Half of the weight on my shoulders drops off as I nod. "Okay. We have a pattern. That makes me think there must be something to it other than hallucinations, right? I mean, why would yours be the same twice in a row and the same as Calista's?"

Kai keeps his gaze trained down, studying the hot chocolate with such intensity, I'm getting concerned there's something wrong with it. "I saw you."

"Huh? What do you mean?"

"I saw you doing CPR on me."

"Like an out-of-body experience?"

He nods, and I weigh my head from left to right. "Okay. But your brain could've filled in what it should've looked like—"

"You dropped the BVM. It fell and rolled under the Freezer. You got it back with your foot."

I stare at him, open mouthed. There's no way he could've known that. Even if he had been fully awake in the CryoTherm he wouldn't have been able to see that because of the chamber's walls. "Holy cow," I whisper as realization strikes. "Your soul really left your body."

Kai swallows. "That it did."

For a moment, we sit in silence, both digesting the magnitude of what just happened. No, I didn't just stop Kai's heart on a whim. I had somewhat believed there was a chance of an afterlife, thanks to Kai's and Calista's stories. And, I guess, I hope springs eternal. That being said, him seeing me seals the deal.

I imagine Kai's soul, floating above me, watching me—

A rush of heat swamps my system: He was watching me.

I pick at my cuticles. "What... what else did you see?" Like, me touching your cheek and whispering to you. Please no. That would be a new high for embarrassment.

There's a slight pause before he replies, enough to make my heart skip a beat. "Nothing. Why? Should I have seen anything else?"

"No." Not at all. Nope. Nope-di-nope. "Just, uhh, curious."

The corner of his lip twitches, but he keeps his gaze trained into that hot chocolate. "Okay then."

I clear my throat. "Right. Good, back to the topic. I'm sorry you didn't get to talk to Cole, but..." I suck in my lower lip and chew on it. "Maybe we shouldn't have assumed it was easy to contact somebody in the afterlife." I swipe a nonexistent strand of hair out of my face. "I mean, two days ago, I for one wasn't even sure there was an afterlife, and now you've been back to the Realm. And you've seen Cole. Maybe that's as good as it gets for us. It's also a kind of closure, you know? We don't even know if we can talk to him. We already know bringing him back won't work." Calista said it wasn't possible, and even from a factual medical perspective she probably would've been right.

"Yeah." He nods. "Kind of." He looks out the window at the CryoTherm, and somehow, I don't believe him. This is not the closure he was going for, I know that.

Worry wraps its tendrils around my heart and squeezes. What if I can't talk to Sarah either? It would throw a big, ugly wrench into my plan to apologize.

A melodic beep disturbs the silence. "Oh crap." I dart down to grab my bag from the floor, searching for my phone. "Grampie." I completely forgot about him. I unlock my phone and the message pops right up.

Grampie: Didn't forget about your old grandpa, did you?

Behind it he put a winking smiley and an eye-rolling one, followed by a balled fist and a crying face. I sigh. Should have never shown him how to switch to the emoji keyboard on his iPad.

I throw the phone back into my bag and turn to Kai. "We need to go. Grampie expected me around noon, now it's one, and I really, really don't want him to find out what we did."

"Say no more." Kai turns all business and hands me the cup with what's left of the hot chocolate to buckle himself up. Ten seconds later, we make our way out of the train yard and back onto the road, leaving all the equipment as it was, powered down and waiting for us.

Waiting for another death.

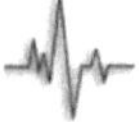

"Excuse me for keeping Gwen for so long." Kai shakes Grampie's hand carefully, as if afraid to break the old man's bones.

Grampie, on the other hand, gives Kai the grandfatherly once over before he nods. "It's quite all right," he grumps, "I remember being young. It's been a while, but still." He adjusts his position in his chair at the kitchen table—the one I'm sure he must have left since this morning's breakfast. I hope. He couldn't have sat there the whole time, could he?

"How are you holding up, son? Dora tells me you've been taking it quite severely to heart?"

Despite Grampie's gentle probing, Kai's whole body tenses, although his voice is light when he answers. "It's been rough, but Cole… seems to be doing fine."

Grampie raises an eyebrow at that. "Well then. I'm glad you're joining us for lunch, Gwen was not herself this morning at all. Maybe this way, she'll at least not daydream of you."

"Grampie!" I call out, smacking his shoulder softly. "I didn't!" I mean, I totally was thinking of Kai, but not the way he thinks.

Although I really want to.

Grampie giggles, while Kai's face spreads into a wide grin. "You daydreamed of me? I want to know all about it." He crosses both arms behind his head and leans back in his chair, boyish smirk on his face.

"Oh, whatever." I place the bowl with the quickly reheated soup onto the table. There is just no winning with these two, it appears.

Over the course of the meal, Kai warms up, literally and figuratively. His face regains some color and he becomes more and more lively as him and Grampie start talking all things Kampton that I don't have a clue about. The more they talk, the more animated Grampie gets as well, the parts of him that used to be mayor for two decades shining through. I wish I had seen him during that time, but when I was born, he was already retired and only volunteered at city functions instead of directing them. Still, the Grampie I know from back then was vibrant, his presence filling the room the moment he entered it. Only the last couple of years have taken that from him, and boy, does he hate it.

At one point, Grampie fishes for something under the tablecloth. "Before I forget it." He pulls out an envelope and places it in front of me, keeping his fingers on it. "This arrived two days ago. Your mom told me to not give it to you, but I figured…" He drops his voice to a conspiratorial whisper. "You decide for yourself." With that, he leans back and leaves the letter in front of me.

I don't need to ask who sent it. I know the handwriting.

It's the same as Sarah's.

"Mrs. Matthews." I swallow hard. Sarah's mom.

On my right, Kai tilts his head to the left, one eyebrow up.

My fingers shake as I reach for the envelope. It weighs a ton, yet when I open it, there's only one page in there, embossed with the Matthews' family seal.

The last time I spoke to Sarah's mom was… before July 31st. After… well, I was hospitalized first. Then under observation. Then not allowed to contact anyone to *not stress myself.*

They buried Sarah without me.

And I haven't even been to the cemetery, because Mom wanted to avoid re-traumatization. After that Dad kept me out of the public eye at home to protect me, but when it became clear the press wasn't going to forget what happened, he shipped me out here faster than I could protest. How fitting Mrs. Matthews is writing me now, hours before I'm going to meet her dead daughter.

Grampie gives me a worried look. "Go." He nods his chin toward the living room. "We'll be fine." Not a second later, he asks Kai some kind of question I don't hear, engaging him into a conversation my brain doesn't process.

Sarah's mom wrote.

I stare at the letter in front of me until I find myself in my chair in front of the window. When I unfold the paper, little black dots dance in front of my vision. Easy. Easy, Gwen. No need to faint. The worst that can happen is that Mrs. Matthews blames me for her daughter's death.

And I'm doing that myself already.

I take a deep breath in and blow it out through pursed lips.

Dear Gwen,

I hope you're doing better. I keep checking in with your mom and asking for you, but she thinks you still need some distance to heal, and I completely understand. Please know that I wouldn't write to you unless I thought it was necessary, and I think it is.

I'm not sure how much you're in the loop of the investigation, but something has come up. The toxicology report lists a couple of drugs in Sarah's killer's bloodstream, but the main one is really hard to get and very expensive. They're wondering who supplied him with that, and they're thinking there could have been somebody else involved.

I shake my head, chasing the fog away. Wait, somebody else? What does she mean? Like, pulling the strings? Not a one-man-con? And how should I know? Why doesn't the DA cut a deal with that monster: talk, and you'll get some years off your sentence?

They've found text messages on the killer's phone to a drug dealer. The killer promised to have money in a day or two, over half a million dollars. Now, I'm sure you can figure out where this is going. Although there was no request for ransom, our lawyer thinks it is a possibility that you—specifically you, Gwen—were targeted by that man for the money he needed.

Huh? We knew that. Kidnap the heir to a fortune is a get-rich-in-an-instant trick, especially because she owns quite a few of these shares already and Daddy has more where those came from.

Anyway, to get to the point... Gwen, I need you to remember what happened that night. Has Niparko said anything? Did he want money? Was there anybody else? What else do you remember? Anything can help. I need to understand why my baby girl is gone, and if this was a targeted kidnapping, it would change everything, for us and for you, obviously.

Forever in your debt,

Christine Matthews

What. The. Hell.

I let the letter sink down to my lap. Every breath I take is raspy and none of them get any air in. At all. My fingers claw at my collar. Must loosen it. Must get air in. Must breathe.

Forever in your debt.

No.

I'm forever guilty, no matter what.

I bend forward and stick my head between my knees, a groan escaping me.

Can't think.

If this was kidnapping.

What does she mean? It's crystal clear this was a kidnapping. Why is that even a question? This was about money and nothing—

The flash of a grin, a hand in my hair, a drink in my hand—

A moan leaves my throat. "No," I breathe. No, no, no! It's wrong. None of that happened. None. I slam my palm against my forehead. I *need* to remember, whether I want to or not.

Only I can't. Nothing's there.

And for the first time ever, that really scares me.

What am I missing? What does Mrs. Matthews know that I don't?

I scan over the letter again: *in the loop with the investigation, expensive drugs, no ransom request*—wait, no ransom request? It was *all* about money. None of the lies the press spun are true. *Not* about partying. *All* about the money. Who would kidnap the heir to a fortune and not want—

A knock on the door interrupts my near-panic before I can completely freak out—and let's be honest, I'm already baseline crazy these days as it is.

"Hey, Gwen?" The door opens a tad.

Kai.

As if caught red handed, I straighten up and plaster a smile on my face. "Yeah?"

Kai opens the door wider, brows pulled down slightly. "You okay?" He looks pointedly at the letter in my hands.

"Uh, yeah, yeah, totally." I fold the letter and stuff it behind the cushion on the left. "What's going on?"

Kai shrugs. "I think your grandfather is getting tired. He said I shouldn't bother you, and he's trying to not let me see it, but he's basically falling asleep sitting up." He gives me an apologetic smile.

Sounds like Grampie. "Thanks, Kai." I jump out of my chair, leaving the letter and all the thoughts I don't want behind.

In the kitchen, Grampie plays with the same wooden box he had in the living room the day before. Au contraire to last time, his moves are slow, his fingers not half as sure as before.

"Okay, Grampie, nap time. I'll bring you to your room, okay?" I help him up by the elbow, since both of his hands are busy holding on to the box.

"I'll do the dishes." Kai takes the plates and carries them over to the dishwasher. I don't know what it is, but Kai doing the dishes as if he lived here and it was the most natural thing in the world… I feel like we're a team. Together. It's an odd sensation, part belonging, part excitement, and a whole lot of butterflies.

Then I realize what I just thought.

Butterflies because he's doing the dishes.

Something must be wrong with me. Even more so than we already knew.

"Gwen." Grampie's soft voice brings me back. "He's still going to be here in a minute, you know?" I hear the smile that comes with the teasing.

"Stop it, Grampie," I whisper, guiding him out the kitchen before Kai gets even more of a big head. "It's not what you think."

"Of course not." He stuffs the box under one arm and pats my shoulder with the other hand, as if I was a three-year-old. "That's what I told your Grammie's parents too." He gives the box a small shake. "And speaking of parents." His playful tone is gone. "Your mother called again. You might want to call her back tonight. You know how she is."

Oh yes, don't I know it. She worries too much, and I bet my phone call from earlier didn't help my cause. I blow a raspberry as I help Grampie into his recliner chair in his library. "Yeah, yeah, will do. For now, she can wait." I have more important stuff to do, like… meeting Sarah.

Like getting myself killed.

No. Like, apologizing. Like, finding out what happened.

If it really was kidnapping.

My stomach cramps up, but I won't give in to the rising nausea. Or to the panic coming with it, the panic that I'm more guilty than I know—and I know I'm guilty, if not personally, then at least by association. I'm the heir to MSC. I have money. My dad has money. If it wasn't for who I am and for me wanting to go to that party, Sarah would still be alive.

But what if being the heir to MSC wasn't truly what I'm

guilty of? What if I made some really stupid and idiotic decisions? What if those glimpses my brain showed me are the real deal? A boy, cute. Sarah, me. Flirting. *Drinking.*

Bile leaves a bitter taste inside my mouth.

If those glimpses are real, then… then my guilt changes from passive, to active. Passive, because if it was kidnapping, it was out of my control. But if I was so stupid and got us drunk and to leave the party to who knows where… then that makes me actively guilty. My direct actions got Sarah killed.

My. Direct. Actions.

We don't know why Sarah was killed, Gwendolyn. But we do know none of it was your fault. You didn't kill her, but the kidnapper did. It was his decision, not yours. You're a victim as much as Sarah, it's him who is responsible. Him, not you.

I want to believe my shrink, I really do, but I can't help but blame myself. It's what happens when your best friend gets killed and you survive. Thanks, survivor's guilt. And if I acted irresponsibly and drank…

I shake my head quickly. No. A made-up memory, nothing else. We would've heard if I had alcohol in my bloodstream, or if a boy was involved.

Was there anybody else?

Nope. Wasn't.

I clear my throat and drape Grampie's favorite blanket across his lap. "What's this, anyway?" I tap the wooden box on his lap twice.

Grampie frowns. "Old memories, Gwennie-dear. Pictures. Letters. This"—he gives it one more shake—"is Grammie and me. And I can't get the damned thing to open."

Grammie and Grampie. They were quite the couple, from the moment they met. Also quite the trouble makers, although that's a part Mayor O'Karran likes to drop when he talks about the past. I take the box from him, gently set it on the table next to him, and tug the blanket up higher.

I swallow dry. "Hey, Grampie?" I push his current book closer to him on the table. "You know I love you, right?"

He gives me a skeptical look down his nose. "Of course. Are you worried I'm going to feel left out with that new man in your life?" Only the twinkle in his eyes gives away he's pulling my leg.

"Grampie." I groan. "Whatever." I give him a quick hug, trying to put all the love in it I have for this old man, while not making it too obvious something is going on.

Not an easy task.

Once Grampie is set, I sneak out of his library and back to the kitchen, where Kai waits in front of the window, looking out into the snowy backyard. His hands are stuffed into his pockets, head slightly tilted to the left. He's so completely lost in thought he doesn't hear me come in.

For a moment I stay right where I am, door still open and in my hand, and enjoy the view.

And dang if it didn't make me... happy.

It's completely messed up—the way we met and what we did—but yet I'm glad about it.

I close the door quietly and step next to him, arm brushing against his and burning where we touch. My gaze follows his to the snow-covered trees, the birds trying to find some seeds that have fallen off the feeder, and the clouds rolling in, a promise of more snow for this afternoon.

Kai's shoulders heave in a silent sigh. "I need to go back in. I need to try again."

And *boom,* the peacefulness is gone. "What?" I can't have heard that right. "You just were there, Kai. Over four minutes, you can't just—"

"I have to." The despair echoing in those tiny three words weighs a ton.

Shaking my head, I cross my arms in front of my chest. "We never said we'd do it more than once. That's—"

He turns around and takes me by the shoulders. "I know. I know. Believe me, I know. My chest hurts like a… well, badly, from the defibrillator and the compressions, but I have to go back in. I was so close. *So* close. The least I want to do is talk to him. I want to say good-bye, and no, I don't want to use your aunt. I have to say good-bye in person. Myself. I can't let him go *just like this.*"

I open my mouth, then close it again. It's not that I don't get where he's coming from. To a degree, my problems are the same. Still, I shake my head. In a hospital, he would have been observed in the ICU for at least a day after that much CPR. You don't die and go right back to business—and for sure not right back to dying, unless you want to stay dead. "You just died, Kai. This isn't like getting another tattoo where the old one still hurts. This is us completely shutting down your body. We never said we'd do it twice. Once is crazy enough, and—"

"Please." He smooths his thumbs over my shoulders in idle circles, the sparks they're causing working their way into my heart and setting it on fire. "I can't do it alone, and… *please.*"

Argh. I close my eyes, trying to shield myself from the emotions, the misery, the heartbreak, but to no avail. "Maybe." I'm weak in even giving him that much, but I can't pull that rug from under him with a clear *no*. On the other hand… I can delay the problem.

I meet his gaze and shake my head once more, for emphasis. "Not today though. You have to give your body time to recover." And I need time to come up with an excuse, or a reason why he can't go in again. Once is reckless and idiotic already, twice is pushing our luck.

One shot. That's all.

I look up into those brown eyes. "Now it's my turn."

Chapter Sixteen

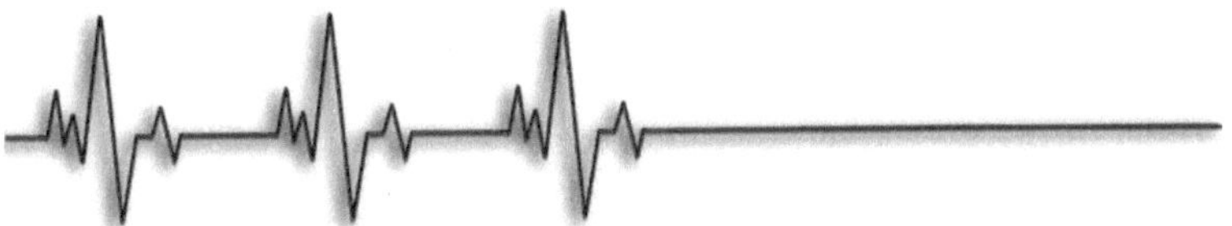

Favor, Returned

This time around, I work much more mechanically.

We go through the same moves we've executed twice now, once for practice and once for Kai's trip to the Realm. Now we're doing it for mine.

Since we made our way back to the train yard, I've started calling it *my trip to the Realm*, rather than what it is: my impending death. I find it much easier to cope with this way. It's a trip to the Realm and back, nothing more, a short journey of four minutes, although I added another task to my list. Yes, I need to apologize to Sarah. Big time. That much hasn't changed. But I also need to find out what she remembers, because obviously my mind is a really big help when it comes to that.

Not.

So, I've gotta find Sarah, apologize to her for taking her to the party with me, find out if she remembers what happened, and then come back.

Piece of cake.

I ignore the shaking of my hands as I recheck the programming and the defibrillator. This morning I thought I could never do what Kai did, take somebody's word for it and trust myself in their hands, not knowing if this would work or not. I thought I'd never have that kind of courage, going first. Now my point of view has changed. Now I think going second is much harder, especially after how difficult it was to get Kai back.

The person I was before the kidnapping would've called me crazy for what I'm about to do. She'd never have considered anything so risky, for herself or others. The person I am now has a different point of view. She accepts that there are risks involved, but she also knows the potential gain outweighs them.

I sigh. Part of my naiveté is gone. I know it might not work out to see Sarah, or to get me back to life. I know I might stay there permanently. Might stay *dead* permanently. A tiny part of me whispers that I couldn't really complain if that happened. In fact, it would be appropriate payback for what I did.

And maybe that part is right.

But it should also shut up right now.

I wipe my palms on my thighs, blow out a deep breath to ground myself, then list everything off my fingers. "Okay. I've got the CryoTherm programmed for my weight and shape, the defib is set, oxygen is on, and you have your instructions, but in case something goes wrong, there's a flow chart of what to do, and if then—"

Kai lays a finger under my chin and lifts it up. He's right in front of me in all his Kai-ness, tall, wide, dark. He glides the same finger from my chin up to rest across my lips, and I almost die right there.

Who needs a CryoTherm for that?

My heart hammers like a drum, feverishly enjoying what might be its last hurrah.

"Nervous?" he asks with that soft smile of his.

"I'm not nervous." I breathe against his finger, the sensation of my lips on his skin electrifying me. This is better than the defibrillator. Much, much better.

The smile widens. "Obviously not." His finger brushes over my mouth and down my neck until he reaches my pulse running amok, feeling it. "You know… you don't have to do this."

Maybe he's right. But it doesn't change that I opened this Pandora's Box, and now I'm going to check what's inside. "I know."

"Then don't." His gaze drops down to the ground. "Don't." His jaw tightens, and I get how he feels. It was the same for me this morning, carrying the responsibility of another person's life on my shoulders.

"I'll be fine. You won't let anything bad happen to me." I'm sure of that. I feel safe—or as safe as one can five minutes before inducing cardiac arrest.

His jaw sets. "It's not worth it just for the experience,

Gwen! I needed to see Kai, but for you it's curiosity and nothing else!"

I step back, breaking contact with his finger. My skin feels cold right away, like something was missing. "I'm doing this." I unbutton my coat and throw it past Kai onto the bed of the truck. "Now." The sweater follows stat, leaving me in a shirt. Goosebumps break out. This is so not going to be fun.

"Gwen—" Kai stops in mid-movement the second my shirt goes and I'm left in a bra. His eyes pop open, and he's staring. Flat out staring.

And, despite the cold, it feels damn good.

His gaze stays on me when I kick off my boots and tear off my socks.

It stays on me when I'm doing my very best to at least pretend the cold wasn't bothering me too much, as if the snow wasn't burning under my feet, cramping up my muscles and shooting pain up my calf.

It stays on me when the jeans are next—but once it gets interesting and I slide them down over my butt, Kai looks away.

The apple in his throat bobs up and down before he works a hand through his emo-hair. "I'll get the lid open some more for you." His voice is rough as he turns toward the CryoTherm just before my pants are completely gone and I'm left in crimson-red underwear with goosebumps all over my pale skin and nobody checking it out. Disappointment hits hard, but I push it aside. Not what I want to feel in my potential last moments alive.

Hopping from one foot onto the other with my arms wrapped around my chest, I make it to the freezer in two seconds. All I want is to crawl into the truck and turn the heater on, I'm *that* cold already. Imagining having to crawl into the cold CryoGel and being cooled down even further is completely unappealing to me. Completely. My feet hurt like a b— well, a lot, and to say the cold was making me miserable would be an understatement.

The moment that thought crosses my mind I feel it like a punch to the gut.

What a disgusting wimp I am.

Sarah died because I was an easy way to get money, and here I am, with an option to apologize, to see her again, and all without dying painfully with a knife buried inside my body— and I'm complaining I'm cold.

I lift my chin up high. "I'm ready." My voice is softer than I'd like to, but at least not shaking.

Kai turns around. "Me too." He holds out a hand for me and helps me up the two steps we made out of old fruit boxes and into the freezer, gaze never dipping down from my face despite all my goods basically dancing right in front of his nose on my way up and into the CryoTherm.

Disappointment ducks under my defense and delivers a mean sucker punch this time, and it makes me mad at myself. Priorities, Gwendolyn.

I shove my legs through the cold gel cushions down into the freezer. It feels much nicer than anticipated. Not as… well, freezing. Maybe part of that neurotoxin still clings to the plastic and takes off the sting. Easing myself down, I rest my head in the groove designed to surround it as much as possible to guarantee rapid and successful brain cooling. Above me, Kai untangles the EEG electrodes and sticks one onto my right, and one onto my left temple. When he pulls his hand away, he sweeps a careless finger over the side of my jaw, bringing my heart to stumble in response.

Am I glad the EKG isn't on yet, or he would've totally seen my heart on display, as if my crush on him wasn't already embarrassing enough.

Kai peels off the sticky tape of the red, black, and blue electrodes. The first two go under my clavicles and the third on my left side, right under my bra. He doesn't meet my eyes, instead works mechanically, checking the settings before he finally looks at me again.

"We're good," he says, tapping a button, and the slight sound of the EKG's beeping with every heartbeat of mine disturbs the silence.

Suddenly, the *beep* turned real. By turning on that EKG, everything became so final.

So much scarier.

"Kai?" It's a wonder he can hear me, but he does.

"What?" He leans closer into the chamber, his expression softening when he sees my face. "You don't have to do this, Gwen. We can just forget—"

That's the problem, I have forgotten already. "No. I'm doing this. Push the button, Kai." I'm not balking at the last moment. Sarah didn't choose to die. She didn't need to die. This is what I have to do. This is my closure, my good-bye to her, no matter how it goes.

"Any letters?"

"Huh?"

"For your parents?"

I shake my head. "No. No. Not necessary." Won't need it if I come out alive, and if I'm dead… they'll know it's because of Sarah.

Kai's gaze bores into mine as if he could read me. Without taking his eyes off me, he fumbles with his right hand to find the big red button. "Okay then," he whispers and pushes it.

The change is instantaneous. "Holy crap," I breathe, as the gel around me turns into a bath of ice water. "Cold, cold, cold." The CryoTherm adjusts the gel packs around me, engulfing me to the max. My uncovered chest is burning in comparison, just from the lack of cooling packs there.

I know exactly what's going to happen next. I've seen it in Kai.

And I'm afraid.

I'm afraid it'll hurt.

I'm afraid it won't work, one way or the other. That I die, but won't meet Sarah, and it was all for nothing. Or that I'll die and never come back, that I'll never recover from July 31st, that I'll never have the chance for a normal life.

And I'm afraid of what else I might see or hear.

Kai's large, blissfully warm hand pulls my icy and numb one out of the gel and holds it. "It's going to be fine." He works his fingers in-between mine. "I'll watch over you. I'll get you back. Try to relax. It's not going to hurt. It's—"

His voice is all I hear, his large, dark eyes all I see. Part of me notices a short sting all over my body at one point, but it's gone a moment later, and so is the pain from the cold. From there on, I'm surrounded by a growing sensation of peacefulness, with Kai right in the center of it. My vision grows blurry and blacks out, yet I still see him. His voice reaches me from far away, so far away I can't make out what it says anymore, but knowing he's there is all I need.

I don't feel my body anymore, and I only regret it because I can't feel Kai's hand around mine.

Bit by bit, everything fades away. I forget what I'm about to do, I forget who I am. My vision is gone and blacked out, my hearing only brings the soft sound of a voice that means *something* to me, although I can't remember what.

Then a short, sharp sting on my chest, and then…

Nothing.

Chapter Seventeen

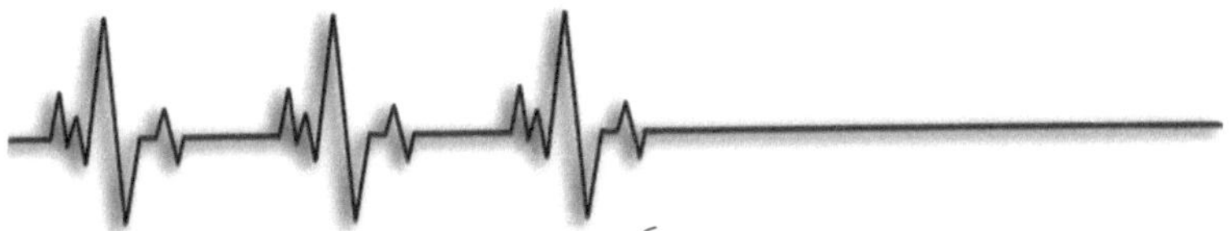

Reunion

'm confused. A moment ago, everything was fading out and now I'm—

Shit.

I'm hovering in the air, maybe a good three yards above my body—my *dead* body. I jerk back, my, uh, spirit body drifting up some more.

"No way," I breathe, holding my hands in front of my eyes and turning them left to right.

They look exactly like they normally do.

I glance down my body. I'm in the same red underwear I went into the CryoTherm with, the same underwear I'm still wearing down there, in the CryoTherm.

Holy everything, it worked!

Kai made my heart stop, and I crossed into the Realm.

Down on the ground, Kai gently swipes a strand of hair out of my face, a gesture so tender it pulls on a heartstring. I should be down there, with him, feeling his touch instead of merely observing it.

As if my thought alone was enough, my body lowers toward the CryoTherm.

"Gwen?"

My movement stops right there, like I was pulled back by a string. That voice—

"Sarah." I crane my neck left-right-up-down until I see her, just like on the day she died, floating behind me, giving me that wide grin I loved so much about her.

A *grin*.

Not a fist to the face.

"You crazy, girl?" She grins wider. "Yeah. You absolutely crazy." It's her best Chris Rock impression, and it makes me laugh out loud in relief, happiness, and grief all the same.

"Sarah." I run toward her through the air as if it was the most natural thing to do. "Sarah." I crash into her, encircling her in a hug, like so many times before, and it feels heavenly.

"Hey, crazy," she replies softly, hugging me back like this was any normal day, any normal hello before we'd go and spend the afternoon together.

I cling to her neck so hard I'd surely be choking her if she were still alive, only she isn't anymore, and it's my fault.

"I'm so sorry." My voice breaks. "So, so sorry. I should've never taken you to the party, then he would never have taken you either. I should—"

"Stop it, Gwen. Stop it right there. Yes, there was a price on your head, but we couldn't have known. Nobody knew he would do that to us." Sarah pulls me away and gives me a good look. She produces a tissue from somewhere and hands it to me, but I don't take it. "Gwen? Hey." Her hands are on my shoulders, squeezing. "You shouldn't even be here. Why the heck are you? What's going on?"

I stare straight into the blue eyes I've shared most of my life with. "I don't remember," I whisper. "What happened? I need to know, it's all gone, and—"

"It's a great idea." Sarah falls around my neck and giggles. "Let's go." She stumbles a bit. "Whoopsie. Last one was too m'ch, huh?" Another giggle.

"Naaah." My response is about the same level of giddiness. It's too funny though. Everything, I mean.

A sharp pain shoots through my head and I wince. What the—

"Gwen? What's wrong?"

We look at each other like we've done a million times, worry shining in her eyes. I swallow hard, surprised that still works. As much as I want to, I can't ignore those flashes anymore.

Sarah takes me by the shoulders. "Hey. Stop freaking me out. And damn it, Gwen, you need to get out of here." Her gaze drops down to the ground of the train yard, partially hidden in some kind of mist. Everything's blurry to me, like, not quite in focus. She squints for a second before her mouth drops open.

"No way, Gwen O'Karran. Is that boy who I think it is?" She pulls me around by my arm, so that both of us look down at my body in the CryoTherm and the boy with the full shock of dark hair bent over me, back of his hand still caressing my cheek.

As if pulled in by a magnet, I drop a couple of feet, leaving Sarah hovering above me.

She laughs out loud. "So that's what's anchoring you, huh? Kai Harrison? How in the world…?" She comes down to me, and her sheer presence lets me float higher again, away from Kai.

I shrug. "Well, it just happened. Cole is in a coma, and Kai was about to kill himself to find him."

"He—what?" Her jaw drops.

Agreed. It sounds so much crazier saying it out loud. "Accident. Cole was clinically dead for a while before they got him back. Kai thinks his soul is trapped here, so if you've seen him, we need Cole to wake up." A cold breeze brushes over us and brings goosebumps to my skin. Underwear is not the way to go in the Realm, it appears. I wrap my arms around my chest. "Anyway, I figured I'd give him the benefit of the doubt and help him make it into the afterlife, and while we're at it, look for you. Because, you know, I'm sorry, Sarah. I'm so, so sorry. If I could make it undone, I would, I—"

"Forget it, Gwen. Seriously."

I stomp my foot. Feels weird doing that hovering in the air. "I *have* already, Sarah! That's the problem. I can't remember a thing." Sheesh, even tears work here, at least my eyes are watering up. "I don't remember anything. I leave the house, I wake up in the ICU."

She presses her lips into a thin line. "Believe me, you don't want to remember the details."

"Maybe," I whisper. "But I don't even have a rough outline. I feel I'm going crazy. I need your help. Mom sent me to Kampton to get over my PTSD and get some distance from the press, but if I wasn't here, I can tell you at this point I'd even gone and visited Niparko in jail to trigger some kind of memory, at least."

Sarah stares at me open mouthed. "Your mom—? Wait, you'd visit Niparko in *jail*—"

A wave of grey fog rolls over us. Cold, wet, thick—so thick, visibility is down to inches within a mere second. Wha—

Sarah grabs my forearm through the grey mist. I can't see her, but I feel her grip on me, hard. Panic swings in her voice when she calls out to me. "Gwen! Seriously! Your dad! The police need to examine—" She yelps out as a gust of foggy wind crashes into me and rips me out of her grasp.

Her fingernails scratch over my skin. "Sarah!" I stumble and only barely catch myself. "Where are you?" I can't see her—I can't see the hand in front of my face, it's too foggy! No more wind, only fog, fog, fog—milky white fog freakin' everywhere!

I whirl to the left, the right—where is she? "Sarah!" What did she mean—Dad, police…?

A short gasping sounds comes from somewhere, a grunt—and then nothing.

My hearts drops into my stomach. Oh, shit. "Sarah!" That didn't sound good. What happened? Where is she? Where am I? I can't see the CryoTherm with all this freakin' fog—

Another wind-fog-wave crashes into me. "Ugh!" I stumble,

but to no avail. Like I'm nothing more than a leaf falling off a tree, it knocks me off my feet and makes me tumble down. Or up, I wouldn't know. I yelp out once, trying to regain my balance, trying to stagger back to my feet, but to no avail. "Sarah!"

Nothing.

Another gust of stormy fog blows into me from behind, this one so harsh it throws me forward onto all fours.

If I wasn't dead already, I'd say this thing was trying to kill me.

"Sarah!" My heart is pumping harder than it ever has when I was alive. "Sarah! Cole! Somebody!" I yell at the top of my lungs, scrambling to my feet against the wind, against the fog, every breath wheezy, every motion shaky. I barely make it to standing before I get thrown off my feet again. "Ouch!" My head snaps back into my neck, accompanied by a cracking sound of my spine. "Sarah! Cole! Help, I need—"

Like a switch is flipped, the wind seizes and the fog parts. Some of its tendrils still waft through the air, but at least it's not all white around me.

"Holy cow." I stay down on all fours, sucking in one harsh breath after another. Air. Feels good to finally suck in a big breath of air. How ironic, given the fact that currently I'm dead.

"Who are you?" The voice coming from in front of me is soft and curious, deep and warm.

And I know it. Because it's Kai's voice, only it isn't.

I jerk my head up, and there he is, just like I remember from the river. "Cole," I breathe. As fast as I can I sort my extremities and scramble up to standing, each movement bringing up more of that fog around me again.

He narrows his eyes. "Do I know you? Wait, I *do* know you."

It takes me quite the self-restraint to keep myself from rolling my eyes. I can't believe I'm about to say it, but then, time is of the essence. "I'm the girl in the frog bathing suit. From the river. In summer."

Apparently, that's enough of an explanation, because his eyes light up. "Hallelujah—the frog bathing suit, no way. What brings you here?" His face falls. "Aw, sorry. Insensitive. You just died? I've been dead for a while, it's not as bad as you'd think." He winks at me, and it makes him look so much like his brother I drop down another foot again, like I was pulled back into my ice-cold body.

Dead? No, not dead! Crap, not the kind of talk I can pull off in a couple of seconds or however long I still have, because there can't be much more time before Kai begins to revive my body. "Actually, Cole, it's complicated. Kai's looking for you. He was here to—"

"Kai is dead?" The horror in his voice matches the look on his face. "Why don't I know, I should—"

"Listen, Cole, no. Kai isn't dead, but neither—"

I yelp out once as the mist in front of me explodes into something bright and much, *much* whiter than before, bringing up another wall of fog so thick it would suffocate me if I was still breathing for real. Like before it makes it impossible to see through. "Cole, where—"

"Get out," a female voice hisses at me a split second before I get shoved in the shoulders and thrown back.

I land on my butt, catching my fall with my hands outstretched behind me. "Hey, what—"

"No 'hey', no 'what'. Shut up. Get out of here, or I'll make sure you join us. Permanently." Another shove, and this time I catch a glimpse of blond, curly hair and a pretty young face that rings a bell somehow.

"Back off." She hisses, and it doesn't sound friendly at all.

Zzzing!

A burning, stabbing pain shoots through my chest, like a bomb going off underneath my sternum. Holy cow, what is she doing to me? I scream out and drop down a couple of feet. "Cole!" I reach up, but Cole is gone, swallowed by the fog. I'm alone with the scowling girl towering above me, hands on her hips like an archangel serving justice.

Another explosion inside my chest shoots pain from right to left. I scream out as I drop farther down, away from the girl whose eyes widen in surprise.

That's when I get it: It's not her doing this to me. It's Kai.

It must be Kai shocking my heart.

It's time to go back, and I want to go back. I want to be back with Kai.

As soon as the thought crosses my mind, I sink lower, the fog clearing below me. There he is, paddles in his hands, shocking me for the third time. "Come on, Gwen, come on, don't make it difficult for me!" He curses, the emotion in his voice drawing me even closer, like a magnet. How do I get back into my body, do I just dive in or—

"Not so fast." The girl wraps her fingers around my forearm and keeps me from descending farther. "You stay away from us, understood?" Her grip is much stronger than I would have thought.

I look up at her—

Blonde. Young. My age. Mad.

Her face is distorted in anger, and her grip on my arm would leave bruises if I was still alive. She's pulling hard and up, away from Kai.

Oh, hell to the no!

"Let go of me!" I grunt, and claw at her fingers to break free of her hold.

She laughs. "Let go? Look, I don't know you, but here you are right after Kai comes in and tries to take away Cole. This is not how we play this game. Back. Off."

Zzzing!

Another fiery pain shoots through my heart, bringing another pulling sensation from below, threatening to tear me apart.

"Come on, Gwen! Crap!" Kai. From far, far away.

The girl's hold on my arm tightens. "I can keep you here. I can keep you, and none of them will be the wiser."

"No!" I pull back. That girl is crazy. "I won't let you—"

She laughs out loud. "You really don't know anything." She giggles, but it sounds artificial.

"Gwen! Gwen! Heartbeat! Like, now! Come back! I know you can hear me!" Kai sounds more and more desperate.

The girl's eyes drop down. "Huh. Interesting. Didn't expect that from Kai."

"Gwen, I'm here, you can find me! I'm here!"

My chest hurts again, like a gigantic bruise was forming on

it.

"Gwen, please. Don't leave me here. Come back! *Please*." The last part he said so softly it wasn't more than a whisper. Yet, I hear it the loudest.

My vision fades, a hum starts in my ears and gets louder, like the pain in my chest is getting achier by the second.

The girl releases me with an exaggerated move, as if she had touched something disgusting. "Just remember, back off. Either of you come here again, you stay. Especially *him*."

After that all sound is gone, all vision is gone.

All that stays is peace, the sensation of belonging—

—and then everything is black.

Chapter Eighteen

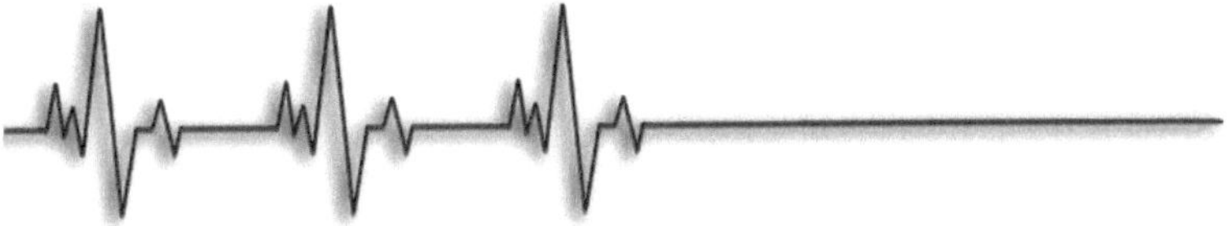

Kai's Home

Kai all but kicks open the bright blue entrance door to his house and ushers me inside.

"Come on. I'll make us some tea." He has his right arm wrapped around my shoulders so tight as if he could warm me up to more than freezing temperatures with it. Interestingly enough, it works. Wherever my body connects with his, I could swear I'm heating up to about a hundred degrees—centigrade, that is—although it doesn't tune down my shivering at all.

And right now, I'm a shivering mess, courtesy of the CryoTherm… and the last two hours.

The girl: *I can keep you here, and none of them will be the wiser.*

Mrs. Matthews' letter: no request for ransom.

Sarah: *Your dad, the police needs to examine—*

All of these tidbits run amok inside my head, chasing each other for the lead. Examine what? What am I supposed to make of that? Of any of that? What do I tell Kai when he asks what I saw in the Realm—and he will ask, I'm sure of it.

A bout of wind brings in some snowflakes before Kai kicks the door closed with his heel. "Up to the right, the stairs—"

"Kai? Would you mind—oh."

Both of us turn around to the older lady standing in the hallway, a jar of *something* in her hands. She must be at least in her mid-eighties, white curls on her head and freckles over her nose. Kai's grandma, no doubt about it.

"Moms." Kai growls under his breath. "Now's not—"

Yeah, no, we don't need her to know I'm frozen to the core, nor does she need to even get the inkling of why that's the case. Her and Grampie, they talk. I hold out my hand, on my best behavior. "G-good morning, ma'm. Gwen O'K-Karran."

The old lady breaks out in a wide smile. "Owen's granddaughter. About time I meet you, Gwendolyn. I'm Dora." She gives my hand a surprisingly strong shake. "I've heard so much about you."

And there it is, the slight dim in her eyes, the only hint at the extent of what exactly she heard from Grampie—and I'm sure she heard everything.

She—

The boy takes my hand, and I let him. "You know about the afterparty?"

I wince and cover it up with a fast smile. That same face again, the same boy. What the hell? I've never had great imagination, which makes these… *images* flashing in front of my inner eye even more disturbing. With this level of detail, can I still blame them on my mind making them up?

The answer to that question is bringing the acid in my stomach to rise.

"Moms, she's freezing." Kai takes the jar from his grandmother and pops it open before he hands it back to her. "We'll be upstairs." He drags me past his grandma and toward the stairs on the right.

"N-nice to m-meet you, ma'am." A wave of said bitter bile rises up my throat.

"Call me Dora, honey." Kai's grandma stays at the bottom of the stairs and watches us walk up, me wrapped in Kai's arm.

I can feel the arrows of her pity penetrate my skin.

And I hate it.

Because you can't accept what happened. What you might've done.

Oh, screw that shrink, I don't need that kind of talk, I'm giving myself enough of a hard time as it is.

I speed it up and let Kai hurry me up the stairs. The faster I'm away from those sad and knowing eyes, the better, because… the last hour gave me enough to digest.

We walk through a short hallway with soft, beige carpet. At the end, two doors sit across from each other, one decorated with the poster of a '59 Charger—which I only know because it says so on the poster—and the other one with a stylized red rose on a black background.

For that one I don't need to read the text to know it's Depeche Mode.

That one must be Kai's.

I appoint myself a score of a hundred points when Kai opens the Depeche Mode door. "Welcome to my room and excuse the mess." He lets go of my shoulders, grabs a couple of things off the floor and throws them into the corner behind the door. It doesn't make much of a difference, because his room isn't what I'd call cluttered. My mom would take me out for a mani-pedi if I kept my room at Kai's level of tidiness. I let my gaze roam around, a smile forming on my lips, despite the cold. This room is pretty much perfect, and fits Kai like a glove.

Two of the walls including the one with the bright white door we just walked through are painted in the most vibrant crimson red, but it's the other two to the left and right that make this a perfect Kai room. Divided into thirds, the lower third of the walls is painted in grey, the middle one in black, and the upper one in white. A couple of posters decorate the walls, more Depeche Mode, one larger Two Steps from Hell, and some photo collages. His desk, black of course, sits in front of the window, a laptop on its surface, screensaver on and waiting patiently for his return.

The eye catcher of the room though, at least for me, would be the Queen-sized bed against the three-colored wall on the right, because yes, of course my mind goes there. Matching the room with its black sheets and black covers, the bed melts into the background, only a small, green, stuffed animal frog sitting in the corner provides a splash of color. Oh, and the bright-red electric guitar leaned against the wall next to the bed.

Kai drops his jacket onto the floor and steps out of his boots, feet sinking into the fluffy grey carpet. He opens his closet—black wooden shutter doors integrated into the right wall—and rips out a blanket.

"Get out of your jacket. Too cold." Before I can as much as unwrap my arms from my body, he all but rips my jacket off of me and drapes the blanket around me. "Shoes off. We have heated floors."

I stumble when I kick off my boots, but the moment my feet sink into the soft carpet… Heaven.

"One minute, okay? Be right back with tea." He's out of the room in a heartbeat, fast steps bolting down the stairs to somewhere on the ground floor.

And just like that, I'm alone in Kai's room.

I turn around my axis. Me, in Kai's room. My younger self would be ecstatic, and if I wasn't still shell-shocked, I'd be ecstatic right now. But, as it is, my knees are wobbly. My stomach's in knots. I can't feel anything besides numb panic. Pulling the blanket closer to my body, I walk to the desk and its chair, because, let's be honest, I don't dare to sit on Kai's bed.

I fall into the chair and bury my head in my arms on the desk.

My chest hurts from the shocks and CPR. My body feels like it has been through the wringer. Twice.

Yet it's nothing against the pain in my heart.

What happened in the Realm? The fog, that girl?

Even more important—what really happened out there? On July 31st? Who's that blond boy? I'm sure I've never seen him before, but—

Wait.

I sit up straighter. Maybe this is what Mrs. Matthews meant, the *somebody else* who was there. It could've been him. But if the blond boy had been there, he would've been in the news. As far as I know, it was all about Sarah and me—Sarah, me, and *him*: Niparko. Nobody else was there, no matter what Mrs. Matthews might think.

So no, it must be something other than that.

I groan into my arms. What did Sarah mean with my dad and the police? He has more than cooperated with them. His invention was the reason we were found relatively fast. So, what does he need to give the police to examine?

If only I'd had more time in there, with Sarah. The fog came in just when things got interesting. I rub my eyes across my arm on the desk. Maybe there's still a possibility my brain made all of that up. Maybe I'm crazy—I mean, I'm half-way there already these days. My subconscious could have shown me what I wanted to see. The last spasms of a dying brain.

Harr-harr. Fat chance, at this point.

I groan and bang my head onto the desk twice, then let my forehead rest against the cool surface. Thinking is like quicksand. Whenever I try to focus on *that* night, I get nothing and end up replaying the same couple of scenes. I wish I could think more clearly. A dry huff leaves my throat. Yeah, maybe dying doesn't exactly improve that quality.

My phone vibrates inside my pocket. Without lifting my head, I fish for it and retrieve the buzzing thing from my pocket. If that's Grampie or my parents—

Nope. Calista.

Yeah. Definitely not in the mood right now. I reject the call the same time as the door opens and Kai comes back in, carrying a tray with two cups and a teapot, the strings of three tea bags dangling from it.

"Two more minutes and it's done." He sets the tray down on the desk to the right of me. When he pulls his hand back, it knocks over a framed picture. He puts it back up in one move, aligning it with the desk.

My stare sticks to it like hair to Velcro as recognition hits hard and nauseating flutters begin to churn inside my gut. Oh, damn. Blonde hair, a pretty face, and, unlike when I saw her in the Realm, a beautiful smile pulling the corners of her lips upward.

I point to the picture, my finger shaking. "Who's that?" And why does Kai have a picture of *her* on his desk? I pull the blanket tighter around me. Suddenly, it's chilly here.

"That?" Kai takes the picture and sits down on the bed to my right, the little green stuffy frog falling over from the shift in weight. He leans forward, one finger gently brushing over part of the photo. "That's Cole and me after last year's BJJ championships."

I kind of figured that part. I know those two boys in their martial arts uniforms, hoodie-sweaters pulled over their bodies, both with a wide proud grin on their faces and a trophy in their hands.

"Nu-uh." I shake my head and point at the girl next to Cole, the girl I've seen before.

The girl who threatened to keep me and Kai in the Realm.

Kai gets my point. "That's Claire," he says, wistful smile on his face

Huh? "Claire?" Looking at the way she's wrapped around Cole, I don't need to ask, yet still I do. "Cole's girlfriend?" What the hell then is she doing in the Realm? How did she enter? And why? To find Cole, just like us?

For a moment Kai is lost in thought. "Yup. Cole and Claire got together about a year before our accident. You know where we were coming from, when it happened? Our accident?" He pauses, waiting for me. "We were on our way back home. From Claire's funeral."

From Claire's— I choke on my next breath. "Her funeral?" She's dead? That would explain why she was in the Realm.

Kai's eyes take on a distant quality. "Cole and Claire… they were like the dream couple. Madly in love, actually so much it started to piss me off." He blushes and turns the picture in his hands. "Not that I didn't want him to feel that way, it was just…" He shrugs. "It's tough if your twin finds exactly what he wants, while you… while you know it's highly unlikely you and your long-term crush will ever work out…" He gives me a small smile and wink, but it can't make up for the bucket of water he just verbally dumped over my head.

His long-term crush.

Kai has a long-term crush.

It shouldn't mean anything, yet it still it feels like a rejection. No wonder nothing happened between us. No wonder he didn't kiss me. No wonder he didn't react to me in my underwear.

So stupid. I let myself believe that maybe—

So. Stupid.

He's *my* long-term crush alright, but that doesn't mean I'm his.

Obviously.

I force my face into a neutral mask to hide the disappointment. I have no right to it. All we did is hold hands and help each other through a rough time.

Nothing more.

Kai notices the fallen over stuffy frog, sits him back up, and gives him a gentle poke in the belly. "So, Claire plans this elaborate romantic picnic for them on the roof of their house. Two stories, right on top of her awning window, great view. They climb up, she missteps and falls two stories right onto a fence post. Impales herself on it, boom, gone." So is his voice. He closes his eyes. "Cole blamed himself. He should never have let her get up there, he should have caught her, he should have… Part of him died that day, when Claire fell. And then when our accident happened and I came back from the Realm and he didn't… I thought, at least he was with Claire. It was the only thing that made leaving him in the Realm bearable." He smiles ever so slightly. "It made it better to know that he's with her."

This would be the perfect moment to tell him what I saw. Whom I saw. But the problem is not what I saw, but what I heard: Cole thinking he's dead. Claire threatening to kill me— and even more importantly, to kill Kai. To keep us in the Realm, if we tried to take away Cole.

I don't need to be an expert in psychology to know how this will play out. One, I tell Kai about Cole. Two, Kai insists on going back in, which is what he wants to do anyway. Three, Claire keeps him. Four, I'll be at fault for a second death.

But what's the alternative? Not tell him anything? Is that fair? It's safer for sure, that much is clear. I—

"Anyway, enough about that. How are you feeling? Warming up?" Kai gets off the bed and places the frame back in its corner before he dumps the tea bags from the pot into the trash next to his desk.

I suck in a sharp breath that does nothing to clear my mind. "Uhh, kind of." On the outside at least. The inside keeps its chill, although at this point, it's courtesy of Claire, not the CryoTherm.

Kai pours us some tea. "You scared me, Gwen." He says it completely calm and level, but maybe that's why it shoots all the way into my heart, no matter his previous statement.

I grimace. "I didn't mean to." Wasn't by choice it took me so long to return. Thanks, Claire.

He chuckles. "Yeah, I know. It can be distracting in the Realm, can't it?" He hands me a cup. "What… what did you see in there? If you don't mind me asking."

And there we go.

I take a slow sip of my tea to buy myself some time. My heart hammers as if it needed to make up for beats missed while I was in the Realm. "It was all so foggy." That's a good opening. Right? Right?

Kai sits back down onto the bed, careful not to spill his tea. "Yeah, for me too. Worse the first time, during the accident. A bit better this time, as if my brain had aligned itself with the Realm."

A shudder runs down my spine. That's as scary a thought as I've ever heard.

"What else did you see?" He takes a sip of his tea.

I wrap my fingers around the hot mug until they sting from the heat and make an executive decision. Kai can't know about my experience with Cole or Claire. If he did, he'd be even more gung-ho on going back into the Realm, either with my help and the CryoTherm, or without it. I'm sorry if Cole is staying in the Realm under false pretenses, but I can't change that. The twin in front of me is my priority at the moment, especially in light of Claire's threat to not let him leave the Realm, should he re-enter.

So, I blow some air over my steaming tea and sigh. I've got to sell this well. "What I saw? Not much. It… it went by so fast; I didn't know what to do." *Lie.*

Kai's brows scrunch into a V. "You didn't see anybody?"

Either of you come here again, you stay. Especially him.

A wheezy breath leaves my throat. I rub my forehead. Basics. Start with the basics. "I saw myself down in the CryoTherm." And I saw Kai how he didn't move an inch but held my hand the whole time.

His cheeks turn the slightest hint of red. "Uhh, yeah. So, you were definitely in the Realm." He looks down into his tea. Silence hovers, and it is heavy, full of loss and missed opportunities.

Kai turns the cup in his hands. He sucks in a long breath and holds it for about five seconds, before he speaks. "I wanna go back in, Gwen. Tomorrow."

Just like I feared. My gaze flies up to his. "No way." And I thought I had time to come up with a better plan to discourage him from going back in, but I stand corrected. Obviously, I didn't factor in Kai's persistence, i.e., love for his brother. "Seriously, you just died, Kai. Nope."

There's no freaking way we can go back. How am I supposed to know how serious to take Claire, or what she can do? She held me by the arm, and I couldn't descend down to my body. Repeat, for emphasis: I couldn't descend to my body. If she had held on longer until it was too late...

Yeah, I would have died, or rather... I would've stayed dead.

Either of you come here again, you stay. Especially him.

Would she really forcefully keep her boyfriend's brother trapped in the Realm? And why? Isn't that exactly the opposite of what she's telling me? I'm supposed to keep him out of the Realm or she's going to keep him in? That doesn't make any sense. And does the why even matter at this point? Because Kai can't enter the Realm again. Period. And even on the off chance my brain made up Claire, I still don't want to stop his heart again.

Once was scary enough.

A muscle in his temple twitches. "I told you. I have to try it again." He scoots forward, closer to me, chewing on his lower lip. "Seriously, it was different this time. I could see more clearly. I saw Cole! I'm thinking if it gets better every time, I'm pretty sure I can reach him when I go in again. I can... I don't know. At least say good-bye." He lays his right hand onto my knee, carefully so, as if he was afraid I'd pull away. "Please, Gwen. One more time. That's all I ask."

My chest is tight with a whole buttload of conflicting emotions. It's not like I didn't get it. I really do.

But I also think we stretched our luck to the max already.

"Please." His eyes are so deep I could drown in them, and boy, that doesn't make what I have to say any easier.

"Kai—"

"Four minutes. This time I know what I'm doing." He squeezes my knee.

"You just died, Kai. Not even six hours ago!"

"But—"

"I like afterparties more than the real parties." Sarah takes a swig from the bottle and hands it to me in the front of the car. I'm drunk already, but not drunk enough to not realize we're gonna be completely screwed if the police stop us with an open bottle of alcohol in the car. Oh, well. I'm sure my mom can talk me out of whatever mess I'm getting into. She knows everybody here and in my parents' hometown. Everybody. Plus, I'm an O'Karran. I should start using my last name more—I'm kinda invincible that way. A giggle escapes me. Invincible. Hehe. I take another swig and hand it over my left shoulder to the rear and Sarah.

She takes it and gulps down half of it. "Afterparty of the year, coming right up."

"—why I need to go back in."

For a moment, I can't make sense of the last part of Kai's sentence. My head's being split in two by an axe, but it's nothing compared to the pain cutting through my soul. I can't close my eyes to all these bits and pieces… they're too clear to be a figment of my imagination: Sarah and me drinking. That blond boy from the last time my brain pulled this number on me. I couldn't make that up if I tried. As much as I want it to be made up by my mind, I don't think it is anymore. I'm afraid it might be a memory.

And that's not good.

If all that was true, if that did happen, then… we were easy targets that night. I know I shouldn't be blaming myself for what happened. I didn't kidnap us. I didn't kill Sarah. But being loaded and a welcome target for extortion did make me the reason why Sarah was caught up in a mess that only should've affected me. And if I flirted with a guy and drank, when I promised I wouldn't, I behaved irresponsible and might've made us easier targets. Who goes to afterparties? Not me, usually!

Nausea rises, and it brings the bitter taste of guilt with it. How weak of me. Enter a pretty boy and I forget my promises.

Disgusting.

But then, if there was a boy that night and Sarah and I drunk—why is he nowhere mentioned? Did he drop us off for the afterparty? Did we not go? Did we not make it there? Nobody ever mentioned him, everything was about only Sarah and me, the heir and her friend. Mom didn't say anything. Dad didn't say anything. Police didn't say anything. Only Sarah's mom brought up that possibility in the letter she sent, and I doubt she meant my party-flirt.

I cringe and blink a couple of times—and then, everything is so clear, like a curtain pulled back and revealing a clear view of what lies behind. So obvious. Kai isn't the only one who needs to go back into the Realm.

But he is the only one who shouldn't.

Me on the other hand… The benefit of possible answers outweighs the risk Claire poses. I need to know what happened, and there's a black box of memories Sarah has the key to. She was there. All I need to do is ask, and this time faster, without wasting precious minutes. Here's my subconscious, apparently trying to get a message across with these… *memories*, so yeah, I need to know what happened to that boy. With him. Who is he and what does he know about the man who killed Sarah? Is he the key to everything, or—

Like ice, horror shoots through my veins.

What if… what if nobody mentioned the boy, because Niparko killed him too? In those short clips playing in my mind he's still so young, barely a bit older than us.

Oh, god.

No. No, no, no. Somebody would've found him. I'd know about that. We'd know. Mom protected me from the news, but she wouldn't have left another death or a missing person out. I would've known if the boy was somehow part of it all.

I suck in a sharp breath. Okay. Okay. Good. Whatever stupid thing I did that involved the boy, it didn't *involve* the boy. Only one person got harmed because of who I am, not two.

So, what's the missing link? How does everything connect? Was it me being irresponsible and breaking my promises? I bite down so hard, my molars hurt.

I could swear I didn't drink. I didn't flirt. I didn't drive under the influence. I learned my lessons the hard way, and I *promised* my mom. Problem is, the things I'm seeing in these quote-unquote flashbacks, they feel… right. They feel true.

And that is scary as hell.

I wrap my fingers tighter around my cup.

My biggest hope is that Sarah knows more. His name. A school he goes to. Anything. If he is real, if he was there, he might be the key to unlock my memory. Where did we split? Did he see who picked us up? What's my part in all of this?

What. Is. My. Part.

What did I do?

There's no way I can let it rest. The doubt is there, a nagging feeling tugging at my very core that maybe I'm not quite the victim I thought I was. That maybe I messed up and threw caution to the wind. That maybe it's not only my status as heir to MSC that got Sarah killed, but my idiocy as well.

Only one way to find out. I look Kai straight in the eyes and sit up straighter, my mind made up. "I'll go in first tomorrow morning."

"What?" Kai all but recoils. "No. We said—"

I know. And I'm applying a different standard to my needs than his. Still, I cut my eye at him. "Come on. I didn't see anything in the Realm." A white lie, a necessary one. "So, let's make it even. You died twice already and you think it cleared your vision. It's my turn. Second time, clearer vision." That's logical reasoning, right?

Kai glares at me. "You just died. Not even an hour ago."

Touché.

I shrug again. "Well, it's my machine, and you're leading the scoreboard with two deaths versus one of mine. I want to see it the way you did."

I want to know.

And I don't want to endanger Kai. Kai is a good guy. Kai's family has suffered enough. If Claire kept him in the realm… Nope. I can't put him or his family through this again. Me on the other hand…

Kai takes a barely controlled breath in. "Seriously, Gwen. Why? You don't have to do this. Why risk it again? I almost didn't get you back, and…" He shakes his head twice. "I really don't think you should do this."

And right he is. Neither of us should, but at least one of us will.

I hold his gaze. "I'll look for Cole as well. Double the chances. Besides, it's me, or we take the CryoTherm down." I mean it. Anything to keep him out.

A muscle thrums along his jaw. He knows he's trapped. "Fine." Kai clenches his teeth. "Fine. But then it's my turn."

"Of course." Another lie.

The only way I'll let Kai ever enter the Realm again is over my cold and dead body.

Chapter Nineteen

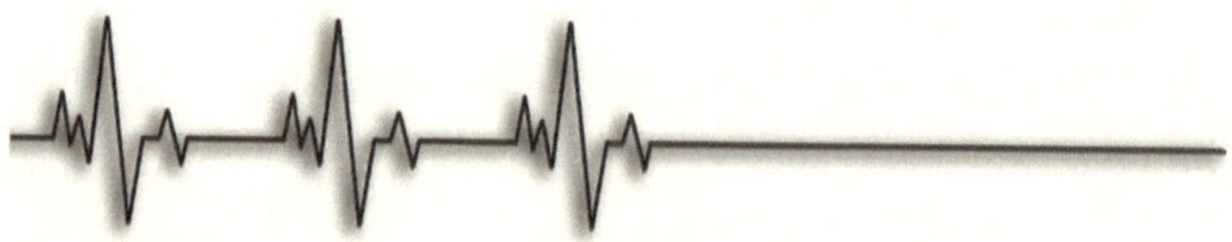

Night After

"No, Dad, I haven't heard back from anybody." I don't roll my eyes. I don't stick out my tongue. Instead, I keep my smile trained at my father on the other end of the iPad.

Dad scowls. "It's taking them long. One should think with your qualifications—"

Yeah, well, had I truly submitted the applications to med school, maybe then. But I haven't, and I won't. I have, on the other hand, wondered quite a bit what Sarah meant: *your dad— the police need to examine…* examine what? Why? "Dad, have you spoken to the police lately?"

My dad jerks, the amber-colored liquid in his glass

swishing up and over from the sudden movement. "W-why would you ask that, Gwendolyn?"

Gwendolyn. Not Gwen. Not Gwennie.

I tilt my head and shrug. "Nothing, just wondering if they've examined…?" I leave the sentence open for my dad to fill. Fishing for information works best with him if he doesn't realize that's what I'm doing.

He huffs. "Nothing they haven't examined a hundred times, believe me." Dad sets the glass of whiskey on his mahogany desk. "But thank you for bringing that up. I've been thinking. Honey, whenever you think you're ready, you should give an interview."

"What?" I shoot upright from the slouched position on my bed. "No way, Dad!" That's why I'm here, in Kampton, Oregon—*northern* Oregon—to get away from all of this, to—

"Easy, Gwen, easy." My dad holds up a calming hand. "I meant a short, controlled statement to give your side of the story. To clear up some of the… confusion that's going around right now."

An icy palm grips my heart and holds it tight. "What kind of confusion, Dad? How can there be confusion?" The ice spreads into my bloodstream, freezing my body. There shouldn't be any confusion. We got kidnapped. Sarah got killed. I got out.

Or is that not what happened? Because the ever-increasing problem is, I'm not so sure anymore. "What is it you're not telling me?" And does it have to do with a blond boy, by any chance?

Dad takes another sip from his whiskey, followed by a

quick swallow. "Nothing, Gwen. I just… well, I figured with the stock market tanking for MSC it would be beneficial if people heard from you. How MSC saved your life, I mean."

Anger lights up. Ah, of course. That's the confusion he's talking about. Business. It's always about business. "Dad—"

"And we did save your life. Without the GeneTracer, they wouldn't have found you that quickly, and then…" Dad fills the silence with another sip of whiskey.

Yeah, and then I, too, would've been dead thanks to those drugs, most likely.

I grip the iPad so hard my knuckles turn white. "So sorry I inconvenienced you and the company, Dad. Next time I get kidnapped—"

"It's not just an inconvenience, Gwendolyn." My dad barks into the camera, jaw set. "This thing almost ruined me! It backfired so badly I can't even begin to assess the damage, especially after we hit that record high once the police found you with our very own MSC-technology! Least you can do for me is damage control!"

Like a whip, his words lash out and cut me open right where it hurts the most. A choked breath breaks from my throat, one that holds way too many tears already.

Yes, my dad first and foremost is a businessman, and to be honest, I've never come first for him. Or second. Third. Fourth. Depending on the number of projects he was working on.

But he has never put my life or well-being on the bottom of the list before.

Dad takes another big gulp of his whiskey, more than he normally drinks. Maybe it's the alcohol talking. Or… it's the truth finally coming out. He sets the glass down, his shoulders slumping forward with the breath he releases. "I'm sorry, Gwen, I—"

"No." I shake my head so fast I turn dizzy. "I don't want to hear it, Dad. I don't." I don't want to hear how I ruined everything the day that ruined me. How he blames me for the bad press and business. I do that enough myself.

"Gwendo—"

I end the FaceTime call.

Screw this.

Screw *him*.

I drop my iPad on the floor next to my bed and rub both palms over my eyes. If today hadn't been the weirdest, scariest day since July 31st, or maybe since ever, given I don't remember that much of *that* day, maybe then I wouldn't be so sensitive.

Honey, Dad always loves you, you know that—said my mom about a thousand times to me whenever the company came first. So yes, I'm sensitive with this for a reason.

Add seeing Kai die.

Add dying myself.

Add seeing Sarah again.

Add meeting Cole.

Add Claire…

I huff to myself. What a day.

Finding Sarah almost pales in comparison to meeting Cole and the appearance of his feisty blonde GF.

What was Claire about? What's her agenda? It sounds like they were all friends, when she was alive. Why would she threaten to keep Kai? Is she afraid of him telling Cole he isn't dead? What is she doing to Cole? With Cole? Are they playing happy couple in the afterlife, with Cole being oblivious to his true fate?

And, most importantly, can she do what she said she could?

Everything's a blur inside my mind: the transition, what I saw, what I felt, coming back… Is that what Calista was talking about, provided she was actually being honest and she is indeed connecting to the Realm? And what part of me was crossing, coming to think about it? My soul? My quantum information? My… Whatever. Does it matter?

I fall back into my bed. Maybe I should tell Kai everything. Come clean, tell him about July 31st, about what I saw… He should know what to make of Claire. I should tell him.

Starting to build some trust, aren't we?

My cheeks burn. Why my mom is still paying that shrink is beyond me, since apparently, I have her integrated into my daily living at this point. Not much else could be more annoying, quite frankly, than hearing her voice. Well, besides not remembering.

I slide under the blanket, for a moment reminded of doing the same thing when getting into the CryoTherm. My fingers hover over the switch of my nightlight, then pull back.

Maybe this is a night to sleep with the lights on.

I pull my blankets up high and lay back, one hand on my chest above my heart. The skin isn't red anymore, but every bit of pressure hurts. Guess that's what I get from going through CPR.

When I came home and Grampie asked how my afternoon was… I was this close to spilling the beans. This. Close.

I wish Sarah was here. Somebody to talk to. But then if she were here, I wouldn't need to talk about the afterlife, 'cause I never would have gone.

With every passing second, my body relaxes more and more, and with it my mind. It circles through everything that happened today, but always, *always,* comes back to Kai.

Kai lifeless in the Freezer. Kai brushing a strand of hair out of my face. Kai's arm around me on the way to his room. Kai saying he'll never feel the way Cole did with Claire.

Pathetic, given that he told me about this stupid long-term crush of his, but I died today. Pathetic is all I have left.

Kai—

I'm in a doctor's office, in a gown, sitting on the exam table. The nurse comes in and smiles at me. "The doc told me to give you this." She hands me a prescription. "It's going to ease the symptoms, she says. And you're supposed to come back in a couple of days. Recheck. Okay? And no worries, you can keep coming here until you're twenty-one. Two more years."

I nod and hold on to the prescription as if it meant my life. "Thank you." My voice is deeper than normal, a bit raspy. Can't cry in front of the nurse. Men don't cry. I force a smile as if this was any other day and not the day that could change my life. At least somebody cares for me. The doc is always in my corner.

A wave of gratitude and warmth washes over me—only to be replaced by white, hot, blinding fear. "You fucking moron!" Something hard hits me over the head. Pain explodes above my right temple, the kind of pain that makes thinking hard." You were supposed to sell half, not all. Half! You're going to make up for it!"

Another blow to my head, but this time the pain doesn't come. Instead, I'm at a party, the kind that spoiled high school students have all the time.

I've been standing in the corner of this fancy living room for the last ten minutes, observing. Music plays in the background. It's crowded. At least fifty teens between sixteen and twenty party around me like they had no care in the world. Yeah, right. They don't.

I scan the crowd, dismissing everybody who isn't her. Ten seconds later, my face pulls into a grin. Long, curly brown hair, a body with curves to die for, and an outfit that cost more than we got to spend on food the last two months. But that's a thing of the past. She says something to her friend and laughs, and that laugh… it's young. Without a worry. It's a laugh that won't return in this form once I'm done with her.

For a moment, I hesitate.

No.

No choice.

So, I swagger through the room straight at her—my ticket to freedom. "I could start with a boring one-liner, but that's not me." Her eyebrows shoot up, but she doesn't walk away. She's intrigued. Cute.

I step closer. "I have a different suggestion. You, me. Fun times." Her mouth opens and closes again. My grin widens. Figured she wouldn't know what to say. Too sheltered.

"Tom." I hold out my hand. She hesitates, but still takes it.

"Gwen," she tells me what I already know. "Gwen O'Karran."

With a scream and jolt I sit up in bed.

My heart sprints as if it needed distance from what I just

dreamed, every beat reminding me to not take it for granted.

Holy everything!

It was completely realistic how I saw myself at the party, and—

My hands shake as I rub both palms over my eyes. Is that my brain making up the other side of the story? Why? *How?* It was so detailed, so… lifelike, I… Damn it.

I fall back into the pillow and blink into the near-darkness.

Holy cow. Holy cow, holy cow—what is my brain coming up with? I blow a strand of hair out of my eyes. Okay. Easy, Gwen. The last part, it could've happened. The Party. Sarah and Me. *Tom.* The… boy? Is he the boy? He must be.

I squeeze my eyes together so tight, stars dance in front of my lids. It's the first part of this memory-dream-thing I'm having a hard time with. What I just saw, doesn't that crazy stuff prove my mind is making it all up? Who sees themselves through somebody else's eyes? Heck, I felt I was a guy in the first part! How freakin' crazy is that?

So, if my mind is making that up, how much can I trust it to give me the truth when it comes to everything else? Relief washes over me. Then, I didn't drink. I didn't flirt. I didn't put Sarah and myself at risk.

Or did I?

No ransom request.

If it truly was a kidnapping.

I take a shaky breath in.

Something is off here, and I'm afraid whatever it is, I won't like it.

Not at all.

Chapter Twenty

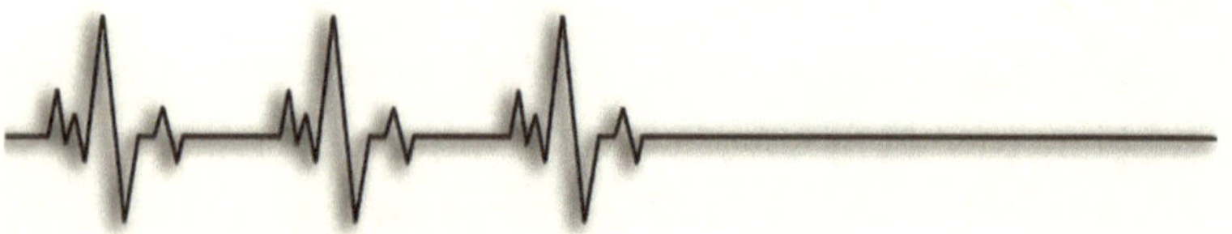

Second Round

The next morning I'd take the hit-by-a-truck look over whatever look I'm sprouting today.

I feel like crap, and it shows. The reflection staring back at me from my computer screen is way too pale. To top it off, my eyes are adorned with circles way too dark and deep to still be attributed to sleep deprivation.

I stick my tongue out at the image.

Whatever.

I fish for my pill box with my left hand while banging my right against my temple. Pull yourself together, brain. Work with me. I pop one of my painkillers but ignore the others. Hello, sanity, where are you? It's me, Gwen. Long time no see.

Maybe not the best time to get off Mom's regimen, but oh well.

My phone chimes, and one glance at the display makes me groan. Calista again, speaking of headaches. How does she have my number anyway? I reject the call with one click, but before I've lifted my finger away from the screen, the thing rings again. This time I swipe the green bar to the right. "Grampie, I'm only up one floor, you know?"

Grampie's image on the screen frowns. "I know, but stairs and me are not friends anymore."

Point taken. "What do you need?"

"Nothing, my dear. This is just a courtesy call that the Harrison boy has pulled up in our driveway. He's waiting in the truck, and from what I can see, he's a bit nervous." Grampie winks at me. "Might want to go down before he chews his nails off completely." He chuckles, and out of reflex I grin back, although there is nothing funny about Kai being nervous.

"Will do, Grampie. On my way down, thanks." With the tap of my finger, I disconnect my grandfather, and I make it out of the house in less than a minute. New record.

Like Grampie said, Kai's in his truck. "Hey." I give him a short smile and hoist myself up into the cabin. The vents blast heat on full power. I shoot him a sly grin. "You know, the more you warm me up, the longer it's going to take to cool me down."

Wrong one-liner.

Kai throws me an angry glance. "If I had my will, you wouldn't go in at all." He shifts the truck into reverse and backs out of our driveway.

"Kai—"

He holds up a hand. "Let's not talk about it. I wanna get

this over with."

Right.

I drop my gaze down to my lap. Despite the heat set to like a hundred degrees, a shiver runs down my back.

We don't say another word during the short drive to the train yard, nor do we say anything as we go through the preparations mechanically, like the last two times.

We don't speak as I strip down to my underwear—and that's the silence that weighs the heaviest.

Kai, ever the gentleman, keeps himself turned away from me until I'm about to crawl into the CryoTherm.

"Gwen—" He catches my hand before I take the few steps up our improvised ladder. The warmth of his hand on my icy skin, it's heaven.

I turn toward him.

Big mistake.

His eyes are so large they're all I see. Wide. Scared. Worried—for me. For a split second, I forget there's a long-term crush of his somewhere. For a split second, I relish in the gift of possibility. For a split second—and then it's gone.

Kai sucks in his lower lip and chews on it, his fingers entwining with mine, a move so natural it makes my heart ache. "Please don't."

I dance from one foot onto the other. "We made a deal." Which I'm not planning to uphold. But it's for the better. My way to sanity lies in my next trip to the Realm. It's risky, yes, but I'm in for a penny, in for a pound. There's no way I can stop now, not with answers so tantalizingly close, and the risk so... Huh. I actually don't know how to finish that sentence.

Since Sarah died and I didn't, I haven't been as rooted to the idea of living as I was before. I used to love life and live it to the fullest. Now…? Now I'm alive, but I'm not living. And who would care if I stayed in the Realm? Yes, Mom. Grampie. Dad? Probably only if it affected his business in one way or the other, let's be honest. Guess my point is, I know what I'm getting myself into, Claire included. Kai doesn't, and he can't know, or else he'd throw all caution out the window and jump out right after it. I don't have much to lose anymore, but Kai does. I need to know the truth, or it'll break me, Kai doesn't, or it'll break him.

For me, it's worth the risk. Period.

Kai shakes his head. "I—"

I place my finger across his lips. His eyes pop open wide, even wider than they were before, gaze intently searching mine. A series of shivers dances over my skin, and none of them have anything to do with the cold out here. "I'll go in, Kai. I'll see if I can find Cole." That must convince him, because if he keeps looking at me like this, I'm not sure I can pull through with my plans.

Before I can change my mind and take an axe to the CryoTherm, I break our connection and crawl into the machine. Kai stays rooted in his spot for a good ten seconds, eyes closed, face turned upward at the partially destroyed ceiling. Then, he sighs and opens his eyes. "Beginning cool-down procedure."

EEG. EKG. Rechecking the defibrillator.

But this time, he doesn't take my hand.

I wish he would.

One should think dying for the second time wasn't as scary, but it's still scary as shit. I try to look anywhere but at Kai. I don't want him to see how much his withdrawal hurts.

I clear my throat. "K-Kai?" I squeak. "Uh, just thinking… When—*if*—I see C-Cole… w-what should I say to him?"

For a moment, I fear he is going to ignore me.

He closes his eyes and swallows hard. "That I miss him every freaking second of the day. And that he needs to get his ass out of that coma." He sucks in his lower lip. "The rest I'll do when I go in."

Or not.

My teeth chatter so hard they echo through the empty train yard. "O-okay." Just saying this one word is *hard*.

Everything is hard, especially thinking.

The CryoGel cools my body more and more until none of those conscious thoughts stay. They become lighter and lighter until they float away, taking what is me with them. All there's left is cold, confusion, and a slight sting all over my skin that makes everything better.

I think my lips move, but no sound comes out.

I think Kai moves closer, but I wouldn't know.

I think I feel something wet and hot dripping onto my skin, but it doesn't make sense.

I think I hear whispered words, but I don't understand them.

Then, a sharp sting across my chest, and then, for a short moment, nothing.

Then, a tug on my hand. "Hey. Shh. Come on."

Another tug.

My eyes fly open and I fall right into Kai's darker ones, brows scrunched together from worry. The hair that just fell into his face is now spiked up and—

"Whoa!" I jackknife up into a sitting position. "Cole!" Not Kai. *Cole!* Kai's still on my left, now finally holding on to my hand, jaw set so tight it's going to break his molars in two, and… tears in his eyes.

I almost get sucked back into my body right there and then.

"Yeah, well, me. We kind of got interrupted last time." Cole tugs on my hand again and helps me up out of my, uhh, dead body.

Freaky. Absolutely freaky.

But also, Kai was right. Things seem sharper, more in focus. As if I was a newborn whose vision was adjusting to the environment over time.

As soon as I'm hovering above the CryoTherm, Cole lets go of my hand. "What the hell are you doing, butthead?" he whispers, floating down to Kai and my body. "Kai…" One hand reaches out, yet he never touches his twin. "So, this is how you two got here? With this? It felt wrong when I saw you, and—" He shakes his head. "What the heck?"

I'm not sure he's talking about the CryoTherm or his brother holding my hand. "Kai wanted to say good-bye, Cole."

He whips his head around. "Say good-bye? Hell, what kind of BS is that? I'm dead! I assume he's sad about it, that butthead, we're twins. Who gets to say good-bye? Come on! This here?" One more shake of his head. "Crazy."

Well, he's right with that, although I feel like I need to defend Kai, as long as truly-crazy Claire hasn't shown. Maybe she doesn't know I'm here. How does that work anyway?

"He's miserable without you, Cole. He regrets it every day—that he drove, and that he is fine."

"But I don't blame him!" Cole yells. "That idiot! I don't blame him for that. It was an accident. Shit happens. I don't want him to do *this*." Another accusing finger points at the CryoTherm. "And neither should you be doing this. What the—"

"He visits you every day, you know." I don't think Cole understands how devastated Kai is.

Cole snaps his mouth shut and works one hand through his hair, a gesture so much like Kai's, it hurts. "Well. He better. Those flowers need watering."

Huh? Oh. Crap. Get to the point, Gwen! I facepalm myself. Priorities. "No, not the cemetery. You're at Silverlake."

"Silverlake?"

I shrug, about to stuff my hands into my pockets, until I remember I'm floating in front of Cole's face in my underwear.

Oops.

Didn't really think that through.

"Uhh, yes. Silverlake." I cross my arms in front of my chest. "You're in a coma, Cole. Not dead. A coma."

Cole recoils as if I had slapped him. "What?"

"I'm sorry, you—"

"Coma? I'm not… dead?" His mouth opens and closes. He turns his hands in front of his eyes. "I mean, it would explain why… But she never… Are you sure? Because—"

"I visited you too. At Silverlake. And, Cole?" Now let's cut to the real reason why I'm here. "I need two things. First, I need something I can tell Kai to keep him from coming here again. Something. Anything that'll give him closure and keep him out. And second, I would need to see my friend Sa—"

A wave of fog rolls over me so quickly I have no time to brace myself for it. I yelp out as it grabs me and throws me around, lifting me up to somewhere until I can't see Cole, can't see the CryoTherm, can't see anything besides grey fog around me.

"Cole!"

The fog cranks it up a notch, its force snapping my head back and bending my spine close to the breaking point. I gasp and try to curl up. If I wasn't dead already, I'd say it was trying to kill me. Again.

"You're back." The snide female voice comes with a drop in the fog's power. Like a winter storm had lost its thunder it subsides, dropping me to all fours.

And I have no clue where I am.

No, not true. Twigs and leaves lie in heaps under my knees and hands, but I don't feel them. My body doesn't leave any impressions in the soft ground. This... this is the forest behind the old train yard, at least a mile away from the CryoTherm and Kai.

Crap. How do I get back to my body? Do I run? Float? How much longer do I have?

Claire steps out of the fog and into the light. "I warned you. I let you go. You do not come here, and you do not mess with Cole."

"But—"

Claire growls—she actually growls—and squats in front of

me. Before I can pull away, she has wrapped her fingers around my wrist. "We have a good thing going here. I don't wish you any harm, but I warned you." She tilts her head, looking down at our connected hands, a surprised huff breaking from her throat. "Now look at that. You're stained, I was right. Stained. And entering the Realm. How stupid."

Stained? What—

A jolt shoots through my chest and I cry out. This time I know what it means: Kai is shocking me, trying to get me back. My body moves on its own account, as if pulled toward the train yard, but Claire's grip keeps me anchored.

"I warned you," she whispers. Something close to regret crosses her face, but not for long.

A second jolt, a second twitch of my body she prevents.

Oh, crap. She's really trying to keep me here.

That thought sends a shockwave through my body strong enough to shake me out of my daze. "Let go!" I yank on my wrist, but it's like her hand is glued to my skin. "Let go! I need to go back, I—" Another jolt, another cry. It's the third shock, Kai must be starting CPR now.

Which means I don't have much time left. My body is warming up, and a warm and dead body is a truly dead body.

I jump to my feet, disregarding the stinging pain in my chest.

Compressions. Those must be the compressions.

"You take your hands off me!" I pull, I push, I punch and kick, but I can't get to her. As if she knew what I was going to do she sidesteps all my attacks while keeping me anchored to her.

"Like I said, I warned you. And for what it's worth, I'm sorry. You'll understand once you cross for real."

I aim for her face. "I don't want to cross for real!" And for the first time since that fateful day, I mean it. I don't want to die. I survived a kidnapping. I survived a trip to the Realm. I've met Kai. My life has just started to make sense again, at least borderline, and I'm not ready to die.

I'm not ready to die.

And I'm not missing neither the timing nor the irony of that thought.

Zzzingg—one more surge of energy, one more pull on my body I can't follow. This is the fourth, if I don't—

"Sarah!" I yell at the top of my lungs. "Sarah! Help! Sarah!"

She's my only chance. Claire's hand is glued to mine, there's no way—

"What. The. Hell."

Sarah.

Like the day she kicked Charles Dean's butt for messing with an eighth grader she's all amped up and ready to go. She only needs a split second to take in the situation. With her hands on her hips and fire in her eyes, Sarah is ready to kick some butt.

And don't we know I need it.

Claire yanks me closer to her. "Stay out of this. I have no beef with you."

Sarah chuckles drily. "You do. She's my beef." She nods at me. "And it was you separating me from her yesterday. I don't like that. At all."

The fog. Claire was the fog. Gosh, it makes total sense, but

I didn't know that was something someone could do.

The pain inside my chest becomes unbearable. Last time it wasn't this bad. "Sarah," I croak, "need to go back." Gone are my good intentions, gone are the questions I wanted to ask, gone are the apologies. All that matters is getting out of here.

Going back.

Going back to Kai.

To life.

"No kidding." In the blink of an eye Sarah is next to Claire, one hand on her wrist and one on mine. "Dead or not, you don't mess with my friends." And with that, fire shoots through my wrist and into me, burning me alive, killing every cell in my body and every conscious thought I've ever had. The afterlife turns dark around me, swallowing me whole into an abyss I opened myself.

I sink deeper and deeper, tumbling down into a black abyss, like I'm dying all over. *Grunts, shoves, pulls, kicks*—and then my arm is free.

"Gwen, fast! Back to Kai. Go! *Kai*, Gwen! *Kai!*"

Kai.

As if that thought was ignited jet fuel I shoot back, through the trees, across the clearing and into the old train yard.

Kai.

I don't see, I don't feel, I only hear a desperate curse.

"Crap, Gwen, come back! Come back! I'm begging you, come—"

Then, nothing.

Chapter Twenty-One

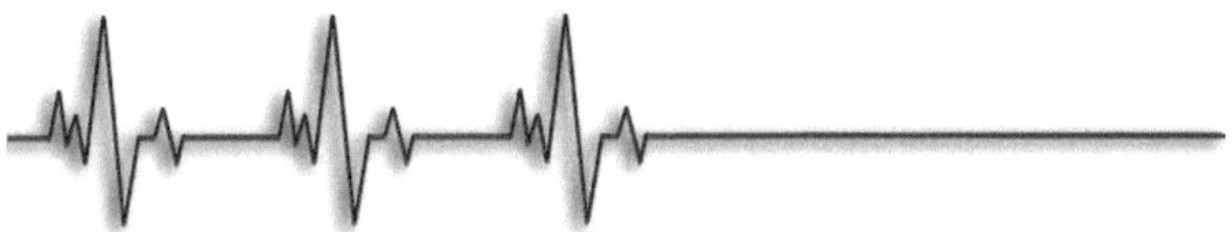

Closer

First, I'm not quite sure what's happening.

I'm awake yet I'm not, I can see and yet I can't.

"Gwen," a soft voice whispers, then everything shifts into focus, shifts to the deep brown eyes set in a face filled with worry, to the tousled head of dark hair.

Kai.

Warmth spreads in my chest, reaching for my heart.

"Gwen," Kai repeats, and then I'm all but ripped out of the CryoTherm. Strong arms press me against a wide torso as the vibrations of running shoot little pangs of pain through my sore chest.

Not quite awake yet, I cling to him like a baby monkey,

hands around his neck and face buried in his jacket that smells so good of Kai, of cookies, of home, and of life.

I'm back.

I didn't think I was going to make it.

Sarah saved me. Sarah saved me from Claire. If she hadn't been there—

Kai rips the door of the truck open, squishing both of us behind the wheel, one hand finding the button for the engine, the other one to slide the seat back. "I got you." His voice shakes. "I got you. Shit, you scared me." He wraps his opened jacket around my sides as far as it'll reach, trapping me against his chest.

No, not trapping.

Cradling.

Kai keeps me cradled in his lap, my feet dangling over the middle console onto the passenger's seat, my upper body pressed into his chest. His heart hammers against my body, fast and strong, every beat music to my ears.

A violent tremor rocks through me.

"You're still frozen." Kai's breath dances down the side of my face. For one short moment he hesitates—and then he glides his hands over my skin on my back, rubbing it warm.

I must feel like ice to him, because to me his hands are made of fire, igniting me one inch at a time. A strange kind of heat pools deep in my body, one that has nothing to do with the car's temperature set to max.

Kai rubs his palms frantically over my back and arms, the friction of his skin on mine heaven and hell at the same time. It's nothing but an innocent touch, intended to warm me up.

But then something changes.

First, the rubbing slows down until it's not much more than a soft, ever-so-gentle touch across my back and sides, like a butterfly's wing brushing over my skin.

Then I notice his chest rising and falling out of rhythm, his heartrate so fast, I can't distinguish single beats anymore.

My heart isn't faring much better, doing a weird fluttering thing, like I was still in V-fib, but in this very moment I'm not the girl who died a few minutes ago. I'm the girl who's more alive than she's been in months.

Every fiber of my being wants to melt into Kai, wants to touch him and be touched.

Wants to *live*.

Kai skims his fingers over a soft spot on my lower back, and it releases the safety inside my brain. I sneak my arms around his neck and snuggle myself closer to him, nuzzling my face into his neck.

There might or might not have been a brushing of my lips over his skin.

Kai gasps and freezes, his hands on my sides. A harsh breath of air leaves his throat, yet he doesn't move.

But neither does he push me away.

His hands begin to shake from the effort of holding them still. "Gwen…" he whispers, and it comes with an undertone of *something*.

My heart skids to a screeching halt. Of course. Kai is a good guy.

I close my eyes and allow myself one moment to make a decision. It comes surprisingly easy. "It's okay, Kai. I'm okay you're still thinking about your long-term crush." Funny enough, the words are true. I'm not even disappointed at myself for choosing to be second-best. If I've learned one thing from my visits to the Realm, it's that life needs to be lived. You can't hold back. Maybe I'm selfish—actually, I know I am—but I want this. I want Kai.

And I'll deal with the consequence of my action later.

I brush my lips over the soft spot just below his ear, right where his pulse is beating like a jackhammer.

Kai sucks in a sharp gasp as his body stiffens under mine. "Gwen you a—"

"Yes, I'm okay with it." I purse my lips and drop the softest kiss possible under his jawline.

For an eternal second nothing happens.

No reaction.

Then Kai's fingers twitch at my sides. "Gwen." It's nothing more than a faint whisper, yet the way he says it deafens me.

Kai turns into me and presses his lips against my temple.

Oh, holy hell.

Lightning zips through my veins, electrifying me from head to toe.

He takes me by the shoulders and peels me off his chest, pulling and pushing on my legs until they find the space next to his thighs and I straddle him. Holding me by the hips, down by my crimson-red underwear, his gaze scrolls above every inch of my body. His lower lip is tucked between his teeth, the apple in his throat moving up and down in a hard swallow.

The vents behind me may blast hot air on full power by now, but they have nothing on the heat building up inside of me—a heat that's all from Kai, from the way he looks at me.

I cup his face with both my hands. His cheeks are soft, with a little bit of stubble. Manly.

Kai flattens his hands against my sides, spreading his fingers. His eyes are wide, dilated, and so intense, it tears my heart wide open. There's something in his gaze that melts me. I've dreamed about a moment like this for years. Everything about him causes my body to feel more than revived, like I was energized on a whole new level.

He parts his lips as I glide my thumb over them. "Kai," I whisper, my heart making a silly little jump when he drops his gaze to my mouth. Both of us lean in at the same time, no idea who moved first, and it's not as if it mattered. All that does is that first tentative brush of our lips, the first probing, careful connection.

It's all and more than I've ever wanted.

Sparks shoot across my body with the first touch of our tongues, ripping my heart and soul apart in a supernova of heat. My senses go into overload. This... this is *everything.*

He tugs me closer, bringing our bodies flush together.

And I can't say I mind it. How could I, while I'm enjoying every second of him roaming his hands across my back, my sides, down to my hips again. I lean into him, pushing forward to touch as much of him as possible. I can't miss out on a single square inch of Kai.

Kai groans into my mouth. He gently nibbles my lower lip, every bite speeding up my heart. I want more. Need more. Dropping my hands onto his shoulders I fumble for his jacket and push it off. He's wearing way too much. How unfair.

I don't need to spell out for him what I'm about to do. Kai leans forward, never breaking the kiss, shrugging out of the jacket I brush off his arms and throw into the back. As soon as it's gone, I fish for the hem of his sweater and shirt, grab them and pull them over his head.

He's not exactly fighting me on this.

The second his shirts are gone, I have to take a moment to appreciate the view.

Kai is… marvelous. Strong. Manly, with a little bit of chest hair and a very fine trail leading down the middle of his stomach, vanishing under his belt. The pulse in his neck beats like crazy, making mine speed up just the same.

His gaze holds mine captive as he slowly and gently brushes his fingers from my knees up to my thighs. The heat of his gaze together with his touch… Maybe I'm imagining things, but I don't feel second-best, I feel like I'm *it*. My breath hitches and my toes curl. Something flares up in his eyes, but his hands continue their scenic route, dragging up my sides and toward my back. Such a light touch, yet I feel it everywhere in my body.

I arch forward and into him at the same time he sits up straighter and pulls me closer. Our chests touch, soft skin on rough, fire on ice, boy on girl. He looks at me with such affection, I wouldn't be surprised if my heart stopped yet again. Slowly and deliberately, he tilts his head and places the softest kisses down my neck, until he reaches the corner of my mouth.

"Gwen," he whispers. His warm breath against my skin… hello, goosebumps.

"Kai," I whisper back at him. He nips at my lips, grazes over them, each touch releasing a firework inside my chest. I'm hyperaware of every bit of skin we're connected by—his chest pressed against mine, my legs straddling his thighs, our hands exploring, searching, covering every inch of each other's body.

This is what I dreamed about when Sarah and I lay awake, talking about the Harrison twi—

I jerk back when memory assaults me.

Sarah.

Sarah helping me, rescuing me from Claire, Cole being chased away from her, Cole who doesn't know—

With a jolt I sit up, head brushing against the low ceiling, heart cramping inside my chest.

Kai cocks his head, but keeps his hands resting on my hips, his thumbs moving in idle circles, drawing my every thought to his touch, like moths to the light.

"Wait." I drop hands to his, stilling their movement. I can't think otherwise.

"What's going on?" He lowers a worried eyebrow. "Too fast?"

I swallow dry. There's absolutely no moisture left in my mouth, all evaporated in the heat of the last few minutes. I feel like I ran a marathon, but one where I don't know if I want to cross the finish line. Blinking rapidly, I try to gather my wits. The Realm, Cole... Cole didn't know he was in a coma and not dead. While that's a biggie for Cole, it won't make a difference to Kai: I don't need Aunt Calista's clairvoyance to know what he's going to say the second I tell him about Cole and Claire. He will want to go back, now even more than before.

And that can't happen.

Not after what Claire said. What she did. What she's truly capable of.

Icy horror shoots through my veins, courtesy of those memories. I was *this* close to not making it out of the Realm if it wasn't for Sarah, and I can't be responsible for Kai—

Kai sits up straighter beneath me. "Hey." He cups my cheek with one hand. "Too much, too soon?" He pointedly looks down at my sparsely clad body.

"No," I breathe, shaking my head, "oh gosh, no. If I ever die again, this is how I want to come back." I hesitate and push my fingers in-between his. What do I tell him? How much? And how do I keep him from crossing again?

How do I keep him alive?

Well, I lie.

Kai smooths his thumb over my cheek before he drops the hand back to my waist, a lopsided grin tucking on his lips. "No need to go through extremes. A dinner and some flowers would do." He winks and squeezes my sides.

I open my mouth, then close it, my mind stuck on what happened in the Realm.

He must've read *something* in my expression, because Kai turns serious. "What is it?"

I blurt out the words that aren't clearly a lie, yet I make them one. "I remember. I saw Cole. I spoke to him."

Surprise flickers across his face, morphing into an awed expression. "You—"

I place a finger across his lips just like I did before going into the CryoTherm. "Yes. I saw Cole, I spoke to him, and—" My jaw tightens and I suck in a deep breath. This is where the lying begins. "You were right. He's happy." I smile, but it feels so incredibly fake I wonder how he can't see it. "He says hi, and he wants you to move on."

Because if you don't, it's going to kill you.

Chapter Twenty-Two

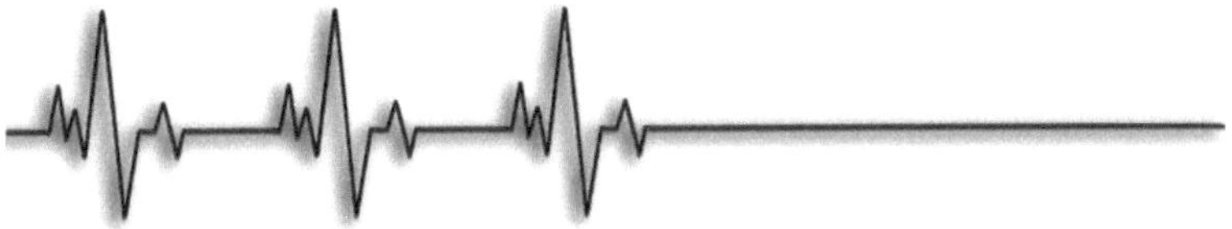

Parental Concerns

Kai stares at me for what feels like an eternity.

And like with Grampie's stare, not much's missing and I'd crumble.

But I don't.

Kai's life depends on me, and if all it takes is a little bending of the truth, I'll gladly do that. Sarah died on my watch, I have absolutely no desire to add a second—

Bright, hot pain shoots through my head.

"No, sir, we did not find any other person. No ransom note either." The police officer looks over at me on the ambulance's gurney. He wobbles. Warps. Or maybe it's me. Everything's blurry, the colors

are off. Reality feels wrong somehow.

The other man sighs. "Didn't find any bruises on the preliminary exam. No defensive wounds, nothing." He shrugs. "Could've been a threesome gone wrong. Happens when kids mess with drugs." His eyes are full of pity when they land on me. "And she doesn't even know what she's done."

"Move on?" Kai chokes out. "He told you I should move on?"

I blink once, twice. What the f—

"I can't just *move on*, that's the point, that freakin' idiot!" Kai slams a palm into the door on his left and I jerk. His expression softens. "Sorry, I didn't mean to yell, it's just…"

"Y-yeah, it… it hurts," I stutter. Holy cow, what kind of flashback was that? A threesome gone wrong, no defensive wounds, drugs… what the heck? I squeeze my eyes shut until they burn.

And she doesn't even know what she's done.

What. Have. I. Done? What have I done, dammit! It can't have been what my brain is teasing me with—or maybe it was *exactly* that and I've buried the evidence of my own shortcomings under layers and layers of PTSD.

"Yeah, it hurts," Kai whispers. A sad smile plays around his lips. "He's not just my brother; he's my twin. I can't just move on, I…" He sucks in a deep breath. "No offense, but how do I know…" He cocks an eyebrow. "What if your brain came up with that and—"

"So now we're picking and choosing again?" Take whatever we like, whenever it's convenient?

Kai scowls. "Well—"

Okay. I have to give him something. Something that'll convince him. "What do you want to hear? He looked like you, with spiked hair. Okay, my brain could've made that up, after all, I've seen him before."

"What did he say?"

"Besides that you're an idiot for doing this?"

Kai grimaces. "Okay, that sounds like him, but also like something anybody who met me could say. What else?"

"Butthead. He called you a butthead."

"Did he... did he recognize you?" He swallows hard and drops his gaze.

I narrow my eyes at him. "Why would he recognize me, and how would that information make you believe I really saw him?"

Keeping his gaze lowered, he shakes his head once. "Just... just tell me, okay?"

I sigh. "Not at first. But once I told him I was the frog bathing suit, I guess so, since he said halle—"

"—lujah." Kai whispers the word together with me in unison. His fingers on my hip shake the slightest. "Then it's true. You saw him. You spoke to Cole." When he looks up, his eyes shine with tears. "Damn that idiot."

I brush my thumb over his cheek, catching one tear. "You guys are weird. Hallelujah." Wouldn't have been my first guess.

"Insider. Twins, you know?" He lets his head fall against the headrest behind him, eyes closed. "I need to see him one last time. No matter what. It's great that he's happy, but I'm not. Not like this." He opens his eyes, gaze loaded with determination. "I wanna go in. Now. As long as he's still around. Maybe this time I can catch him, and—"

Oh, hell to the no. "Kai, I don't—"

"We made a deal, Gwen." His jaw sets.

Damn it. "I know, but Cole… was really insisting you don't enter the Realm. He was mad, Kai." Not a lie.

He huffs dry. "As if I cared if he's mad or not. He's also gone and I'm here. I'm going in." He checks his watch. "Do you feel up for CPR now, or do you want to wait half an hour or so?"

I stare at him open mouthed. So much for thinking telling him Cole was happy would make him forget his desire to see his brother once more. "Kai… it's—"

From somewhere inside my purse, Taylor Swift chimes. "Grampie." Thank whomever for the distraction. I scramble half off Kai's lap and fish for my bag in the foot area of the passenger's seat.

"Gramps." I put the phone on speaker, and Grampie's voice fills the silence between me and Kai.

"A little heads up. You might want to be here in the next fifteen minutes and on your best behavior. Your parents have just entered Kampton County, and I don't need to specify what that means." He hangs up on me without good-bye.

Oh, crap. That's bad with a capital B.

Kai's eyes narrow. "What does he mean by that?"

"Nothing." The answer comes like a reflex, curtesy of six months of insecurity and mental instability.

"Didn't sound like nothing." He cocks an eyebrow.

And right he is. My blood pressure spikes, courtesy of an uber-sized adrenaline-dump. My parents find me out of the house… a couple of things are going to happen. One, Dad is going to throw a fit. First, I drag down his company, and instead of working on med school or helping Grampie, I "have fun". Not good.

Two, while Mom's reaction is not going to be about med school, it is going to be about hanging with a boy. July 31st has left a bitter taste in everybody's mouth, and especially hers. She was the one who let me go to the party, and twenty hours later, they find me in my underwear, a dead girl next to me.

"Gwen?"

I draw in a wheezy breath. Three, even worse: the CryoTherm. Shoot. "I need to go. Drop me off at home. Please. If they find the CryoTherm is gone… We'll be in deep." Like, really.

I can tell when realization of what kind of mess we're in hits him. Kai curses. "Shit. Okay." He helps me scrambling off his lap, fingers lingering on my thigh. "But," he holds me back until I look at him, "but as soon as there's an opening, I'm going in."

And the way he says it, it won't be easy keeping him from it.

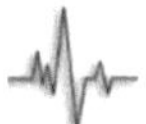

We make it to Grampie's house in an impressive nine minutes—and that includes me getting dressed in the passenger's seat while Kai's driving.

Despite the near-panic that has me, I catch him glancing

over to me when he thinks I'm not looking, and that's when I wish it was ten minutes ago, and we were still kissing. My parents' bad timing is epic.

As soon as I'm dressed and locked into my seatbelt, I drop my hand on his thigh. Without missing a beat, he wraps his fingers around mine, and boy, does that make the butterflies in my stomach lift off and dance. Once he pulls into our driveway, he holds on to my hand. "Text me. Call me. Come over. Anything, okay?" His cheeks turn the slightest hue of pink.

"All three," I say and bend over to him.

The kiss is sweet and warm, and entirely too short—and then I'm out of the truck, and Kai is gone.

I hurry inside, drying my shoes to avoid the wet tracks that will give me away to my ever-observant dad. "Grampie?"

"Here." The living room.

I throw my jacket over the garderobe behind the door and speed-walk over to Grampie. "Where are they? Did they call or—"

Grampie lifts his iPad so I can see the screen. A blinking dot slowly moves across a map of Kampton, Oregon. "Main and 6th. My alarm went off as soon as they crossed the county line."

I arch a brow. "Your alarm." Right.

"Well, yes. I don't like to be surprised by visitors if I can help it. I track your parents' iPhones. Have been, since your mother decided an old man can't live by himself in peace and quiet no more."

Despite the annoyance of my parents' visit I burst out laughing. "Grampie, you rock," I giggle. He's tracking my parents' phones—I should have that app; it would be beyond convenient!

"Why, thank you, dear Gwennie." Grampie pretends to bow in his chair. By the looks of it, he's quite pleased with himself.

I'm still laughing when my parents pull up to Grampie's McMansion and enter the house—without knocking, since they have a key.

Grampie gives me a knowing glance. "See? That's why I like to be prepared."

The entrance door closes. "Hello? Owen? Gwen? We're hee-heere!" My mom. That's her spreading-positive-vibes voice.

It means nothing good for me.

Still, I plaster a smile on my face. "Mom? Dad? You're here?" I'm pretty proud of my performance. No nervous fiddling. No quick glances. Just a hug for my mom and an even faster one for my dad when they enter the living room.

Mom takes me by the shoulders. "Just thought we'd drop by. I realized it's Grampie's birthday this weekend, so we wanted to surprise you." If it wasn't for the quick glance at my dad, the one that screams *say something, Rob,* she could've fooled me.

Yeah. They're not here for Grampie.

They're here for me.

A lump settles inside my throat. Not good. I don't need questions—of any kind—or supervision. Or somebody checking on Dad's tinker place.

My dad awkwardly pats my shoulder. "And it's good to see you, Gwen." Said the man who barked at me last night about his precious company.

Right after they found me—right after the ambulance brought me to the ER and I woke up in the ICU enough to know who I was—right then my dad hugged me. He hugged me like when I was little and could do no wrong, and like he was happy I was there.

For a moment, I was stupid enough to believe it. Until that bubble burst about ten seconds later when he whispered in my ear. "You won't believe it. We're leading the stock market today. All because of you, because we found you. Well, the GeneTracer. They all love that story. I'm so glad you're back, my angel." He kissed my hair, and then took a phone call from his manager in the Shanghai office, who'd just heard about what happened.

My mom was the one to pick up the pieces of what was left of me and try to put them together again. Not my dad.

Still, I pull myself together. If either of them finds out what I've been doing, Mom's going to get me hospitalized on a 5150, or whatever the equivalent in Oregon is for an involuntary hold in the mental ward. "Good to see you too, Dad."

Another glance from my mom, this time with a jerk of her chin. My dad can read it as well as I can. *Talk to her, Rob. Come on.*

"So, uh, Chris Wellington says hi. Met him and his parents at court—"

A shooting pain behind my eyes, a short flicker of light—

I'm standing in front of a judge, maybe in his fifties, white hair, cold eyes. He reads over the paper I gave him, then looks at me. "It'll take more than a medical clearance to make this work, son."

Son.

Nobody ever calls me son, but I'll take it. "I know, sir. I was hoping it was a good start. I tested negative—five times over the last months. That should count for something, right?"

Please let him say yes. I can't be behind bars, or I can't make the money I need to buy the freedom I want. Away from all this. It's a once-in-a-lifetime chance.

And Edan's only one, let's be real.

The judge looks at me, and finally he nods. "Okay then. I'll give you a chance."

Whoa. Ow. I shake my head once to clear it. The same inside-somebody-else's-body experience. A judge, the sensation of fear, of losing something worth living for, so profound… it makes no sense, where is that coming from?

"… and well, in case you were wondering, we did recover from the blow we took back in July. We've almost caught up to where we were—"

That gets me back into the here and now like a jab to the chin. "Really? Really, Dad? You're talking to me about recovering from the blow your company took? What about me? The blow that I took? That *Sarah* took?" But yeah, let's worry about the company, by all means!

Tears shoot to my eyes, but before they can fall, I turn on my heel and storm out of the room. Only because I know Grampie hates it, I don't slam the door behind me.

I wish they'd all go away. I wish all of this would go away, and I finally *knew*, no matter the cost. I feel like I'm stuck in limbo without a chance to escape. Everything's chaotic in my mind—has been for months—and all these weird pseudo-flashbacks don't help. I'm not helping myself either sometimes accepting them as real, then as fake. No idea what to believe anymore—no, not true: In the end, no matter how realistic, they must be dreams. Last time I checked, I'm not a guy, and I was definitely a guy in the last two. Made-up figments of a traumatized mind. Or maybe, like my mom said in the hospital, it must have been the stuff *he* gave us. What did Sarah's mom say in her letter? New and expensive drugs.

Did *he* give us that? Niparko? To make us comply?

Or worse, was it something we did before, with… with blond boy, with Tom? Something we took voluntarily, for fun?

Bile rises up my throat. No. Been there, done that, and decided it wasn't for me. Took me a while, but no pill has ever made Dad understand me more, so why risk ruining my brain? So nope, I don't do drugs anymore. Alcohol… well, maybe. But drugs, no.

But suppose I did. Suppose I was mad at Dad. Suppose I wanted to have fun. Yeah, if I ever took anything again, I'm sure I would go for expensive. I'd have the money for it, I'd think it was cool.

The noose tightens around my neck and it makes my breath come out choppy.

Not about ransom. No kidnapping. I can't ignore the little I know, the little that will make a giant difference.

Not a kidnapping.

But what did Niparko want? What does this Tom have to do with it, if he is real?

"Why, why, why?" I groan and bang my palm against my

forehead. It's maddening. I can't add one and one together. I feel like a mental amputee. Every time I try to remember, I—

"Why what, Gwennie?"

Geez!

I twitch as my mom sneaks her arms around my body and hooks her fingers into the loops of my jeans from behind. A whiff of something flowery wafts over. "Are you part-time ninja now, Mom?"

She laughs softly. "Need to be able to sneak up on my patients for their shots. No toddler ever liked to get poked."

A short snorty laugh escapes me. "True that."

She taps my hip with her fingers. "What were you facepalming yourself for, honey?"

"Nothing, Mom." I sigh and lean my head back onto her shoulder behind me, like I've done a million times before.

"Didn't sound like nothing, baby." My mom presses a kiss onto my temple. Not even half an hour ago Kai did the same thing.

Kai.

Maybe it's the thought of him, maybe my mom's calming presence, but everything comes to a head in this very moment: July 31st. Its fallout. The flashbacks. Stopping my heart and almost staying in the Realm. The risk Kai is in. The pressure on my shoulders to keep him safe. To find out what really happened July 31st.

I'm not a crier. Not at all. But maybe we all have a reservoir where all the sad stuff goes to keep us functioning—only mine is flooding over in this very moment. The first tear falls, and while it's silent, my mom, pediatrician extraordinaire, isn't fooled.

"Honey?" She lets go of my belt loops and turns me around with *that* look on her face. The one that screams worry. "Honey? It's okay. I'm sure… I'm sure Dad didn't mean it that way. You know how he is with the company." She smooths down my hair. "I've told him about a million times he shouldn't be thankful that the GeneTracer found you, but that you were found, period." She pauses, one hand in my hair on the side of my head. "Be honest, Gwennie. Do you remember something? Is that why—"

"I wish, Mom. It's all so frustrating." I stomp my foot like a toddler who doesn't get her way. "I know you told me over and over to stay away from all of it, and I have, but I really need to remember. I was thinking about googling a couple of articles—"

Mom's gaze softens. She reaches up and cups my face with both hands. "Don't, Gwennie. I've dealt with PTSD enough to know that it's not going to get better from reading made-up stories. Or news stories. It won't help you, but it'll make it worse. Trust me that there is nothing out there you need to read. Please stay off the web." I get another warm smile, the kind that disarms me each and every time.

I deflate. "It's not like I'm looking forward to reading that crap, but maybe there was something in there that could help me spark a memory. There are bits and pieces, mini-flashbacks, but I don't even know what they mean. If they're even real. And it's driving me nuts. They can't be my thoughts. They can't be what I saw, and…" I look at her through the tears blurring my vision. "Do you think I'm going crazy?" It surely feels like it.

My actions speak for themselves, I'd say.

"Gwendolyn O'Karran." Mom uses her best maternal tone. "You are not crazy. You are sick, and that is okay. Anybody would be. You will heal." She pulls me into a tight hug.

I will heal.

I wish I believed it.

Chapter Twenty-Three

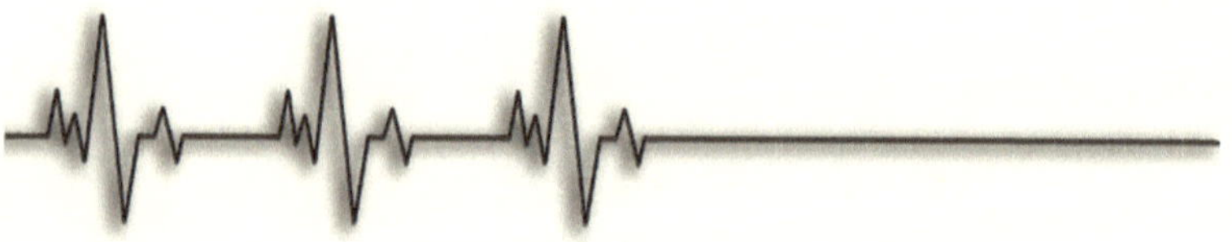

Nighttime Visitor

I take one good look at Kai in the picture he sent me before I click my cell phone off. If I had to guess I'd say it's a picture from *before*. It's something about his eyes that's more alive than I've seen over the last couple of days—well, if I don't count today's make-out session in his truck.

The mere thought of those few precious minutes… Holy hell, do those butterflies dance a cha-cha inside my stomach. I hope it's the same for him—for many reasons, one of them being that well, I don't want him to go into the CryoTherm again tomorrow. Easiest way to distract a guy? A make-out session. Mutually beneficial plan, I'd say.

I lay my cell on my nightstand and get off the bed to get

myself some warm milk, my go-to recipe against bad dreams and nightmares. It's late already, so I tiptoe down the stairs in my socks, careful to avoid the creaking step in the middle of the staircase. The light in the hallway is off, but the living room is still brightly illuminated. Grampie is probably still surfing on his iPad, he doesn't sleep more than six hours a night anyway. I'm about to walk past the door when I hear my name. My mom. Something in her voice makes me freeze in mid-step.

"… really has me worried."

"We're all worried, Michelle." That's my dad, easily recognizable by the cold tone.

"No, Rob. More than usual. I think, she—" My mom pauses.

"She what?"

"I think she's bad enough she might try to kill herself."

I jerk back as if slapped, while Dad laughs out loud. "What? Gwennie? You're exaggerating. She's fine, Michelle. She'll be found innocent and she'll recover. It was an accident."

Found innocent?

An icy fear clamps its fist around my heart.

Found innocent? What does that mean? Who will find me innocent? There's nothing I could be found innocent for! I *am* innocent! I didn't do anything besides take Sarah to a party!

I can hear my mom sigh through the closed door. My heart bangs around inside my chest like it wanted to rant me out.

"I'm not so sure. She's bad. She's been asking about death, and—"

"Nonsense." That's Grampie talking. "That kid is resilient. Now, remembering what happened would help her, I'd say, but

I ain't no doctor."

But right he is, nonetheless.

"Right you are, Owen. You're no doctor."

Boy, is my mom testy today.

"All I'm saying is that I'm worried Gwen is going to harm herself, and that we should keep an eye on her. Maybe take her back home in a day or two."

I barely keep in the little yelp that would have given me away. I'm not leaving. I'm not leaving Kai. No. Not now. Not now that I've finally found—

I feel a finger brushing across my lips. "Open for me, sweetheart. Come on, just a little bit." It tickles, so I grin.

The world's already blurry. Blurry and fun. Parties are awesome. Afterparties are even better.

"Good girl." The fingers push something small and round between my lips. "It's only your second. Good against hang over. Now swallow. Nice."

He trails the same fingers down my neck until it meets my shirt. "You're delicious."

A short bout of dizziness sweeps over me like a passing breeze, and then I'm back in front of Grampie's living room door.

Drugs.

No, no, no, no.

I didn't... not willingly. I promised, I wouldn't be so stupid—

Is that when... Was that a memory? Was it real? Was that Tom giving me the drugs?

Drugs.

I rub my palms over my eyes. I haven't taken anything since med school became an option and I got over my short rebellious phase. The only possible reason I could imagine my self-control slipping… I was so mad at Dad for pushing and pushing and pushing… maybe I did take them, just to show him he can't control me all the time. Maybe, if Tom is real, I felt flattered by his attention, maybe I made Sarah take them and therefore us defenseless against Niparko.

It's possible.

Rebellious me, leading the way down the rabbit hole.

Frack, frack, frack! How else could it have played out? Because, by now it looks like a classic teenager thing: go out, party, drink, take drugs—and then things went wrong.

Only I don't remember how and where.

As if in trance I sneak back up to my room, the warm milk forgotten, replaced by the weight of the world wearing me down.

No, the weight of a life lost wearing me down.

Every time I have another one of those little snippets pop up, I like less and less what I see.

I sink into my bed, a hollow feeling inside my stomach and an alternative reality playing in front of my inner eye.

Sarah and I, at the party. We see the boy, Tom. He hits on me, and I don't mind it. He gives me a pill. We drive somewhere. I'm drunk, and most likely so is Sarah.

And in the end Sarah is dead, and more questions are left than answered, like, where is Tom? Is he truly a third person, or is he… could he be… *involved,* somehow?

It doesn't seem likely, after all my snippets show me a cute, outgoing guy. Somebody I could fall for. Somebody I did fall for, it appears. My age-ish, maybe nineteen, twenty. Not somebody working with a killer.

But then, why haven't I heard of him again?

Okay, I haven't read any news, but… shouldn't I have heard something? Anything? Mom mentioning him? Anybody?

I stare up at the ceiling. It's so frustrating. I should be able to tell what the man who killed my best friend looked like, but my brain is keeping the information locked up behind ten firewalls.

The longer I stare straight up at the ceiling, the more all colors bleach out of my vision. My eyes begin to tear, and I shiver. Cold here. I wrap my arms around my chest. I mean, the heater is on, but those doomsday-thoughts would do the trick. Another shiver runs down my body and I reach for my blanket, about to pull it higher.

"Getting cold?"

I yelp and jerk up, heart racing, yanking my hands up, ready to defend myself against—

The next breath gets stuck in my throat as my gaze falls onto the person right in front of my bed.

Blue eyes, blond hair: The boy from my flashbacks.

Tom.

Tom, who flirted with me.

Tom, who gave me pills.

He shoots his hand out lightning fast and grabs me by the forearm so tight, it hurts.

Déjà vu hits hard as my heart freezes to its core. I *know* that voice, and I *know* that hold. I *know* that hand on my forearm.

I remember it.

All I see, all I can focus on, are rough fingers wrapped around a sturdy knife. The fingernails are dirty, chewed off. "Easy, honey." He presses the knife against my throat, a lock of blond hair falling into his forehead.

Panic surges. I'm going to die here.

A scream dies in my throat on its way out, turning into a soft pitiful squeal instead. I yank my arm out of his grip and scramble back as fast as I can, pushing myself into the wall, legs up and drawn in, as if they could provide any protection from the monster in front of me.

Tom. Tom is—

"Niparko," I whisper. With each syllable of his name leaving my tongue my soul dies a little bit more.

Tom is Niparko.

The boy I flirted with is the boy who killed Sarah.

And he's here, in my bedroom.

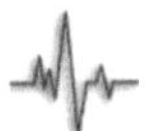

Tom—Niparko—squats down in front of my bed so we're face to face. "Oh, hell yeah it's me," he whispers, "glad I left an impression. Was wondering if you forgot me by now. And before *I* forget it, I appreciate you opening the door for me."

My gaze darts to my bedroom door—my *closed* bedroom

door. It takes all the guts I have to come up with a reply to the guy who turned my nights into nightmares and my waking hours into grief. "How'd you get in? How can you be here?" My voice turns into another squeak at the end. He's in jail, locked away, and even if he escaped, Grampie has alarms all over the—

That's when I notice the difference in my room.

Everything looks faded, black and white-ish with a hint of sepia to it, like a washed-out photograph. And that's not all. Tom might be squatting in front of my bed, pale blue eyes, blond hair, a certain boyish charm like the night we met, but there's no shadow, no impressions in my bed where his elbows touch the soft mattress as he's leaning forward, boxing me in.

And that can only mean one thing.

I whip my gaze to the left where my pillow is, half expecting to see myself lying there, asleep or dead—yet nothing.

Tom grins in a condescending kind of way. "Trying to make sense of it, are we? Now, I hear it can be confusing in the beginning, sweetheart." He reaches out to touch my leg, but I'm quicker and draw it in closer.

No touching.

Never again.

His face turns into a frown. "It seems you don't quite understand the severity of your situation." A cold smirk replaces the frown. "Let me indulge you. Remember this day?"

Dizziness, nausea—and then I'm looking into the same eyes as a moment before, but this time they're smiling. Warm.

"You're cute when you're buzzed." His speech is a bit mumbled, his eyelids droopy. Buzzed too.

I giggle. "I'm always cute."

His smile widens. "Probably." With one lazy finger, he brushes a strand of hair out of my face, the intimacy of the gesture bringing goosebumps to my skin. "You cold?"

"Maybe?" I suck in my lower lip. This shed is cold, but I'm warm. Thanks, alcohol. I knew we were buddies. "And if I was cold, what'cha gonna do about it?" My heart hammers like crazy. I'm daring tonight. Bold. Exciting.

"I might have just the idea." Tom tilts his head and lowers his mouth to mine until our lips connect.

Niparko looks straight into my eyes. "Does this refresher make it better? Let me help you remember what you never should've forgotten. And please, enjoy it from my point of view."

Another bout of dizziness, another wave of nausea.

I'm back in the shed, but in the far recess of my mind I know I'm not me, I'm... him. I'm lying on top of a soft, curvy body. There's a knife in my hand, not sure why. It's sticky, don't know why either.

Doesn't matter.

Only she does.

She's beautiful, looking up at me with those wide eyes. Her breath comes out quick, shallow. When I saw her at the party, I wanted her. Now I'm about to have her. "We'll have sh-ome fun."

First things first though. "But I won't knock you up."

I fish a condom from my back pocket, then reach my left hand between my legs, opening the last button of my pants. Things are blurry around me, swaying, but it doesn't matter. It's all about forgetting. About fun. About living in the moment. It's what we both need. Screw everything else. For now, at least.

Lol: Screw.

She bucks her hips. "Ge' off me." It's slurred. It's cute, kind of, because my brain's too foggy to take her seriously.

I chuckle. She flirted with me. She wants this as much as I do.

I lift my hips to the side and slip my hand between her legs. So warm. Rubbing over her sensitive parts feels... fantastic.

She bucks again. "Shtop id, I s'd." She bucks harder, and I like it. Brings her closer.

I fumble for the hem of her underwear until I lose patience. A ripping sound tears through the silence when the fabric gives up its hold. "Oops." I giggle. Oopsie-daisy. Ripped her underwear. Rawr.

Finally, I got access. I slide my hand down her body.

"N-no."

I ignore her. Oh hell. She's warm. Wet. So hot. Yeah. Yeah. That's it. I push my groin into her body and groan. The knife in my right hand slides down a little bit from the shift in weight—

—and all of a sudden, she grabs my wrist, twists it around, and throws herself up and forward.

I don't have time to react.

She drives the knife right into my heart.

I yowl out once, the sound turning into a bubbly choke a second later. Blood spurts out of my chest and mouth, heart cramping in a desperate spasm before it beats for one last time. My whole body is made of burning, soul-devouring pain, and all I see are the wide eyes of the girl who stabbed me with my own knife.

And they don't hold any remorse at all.

A gut-twisting pain, the short sensation of suffocating—

—and then I'm back in my own body, pressed against my

bedroom's wall, panting, sweating, a complete mess.

Unlike Niparko in front of me. Still on his knees and leaned onto the mattress, he watches me with an unnerving intensity. "That's what you don't remember," he whispers. The apple in his throat moves up and down once. "You don't remember me dying. You were my one shot. My ticket." His voice lowers as he crawls up my mattress like a prowling animal, coming closer and closer, just as close as he was when he tried to rip off my clothing.

Panic hits, hard. I can't make sense of what I saw, of what I felt, and what I don't remember, but experienced right now. My breath comes out in short bursts, my heart hammers at a dizzying speed, and little stars dance in front of my eyes as my gaze darts left and right for a way out. Only, there's none. I'm backed into the wall, trapped by him and trapped inside a murderous memory, nausea rising with every inch he comes closer.

Like a toddler, I pull my blanket up to my chin, as if its warmth could provide any sort of protection against the numbing cold in my center, or against him. I shake my head, like a crazy person. "It didn't happen. It didn't. Didn't. Didn't. Didn't..." No. No, no, no. I didn't do that. I didn't kill him. "That never happened." I press both by palms against my temples and squeeze my eyes shut. I didn't stab him. It's a lie. I didn't kill him. Did. Not. They would've told me. I would've known. It never happened. "It never happened."

"It never happened?" he yells, one hand slamming into the mattress next to me so hard, I swear I feel it. I squeak and drop my hands, yanking my eyes open only to find him glare at me.

"Hell yeah, it happened, Gwen! How else do you think I died? How else do you think—" He sucks in a sharp breath of air, the muscles in his jaw tightening. "Nothing would've happened if— Damn it! You came willingly. You wanted fun. Daddy was mean to you. You wanted to fool around, you wanted to be wild. It should've worked out fine."

I squeeze my eyelids together again, shutting out the world, him, all those images I don't want to see, pressing them together so tight it hurts. His words though hurt more. Could he be right? No. I did none of those things. I'm not reckless like that. I'm better than that. It's not true.

Niparko leans closer. "The moment I took you from that party, you were worth your weight in gold. And maybe I wouldn't have done it had you not wanted to, despite everything. But you wanted me, and that sealed the deal." He chuckles once, cold. "Your friend, she was the one who didn't want to come. You did. You convinced her. And when she fought..." For a moment something else is there, something behind the mask of anger and hate, something that reminds me more of the boy we met that night, not the murderer. As quickly as it came it is gone. Tom's—Niparko's—voice turns into a whisper. "I didn't have a choice. Not my fault. *Yours.*"

"G-go away," I whisper hoarsely.

He shrugs. "I will. But it won't help you." He slides a finger over the exposed back of my foot. I scream out and jerk back from his ice-cold touch. Feels way too much like somebody had used a razor-sharp ice cube and sliced my skin open.

His eyes lose the mock playfulness and turn hard. Unforgiving, like it must've been when he pressed that knife against my throat.

Like when he killed Sarah.

A wail escapes my throat. *Sarah.*

"I don't want you to forget me, Gwendolyn O'Karran. Ever. You took my life from me. You took my only chance to—" His hands ball to fists on top of my sheets. "You opened the door for me, and a little blonde angel threw me a hint. I owe her."

His face is inches away from mine.

Too close.

Too much.

Too much like that night—

"And you owe me for what you did to me. You owe me big time. I'll be back to remind you of it. And to collect." He pushes off my bed into a crouch right in front of it.

I suck in a desperate breath.

"A warning. That friend of yours, do yourself a favor and keep him on a leash. Because I made a promise to my blonde angel. If he enters the Realm, he stays. I'll make sure of it." He blows me a mock kiss. "Sweet dreams, Gwen. I'll see you soon."

And just like that, Niparko is gone, and *click*, everything is back to normal. The colors, the temperature.

Niparko was here.

Niparko.

My stomach cramps.

I barely make it to the edge of the bed before I throw up right onto the floor.

Chapter Twenty-Four

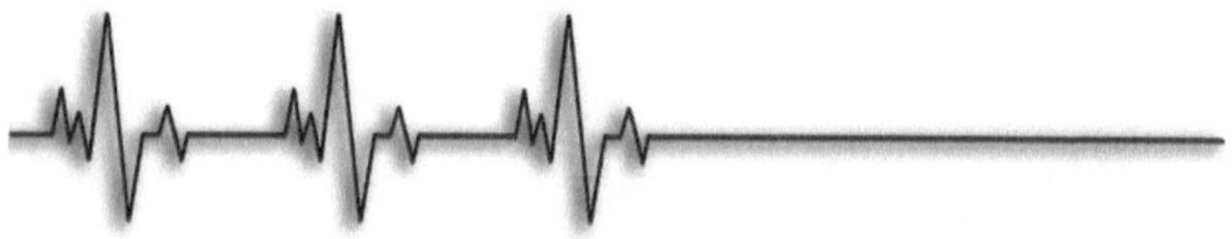

Panic and Doubt

Needless to say, the rest of the night doesn't bring me any rest.

I'm second-guessing everything.

Everything I went through with Tom. *Niparko.*

Everything I saw in the Realm.

Everything.

And yes, it changes *everything* as well: It wasn't kidnapping.

It. Was. Not. Kidnapping.

Nobody wanted ransom. Nobody wanted me for my money.

Instead, I wanted to party, and that's what I got.

Quite the party.

I take a deep, shaky breath in.

Niparko killed Sarah.

I killed Niparko.

Knowing I ended a life… Does it make a difference it was self-defense? Me against—I don't know, a possible rapist? Because that's what was on his mind: having sex with me. Against my will. At least at that point. Maybe I came with him willingly. *Probably*. But what I experienced, what he showed me… I shake my head and drape an arm over my eyes. I wanted him to stop.

He didn't want to stop, and now he's dead.

A hot wave of nausea sweeps over me.

My fault. My fault, my fault, my fault.

I flirted. I made him think I wanted sex.

And then I killed him.

My fault.

Somewhere in the depth of my mind, the last bit of common sense rises up and fights to the surface. No. Not my fault. I'm allowed to change my mind! I'm allowed to defend myself. He had killed Sarah already, for crying out loud! He might've killed me after he raped me! Self-defense, because that was about to happen—he was about to have sex with me against my will.

Under drugs.

Expensive drugs, as Mrs. Matthews wrote.

Click.

The pieces fall into place right in front of my eyes, building a shaky bridge over the abyss I'm staring into. Oh, in the name of all that's holy, it must have been me buying those drugs. I'm the one with money. I'm the one who was pissed at the world and wanted some time off.

A lump forms in my throat. When I thought I wanted to remember, I was wrong. Remembering isn't good. Looks like my brain had a reason to deny access to those memories.

If I bought the drugs... Then I'm responsible for everything. Not just for shlepping Sarah to a party where we got kidna—where we met Niparko, but then I'm also responsible for drugging Sarah and Niparko—and then for Niparko losing control and killing Sarah.

And I'm also fully responsible for killing him, self-defense or not. I brought the situation onto myself.

I chew on the inside of my lip so hard it bleeds.

I didn't want to kill him, only wanted to get him off me and get out, that much I know.

And I didn't want to end up dead like Sarah.

At that point everything was so blurry, so unreal, like reality had lost its edge and turned fuzzy. How could I have known his wrist would flick over that easily, or that a knife enters a human body through the ribs with about as much resistance as going through butter?

I couldn't have known that.

But you accepted it as a possible outcome. The nasty voice inside my head scolds me.

And now, I have to pay the price.

I groan and rub both hands over my eyes.

What did I do?

Is he right? Did I start it?

If I did, I don't know how I could live with that.

My stomach cramps and I double over.

If this is true, why has nobody told me? *He's in jail,* is what they said. Jail! Not *grave.* It's been six months! How could I not have known Sarah's murderer was dead? That I killed him? Is that why they kept me off the internet and here—not to protect me from the press, but from *that?* Is that what Dad meant when he said they were going to find me innocent? Innocent of *killing* Niparko?

I have to focus on my breathing to not faint.

Tom said a little blonde angel opened the door for him. What door? From the Realm to here? And more importantly, how can I close it again? If only I knew—

The outline of an idea shoots through me. Sucking in a sharp breath, I look to my right at the clock. It's almost six in the morning.

Old people don't sleep that much, do they?

She's my only hope.

My heartrate speeds up as I unplug my cell from its charger and go through my missed calls, finding the one I ignored twice. Redial.

Three rings later Calista picks up. "Gwen?" She sounds sleepy.

"Yeah, I'm—"

She cuts me off. "Did you get my messages? Have you seen anything?" The sleep is gone from her voice. Something rustles in the background, like a blanket.

"Huh? What messa—oh." She called me twice. She left a message. Twice. I just didn't bother checking it. I clear my throat. "No, I haven't, but—"

"Whatever you did and however you did it, you cannot go in again, Gwen! You can't. Do you understand? The moment you went in, the moment both of you did, it set off alarms. It weakened the barrier." More rustling and some grunting on her part come through the line.

It weakened the barrier. Nonsense a day ago, now precious gospel. "Is that why I…" I swallow hard. "Is that why I saw Niparko tonight?" Saying it out loud hits a new high on the crazy-scale, but it's Calista. The scale is adjusted when it comes to her.

The rustling stops. For a moment, there's only white noise on the other end. "He came to you?"

Tears spring to my eyes, some of them from relief that she believes me, some from the aftershock of seeing Niparko, of seeing the boy I killed, of re-living driving the knife into his chest.

It's official, I really was wrong. I thought remembering might help me, but *this* is making it worse. Still, I nod. "Yes. Why did nobody tell me? Why did nobody tell me I killed him?" How could they keep that from me? Who gave them the right to make that decision?

Calista sighs. "From what I know—and mind you, Owen only left a brief message on my answering machine instead of speaking to me directly—your mom was worried it might… it might drive you over the edge."

"Over the edge," I parrot. That doesn't even make any sense.

"Yes. She felt in your state of mind you couldn't have handled it, PTSD and all, so we were all instructed to keep that part to ourselves."

I blink twice. "And that's why she sent me here? Less exposure?"

"Possibly, but it's not important now. Niparko is. What did he—"

"He said we opened the door, and—"

Calista curses. "Then it's worse than I thought. Somebody on the inside must have noticed you."

I'd say that is a safe bet at this point. Enter Claire. "So, can he hurt me? Or Kai? Can they hurt Kai?" I need to know the level of danger we are in.

Calista sighs. "Normally not. Well, it depends on…"

Shoot. "What do you mean?"

"Spirits can't make themselves visible just to anybody, or else I'd be out of a job. Once you've been to the Realm though…" She pauses. "A piece of you stays every time you go. That's what connects you—or Kai—to the Realm. I crossed once when I overdosed, and everything was fuzzy, foggy. With every contact I have with the Realm, and I'm talking spirits appearing to me because I'm connected to the afterlife, things become clearer. For you, that's emphasized because you're truly crossing, not just a passive observer like me. But that's also why you are more visible to the spirits. Because you're actually crossing."

I bite on my nails. "So, what does that mean for us? If we went back in, could they keep us? Or out here, what could they do?"

I hear her take something out of a cabinet and open the fridge. "First, I'm the first to understand what you did and why you did it, but I'm also the first to tell you crossing is not worth it. I don't want to know how you did it, but you need to stop. And yes, Gwen, that's what I've been trying to tell you. You can't—you *must not*—go back into the Realm. What I saw, what I heard… I can guarantee you, you won't make it back out. If they decide to keep you, they can. Provided your body doesn't die, you'll be in a coma, just like Cole, and you'll never come out until your body dies."

The world spins around me. "Never—"

"The longer you stay, the less likely it is, I told you that. Only a soul can buy another one's freedom at that point."

I'm about to roll my eyes just like the last time when she said this, but I don't.

Not anymore.

Not after I met Claire and she tried to keep me in the Realm.

Not after Tom came back and threatened to keep Kai.

Oh.

I smack my forehead. "Of course." Sometimes I'm surprisingly slow, but I'll blame it on the ever-present headaches, or the slight emotional turmoil over the last days. It's so obvious I should've done the math. Niparko mentioned the blonde angel. Claire is blonde. Claire has threatened the exact same thing Niparko has. Ergo, she's Tom's blonde angel.

She's the one who's going to make Tom keep Kai in the Realm if he ever goes back. She couldn't keep me alone last time, so she's recruiting Tom to make sure she can keep Kai, and therefore, Cole.

Which means, I cannot let him enter again, not that I

wanted to in the first place, but now even less so.

"Of course, what, Gwendolyn?" Calista pours something into her cup.

"Nothing." I shake my head although she can't see it.

Calista slurps on a sip of something. "Gwen, why don't you come back with Kai, and we'll talk it through. I'd say—"

The stairs creak—steps. Somebody is coming closer to my bedroom door—hard-heeled business shoes. Leather. Expensive.

"Calista, I need to hang up, Dad's coming. I'll call back later." Without waiting for her reply, I press the red button and end the call.

Not even a second later, a soft knock comes from my door. It's way before seven o'clock, why is he—

The door opens before I can say enter.

"Gwen? Honey?" My dad peeks into the room.

"I'm awake, Dad." I push my blanket off and sit up completely, criss-cross applesauce. "You're up early." Or maybe up late. Sometimes he works through the night.

My dad sneaks into my room and quietly closes the door behind him. Nope, shaved and fresh shirt, unwrinkled. He slept just fine.

Au contraire to me.

He pulls my desk chair closer to the bed and sits down, arms resting on his knees, his phone in his hand. "Gwen, I was wondering…" He turns the phone over twice. "Well, I was thinking, if you don't want to give an interview to the press, maybe you could speak to Uncle Doug? As our lawyer? I'd like him to go ahead and issue a statement on your behalf about that night. Something along the lines of you can't remember, and that if you could undo it and stay home, you certainly would. What do you think?" He holds out the phone for me to take.

"Dad…" I stare at it like it was poison. And yeah, now I know that's why the press was so bad. Not because we partied and Sarah died. Because we partied, Sarah died, and MSC's heir killed somebody.

Nausea rises up my throat.

Dad gives me a small smile. "It would really help the company. Bring us back up, you know?"

I deflate. "Dad—"

He lets his head hang down. "Seriously, Gwen. When I said last night we're recovering it was more a euphemism. We're not going bankrupt, but at this point press is so bad, I'd pay money to have the public opinion of us change. My marketing team is working on spinning it, but the moment we fell from finding two girls with our own tools to—" He stops himself and shakes his head.

I freeze. "To what, Dad?" Say it. Say I killed Tom. Say it!

He clears his throat. "Nothing. Anyway. Just one call. Please, honey. Your statement is worth a lot, really." He holds out the phone to me, but I can't take it.

Because this very moment, the clouds have lifted and granted me a rare glimpse at sanity.

What if… what if Sarah meant something else than I assumed? *Yes, there was a price on your head, but we couldn't have known. Nobody knew he would do that to us.* And what she said about Dad? *Your dad—police needs to examine…?*

I assumed she meant Niparko with the first statement, and

with the second she meant Dad had more tools or insights he was supposed to use. Both would've made sense.

But what if—

"Honey, are you all right?" Dad lays a hand on my shoulder and squeezes, but I don't feel it. I'm busy enough not losing the ground under my feet, because—

No. No, no, no. He'd never do that. He'd never do that to me. To us.

I force myself to smile. "I'm fine, Dad. Just... tired."

He blows out a big puff of air. "Gwen, I... I worry about you. You scare me. If it was up to me, I'd take you off all meds and let your body heal itself, but..." He shrugs. "Your mother insists those pills will help your mental health and memory."

Oh, my mental health is down the drain at this point, but my memory is just fine. Too fine, to be exact. *The moment I took you from that party, you were worth your weight in gold.* That's what Tom said last night, and I thought it was odd if there was no ransom request, no obvious kidnapping, but no odder than a dead man's spirit in my room. So, it kind of got lost between the major issues of this reunion. But now... now it makes sense.

Ice-cold poison runs through my veins, freezing me and killing what's left of my soul.

There was no ransom note, because it wasn't necessary. This game started long before I even entered the field. Who profited most from my kidnapping?

My dad's company.

His stocks skyrocketed after they found me with their very own tools. All he's been worried about since July 31st is his company. His stocks. First the elation when they went through the roof, and ever since the press spun this whole thing around, he's been trying to catch up to it and do damage control. But first, he profited. Majorly.

Dad stands up from the chair. "Never mind then. Get some more rest. Maybe some other time." He gives me a small wink.

I look straight up at the man who might be behind everything, who might be the reason Sarah is dead. The reason why I killed a man.

"Yeah. Maybe some other time."

Chapter Twenty-Five

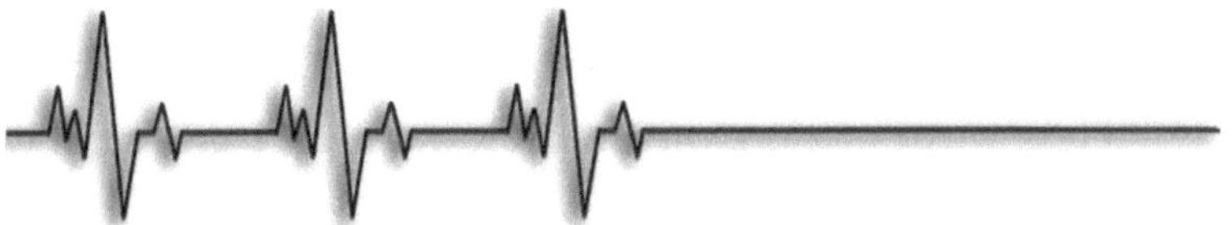

Nice Morning

Half an hour later, I get dressed with hands so shaky, it takes me three attempts to get my socks over my toes, and when I finally make it downstairs, I realize I have my shirt on backward.

Cold sweat dots my forehead. Could be courtesy of my early morning revelation, or my nighttime visitor. I've got enough demons to choose from. An embarrassing high-pitched and borderline-crazy giggle bursts from my throat.

Before I open the kitchen door, I take a deep breath. Keep calm. I don't know what I'm going to do, but panicking won't help. Maybe talk to Kai. Maybe be honest. Maybe—

I open the kitchen door to an unsuspecting Grampie in his

favorite chair, cane leaned against the table and the same wooden box in front of him he's been playing with for a while.

"Damned thing, will you move!" Frustrated, he drops a screwdriver onto the kitchen table and shoves the box away from him. "Shit."

Despite everything, I burst out laughing.

Grampie whips his head around. "Oops. Gwennie." He blushes. "You didn't hear that."

"Hear what?" I close the door behind me. "I don't mind you cursing. People who curse say the truth, I've heard somewhere." I pull out my chair across from him and sit down. "Can't get it to open?"

"Doesn't budge. I don't want to break it, but I'm going to. I doubt the key is just going to magically appear."

"The key?"

"I looked everywhere. Probably lost it. Or it's somewhere safe." He forms makeshift air-quotes around the last word.

Tell him Laura said hi. The key is taped to the inside of the medicine cabinet, the only place where he wouldn't voluntarily look.

Uhh… Heat rushes to my face. I took her for a crook, but I've come to revise that statement of mine. So far all she's said made sense. At least in retrospect.

I look at Grampie, my best friend in life.

I look at the box that holds the pictures of *his* best friend in life.

Oh, what gives.

"Are you sure you've looked everywhere? I mean… like, everywhere? Just asking, because if it was me, I'd hide it well, somewhere you wouldn't want to look, like… maybe tape it to the inside of the medicine cabinet?" I shrug and turn the box around, checking it.

That's why it takes me a second to realize Grampie doesn't say anything.

Instead, he stares at me, mouth open and eyes wide. "What… what did you say?"

"Uhh, it might be taped to the inside of the medicine cabinet? Or not?" I add a shrug. Great idea listening to Calista.

Grampie closes his mouth. "Who put you up to that?"

"I—"

"No." He holds up a hand. "I know. That old witch. I'm sure it was her idea." A fire burns in his eyes hot enough to, well, burn that witch.

Instead of taking the bait, I push the box back over to him. "You know what, Grampie? I've come to think she might not be as crazy as we think she is." With that, I stand up and press a kiss to his cheek. "Love ya, old grump."

"Huh," Grampie grumps back, "love ya too."

I prepare Grampie his eggs and sit down across of him, staring down into my own plate and tea. No appetite.

After two or three bites, Grampie tilts his head to the side. "Are you finally ready to tell me what's going on in that head of yours?" He reaches forward and taps my temple twice. "You were off the last days, Gwennie-girl."

Off is putting it mildly. I drop my head onto my arms folded on the table. "Sorry, Grampie."

"No need to apologize. All I am is worried about you. You're too sad. Only when that Harrison boy was over it was like a ray of sunlight opened up the clouds." He makes a theatrical, wide hand gesture.

I lift my head enough to cut him an eye. "Wow, Grampie. Dramatic much?"

He shrugs. "Just observant."

"Uh-huh."

"Gwennie?"

"Yes, Grampie?"

"You're not being stupid, are you?"

I lift my head for good this time. "What do you mean?" Because there are indeed lots of things I've been stupid with, it appears.

"What do you think I mean?"

"Really." I lean back and cross my arms in front of my chest. "Using the same technique my shrink does. Didn't I mention I hate it when she does that?"

"You might have."

"And still, it doesn't make you change your tactic."

"Not in the least." He keeps his attention on me, fork still in his hand, waiting.

I sigh and rub a palm across my eyes. "It's nothing, Grampie. Just having a hard time… a hard time dealing with death." Everybody's death. Sarah's. Niparko's. Kai's. Mine.

Everybody's death.

Grampie flinches. "I would think that you did. What happened to you was hard. Traumatizing."

"Gee, thanks for the reminder."

"But it was also not your fault."

My mouth opens and closes. Not my fault. Wonderful

words, if only I could believe them. I drop my gaze to the table. "How can you be so sure?" It's nothing more than a whisper.

Grampie's eyes harden. "Because I know you, Gwennie. I know that night messed with you in more than one way, but I also know that you're a fundamentally good person."

Tears sting in my eyes. "How can I be a good person if I got Sarah killed?" And… and when I killed Niparko. I took a life, with my own hands.

I took a life.

"No. That man got Sarah killed. Not you, Gwennie. Don't you ever think that."

"But—"

"No but. Sometimes, you look like you'd rather be dead yourself, and I get it—but I won't have it. The only person here allowed to look forward to death is me."

"Grampie!"

A grin spreads across his wrinkled face. "Easy, Gwendolyn. But thank you for your outrage, it helps to bring my point across. Imagine how much it hurts me to see you suffering like that. Live, Gwen. Go and get to know that Harrison-boy a bit better. But don't live in the past. Or wait for death."

My lower lip trembles. "I—"

Fast steps come down the stairs, and five seconds later, the door opens to my mom. "Good morn—"

"*I like to eat my beans, beans, beans—*" Her phone starts ringing, and she rolls her eyes. So do I, albeit for a different reason. Maybe we have to talk about that ringtone. Might be time to change it.

"*Hear the noise they're making in my Jeans, Jeans, Jeans!*" To my utter relief Mom doesn't wait for the second verse before she picks up. Either she's on call, or it's the lab, and it's about her research. She wiggles her fingers at me and Grampie, giving us an apologetic wink, not picking up on the mood in the kitchen at all.

Both of us fall into impeccable behavior the second she enters the room and nod a wordless greeting back at her. We know how it works: stay under the radar. My mom can be very perceptive.

She drops a slice of bread into the toaster with one hand, the other still holding the phone to her ear. I don't think there was ever a day where she wasn't working. "No. You just repeat the set-up, only this time you increase the amount of lev-metaminozole by point two milligrams. That's it." She pauses and smiles, her mind hundreds of miles away in the lab. "No worries. You can do it."

A wave of headache, my mind splitting in two—

—the world is blurry around me. It's cold, but not too bad. I can't really remember why I'm on the ground. Doesn't matter, because Sarah is cuddled into me. Once in a while she giggles under her breath. I don't. I feel off. I'm done with after-partying.

"Tom?" I wish he'd stop pacing. It ruins the peace.

He ignores me, just as before.

I try again. "Tom? Can you drive us home?" My head lolls to the right, can't hold it. It bumps into Sarah's. He drove us here. My car. Don't know where he put the keys.

Tom doesn't listen. He keeps on pacing in this little shack, talking to himself. I don't hear much of it.

"You can do it, Tom. You can do it. You can get her there. Either way. Yes. Either way. I can do it."

It's a little bit scary. "Tom?"

He looks up from the ground, straight at me. "Gwen?"

Something in his eyes—

I jerk upright, and Sarah slides down my side. "Ey!" she protests, before she falls into another fit of giggles.

"What is it?" He staggers over to me, not at all like the confident boy who hit on me. This Tom is nervous, pale. He had what, two pills? Three?

"I wanna go home," I squeak. I'm not nearly as drunk as before anymore. I just want to be home. Mom's gonna be worried, and Dad—

Lightning fast, Tom squats down in front of me. If I could, I'd back up.

"Not yet, darling." With one finger, he brushes a strand of hair behind my ear. "Now the fun begins."

He fumbles in his pocket for the same small clear plastic Ziplock baggie he pulled out before. For a moment he stares at it, jaw tight, but then he sighs to himself. "Only one more. I can do it," he whispers so low under his breath, I can't be sure.

He pops one pill himself and holds another one up. "Let's make mommy proud, sweetheart. You can swallow pills." With a devilish grin, Tom takes the pill between his teeth and leans in. Before I can scoot back, his hand is in my hair, bending my head back.

"Nu-uh," he mumbles through his teeth—and then his other hand pinches my nose closed.

"Hey—"

His mouth is on mine the second my lips part. Just like the kiss before, only this time I can't breathe, I can't—

He drops the pill into my mouth. It lands on my tongue, but I don't want to swallow it. I don't. It was fun, but not anymore. I raise my hands to push him away, but he's faster, catching them and holding my wrists together with one hand, the other controlling my head by my hair.

I gag, I move, I try to get away—but Tom is everywhere. As if he liked my fighting, he presses himself into me—and then, when the need for air becomes overwhelming, I swallow. I feel his lips pull into a smile the second I do.

"Good girl," he coos, finally giving me room to breathe. "Good girl." Then, once again under his breath. "I can do this."

"Gwennie? Honey? Are you all right?" My mom has a hand on my shoulder, but when she put it there I can't say. Holy cow. My head pulsates like a neutron star.

Me.

In the shed.

I took another pill, but it wasn't voluntarily. Relief floods me, so potent, my hands shake. It wasn't voluntary.

"Honey?" My mom squats down in front of me.

"Huh?" What did she say?

Her eyes turn from worried to that pitying look that makes me feel guilty for doing that to her. To them. For adding this burden to their lives.

I come up with a quick smile. "Nothing, Mom. Just a headache. Happens."

She gives me the look—the one that tells me she doesn't believe me. Mom sighs and stands up to grab a pill container from the shelf behind Grampie. "Okay then. Look. I know you're on enough meds, but…" She cups my cheek, thumb caressing across my skin. "I've got something for you. And it's going to help, Gwennie. The newest of the new."

I stare at the pills as if they were poison. It's ridiculous, but still… I can't help it. My body screams to run away from these things, as far as I can. Which basically proves I need more meds. Crazy is cranking it up on me. "Mom—"

"Please. Seeing you like this… I can't stand it. I'm worried, honey." She pats my cheek gently, then opens the container and counts out three pills. "You have to take them all three together, Gwen. It'll do the trick."

Her voice is so full of hope for me, of optimism—how could I say no?

"Thanks, Mom." I take the pills and put them in my pocket. "Will take'm after breakfast."

"Why don't you take them—"

"Oh, for heaven's sake, Michelle, cut that girl some slack."

Mom and me whip our gazes over at Grampie, and boy, is he in a mood. His light eyes seem to spit fire at my mom, and the hand that holds the fork… yeah, maybe no more forks for Grampie either.

My mom deflates. "Owen—"

"Don't you Owen me, Michelle. Gwendolyn came here to recover. Having you and Rob all over her does not qualify, and you know that."

"As a doctor—"

"Yeah, yeah." Grampie waves an impatient hand. "I know. But as a senior citizen, former mayor, and man with experience in raising kids, I know that she needs time. And trust. Trust that things are going to work out."

My mom opens her mouth but snaps it closed when the door opens to my dad.

"What a nice morning it is when the first words I hear my father say is the motto he raised me by." Only then does he realize my mom's still squatting in front of me. His brows furrow. "What's going on? Michelle?"

My mom pushes off. "Nothing, Rob." She wipes her palms on her thighs. "You need to refill coffee beans in the espresso machine. It's empty." She sets the pill container onto the shelf behind Grampie and walks out of the kitchen.

With her coffee, without her toast.

Maybe she feels it too. That something is off with Dad.

Dad fishes the bread out of the toaster and bites into it, plain and all. "What's going on?" He nods at the door that closed behind my mom.

"With her, with Gwennie, or with the two of you?" Grampie asks, and it carries some bite.

Dad raises his hands, one still holding the gnawed-on toast. "Easy, Dad. I just feel like I'm late to the party here, but anyway. Gwen?" I get a smile and a thumb pointing toward the backyard. "I figured I'd get some stuff done while I'm here. Visit the Kampton branch of MediSync Connect and then see if I can come up with anything new. Would you maybe…?" He lifts and drops his left shoulder. "Well, I thought maybe you'd like to join me? I mean, in the tinker place? Could be fun, you used to be in there with me a lot, and you've actually helped a bit here and there."

The sip of my tea finds the wrong way down, and it's not

because of my dad's almost-insult hidden in there.

Barely in time, I cover my cough before I spatter Earl Grey all over the breakfast table. "The tinker place?" I wheeze. Oh no, no, *no*—Dad can't go into the tinker place. He'll notice the CryoTherm is gone, and from there, it's only one logical conclusion further to who took it, and then to getting me hospitalized for suicidality. And maybe even Kai.

Neither of those can happen.

I cough some more, every breath whistling on its way in and out. Dad pats me on the back. "Easy there. Swallow before talking." Two more claps. "Yes, the tinker place. I remember you liked working there."

Yeah, when I was like seven. I take one more wheezy breath. What's his angle? Why does he pretend to want to spend time with me? Or, does it really matter? Because at this point, I'm royally screwed.

My dad takes the jar with coffee beans from the counter and pours two handfuls into the espresso machine's slot. "Oh, by the way, Dad. There might be a reporter coming by later today, just FYI. If I'm outside, buzz them in, okay?"

And there's my reason, clear as day: good press. He can't get my statement, so he'll go for the next best thing, father and daughter working together. An easy equation from where he's coming from. Show them father trusts in daughter, watch the stock market improve. Problem solved.

All the anger that rises, all the shame for being used, all the fear of Dad being the instigator—I push it aside. My heart hammers like crazy. "Dad? Can you wait with the tinker place? I have stuff to do this morning, going shopping for Grampie and stuff. But later would be fine."

Come on, come on, bite. Bite, Dad.

For a torturous long moment my dad doesn't react, but then his face lights up. "Wonderful. I'll call Andrew and let him know to come later. Afternoon?"

Yup. Not about us spending time. About the company, as always.

I let go of a breath I didn't know I held. "Okay." I add a small smile and stand up from the table. That'll give me enough time. "Well, I'll get going, so we can start sooner. But wait for me, okay?"

"Sure." Dad nods absentmindedly while scrolling through his phone.

Grampie, on the other hand, looks from one of us to the other and back, eyebrows scrunched together. "Gwennie, if you don't mind, drive over to Porthos as well. I'm in desperate need for some of their baked goods." He winks at me, and a weight falls off my shoulders. A pseudo-trip to Porthos will be another half hour at least. The lines are always long. Grampie just bought me time I don't need to explain my whereabouts for. Him and I, we both know he doesn't eat any of that. Not a health-nut like Grampie.

"Will do, Grampie." *Thank you,* I mouth at him as I sneak out the door.

"Rob, sit. Tell me about your latest project." Grampie pats the chair next to him, and just like that, he also bought me the guarantee Dad won't get up for at least another hour.

I have until noon the latest to bring the CryoTherm back, or I'm in deep.

Chapter Twenty-Six

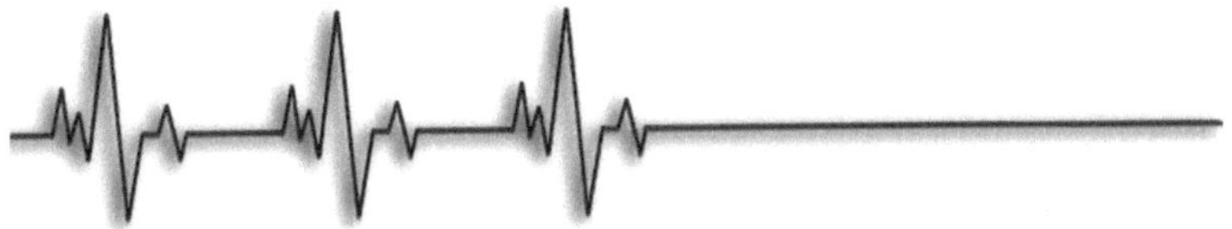

Change of Plans

I park my Volkswagen Beetle in front of Kai's house. It's the first time I drove here instead of walking, but every minute counts. Plus, that's why I got my own car. Granted, not the most practical one for icy and slippery weather, but still cute as a button, despite the circumstances surrounding it. It was my birthday gift last August, replacing my used Prius. Biggest gift ever, since it was supposed to make me feel better after July 31st.

Surprise: it didn't.

Next surprise: It didn't not make me feel better because I'm a spoiled billionaire's daughter who's already a partial shareholder and going to become an even bigger shareholder-slash-even richer at age eighteen, but because it didn't feel fair.

I get rewarded with a car, while Sarah… Yeah.

Dad didn't get it, but whatever.

I get out of the Beetle and lock it. We'll need Kai's truck to get the CryoTherm back. Well, and Kai's muscles. Tiptoeing up the narrow way to Kai's house I make it to the door without falling. Part of the snow must have melted and frozen over again, it's super icy and slippery.

This time it takes at least twenty seconds before I hear steps approaching after I ring the bell. Kai's Grandma.

"Good morning, Dora." I fake a half-curtsy, don't know why. Kind of a reflex with an older, white-haired lady.

Dora smiles at me. "Gwendolyn, good to see you again. Kai is—"

"Right here, Moms." Kai peeks over the railing from the second floor. "Come on up, Gwen." He waves a hand for me to come inside.

Unbelievable what one look at him can do.

Gone is the pressure, gone is the worry, gone is the dark cloud hanging over me since last night. All of it is chased away by an army of kick-ass butterflies that took over my insides the moment I laid eyes on Kai.

I'm out of my boots and up the stairs in no time. Kai walks ahead, jeans a perfect fit for his body, his feet bare. He holds the door open for me, and the second I walk through I'm chest to chest with him, breathing the same air he does.

Especially when his lips touch mine.

Oh, hell.

No: Oh, heaven.

My whole world falls apart and comes back together in

pinks and reds and hearts'n stuff. CryoTherm? We've got until noon. Maybe early afternoon. Kai nibbles on my lips before he parts them with his tongue. He runs his hands down my back, and mine find his waist, fingers digging into his shirt. I need it gone.

"I missed you," Kai whispers into my mouth. One by one he unbuttons my jacket and slides it off my shoulders.

"Me, too," I whisper back. Truer words have never been spoken. The chaos that was my mind a mere thirty seconds ago is gone: Calmed down and excited at the same time, all by him. All by Kai.

His abs contract when I sneak my ice-cold hands under his shirt.

Goosebumps.

On his skin as well as on mine.

I rake my nails across his stomach, and Kai gasps, his grip on my waist tightening.

His tongue flicks out at mine, each touch shooting fireworks through my veins. I abandon his abs and instead press myself harder into him. There can't be any part of my body not connected to him. If I could, I'd crawl into him.

Kai makes a deep rumbling sound in the back of his throat, and it's the most sexy thing I've ever heard. His kiss deepens as he slides his hands down my back, hesitating a tiny moment, before he cups my butt.

My eyes roll back, and now I'm the one making a slightly embarrassing moaning sound.

"Kai!" Dora yells from downstairs.

Both of us twitch.

"Kai! Door open, please!" She claps her hands twice, probably in an attempt to get our attention.

And well, it works.

Sighing once, Kai lets go of my butt, but holds on to one of my hands when he turns toward the open door. "It's open, Moms. Otherwise, I wouldn't be able to hear you."

The only response is a grunt before soft shuffling steps walk off to somewhere on the first floor.

Exactly three seconds later, Kai closes the door without a sound, giving me a shrug and a grin. "Won't come up to check. She's bad with stairs these days." There's definitely a mischievous twinkle in his eyes.

I laugh. "Your family doesn't strike me as the open-door-policy type, hippie house and all."

Kai steers me toward the bed and lets me have a seat on the soft mattress. All butterflies lift off at the same time just from the knowledge that I'm sitting on his bed, where he sleeps. Imagining what else could be done here doesn't exactly help to calm them down.

"You're right, we're usually not that kind of family." Kai shrugs. "Moms is just the only one… well, the only one who at least has an inkling about what was going on inside my head." He taps his temple. "She was suspicious I might try to kill myself, although she was nowhere near the true reasons for it."

Speaking of: the CryoTherm. "Kai, we—"

He lifts one finger and grins. "But now that I have you and the freezer things have changed. I can actually go back there and say good-bye to Cole. Let him go, you know?" The last part comes without the swagger that accompanied the words before.

The butterflies that were just getting used to new heights sink down to the pit of my stomach, motionless. "Kai…" I don't know where to start, or even how to start. Nerves bubble inside me as I think about it. He can't go in. Tom is going to keep him. Mean-bitch Claire is going to make sure of that. The afterlife just became much more real than I ever thought.

Kai kisses the back of my hand. "Just one more time, Gwen. One more."

Oh hell, it's going to break his heart, but better to break it, than to permanently stop it. "Kai—"

"I can't wait." Kai all but jumps out of his chair and walks over to the shelf against the other wall across from the bed. It's filled with stuff—books on the bottom, star ships in the middle and on top—only at eye level is one shelf reserved for nothing but pictures. Cole is in close to every one of them, and Claire in at least two more.

Kai picks up a picture with himself and his brother. "Those were the days," he whispers to himself and sets the frame next to one of his parents. He grabs a little green stuffed animal frog in a bathing suit and leans it against it. The moment he picks up the frog, a small white envelope falls out from under its butt, sailing down to the ground.

The letter.

The letter he wrote to his parents in case… in case something went wrong in the CryoTherm.

Kai bends down and picks it up, turning it back and forth in his hands, before he slaps it over his palm twice.

"Guess I'll still need you, huh?" He slides it right back under the frog, only now closer to the frame. His gaze rests on the frog and the picture of his brother, shoulders heaving up and down twice. "I have to do it, no matter the risk, Gwen."

Something cramps up inside of me, threatening to close off my throat. I feel like the biggest ass. I get it. I really do, but it's not going to happen. "Kai… we can't."

"Of course we can. We did it once."

I wince. "That's not what I mean. My dad—"

"*You*'ve done it twice." He boops the little froggie onto its nose.

Yeah, I did go in twice, and the second round bought me a visit by Niparko. Nothing I'd wish on anybody.

I close my eyes for a short moment. "I know. But we literally can't. My dad is going to work in his tinker place this afternoon, and once he sees the CryoTherm is gone—"

Kai whirls around, his frantic gaze darting first to me, then to the left at the alarm clock on his nightstand. "We still have two hours. We can do it. Five minutes to get there if we're fast, five for set up, cooling down maybe ten, add five for me in the Realm—"

"No." I hold out a hand. "Seriously, no."

His expression turns pleading. "Don't let me hang here, Gwen. I need this. It's tough enough to live without Cole, but without a good-bye…" A slow shake of his head. "Can't do it."

A wave of his desperation washes over me and sweeps me off my proverbial feet. Deep breath. "We don't have time." I mean, he's right, we do, it's just that—

"We do. It works out fine."

I suppress a groan. Geez, get a hint, Kai! "It… it might not be enough." I'm this close to telling him what happened. *This* close. Only, it would do him no good. I'm talking to the boy who wanted to drown and electrocute himself to find his brother. Not a huge leap to assume he's going to come up with something to get the same result, with or without me.

And if it's without me... I swallow hard. Without me there'd be no safety net, only death waiting patiently to catch him when I don't.

"We'll be fast." Pause. "Please, Gwen."

I rub a palm over my eyes. "Kai—"

Out of nowhere, a cold breeze brushes across my body, so cold, I draw in a sharp breath of air. In an instant the colors are gone, the world bleached out like in an old photograph.

"Shit," I whisper.

My heart drops to my knees. Not good, not good, not—

"You remember what I told you? Because I wasn't lying, Gwen."

I jerk from the voice so close to my ear.

Hell.

On my left, on Kai's bed—*on Kai's freakin' bed*—sits Niparko, an infuriating grin on his face. "I will keep him. And then you. I don't care."

"*Shit* what, Gwen?"

Huh?

It takes an effort close to moving a mountain to focus back on Kai in front of me. "Kai, there's—" I turn my head left and right, from Kai to Tom and back, but Kai doesn't even glance to my left. Instead, he narrows his eyes at me.

"No, really, Gwen. *Shit* what? *Shit* as in you're afraid? Well, so am I! I don't want to die, but we've been over this. It's something I have to do. *Shit* as in you won't do it?" He sucks in his lower lip. "Then we have a problem."

Niparko snickers. "Uh-oh. I guess you have a problem."

Kai keeps his gaze trained on me. Not on Tom—his show is for me. Only for me.

I force in a wheezy breath and a swallow down my throat. Maybe I should thank Tom. He's the best reminder I could get why Kai can't go in. I have to protect him, no matter what, so I do what I have to, and put on my big-girl panties. "You can't go back in. Period."

Silence.

For the longest three seconds of my life, Kai stares at me as if I'd stabbed him—and I have, only with words instead of weapons. Then his expression turns blank as he nods once. "You know, you never really told me why you wanted to enter the Realm. Twice." His voice is still quiet, yet it almost deafens me. He gives the frog on the shelf another tap on the nose. "First-hand experience my ass. You never wrote a letter either." He turns around, head slightly cocked to the left. "What is it that you're not telling me?"

"Yeah, Gwen. What is it that you're not telling him?" Tom glides a finger down my shoulder and I jerk.

"I—" I blink rapidly. Kai... I mean, what am I supposed to say, I—

And then I see it.

The trace of pity in his eyes that wasn't there before.

And it changes everything.

Everything.

I jump to my feet, anger propelling me up. "What did your

grandma tell you?" It must've been Dora. Her and Grampie talk.

Kai holds my gaze. "Enough. Enough to explain why you wanted to cross into the Realm."

Dizziness—and then I'm not me anymore, but—

"Enough!" I grab my brother's collar and stop him from running. "Get a grip, Edan. You're going to school and that's it." I keep one hand on his shirt while I fish for his backpack with the other. "Here." I shove it into his arms. "If I catch you playing hooky again, I promise I'll tell Dad."

That does the trick. Edan's face turns white.

"All right, all right," he mumbles. "Just figured you used to skip class, so I don't see the point—"

Screw that little idiot. "The point is that I don't want you to have to do what I'm doing, so you better graduate, bro. Or else I can take you to the dealers Dad introduced me to when I was... yeah, about your age." I yank up my sleeve and shove my arm into his face. "Care for any of that?"

Edan turns away. He doesn't do well with scars. Or blood. Or anything, really.

"No. I know how you got them."

I know he does. Because he was the one applying the antibiotic ointment and changing the dressings, while our dad was on a binge, and I was too high on the stuff he shoved down my throat to keep me from screaming the whole neighborhood together.

I pat Edan's shoulder. "See? So bugger off." I turn him around and send him in the right direction, watching him as he crosses the street and walks toward the Middle School one block down.

He will graduate.

But even if he doesn't, I have a plan to keep him out of trouble. Nothing could be more important.

A headache pierces my skull with the force of an axe. "Ugh," I grunt, rubbing my temple.

"You should have told me."

Wait, wha—?

Right, Kai.

"You should have told me. I mean…" He sighs. "It's a big thing, Gwen."

A big thing? Anger surges, drowning out the confusion the last few seconds have left in their wake. I drop my hand off my temple. "A big thing? Seriously? That's what you call it? A *big thing*?" A brain-splitting headache assaults me. I need my meds. I need something to keep my wits together, I can't afford to lose the last bit I have left. Shoving my right hand down my pocket, I fumble out the three pills my mom gave me, while glaring at Kai. "It was a *freaking* big thing, Kai! My best friend is dead, and I killed a guy!" Out of reflex I throw out a hand and point at Tom on Kai's bed—whom Kai can't see.

His brows scrunch as his gaze follows to where I'm pointing before it darts back to me. "Which is exactly why you should've told me! I would consider that vital information, pun intended!"

In a snap Tom is in front of me, one knee on the ground, one foot plated next to mine. I jerk back from the unexpected invasion of my personal space.

"What did you just see?" He growls at me, but it sounds… fake. He's pale, a couple of droplets of sweat forming above his eyebrows. "Did you—"

Kai curses. "Sorry, Gwen. I… I didn't mean it to sound like that. But I would've appreciated some honestly."

Oh hell to the no! I focus back on Kai. "Honesty? I never lied! And you know, maybe what happened to me, to us, is not something I particularly enjoy talking about! I—"

"Screw that, Gwen! I told you everything—*everything*— and you can't even tell me the reason why you want to die? You didn't write a letter either, wanna know what that tells me? It tells me you don't care if you're dead or alive!" He makes a slashing motion across his throat with the last word, chest heaving up and down in a fast rhythm.

Tom grabs may forearm, his grip hard and ice cold. "I'm talking to you. What. Did. You. See."

Kai carries on, unperturbed by Tom's presence. "Now imagine I didn't get you back, and you died. How the hell would you think I would've felt after I found out about your past? Knowing I could've talked you out of it—"

I slam my free hand into the mattress. "Just like *you* are letting yourself get talked out of it by me?" Because it ain't working from where I'm coming from!

Tom gives my arm a nasty tug. "Has that happened before? *Talk*, damn it!"

I yank my hand out with all my might, a move that earns me yet another raised eyebrow from Kai, before he throws both hands up and yells. "It's different for me!"

"Heck, no! It's not at all—" I suck a harsh breath in as both, Kai and Tom, lash out at me.

Tom: "I'm asking for the last time, or—"

Kai: "Plus, even if it wasn't it doesn't change the fact that this is about trust and you broke it!"

I shake my head, doing my best to ignore Tom and focusing on Kai. "I didn't—"

Tom: "Hell, Gwen. I swear I'm going to make your life hell if you don't tell me what you saw!"

Kai: "All I asked was that we do this together—"

Tom: "You little bitch, I'm talking to—"

Kai: "—and I need you for this, or else I don't know what's going to happen!"

Tom: "Gwen! Talk!"

Holy frackin'…! I press my palms against my ears, the pills I held in my hand dropping to the floor. "Shut. *Up!*"

Silence.

Sweet silence.

Kai breathes heavily in front of me, and—*click*—everything's back in color.

Tom is gone.

I let my hands sink down from my face. They feel like they're loaded with lead, while I feel drained. So tired. So exhausted. I gulp in air. "Kai—"

He shakes his head and takes a step back, a hurt look on his face. "I was willing to overlook it. I figured, everybody processes things differently, and maybe you weren't ready. I was willing to push aside how crappy I felt when I had to hear from Moms of all people what happened to you—not from you, Gwen. I was willing to ignore the shock when I realized I was stupid for letting you enter when I didn't even know if you wanted to come out of the Realm again." He swallows hard.

"But what I'm not willing to work with is your disregard for my needs. I bore my soul to you. I cried in your arms. And you still shut me out. You didn't even have the decency to be honest with me."

Zzzing—I don't know why, but this time the arrow hits its target dead center, and it must be doing something to my heart. I'm expecting pain, because his words *should* hurt, yet it's not coming. Instead, I feel numb. Blissfully numb, like I was wrapped in a cocoon of cotton. His words can't reach me. Nothing can.

I let go of a small huff. Yes, he's right. I wasn't honest. And I'm still not being honest with him. It's a sad necessity I'm willing to pay the price for.

Brushing my hands off my thighs, I stand up and look at the boy who made me feel more alive than I'd ever been. I make an effort to keep my voice level when I speak. "I'm going to take down the CryoTherm. Text me if you want to—" I close my eyes. "Forget it."

Then I turn around and walk away from the boy I had a crush on since sixth grade, who made me feel more alive than I'd ever been.

Because that's the only thing that's going to keep *him* alive.

Chapter Twenty-Seven

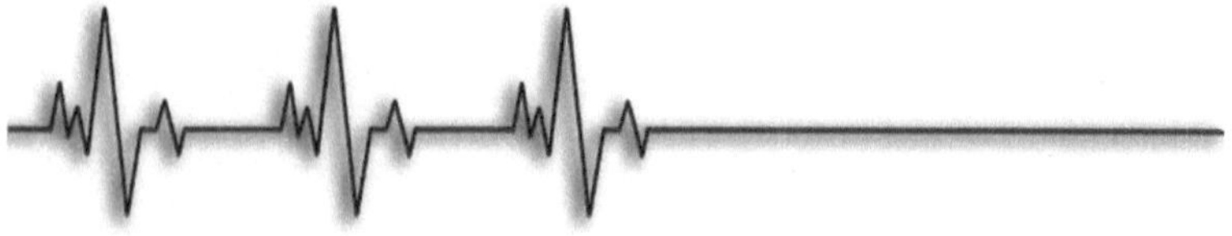

Timing

As if in a trance I walk down to my Beetle.

I think... I think I just broke up with Kai.

A crazy laugh gurgles from my throat when I unlock my car. Is it even breaking up? I'm his second choice, and we made out twice. That hardly qualifies as anything.

And whatever it was, now we're done, I'm pretty sure of it.

I press the button and start the engine. I should've told him. Yeah. Right. What good does telling do? I'd bet it comes with more meds and a phone call to the madhouse for admission. Telling never did anybody any good—and to be fair, I didn't remember half of what happened to me anyway.

Doesn't change that Kai feels I screwed him over royally...

I doubt he's going to want to have anything to do with me.

First, I promised him. And then I broke that promise.

I smack the steering wheel. "For a reason, damn it!" For a *good* reason! I swipe my sweaty palm across my eyes. That headache— Crap. Dropped the pills up in Kai's room. Stupid. I'm so stupid.

Stupid to let myself get pulled into this.

Stupid for agreeing to kill him.

Stupid for dying myself.

Stupid for dying a freakin' second time.

Just plain, old stupid.

I grab a bottle of water out of the holder and down two Motrin from the glove compartment instead of Mom's meds. Then, I pull away from the curb. Damn. Now I've got to get the truck from Grampie's and get the CryoTherm back, all by myself and without Dad noticing. Crap, crap, crap.

My hands shake so badly I can barely hold on to the wheel. Maybe I shouldn't be driving like this.

At the next grocery store, I pull over into their parking lot, but keep the engine running once I'm in a parking spot.

Damn.

I let my head fall back against the head rest. What a craptastic day. My mind is a chaos of thoughts, everything mixing together, yet none of it makes sense. I get my flashbacks of what happened, but what about the other stuff? Where I'm not myself. Was that *his* flashback, Tom's? It would make sense, but… he seemed shocked by that. Shouldn't he be the one like, sending me this stuff, like he did before, because I don't know, Ghost of The Past, or whatever?

A weird, snorting huff leaves my throat. What happened to my life over the last two days? Hell, the last couple of hours? The last six months?

I blow out a slow breath through pursed lips.

Everything's going downhill.

Everything I used to think was important is not.

Does it even matter at this point if I started the whole thing by flirting with Tom? If I had started the drugs? Because, if I'm right and my dad is involved—

My phone chimes.

Whatever.

Because if I'm right and my dad is involved in this… "He can't." But maybe he can. His behavior is more than odd—has been more than odd since the kidnapping.

I count off my fingers, talking out loud. No, I'm not losing it even more. It helps me focusing: "No ransom note, but Tom said *everything was set*." I even give myself air quotes. "So maybe it was all a set-up plan between Dad and Tom," I whisper into the silence of the car. "Maybe—"

My cell chimes again, the reminder a text came in, and this time my eyes fall onto the display.

Kai.

The text pops up once the phone recognizes my face:

Inducing Hypothermia at 10:39 hours.

Nothing else.

I re-read it again.

And again.

And it does nothing against the chill that has me, the tight band of panic cutting off my throat.

I screwed up.

I wasn't fast enough.

Kai beat me to the CryoTherm.

And he's cooling himself down and entering the Realm.

Which he will never leave.

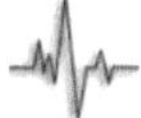

10:50 hours.

"Crap!" I yell. "Crap, crap, crap!" My palm strikes the wheel with every outburst. How stupid and butt-headed can he be? He's going in alone? *Alone?*

"Shit, shit, shit!" I ram the gear into reverse and shoot out of the parking spot. Somebody honks at me like crazy, but I don't care.

Inducing hypothermia—what the heck does he mean? Firing up the CryoTherm? Starting the cooling down sequence? Details matter—timing matters! But no matter what, if his heart hasn't stopped yet, it will soon.

And that means the clock is ticking.

I race out of the parking lot, tires screeching. Never before have I pushed the Beetle that much, let alone over snowy roads like these, but I can't slow down. Keeping both hands firmly on the wheel, I use voice control to start the stopwatch. Details freaking matter!

My heart rate is erratic at best, skipping beats left and right.

Maybe Kai's just messing with me. Or maybe once he goes in, Cole will be there, it'll be a quick good-bye, and then he's out again. Just because Tom and Claire said they could keep him doesn't necessarily mean—

Yeah, but I won't take that risk.

I run a red light at the outskirts of the town, some teenager shaking his fist after me.

Sorry, buddy. Priorities.

I keep my foot down and race over the snow-covered dirt road toward the old train yard, following the thick trails Kai's truck left a mere couple of minutes before me.

"Come on, come on," I hiss at my car. "Faster, damn it!" Another three minutes gone.

Even if I assume he just started the CryoTherm when he texted… at this point he'll be very hypothermic already.

And possibly dead.

Freaking dead.

My eyes tear up and I wipe them dry with the back of my hand.

There. Train yard.

I pull up in the back and jump out of my car, engine running and door open.

"Kai!" I know he can hear me, if not in this world, then in the Realm. "Kai! Come the heck back, or I swear—"

I stop dead in my tracks. The CryoTherm glows in its beautiful blue light, illuminating Kai's still face and high cheekbones.

But that's not what roots me to the spot.

It's the timer next to the EKG.

10:44

10:45

10:46

10:47

Kai has been dead for over ten minutes.

Chapter Twenty-Eight

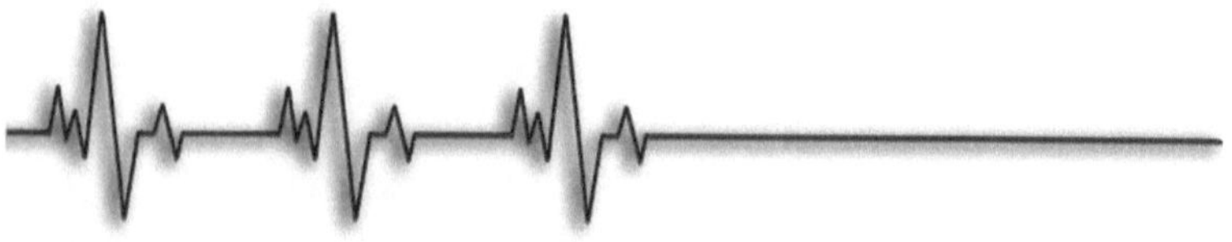

911

"No."

I slap one hand over my mouth. "No."

Eleven Minutes.

Eleven-oh-one.

Eleven-oh-two.

Eleven-oh—

"Crap!" I snap into action. Within three seconds, I've sprinted the distance from the entrance to the CryoTherm.

Thirty-three degrees body temperature.

Thirty-three degrees for over ten minutes.

My palm hits the Emergency Rewarm button so hard, it makes an offended crunching noise.

"Kai!" I yell into the empty train yard. "Come back! Seriously! Now!"

Flatline.

His EKG's a flatline.

That's good, right? Right? It means there's only one way to go.

I jump up the little makeshift stool so that I'm high enough and slide my right index finger up his breastbone from the xyphoid process, finding the same anatomic landmarks I found the day prior.

He's still bruised.

Not that it mattered, and there's no time to lose.

I take one deep breath and push down with all my might.

And again.

And again.

Faster, Gwen, faster! Get the blood going, get it going! It's all about circulation, the studies say. Right?

A strange déjà vu comes over me when, like the day before, I use my whole bodyweight to push down on Kai's chest, flexile ribs giving under the pressure, his head twitching like with a nervous tick with every compression.

I rip the ventilation bag off the hook and give him the rescue breaths, in the far recess of my mind relieved he hooked it up to the oxygen tank.

Compressions. More, faster. Go, go, go!

Thirty-three point five degrees.

I keep pumping. My breath comes out harsh and cut off, while my heart is pumping for the two of us, frantic, panicked. Every beat telling me I'm too late: Too late. Too late. Too late.

Thirty-three point eight degrees.

A sob breaks from my throat.

Cold. He's so cold—but that's good, that's good, it'll preserve his brain function. Just keep on doing what you're doing. Keep it up, Gwen.

Thirty-four degrees.

"Kai, please." A hot tear drips down on him. "I know you can hear me, come back, come back!"

More pumping, more compressions, more rescue breaths, all as fast as I can.

Use the rhythm of the BeeGee's Staying Alive, they said during CPR class. Or Queen's *Another One Bites the Dust*. I thought was funny at that time. Now I don't.

Thirty-four point three degrees.

I pause, panting.

Check the EKG, Gwen! Nothing. Still flatline.

"Kai, don't do this to me, please don't!" I bend over him again and compress his chest—his still, cold, motionless chest. Despite the cold sweat forms rivulets along my brow and the back of my neck, brought on by the physical strain of CPR and sheer panic.

Fourteen minutes.

What has happened? Did he find Cole? Or worse, did Tom or Claire find him?

Pump, pump, pump.

Breathe, breathe, breathe.

Thirty-four point eight degrees.

Pause: Squiggly lines on the EKG. Crap!

Lightning fast, I reach out for the defibrillator. "Loading!"

Its high-pitched whine pierces the silence like a knife. "Clear!" I press the paddles to Kai's chest.

Boom!

200 Joules shoot through Kai's body, jerking it up.

Panting, I check the EKG.

Still in V-fib.

Once more.

Load. Check. Fire!

Boom!

No change.

Again!

LoadcheckFIRE!

Boom!

Nothing.

"Shit!" I scream it out into the train yard. I can't break the V-fib, and without a flatline his heart doesn't stand a chance to restart. If I don't do compressions, he'll die.

He'll *stay dead.*

So I push on his chest, as hard as I can, as deep as I can, as fast as I can. A part of me modifies my compressions like I learned. That part is completely detached from the other one, the one that's raging, screaming, and going into full-blown panic mode.

Thirty-five degrees.

Give me a heartbeat, Kai! Really, any time—

Still V-fib.

One more shock.

Boom!

Another one.

Boom!

A third one.

Boom!

And freaking nothing.

"Kai." More tears drip onto him, wetting the chest I'm doing compressions on.

Thirty-six point five degrees.

Normal body temperature.

Normal body temperature and V-fib I can't break. I don't have any meds, because… because I was so stupid to think I wouldn't need them. And I couldn't have gotten them anyway. Adrenaline? Lidocaine? Not quite over the counter.

"Not good. Not good," I wheeze. Every compression my arms are losing strength. I can't keep this up much longer, it's been…

"Nineteen minutes." Shit. Nineteen minutes dead, that's…

Fear clamps around my heart.

What are his chances at this point? Does it matter if it's because he's held back?

I lift my head towards the ceiling. "Let him go! Let him go! Please!"

No answer.

Of course not.

My hands slip off Kai's breastbone.

Crap.

Re-adjust. Continue compressions. Rescue breaths.

Sobs shake my body, making it so much harder to continue CPR, but I must.

Must.

But if I'm honest to myself Kai only has one chance at this point.

"Hey phone," I call out, then again, louder, when I hear no responding beep. "Hey, phone! Call 911!"

"Calling 9-1-1."

For the eternity of five seconds, I wait, until an operator picks up.

"Nine-one-one, what's your location?"

Last chance.

I glance at the EKG.

V-Fib.

He needs this. Kai needs this.

"The old Train Yard. I have one person in cardiac arrest and V-fib. I need help!"

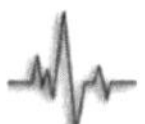

Three long minutes later, I hear the sirens.

Another minute later, they barge in. Four firefighter-paramedics, the first two stopping dead in their tracks.

"Holy crap, what—"

"What is this thing?"

One of the others pushes me off the pedestal. "Taking over. How long?"

I bend over, supporting my weight on my knees, wheezing. "Twenty-three minutes."

The medic curses. "Joe! Lido! Now!"

Around me, the medics jump into action. Medications are drawn, a breathing tube placed into Kai's throat, oxygen attached.

"Satting good, 94%."

Okay. Okay. His brain had enough oh-two. Good.

I wipe a snotty sleeve over my eyes.

"Still V-Fib. Shock."

Boom!

"Shock!"

Boom!

"Shock!"

Boom!

Three more shocks, each and every one jerking Kai's body up.

It looks horrible.

"Lido!"

"In!"

"Two minutes. Check."

All eyes go to the EKG.

"Flatline! Resume compressions."

Flatline. Good. It's something. It's better. My whole body shakes like a leaf. I wrap my arms around my chest to literally hold myself together, but it's no use.

More sirens outside, more commotion around me I don't pick up on. All I do is focus on Kai, his lifeless body.

"Epi. Get it in, get it in!"

They're trying to jumpstart his heart, now that he has a flatline. Now that he has a chance.

Tears stream down my face. "Kai, come on. Please," I beg

the air around me. It's been twenty-five minutes. I know they're going to give up soon if they don't get a heartbeat.

And that can't happen.

Tom. It must be Tom holding him back.

I ball my hands into fists as I spin around, looking for him. "Bring him back, you freaking asshole!"

The medics whip their heads around at my outburst, faces distorted in disgust.

"Not you," I rasp, fingers massaging my temples, "not—"

"Gwendolyn O'Karran?" The voice next to me is deep and authoritative.

"Huh?" I look up to the right. A police officer.

"Are you Gwendolyn O'Karran?"

"Y-yes."

The officer nods and fumbles for something at the right side of his belt.

And then two things happen simultaneously.

"Sinus rhythm! We've got a sinus rhythm!" The medic yanks his hands off Kai's chest, and there it is: a slow, steady heartbeat on the EKG.

Heaven.

A weight the size of a mountain falls off my chest. He's alive. Kai's alive. Kai—

"Gwendolyn O'Karran. You are under arrest for violation of your bail in the case of the murder of Sarah Matthews and Tom Niparko."

Cuffs are being clicked around my wrists.

"Wha—" Murder? Bail? "That must be—"

"You have the right to remain silent and refuse to answer—

"

A medic curses. "He's not waking up, dammit."

"—you say may be used against you in a court of law—"

"Most likely brain damage. After like half an hour—"

"—and to have an attorney present during—"

I don't hear any of it. Not the medics' assumptions, not the officer's arrest.

All I know is that Kai's body is alive.

But his soul is trapped in the Realm.

And I have no way of getting it out.

Chapter Twenty-Nine

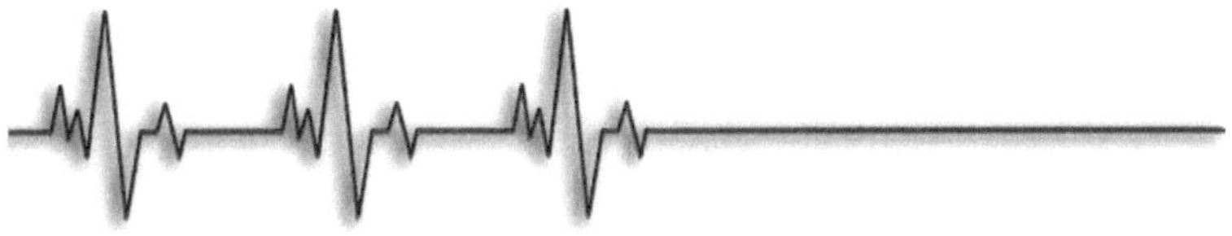

Rockbottom

The ride in the back of the police car is like being trapped in a parallel universe.

I'm in handcuffs.

Arrested.

For what, I don't quite get, I don't quite understand.

The case of the murder of Sarah Matthews and Tom Niparko—there is no case. Tom murdered Sarah, and I defended mys—

Oh.

Oh. The moment the gears click into place I want to facepalm myself, only I'm handcuffed: *She'll be found innocent,* Dad said when I overheard him, Mom and Grampie that night.

Violating bail, the officer said. What else has my family kept from me? Not only that I killed Niparko, but also that… that… that I'm accused of murder? Under investigation?

The pieces align too neatly to be coincidence. What did Mrs. Matthews write? *If this was a targeted kidnapping, it would change everything, for us and for you, obviously.* Because as I understand it now, I'm accused of murder, and out on bail, probably thanks to the O'Karran name.

Air flees my lungs. What's their reasoning? I was the only survivor, therefore I must have killed them both? Okay. Okay. But I only defended myself! It wasn't *murder!*

But the police act as if it was.

I'm being taken into the station.

Searched.

Photographed.

Fingerprinted

And when I'm finally locked in a cell, the air coming through the bars isn't enough to stop me from hyperventilating. I—

Smoke is in the air, and not the good kind. Weed. Some other stuff. I cough and cover my nose and mouth with my forearm. "Edan? Dad?"

I'd leave the door open to air out our crappy apartment, but then the neighbors are going to complain again. So instead, I open the kitchen window. This way the stench could be from us, or the students two windows down.

"Dad?" Damn him, I told him to keep it on the low-down. We're this close to eviction.

I open the door to his room, but he isn't in there. Great. Could've at least opened a window before leaving. What a responsible adult.

With a sigh I enter Edan's and my room—

—and stop.

The next breath gets stuck in my throat.

Completely.

"Edan," I whisper.

Edan lies on his bed, eyes half open and fixed onto the ceiling, sweat dotting his forehead.

And next to him our piece-of-shit father. Sleeve rolled up. Tourniquet around his biceps. Needle still in his vein.

With the roar of a wounded animal, I burst forward and grab my dad by the collar. "What have you done? What the hell have you given him? Answer me! Answer!" I shake him like a doll, but he's too far gone.

Useless.

I throw him back against the wall.

"Edan." I gently wipe the hair from his sticky forehead, while feeling for a pulse with my other hand. Fast, thready, but there.

I kick out back with all my might, hitting my drugged-up dad into the side so hard he falls over. "Fuck you. Fuck you! The one thing I asked you not to do! You've ruined me already, why him? Why him?"

"Hey. Hey!" A hand moves up and down in front of my face. I blink. Again.

"Hey. I'm talking to you. You have one phone call. Five minutes. Make it count." The police officer steps back and leaves me in front of the black phone in this empty room.

How did I get here?

"Five minutes." He points at the clock on the wall and closes the door behind him.

Two more blinks.

Five minutes and one phone call.

Not a tough decision to make. I'm underage. The police are going to call my parents for sure.

Oh god, please let me remember the number correctly.

I snatch the receiver off the hook and punch in the number.

One dial tone.

A second.

A third.

"Hello?"

Thank you, whomever.

"Calista? It's Gwen. Listen, I—"

"Gwen! What is going on? I just visited the Realm and—"

The answer breaks free together with a sob. "He has Kai. Niparko. *Tom.* He told me he was going to keep Kai if he ever went in again, and—" My voice cracks, and with it my heart. "And he did. I was too late. We got his body back, but his soul..." His soul we didn't get.

Silence on the other end.

"Calista?" I need help. I need something. *Anything.*

"Yes. Yes. I'm... I'm here. It's just..." I hear her breathe out fast. "Then Kai is trapped like Cole. If it's been longer than a couple of minutes, five, if he's lucky maybe ten, he won't be able to leave the Realm on his own. Even if they didn't hold him back inside the Realm and with his body still intact and able to receive his soul."

All strength leaves my body. "No." It's barely a whisper.

"I'm afraid so. A soul for a soul, that's the balance of things. Once it's anchored to the Realm only another soul can release it."

That's what she said before, but—

An idea lights me up. "Another soul. So, Kai's soul could release Cole's?" At least one of them free, at least one of them in the Realm of the living.

"Yes. Theoretically."

I groan. "Which means?"

"It means it won't automatically happen. A new soul enters from a viable, receptive body, and it can set the other one free, provided that one has an intent to leave."

"Intent to—"

"Wants to leave. As soon as you want to leave, you will get pulled toward your body if your body is still receptive, like I said."

She's right. She's absolutely right! The two times I went in, whenever I thought about Kai, about going back, my body sank toward him. I close my eyes. Deep breath. Plan. Developing. "Okay. Okay. So how can I enter the Realm and let them know? There must be a trick besides dying. I mean, you do it, so—"

Calista's sigh interrupts me. "Gwendolyn, I have a trick, but it won't work for you. The only way to enter the Realm is if a connected soul pulls you in."

"Like—"

"Like somebody you shared a death experience with. For me it's my friend who overdosed with me when I was young. She died, I made it out thanks to your Gramps, but that connected us. It stained me."

"Then Sarah should be—"

"She won't be able to do it. She died in front of you, sorry to be blunt, but not *with* you. You stayed alive. It's not an event big enough to connect your souls. She won't work as a connected soul." Another sigh. "There is no way into the Realm for you, Gwen. No way besides dying."

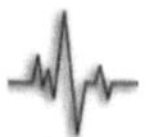

I draw my legs in closer to my body and wrap my arms around them.

The cot is hard.

Doesn't matter.

My muscles ache from sitting in this position for at least two hours, maybe three.

Doesn't matter.

Nothing matters.

Nothing.

Matters.

The sound of steps coming down the hallway breaks the monotony. Fast steps. Heels. Soft shoes, too.

Doesn't matter.

They stop in front of my cell.

Doesn't matter.

"Gwendolyn." My dad. His business voice.

Doesn't matter.

"Gwennie." A whisper. My mom.

Mom.

I lift my head, and it's so, so difficult.

The moment my mom's and my gaze meet, her eyes tear up. "Gwennie." That whisper sounds way more desperate.

Doesn't matter.

She covers her mouth with a hand. It's shaking. "Gwennie."

A police officer and a man in an expensive tailored suit step next to them. Uncle Doug.

"The judge didn't grant bail this time, I'm sorry," the police officer says.

"We'll see about that." Uncle Doug straightens his suit jacket.

The officer chuckles. "No, we won't. No matter you're an O'Karran and a hot shot lawyer from L.A., we have a girl who's charged with murder in one case and accessory to murder in another, who almost killed yet another boy." He pauses and looks at me. "For whatever reason she put the Harrison-boy into that... *machine*, and when the medics came, he had no heartbeat. For twenty minutes." He faces Uncle Doug again. "He's on life-support, and judging from what I heard, it doesn't look good."

A muscle in my uncle's temple twitches. "This is kept confidential?"

"Of course. She's underage. We're not giving out any information until the judge—"

My dad turns on his heels. "No information at all. I don't want her name out. I don't want any of this in the press. We keep her out, we keep the business—"

Everything sways. Nothing stays still. The whole world is filled with colors, and they all taste so good. A door opens to my right, and Tom leans in and over me, un-clicking my seat belt. As if in a trance, I shove my right hand into his hair. So soft.

He chuckles as he pulls back, but stays so close, our noses touch. "Getting the taste for it, aren't we?"

I open my mouth, but he's faster. He licks across my lips. And again. And again. Never thought I'd like that, but tonight I do. I cramp my fingers tighter into his hair, drawing him closer.

He moans into my mouth. "So impatient. But first..." He smashes his mouth to mine, stealing another kiss that leaves me breathless, before he pulls back, breathing heavy. "But first let's give the blood hounds something to search for. You're so good for business. So good for money."

"Gwen? Honey. Gwen?"

I blink twice. Again.

Holy cow. A wheezy breath catches in my throat. That flashback, it must've been... it must've been *before*. Before the shed. *Good for business, Tom said. Just like my dad did.* Me disappearing was good for his company.

"Honey, say something. You're scaring me." Mom wraps her fingers around the bars of my cell.

And my eyes water up.

"Mom." My voice trembles. "Why am I here? I didn't— It wasn't— I haven't—"

My parents exchange a glance, and not a happy one. "You tell her, Rob. I wanted her in psych from the moment we

310

brought her home." My mom crosses her arms in front of her chest.

Dad, on the other hand, keeps a straight face. Straight and serious. "Gwen, there… there are certain things we kept from you."

"You kept from me?" I echo like a pitiful parrot.

"Yes. We considered it better for your mental health."

"My mental health?"

My dad works a hand through his hair. "Gwen, they're still working on Sarah's death. And Niparko, the… kidnapper… Unlike we led you to believe, he's not in jail, Gwen." His eyes take on a certain pity. "He's dead. Stabbed. And… you were the one to stab him."

Silence.

Silence.

Silence.

"Yeah," I breathe out hoarsely. "That was me."

The officer cocks his head. "Is that a confession? Is she—"

Uncle Doug whirls around. "This has already been established. Self-defense. Bail was granted on that account. She's not saying anything else."

Dad ignores his brother. "For Niparko's death… The DA doesn't think it was kidnapping. No attempt to extort money. You all had new designer drugs in your systems. No defensive wounds on you. You had Sarah's and the other boy's blood all over you." He flinches. "To them… to them it could've been partying gone wrong. They're investigating whether you, while under the influence, killed Sarah and then Tom. The other boy, I mean. To them, it could've been you."

The voice appears out of nowhere directly next to me, whispering into my ear. "To me it was you."

I jerk and lift my hands to my ears, then drop them halfway. Just what I need. Ignoring Tom, I stare at my dad. My mom. Back and forth, left and right, left and right... "But... But you never said anything. I—"

"We never said anything because you weren't officially charged. Yet. Besides Niparko, you are their number one suspect, but thanks to Doug's and your mother's connections the judge allowed you bail and house arrest—which we got modified to Kampton, as long as you stayed within the freakin' city borders." His lips press into a thin line.

"*That's* why you sent me here? *That's* why you wanted me to stay close to Grampie's house?" Horror colors my voice. I thought it was for me, to get distance to heal—and heck, under the pretense to help Grampie.

"Yes." Dad's eyes shoot fire. "And what do you do? Violate that. Leave the city limits. I told you *specifically* not to leave the house unless for—"

"I didn't know!" I jump up and off the bench. "How was I supposed to know that? You tell me tons of stuff every day, and most of it—" I snap my mouth shut, but the damage is done.

"Yes, Gwendolyn?" My dad emphasizes my full name. "What do you do most of the time? Please indulge me, because I'm sure it involves ignoring what I tell you."

"Uh-oh," Tom whispers next to me. "You're in deep today."

I whirl around. "Shut up, you—"
Mistake.

Big, *big* mistake.

I realize it the moment my mom sucks in a sharp breath of air. "Gwennie…" Just like before one hand covers her mouth. She takes a step closer to the bars. "Is it… is it getting worse?" She exchanges another glance with my dad. "I told you, she's getting worse."

"No." I shake my head and walk backwards toward the cot. "Nothing's going on, I'm not—"

Tom sticks out a foot and I stumble, barely catching myself.

The pity in my mom's eyes rises to new levels. "Did you take the meds I gave you? Honey?"

I shake my head. My pounding head. "No." None of them, not for a while. And I guess it shows. Guess I should've stuck to what she told me, but I thought I knew better. I thought remembering meant I was doing better.

Disappointment washes over her face, but she gets it under control. "Where are they?"

"I don't know." Couldn't care less at the moment.

"Gwen, where are they?" My mom presses again.

"I don't know."

"Damn it, Gwen, they were prototypes!" The knuckles of her fingers wrapped around the bars of my cell turn paper white. Not happy. Mom's not happy.

Raising two fingers of each hand I massage my temples. "I—"

In the blink of an eye, Tom is gone from my side and pops up right in front of my mom, like, right in her face, hands on his hips, chin up. "Prototypes, huh?"

Mom of course doesn't see him. "Just tell me where they are, and I'll bring them to you—"

Dad says, "Michelle, back off your meds. We'll get her evaluated by Psych—"

"Oh, so *now* you want that?" Mom snaps at him. "After I've been trying to get help for her for the last six months? *Now?*"

"Now things have changed, obviously! I can't afford to not treat her! Do you know what'll happen once the shareholders get wind of this little tweak in the story?" Dad jabs one accusing finger at me.

As I walk back, the hollows of my knees hit the cot and I sit, not having the strength to keep standing. I glance from one of my parents back to the other, both their faces distorted in anger, both radiating a cold it beats the one of the Realm.

It doesn't feel good.

"Mom? I only defended myself." *He was about to rape me.* The words are on the tip of my tongue, yet they don't come out.

Like a hawk's my dad's focus is back on me. "Right, Gwendolyn. Self-defense. You didn't do it." He barks out a harsh laugh as one hand shoots over his head, smoothing down the hair. "In that regard, you're innocent. Can't say that applies to everything else. You know, it's almost ironic how you were the one to bring us together, and now you're the one pushing us apart." He crosses his arms in front of his chest. "Your mother and I, we're getting a divorce."

One-Mississippi.

Two-Mississippi.

Three—

My jaw drops at the same time as the ground opens

beneath me. My last bit of security, of normality, of my life… It's just been swept away from under my feet.

"Ouch," whispers Tom. "Well, kinda did see that coming."

I blink twice.

I didn't.

Never ever.

"Divorce?" I croak.

"Inevitable." My dad shrugs, earning himself an angry look from my mom. "Everything was starting to suffer, most of all the company—"

"The company?" I'm up on my feet again. "Everything is about the freaking company, Dad! What about me? What about Mom? What about—" I suck in my lip and bite down as hard as I can. "What about thinking of us for a change?"

My dad stays silent.

How can he be so calm? His daughter is behind bars, his life is going down the drain—

Or maybe not.

Maybe he is getting it back on track. Maybe I'm the sacrifice on his way to success. Use me for the company, then discard me. My mom, the one who wants to help me—collateral damage, because at this point, it's all about damage control.

I'll give him damage control.

One step closer to the bars. "Maybe I should tell the police Tom said I was good for money."

Another step. "Maybe I should tell them how he was all nervous things could go wrong."

One more. "Maybe they should look into who benefitted

the most from my kidnapping—correction, from finding me, Dad."

Both my parents suck in a sharp breath.

"Gwen, what—?" Dad stares.

"Gwennie, how can you think—?" Mom gasps.

"Aww, sweetie. Adorable attempt, yet so disappointing." Tom.

I stop in front of the bars, hands on my hips, holding my dad's gaze. I'm not backing off. I'm not. I have nothing to lose, and everything to gain.

My heart cramps once. Wrong. I have everything to lose: Kai.

Uncle Doug raises both palms. "Gwendolyn, you're to say nothing more until we've met in private and discussed this matter." He throws a quick glance at the police officer next to him. "You will obviously cooperate with the investigation—"

Cooperate my butt! "If they investigate him as well, yes!" I spit it more at my dad than I say it—and for one tiny, teeny-tiny second, my dad's businessman-facade cracks.

That's my dad behind it.

The softie, who only cared for his business and couldn't pull off raising a daughter on his own.

Who made me a pancake machine when I was six.

Who insisted I'd get my shares to MSC at age seventeen, not at eighteen or once he retired, because he wanted me set for life and start to learn handling responsibility.

That's my dad.

For this tiny, teeny-tiny second, I see him. I see his shock, his hurt, his pain.

And it seems… genuine.

Real.

I rub my hands over my upper arms.

He's acting. It's all for show, nothing else. All for show.

My mom turns to the officer. "I beg of you, we need to get her out of here. Psych. If the judge wants to, he can place her under my conservatorship and make me responsible, but we need to—"

Dad visibly pulls himself together. "She doesn't need conservatorship, Michelle. Gwen needs this to be over and to get out of here. Get your priorities straight."

The rubbing over my arms becomes frantic, the friction heating up my palms. Something feels wrong. Off. A wheezy laugh breaks free from my throat that earns me a worried look from both of my parents for a change.

Something feels wrong.

Yeah. Like, everything. Everything in the last six months. If only I remembered more, if only I knew more, so that I could make sense of all of it and get out of here to help Kai.

My entire body tenses. *Of course.*

Of course.

"Tom," I whisper and turn on my heels. "You know."

There he is, sprawled out on my cot, hands folded behind his back. "Sure do."

"You know exactly what happened." I take one step closer to him.

"What is she doing?" my dad whispers.

"Tell me." I stand right in front of the cot and him.

"Oh my god, Michelle, you were right. She's… losing it."

I ignore him.

I ignore them all, because they're not important anymore. "Tell. Me."

Tom plays with his cuticles. "Why would I? You killed me. I'm a firm believer in quid pro quo. This is your purgatory, rich girl. Not mine. I've lived it all my life."

And—*pop*—he's gone.

"No, no, no," I rasp. "Come back, or I… I… I don't know, I'm going to kill you! I'm not done with you!" I haven't even begun with him. I want Kai, and—

"What's going on with her?" The police officer.

My dad takes a deep, harsh breath. "My… wife was right, officer. She needs to be on 24/7 observation. Mentally unstable, possibly suicidal. A danger to herself, and… to others, it appears. I'm agreeing to the mental hold."

What? I turn on my heels. "I'm not crazy." I'm not crazy. I'm not crazy. I'm not—

The officer shoots my mom a questioning glance. "You all right with that, Doc?"

Pause.

"Mom. I'm fine. I'm fine, I really am, please—"

"Yes, officer. I'd like you personally to transfer her to a mental hospital. A psych hold is definitely in order."

"If you say so, Doc. I'll talk to the judge and make arrangements. She won't get out of there for a while."

No. No, no, no.

I lose all strength in my legs and crumble into a heap of bones right in front of my cot and curl up into a ball.

Realm: one.

Gwen: zero.

Chapter Thirty

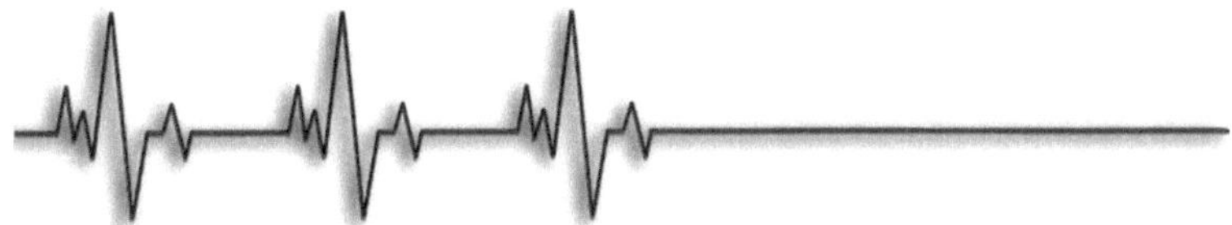

Hello, Darkness

’m in a daze, trapped in the horrors of my own mind, the ones I brought on myself.

As if on repeat, the same scenes replay in front of my inner eye. *Kai. Flatlining. Dead. Sarah in a pool of blood. Tom's eyes glassing over when my knife penetrates his chest.*

Nausea roils inside my stomach.

Divorce. The company. Psych-hold. Crazy. Crazy. Crazy!

It's all too much.

I curl into a ball on my side, facing the wall.

"Still feeling pity for yourself? Am I interrupting the party?"

At this point, I'm so attuned to the drop in temperature,

I'm not surprised when I hear him. "Go away." I see the cameras on the ceiling, and they see me. They see me talking to no-one.

A short laugh. "Nope. Quite entertaining here. Didn't really think I'd get to visit this world again." He settles with his back against the wall, dropping one hand onto my shoulder, patting it. "Actually, thanks for all the entertainment. That friend of yours, Kai, he—"

I twist out from under his hand and sit upright. Screw the cameras, who cares! I growl at Tom. "You're the reason he's on life support now. Screw you, Tom! What has he ever done to you?" Somewhere a security officer is having a ball looking at the footage of the crazy girl in cell one.

Tom raises an eyebrow. "He? Nothing. You did."

"And that gives you the right? Seriously? You killed Sarah! You *killed* her!"

Tom jerks back, a look of disgust on his face gone as quickly as it appeared. "I was high on drugs, damn—"

"And I wasn't? Because if I remember correctly, you gave me those stupid pills! Three!"

"You wanted them!" He pushes off the wall to face me, eyes blazing.

I throw my arms in the air. "Maybe the first! Not the second! For sure not the third!" I pant heavily, my chest constricting. My voice drops to a whisper. "And I didn't want you dead." The truth behind my own words surprises me.

I didn't want him dead.

Off of me, yes.

Not to be raped, yes.

This to be over, yes.

But I didn't want him dead.

Tom stares at me, mouth agape. The apple in his throat moves up and down once. In this moment and for the first time since I stabbed him to death, do I see him as the boy from the party again.

Young.

Too mixed up in something he couldn't dig himself out of on his own.

Both of us.

"I'm sorry." I know it won't help Kai, because the damage is done, but it needed to be said. "I'm sorry I killed you."

His eyes widen—and then he's gone.

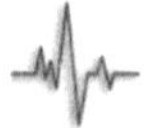

It's another three agonizing long hours before there's movement and the door to my cell is unlocked by the officer from before.

"Come on." He holds the door open and wiggles a pair of handcuffs dangling from his index finger. "Transfer."

Please, no.

I don't want to go to a mental hospital.

I'm not crazy.

I'm not.

"Come on." He rolls his eyes and taps his foot. "Move it."

Not like I had a choice.

I walk up to the officer and hold my hands out.

Click. Cuffs are locked.

Apparently, I'm not high on the danger-scale, at least he

only guides me by my elbow down the same hallway he brought me in in the beginning of the day.

I think.

Wasn't quite paying attention at that point.

Once we enter the lobby, he steps up to a window. "You sit. Wait."

I follow his order and sit in one of the cold metal chairs bolted into the floors. The officer knocks twice on the window, which slides open.

"Kleinman," his colleague on the other side greets.

"What's up, Cy?" My officer points at the pegboard with keys on the other wall of the office. "Can I have a rig? Bringing this one to the nut house." He nods his chin over his shoulder in my direction.

"Oh." The other man's voice drops low. "She's the one who basically killed the second Harrison twin?"

His words bury themselves into my gut like a fist. I didn't want to— I was trying to—

"Yeah. That's the one."

"Damn." Cy reaches for a set of keys and hands it to his colleague. "Worst is, I heard they're going to take him off life-support today. No brain activity. Neither of the twins."

"Off life support?"

"Yeah. Doctors have them both in the same room at Silverlake. They're recommending letting both of them go. Imagine what it must be for their family… I mean, I've got kids and—"

Their voices drop too low for me to pick up on, not that I could hear anything at this point with the blood swooshing through my ears like a river after a storm flood.

Kai.

Kai off life-support.

Kai trapped in the Realm forever.

Kai.

That hurt, it slams into me as brutal as the moment I woke up and was told Sarah was dead. Maybe more.

Kai.

And Cole.

"Sad day." Kleinman takes the keys and pockets them. "Tragic. But at least we get her out of the way and locked up." He takes me by the shoulder and I let him.

They'll take him off life-support today.

They'll *let him go*.

The world turns dizzy around me.

They can't let him go. Taking him off life support will kill him. Literally.

And then my belt will carry a third notch. Sarah. Tom. Kai. Kai.

They can't take him off life-support. They can't. He needs time—I need time. I—

A hole opens up in my heart, split wide open and bleeding from the idea that rammed itself into my soul like a dagger. Kai still has a chance. A small one, but a chance. If Calista is right, he could be bought free. An exchange. A soul for a soul, as long as his body stays receptive, stays alive.

I force down a dry swallow.

It would only be fair.

The officer leads me to the police car. I look up at him.

"When?" How long do I have?

"Huh?" He doesn't get my question.

"When are they going to take him off life support?"

The officer rolls his eyes. "What? Want to celebrate your success?"

I recoil. "No, I—"

"Whatever." He forces my head down and my body into the car.

I swallow. "Please. When?" I meet his gaze.

The officer sighs. "I'd say that's the least of your problems, but from what I heard around 8:00 p.m. The family needs time for their goodbyes." He slams the door behind me, and walks around the car to take a seat in the driver seat.

8:00 p.m.

Three more hours.

Three more hours until Kai is dead.

And this time, he'll stay dead.

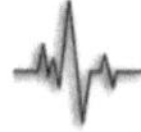

We leave Kampton via the only highway out of this town. It's a two-hour drive, at least.

Two hours, while Kai has only three left.

My cheeks are dry. I've run out of tears, and I can only wait.

The temperature drops around me. *Finally.*

"Here to rub it in how you took Kai and got back to me?" I don't need to keep my voice down. The partition between the officer and me is solid, translucent plastic, and while he can see me move my mouth, he won't hear what I say.

Not that it makes a difference. I'm going to the nut house anyway.

Tom buckles in next to me, a ridiculous move given the fact that he's dead. "Actually, no. Not really."

I close my eyes. "Good."

Because I'm doing enough damage to my soul as we speak.

I'm responsible. I'm the one who brought the CryoTherm. I could've talked Kai out of it. Maybe. But if not, at least I shouldn't have been the one to facilitate his death.

I'm a disappointment to everyone.

And I'm the one who needs to fix this. "Take me to the Realm."

Tom's head whips around. "What?"

"You heard me. Take me to the Realm." I twist in my seat to face him. "Take me and let Kai leave."

His jaw drops. "Yeah. No. Ain't happening."

"Please. Please, Tom. It was my fault—"

"Yes! It was your fault! You killed me, remember? Because of you I'm dead, and—" He balls a fist and bites into his knuckles.

"Please. I beg of you. Take me in! Exchange my soul for his. Please." It's my only chance—it's Kai's only chance.

He lowers the fist and growls at me. "I'm not doing you any favors. And even if I wanted to, what makes you think I can do that? Take you to the Realm?"

"My aunt. She's a medium. She said—"

He huffs. "Well, then it must be true. A medium." His gaze

hardens. "Forget about it. I suffer, you suffer. Don't they say it's easier to do that together?"

Icy fingers wrap around my heart. "Please." My voice wavers, jittery like my fingers. "He's innocent."

"So's my—"

The police car slows down and comes to a standstill on a small surface road in the middle of one of the umpteenth forests in Northern Oregon. When did we leave the highway? Why? Pee-break?

The officer opens my door. "Out."

Here? In the middle of nowhere? "Wait, why? We're—"

"I said out." In one swift motion he draws his gun and aims it at me.

A squeak leaves my throat. What the hell?

"Now," he snarls. "With your back against the car." He points the gun at the trunk.

Holy shit. "Okay, okay." I scramble to get out of the car with my hands cuffed in front of me. What the f—

The officer throws a nervous glance over his shoulder toward the main road. "Faster."

Definitely not a pee-break.

A hot and cold shiver runs down my spine, and it has nothing to do with the freezing temperatures, but everything with the gun trained on me. The next breath gets stuck inside my throat when it can't pass the lump lodged there. "What... what's going on?"

Kleinman scratches his head with one hand, the one with the gun never wavering. "This is you attempting to make a run for it."

"Me—"

"You had to throw up. I stopped. You surprised me with a rock and hit me over the head. We fought, you reached for my gun and I shot you in self-defense." He shrugs. "Sorry."

My mouth opens and closes without any sound coming out. "But—"

Tom steps next to me, checking out the police officer head to toe. "Another minion on the payroll, huh? Look at that."

Horror freezes my muscles. "You're going to shoot me?" Why, why, why? He's a police officer, for heaven's sake!

He sighs. "Let's just say I owe somebody. It's business, honey. Nothing personal."

Business.

Business.

Everything is about business.

"Dad," I croak.

Tom's icy hand wraps around my forearm. "Nu-uh," he says.

"You never gave me your cell number, so how else am I supposed to reach you besides through work? And come on! How much longer do I need to keep them? There are two, not just Gwen! The drugs are wearing off, and—" Tom pauses, listening to the phone. "No, they're still out of it. Kind of. You haven't even told me when to let her go."

He picks up the little ziplock and tries to open it with one hand, but his fingers shake too badly. "I don't like it. I don't do stuff like that." He lowers the phone and puts in on speaker, freeing his hands for the ziplock. "You said it was quick, just scare her and that's it."

One hand finally pulls a pill from the bag and he pops it, swallowing hard. "Yes, I think she's sufficiently scared for a 5150." He picks up the phone again, about to turn off the speaker. Just before his finger hits the button, a melody chimes through from the other side: "I like to eat my beans, beans, beans! Hear the noise they're making in my Jeans, Jeans, Jeans!"

Razor-sharp claws dig into everything that's me and tear it apart.

No.

No.

Not true.

Can't be true.

The ground rips open to swallow me whole.

"That—" That was my mom's ringtone. Our song. My mom's ringtone. Tom spoke to *Mom.* Tom spoke to *my mom about drugging me and Sarah.*

I bend over forward, supporting my weight on my knees. Can't breathe. Can't think. Can't do anything. "Mom."

"Took you a while," Tom says.

Kleinman raises an eyebrow. "Well, yes. The doc called in a favor."

Breathe in, breathe out. Breathe in— "A favor to kill me." My *mom.*

Kleinman rolls his eyes again. "Look, not my choice. Let's get it over with." He racks the gun, and everything slows down.

His movements—the speed of a snail.

The sounds of the birds—a distorted tweet.

My life—passing in front of my eyes.

He's going to kill me.

I'm going to be dead and—

And…

And…

And I'll have the chance to make amends, at least for part of what I've done.

My chance to cross.

I suck in a deep breath, enjoying the scent of nature for one last time. I won't have to carry my guilt for much longer.

Holding my chin up high I step forward to meet his gun. "Do it."

Because there is nothing here that holds me anymore.

I'm ready to die.

Chapter Thirty-One

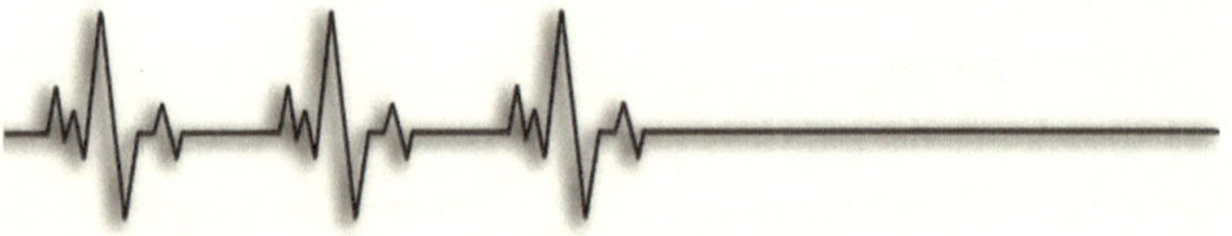

Negotiations

They say in the moment before death you see life the clearest.

They say there is peace that comes when facing the unavoidable.

They say life flashes before your eyes.

All of that is true, and yet it isn't.

My body is flying high on endorphins, maybe a protective mechanism to shield my mind from the pain of impending death, maybe a normal reaction to doing the right thing.

I will set Kai free.

A soul for a soul.

The barrel of the gun touches the fabric of my shirt.

"Do it." I mean it. This here—death by gun—is the only chance I have to cross to the Realm in time to get Kai out. To get Cole out. Ridiculous how easy it is. Get shot. Enter the Realm. Let Cole know he needs to want to leave, which he can, thanks to Kai's soul entering the Realm. Send Kai back home with his brother in exchange for my soul staying.

It's fair.

Kleinman laughs out harsh. "Wow. The doc was right. You're off your rocker." He wraps his second hand around the gun.

No. Not off my rocker: Finally seeing clear.

I feel a pat on my shoulder. "I'm touched. You and me, for eternity. And it rhymes." Tom chuckles.

I ignore him.

Kleinman releases the safety. "For the record, I'm sorry. I—"

A police car turns into our narrow dirt road, flashing its lights and the sirens once.

The officer's eyes dart from me to the tree line to the rig and back. "Crap!" He yanks the gun back and stomps his foot.

The other police car proceeds slowly, avoiding potholes, but it's clearly on its way over to us, and Kleinman knows that as well as I do.

"Shit!" The rig gets a good kick against its tire. "Get in the freakin' car, nut job!"

Get in—

"Get in, damn it!" The officer wiggles his gun for emphasis.

I shake my head. "No. No." No, no, no. "You're supposed to shoot me. You—"

A harsh laugh. "Supposed to shoot you? I'm supposed to pay off my debt to the doc, but that doesn't include getting busted for it. So shut the hell up and get in the car."

My next breath comes in wheezy. "No." No. I'm not getting into the car. This is my one and only chance to cross, and I need to take it. I must take it, or else Kai and Cole will be lost. "Shoot me!"

"Get in the freakin' car!"

I won't. I need to cross. Cross, cross, cross. I dart forward, cuffed hands raised. "Shoot me, damn it! Do it! Do—"

Kleinman raises the gun—

—and hits me smack in the temple with it.

Pain explodes on the left side of my head. I yelp, I cry out, my hands fly up to my head—

Kleinman grabs me by the shoulder and shoves me against the car. "Shut up, bitch! And before you talk about what happened here, think twice. You're the looney toon who killed three people. Nobody will believe you, and I've got the means to make your stay in prison even worse, so shut the hell up!"

The other car comes to a stop a few meters behind us. Two officers step out. "Joel. Unexpected to find you here," says the older male officer.

Pause. A muscle in Kleinman's jaw ticks. "Prisoner felt nauseous."

"Right. That's probably why you hit her with a gun."

"She was attacking me—"

The other officer holds up a hand. "Tell your story to Steve. You're returning to the station. Judge Cortez wants to see her. New evidence. Better hurry, or you're in deep. Taking her without orders doesn't look good, Joel."

Kleinman stares at me, those muscles in his jaw working overtime.

Sighing, the older officer waves at his partner. "Maddie, ride back with Joel, I'll be tailing you guys."

"Gotcha." His colleague walks over and opens the passenger door. "Let's go. Get your prisoner under control, Joel."

Before I can even understand I was robbed of my chance to enter the Realm, Kleinman has grabbed me by the shoulder and stuffed me into the car. He slams the door shut on me and on the last option I had to save Kai.

"No!" I dart forward and slam into the partition. "Screw you! No! Shoot me, damn it! Shoot me!"

I rage, I scream, I throw myself against the translucent barrier separating me from the man who can cross me. Blood smears across the clear plastic from where he split my skull open with his gun. "Please! Please! You promised! You can't go back—"

But he does.

Kleinman starts the engine and backs the rig out onto the main road. The female officer twists in her seat to look at me, then says something agitated to Kleinman he ignores.

It won't help me anyway.

"No." Sobs shake me as I sink down into the narrow space between the seats and the barrier. I know my chance is gone. My brain gets it, even though my emotions haven't caught up yet, and neither has my despair: He can't go back on something like that. He can't promise to kill me and then take it back. He can't. "Please," I whisper. "Please. I need to cross. I need to get him out." *I need to get him out.* An inhuman, animalistic sound leaves my throat and tears through the cabin, more a wail than a shriek.

"Whoa. Ouch. Don't do that again, that hurts." Tom appears on the bench in front of me, both hands covering his ears. "So sorry he didn't kill you. I mean it, really. We'd have had a blast in the Realm." He shrugs. "Oh well. Then I guess I'll have to bug you in this world. Could be worse. Also, it's the least I can do to you, as my murderer." He looks down at his cuticles and blows on them.

Me as his—

An idea strikes, fast as lightning. What did Calista say? Sarah dying next to me wasn't an event big enough to connect our souls—but what about me killing Tom? Claire said I was stained when she saw me the first time, what if that's a stain on my soul from killing Tom? And what if that truly meant—

I reach for his leg and get a hold of his ankle. "Take me! You can take me, Tom! Take me to the Realm! I beg of you, please—"

"What the heck? Let go of me!" He yanks his foot out of my grasp. "I can't do that, and even if I did, you think I'll do you a favor and bring you to the Realm, so you can free your precious Kai? You think I'm going to make this easy on you? Turn you into a martyr who saves the day? Screw you, Gwen O'Karran! You're going to suffer as you were supposed to!"

"Here you go, the newest of the new." The doc hands me a clear plastic bag with a couple of white pills in it. "With your history of

drug abuse, you should stay clear of it. For Gwen it'll be a very nice high though, better than any you've had."

Better than any I've had. The sheer mention of a high makes my heart beat faster and sweat break out of every pore. Thanks, daddy-o, for that little addiction, but I won't give in. I've come too far. "Got it." I push the words out through clenched teeth. I can keep temptation at bay. I can do it.

The doc opens the door to her car. "You're finding this place again, right?" She nods at the small shed hidden between trees and boulders. That's the beauty about California. Nature is vast, and so are its hiding places. "Yeah. I'll get her to drive, or I'll get a car. I'll think of something."

"Shouldn't be a problem. She's young, easily impressed. You're older, Tom. You're cute. Gwen is sheltered, she'll be flattered by your attention."

A flare of nausea rises. Sheltered. Good for her. At seventeen, I was kicked out of school already and dealing for Dad.

"Anyway." The doc plays with a rubber lining the door. "All I need is her on drugs and showing irresponsible behavior. Let her drive when drunk, or let them think she drove under the influence. Scare her, make her lose her wits. The crazier she looks, the better. Everything else is bonus." She smirks. "If you get her knocked up, even better."

My eyes pop open wide. "Knocked—"

"You heard me. The more speaks against her, the better. We're in this together, Tom."

"I know." I drop my gaze.

She sighs and lets go of the door to walk over to me. "Tom. Seriously. All we need is Gwen to lose her footing. Freak her out. Scare her. Something. I'll take care of the rest."

"Okay." My voice comes out as a whisper.

She lays one hand onto my shoulder and squeezes gently. "If we want the court to transfer conservatorship to me, we need ammo. And remember, once I've got access to Gwen's share of MSC, you will get your money." One more reassuring squeeze. "You can get Edan out of your dad's grasp, Tom. The money is all you need. You can get this done."

I swallow down the nausea. "Yes, ma'am." Yes. I can get this done. For Edan, I can get this done.

Whoa.

My chest heaves with erratic breaths. "The shares?" Mom wanted the shares? My shares?

Tom darts forward, eyes spitting fire. "How did you do that? Get the heck out of my head!" He shoves me back into the seat, but it doesn't register.

"She wanted my money." I blink twice. When… why… I mean, was that all I was? A way to money?

"Well, yeah, she wanted your money, genius!" Tom throws his hands up and falls back into the seat behind the driver. He draws one leg up and wraps his arms around it. "Only way to get it after your dad threatened to divorce her."

Oh.

Oh.

Of course. My parents' divorce, their prenup will regulate what my mom gets—and that's not much. Dad has always kept the company close to his heart and protected it with everything he could. Including said prenup. They divorce, and if my mom didn't get a hold of my shares by then, she'd be out of luck.

"She would've sold them," I whisper. She would've sold them, taken the money and done who-knows-what with it. My gaze flies up to Tom. "She would've paid you with it."

No response.

I blink. Again. "For... Edan. Your brother."

"Don't you dare talk about my brother." He growls it more than he says it, but I see the short flash of something other than rage, something warmer, more vulnerable.

With all the strength I have left I crawl up onto the bench, back leaned into the door across from Tom. I pull both my legs in close to my chest and wrap my arms around them. Need to keep myself together. Need to keep my wits, now more than ever.

"Tom?"

No response.

"Would you have done any of this if it wasn't for my mom's offer?"

Silence.

I close my eyes and lean my forehead onto my knees. "So, she tricked you."

She closes the door and starts the engine. She's right, I can do this. Scare a girl, make her look crazy, get my money. What can go wrong—

Shit.

I sprint forward and knock at the driver's side window. "Doc?"

She rolls it down. "What?"

"What happens if something happens?"

Her brows scrunch together. "Like what?"

"Like me getting arrested." Because, let's be honest, if that happened, I'd be screwed. Majorly.

She sighs. "Tom, don't worry about. For one, I have friends in high places. For another, I will honor my part of the deal whether you're arrested or not. As long as I get Gwen's share of the company and you stay quiet about this, Edan will get the money, period. I'll find a way to get him out of your dad's grasp."

A weight the size of a boulder drops off my shoulder. "Okay. Okay then. Just making sure."

Just making sure.

Just making sure.

An idea shoots through my veins like lightning. I lift my head and look at him, still staring out the window and ignoring me. "Tom?"

For a moment he doesn't react, but then his shoulders heave up and down with a big breath. "It's getting old. Stay out of my head." He sounds tired. Resigned. But at least he's talking to me. Not popping out of this world and leaving me alone.

I shake my head. "Nothing I'm doing on purpose, but..." Here goes nothing. "I have a proposal to make. A good one."

He laughs out once, bitter. "Really? I'm all ears. So excited. Can hardly wait." He still looks out the window.

I have one shot at this. Time's dwindling down, and once I'm back in my cell, I'm going to be too late. "My mom promised she'd take care of Edan once she got the shares, right? So... why don't we give her the shares?"

His head flies over to me. "Huh?"

Well, at least I have his attention. I sit up straighter and lean forward over my legs. "For her to get the shares she needed to get conservatorship over me. That was the plan—to make me seem irresponsible and crazy, and then take over. Correct?"

His eyes narrow. "Yes. What are you saying?"

"I'm saying that won't work anymore. My parents are getting divorced. She's too late getting me into the loony bin. Six months ago, yes. But now that it's filed, no judge would grant the non-biological, soon-to-be divorced parent conservatorship. It would go to my dad." And with it, Tom's chance for money from my mom. "So, the only way to get my mom and Edan the money, is if…" Deep breath. Deep breath. "If I died."

Tom's pupils widen. "Are you saying what I think you are?"

Well, duh. "Yeah. I die, and because my parents aren't divorced yet, my mom will get at least half of my shares. I own thirty percent of Dad's business already. It's gonna be less than she wanted, but more than she otherwise would get. She'll have the money for Edan." That's at least what I say. In reality I'm not sure my mom ever intended to pay him out, but I'd rather not bring up that little detail, for obvious reasons. Poor Edan. He drew the short end of the stick from what I've seen. I chew on the inside of my cheek. But at least he's still alive. Kai on the other hand won't be for much longer.

Tom narrows his eyes. "You're trying to trick me. Why would the judge not give your mom conservatorship, but give her your inheritance?"

I shrug. "Easy. At the moment of my death they're still married, and therefore the law grants her half of my possessions.

But for conservatorship the judge is going to look at the overall picture, and then the biological parent will win. Not the soon-to-be-divorced one." I think. Sounds about right.

Tom presses his lips into a thin line. "Whatever. I don't even know if I can take you in—"

"I'm pretty sure you can." I hope. I pray.

"—and even if I did and took you in, you'll still get your will. You get to save the one you love—"

"And you get to save the one you love. Your brother. Fair exchange." My stomach churns with acid. I shouldn't mind leading Tom on, not after what he's done, and not with Kai's life at stake, but knowing what I do now… A woman who sets her daughter up to be kidnapped and drugged might not be the most reliable person to uphold her deals.

The image of Edan on his bed, unconscious, and the panic I felt through Tom's memories pushes the acid up my throat. I swallow it down, hard. Not my problem right now. Priorities.

I throw a quick glance to the side at Kleinman. Driving. Focused on the road, not me. Good. "And by the way, you owe me too."

"What?" He spits it out. "I owe you nothing. Noth—"

"Oh, hell you do!" Because I remember. *I remember!* Lightning fast, I reach out and grab him by the wrist. "Enjoy the ride, bro."

A short bout of nausea, of dizziness—and then I'm back in the one situation my brain has kept from me for the last six months: On my back, helpless, a heavy body pressed into me, one hand twisted into my ponytail yanking my head back, another one pressing a knife to my throat.

"Sh-top shtruggling, Gwen. I promise you'll like it." The blade scratches my skin.

That's what he said to Sarah after the last pill he popped. And then she fought, and then—

I strain my eyes and wish I hadn't, because no matter how much the world spins, the pool of bright, red blood stays right at the center of it. So does the motionless hand with three broken-off fingernails. The pair of eyes that stare but don't see anymore.

My throat cuts off all air to my lungs.

"G'd girl. We don't fight. It ends bad." He sounds scared and high. Scared of himself, and high on those stupid pills.

I cry out, I buck my hips to get him off, but he won't budge. No, he grinds his lower body into mine. I freeze, paralyzed by panic.

"Mh. Feels good. You're s-so soft. Pillsh make't better, eh? They make ev'rythin' better. Ev'rythin'." His eyes roll back. "We'll have sh-ome fun." He lets go of my head and brushes his hand over my right breast and stomach on its way down. "But I won't knock you up." He pulls out a condom from his back pocket, throws it on the ground next to my head, and tilts his pelvis for easier access. Fumbling for the buttons of his pants he pops them open, each pop tearing through the silence like cannon fire.

I can't think well, but I know what that sound means.

"Ge' off me." It comes out slurred, and the buck of my hips doesn't throw him off, it only makes him chuckle. He slides his hand down between my legs, the touch rough and painful. "Shtop id, I s'd."

But he doesn't. He fumbles with my clothing, grunts once in frustration—and then rips my underwear apart.

"Oops," he giggles.

Despite the pills panic floods me like a dam burst open. There's no way out of here for me. He's going to rape me, and then I'm going to die.

I'm going to die just like Sarah.

Tom turns to face me, face ashen. "That's not what happened."

"No? It's what I remember." I hold his eyes. I'm not backing off.

He shakes his head. "No. You wanted—"

"I *wanted?*" I yell. "Maybe! Maybe I did! Maybe earlier I did! But I for sure didn't want it anymore after you killed Sarah! I was scared to death, Tom! Scared you were going to rape me, scared you were going to kill me! I defended myself, can't you see that? I'm sorry I killed you, I'm sorry, I'm sorry, I'm sorry— but I can't take it back. And you," my voice drops to a whisper, "you would've killed me otherwise. I think we both know that. The pills Mom gave you got you good, just like they got me."

Tom stares at me, pushed into the far end of the bench, eyes wide, chest heaving up and down like after a marathon.

For a moment, neither of us says anything. Then, a muscle in his jaw twitches. "I'll try to take you in, and if it works, I will keep you there. That I know I can do. If you think you can trick me somehow, you can't. If I take you, your body will be in a coma, and I promise you, no amount of medical technology will get you back, because I. Will. Keep. You. If they're fast and get you to an ICU, your body will stay alive for a while. If not, it won't. No matter what, your body will die eventually."

Exactly what I was going for. Still, it gives me chills. "I know," I whisper.

Tom shoots forward on all fours until he's so close, my eyes cross to keep him in focus. "You will stay in the Realm."

"I know."

"You sure?"

"A hundred percent."

He laughs. "So stupid. You have everything and still leave it behind. But why not?" He reaches for my hand and takes it. "Say good-bye to the world, Gwendolyn O'Karran."

"Wait, I—"

A short pang of pain—and everything turns black.

Chapter Thirty-Two

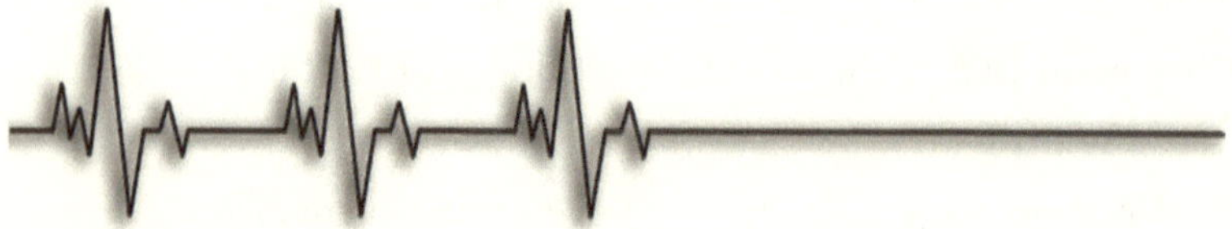

Realm

My vision returns with a *snap*. "Holy—"

The police rig around me has lost its color. Everything's washed out, faded, more subdued—"The Realm." He took me. I'm in!

Tom grunts. "New skill, look at that. Nice. So yeah, welcome to your very personal Hotel California." He lets go of my hand and brushes it off his sleeve. "You can enter any time you like, but you can never leave."

I move forward and out of my, uhh, collapsed body. "Classy, Tom. Really." Everything's so much clearer my third time in the Realm, more in focus, sharper. Like the laceration and blood on my head. I wonder if they're gonna blame my coma and eventual death on Kleinman hitting me. Would serve him right.

And it's not important now.

One glimpse at the dashboard up front tells me I have about thirty minutes tops before they withdraw life support. No matter I'm floating as a spirit, my heart cranks it up a notch at that though. Gotta get to Kai. To Cole *and* Kai, before it's too late.

But how? How do I get there? Damn it, should've thought about that before. "Tom!" I whip my head toward him so fast, the momentum brings my body to a turn. "How can I find Kai?"

"Not my problem now, is it?"

I groan. "Screw you." Screw me, actually. I need to be fast, or else. "Come on, Kai. Where are you? Where the frack are you? Kai…" I close my eyes so tight stars dance behind my eyelids. Kai, come on!

A sudden draft, a sensation like falling—and the temperature around me has changed.

My eyes fly open. "Whoa!" The bridge. The bridge, where I kept Kai from drowning. And there, standing right where he must've stood before he jumped in, are two boys who look almost the same. Almost.

"Kai!" I'm running through the air, feet never touching the ground. "Kai!"

The second time he hears me. He turns to the left and—

"Gwen!" My name—half prayer, half shock. He barely has time to prepare for my onslaught before I've all but jumped him. I wrap my arms around his neck so tight, he'd choke if he was in the real world.

I found him.

I found *them.*

It's not too late.

"Kai." I sob into his neck. "I'm so sorry. I was too late. You were in the CryoTherm for too long and gone too long and—" Not what I should apologize about. "And I'm sorry I didn't tell you the whole truth. I was scared you'd call me crazy, scared you'd find out what I did, and—" And egoistic little me wanted him to be the one person to treat me like before—before I became an accessory to murder and a murderer.

Kai makes a low sound in his throat, and it does wonderful things to my stomach. "Gwen!" His hug squeezes the air out of me, bringing a rush of sensations—need, caring, a yearning too intense to process—before he lets go of me. "What are you doing here?" Wide, warm eyes fix on me. "You shouldn't be here, how—"

"Doesn't matter." I shake my head and take both of Kai's hands in mine. "Time's of the essence though. You both need to get out of here, like, now." My heart hammers like crazy. Funny how that goes, considering I'm in the afterlife and all.

"We tried." Cole holds out a hand for a high-five. "By the way, we've got to stop meeting like this."

Kai's gaze darts from his brother to me. "You—"

"Told ya." I shrug and hit Cole's high-five. "But doesn't matter now. Guys, it should work. Cole, Kai came in here with the intent to release your soul, that's your ticket home. Give it a try." I step from one foot onto the other. "Come on!" I don't know how much time they have left. Who even knows if time works the same in here.

Kai and Cole exchange a glance, but Cole frowns. "I don't think it works. I mean, since I've met you, I've tried. You said I was in a coma, and I tried to get out—"

"And it didn't work, because your soul was stuck. A soul for a soul." Afterlife 1-0-1, according to Calista. I hope she's right.

Something lights up in Kai's eyes. "Try it, mate."

Cole closes his eyes. For a short moment his shape flickers—and then he's back, as solid as his soul can be, a muscle in his jaw ticking. "That's how far I get whenever I try. If I focus real hard, I think—I think—I can kind of feel the other side, but then snap, I'm back, like something was holding me here."

Snap?

I bet I know where *snap* is coming from. "Damn it." I stomp my foot. "Claire." So, it's true: Claire is making sure Cole doesn't leave.

"Claire?"

An angry voice shouts over from farther down the bridge. "Don't pull that crap on me and pop out like this, damn it! I'm keeping an eye on you, and—"

Kai's eyes narrow. "Who's that?"

I grab his arm and turn him away from an angry looking Tom stomping over to us. "Long story. Anyway, Claire. She's the one who made sure I didn't tell you about leaving, Cole. That you're in a coma." The brother's reactions are on the complete opposite ends of the spectrum.

Cole pales.

Kai turns red and growls, "Claire."

"Claire," Cole whispers in a shallow breath. He stumbles a step backwards like hit in the chest—*another drop in temperature, a slight shift in the earth's gravity field*—and I'm no longer looking at the bridge and river, but at Kai and Cole.

In their hospital beds, machines all around them.

And Claire standing next to Cole.

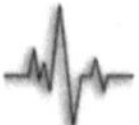

Whoa.

I shake my head to get rid of the sensation of falling, of changing location faster than in the blink of an eye.

Cole, obviously much more a pro in all things afterlife-related than me, adjusts much faster. "Claire!"

She twitches and jerks her head around to us. Guilt flashes across her face. "Cole. How—"

Cole steps closer to Claire and, uhh, himself. "Good question, Claire. Why?" He points at his body lying in the hospital bed. Compared to when I saw him at Silverlake, his body looks even crappier, and that would be because Kai is lying in the bed next to him. Kai, who's had a whole six months of living, while Cole was lying motionless in a coma, muscles wasting.

"Holy cow." Kai pales when he sees his body, an IV in one arm, EKG electrodes attached to his chest, EEG stickers all over his head. One of the monitors shows a strong heartbeat, the other a flatline: No brain activity.

It's the same for Cole.

Claire swipes a strand of blonde hair behind her ear. "Cole. Kai. I—" Her eyes fall on me and widen. "You."

Might as well make this official. "Gwendolyn O'Karran. I would say nice to meet you, but it surely isn't. You need to let Cole go, Claire. Now." I cross my arms in front of my chest. "He has every right to leave, and you know that. Let him go."

"I'm not doing—"

Kai's hands curl into fists. "He can't cross back, Claire. My soul should've released him, and it didn't. Something is holding him here, and I bet it's you."

"I—"

Cole steps closer to Claire, reaching for her hand. "Claire. I… We… we had a good six months here, didn't we?"

Her eyes fill with tears. "Yes."

"But I'm not dead."

"No." She glances at Cole's still body. "Obviously."

"Why?" It's a pained question, loaded with grief.

The first tear falls. "Because… because when I died, I wasn't ready. Not at all. I was here, away from you, from everyone I cared about, and…" More tears run down her face. "My grandparents are here, but it's not the same. I was miserable for missing out on life. I watched you. I saw you cry. I saw you beat yourself up over what happened to me. And when you entered the Realm after your accident—"

"You kept me." The apple in his throat bobs up and down once.

"Yes." Claire lowers her gaze to the hand Cole is holding onto. "First, I didn't know I was doing it. I guess it came naturally. After I found out you were in a coma and not dead…

Then I didn't want to be alone, Cole."

Pain flickers across his face as he pulls her into a tight hug. "I get it, Claire. I totally do. But—"

The door opens to the sound of a woman crying.

"Anna. Be strong."

"Dad?" Kai and Cole say in unison, undivided attention on the door and the incoming visitors. The twins' mom sobs into a tissue. Their dad, one arm wrapped around his wife's shoulder, has tears in his eyes. Dora shuffles in hunched over as if weighed down by the last couple of hours. They all fall into the chairs set around the two beds. Only now do I notice the box of tissues, the crumbled up used ones in the trash, the bottles of water: They've been here for a while. They must've stepped out, that's it.

"Have some water, honey." Mr. Harrison hands one of the bottles to his wife.

"That's not going to make it better, Dave."

"I know. But we only have a little longer left—"

"What are they talking about?" Kai's pained whisper.

My gaze darts up to the clock above the door. Crap. "Kai. Cole. We don't have much longer. They're going to take you off life support. Both. Today. Like, now." I feel like the biggest villain delivering the news.

"What?" Cole's voice is a harsh whisper.

"No," Kai gasps.

I take Kai's hand, urgency in my voice. "Listen. That's why both of you need to leave. Now. Cole, you're set free by Kai's soul. Kai, you're… set free by mine."

Silence.

Three pairs of eyes stare at me.

"What do you mean, set free by yours?" Kai clamps his fingers around mine.

Uhh… "Well, it means that—"

A cold draft of air—

"Looks like I'm late to the party." *Tom.*

I groan. Really, not even in the afterlife can I have a moment to myself.

Kai straightens his shoulders and pulls himself up to his full height in front of me. "Who are you?"

Tom cocks his head to the side. "Me? I'm the one who—"

"He's the one who brought me into the Realm." I step out from behind Kai. "This is Tom. He's… he's the one I killed."

Tom cocks his head. "And I'm the guy who's making sure you're staying here." His gaze falls onto Claire. "Sweetheart. You here, too? Man, I'm *really* late to the party."

Claire buries her face in her hands and groans, the sound drowned out by the growl leaving Kai's throat. "You're the one who kidnapped Gwen. You're the one—" With two large steps, he's in front of Tom, never minding his brother's bed in the way. He passes through it like it was air.

Tom twitches, but never steps back. While he's as tall as Kai, he's much scrawnier. Wiry, instead of Kai's solid muscle. Paler, instead of healthy pink. But he's also much more at home in this Realm. With a quick flick of his palm, he brings up a fog between him and Kai. "Hold it right there, hotshot."

As if he ran into a wall, Kai stumbles back, but Tom isn't done. "If I were you, I'd behave myself. I know the Realm. You don't. I'm the one in control. Am I right, Claire?" He cocks an eyebrow at her.

Cole steps in front of Claire. "Leave Claire out—"

"Hotshot number two, she's in no matter what you say. Sorry to disappoint." Tom pulls off the tone of bored superiority quite well.

Cole looks left to right between his girlfriend and the newcomer. "Claire, what… can you explain? Please?"

"Yeah, Claire." Kai crosses his hands in front of his chest. "And you, too." He gives Tom a challenging look.

Claire shakes her head so fast, her blonde hair whips through her face. "I… I—"

Anna sobs into a tissue, and that sound, that heart wrenching, gutting, desperate sound, it brings my attention back to the issues on hand. "Guys, sorry to be curt, but the summary is that Claire used Tom's help to trap Kai. They worked together. She told him about me entering the Realm, and in return he helped her eliminate the one person alive who could convince Cole to re-enter his body—Kai."

Never have Cole and Kai looked more like twins with their eyes wide, mouths agape, and an expression of disbelief written across their faces. "What the—?"

A knock at the door.

Dave gives a deep, soul-aching sigh. "Come in." He sounds resigned. No wonder.

The door inches open with a slight creak—to the one person I really don't want to see.

"Mom," I breathe.

"Huh. Doc. Look at that." Tom.

"We're sorry to interrupt at such a difficult time, but…"

Mom holds the door open for my dad, dressed in a black suit—and Grampie, also in a black suit, frail-looking and more wobbly than usual. "We wanted to say good-bye while the twins…" She swallows hard. "While the twins were still alive." A single tear runs down her cheek, and if I hadn't seen through Tom's eyes what she's capable of, I would buy her grief. Totally. As it is, I don't.

Anna gets up, and so does Dave. "I don't think you should be here." He doesn't sound friendly, and my dad cringes.

"I would like to apologize that Gwendolyn was able to use an invention of mine to… to…"

"To kill our son?" Dave points an accusing finger at Kai. "No brain activity! None! No chance of recovery! A shell functioning without a soul! *She killed our son!* What the hell were those kids doing there anyway? Playing Russian Roulette? Well, it didn't work out well for Kai! Your daughter killed our son—our only remaining son!" His voice breaks.

Kai reaches for his dad. "No, Dad. No. It was me. I went in… the letter should explain—"

"And Gwendolyn will be punished to the whole extent of the law." Mom presses her lips together. What an actress. "She's been held for murder in three cases, and I doubt she will ever leave the psych ward or jail." Mom apparently hasn't heard about the newest development, my coma.

A strangulated gasp breaks from Kai. "Wait—no, that's not what I wanted—"

Tom snickers. "And that's not what she's gonna get."

He's close enough for me to jab him into the ribs. "Shut up, Tom. Not helping." I turn to Kai. "Listen, you and Cole have to get out of here. Now. Time's running—"

Another knock, and this time the door opens to a man in his mid-fifties in a white coat. "I'm sorry to interrupt, but... it would be time. If you're ready." He folds his hands in front of his body and looks down.

Anna wails once. "Cole. Kai." She sobs and takes one of their hands in each of hers. "Too soon. Too soon."

"Damn it," Kai blurts through tears. "Mom." He lays both hands on her shoulders, and this time they don't pass through. "Mom."

The doctor walks to the two ventilators pumping oxygen into the twins' lungs. "Mrs. and Mr. Harrison, I know this is difficult. We talked about this." He pauses, pulling on a piece of thread coming undone from the *Dr. Isaacs* stitched into his white coat. "We'll switch off the ventilators one after the other. Usually, the body stays alive for another few minutes as the oxygen level drops. We don't expect any changes in the EEG— it's a flatline already. Their heart activity will slow down and then stop." He clears his throat, not looking at either of Kai's and Cole's parents.

"Shit," I whisper. Holy hell. They can't withdraw life support now. Not now, of all times, I haven't gotten them back yet. I twist my body fast, first pointing at Claire, then Tom. "Claire. Tom. Let them go, dammit! Now—"

A long sniffle from Claire. "I can't—"

I stomp my foot. "You must, dammit!" A fast turn on my heels to Tom. "Let Kai go!"

"What the heck, Gwen? I'm not leaving and have him take you for an exchange!" Kai throws both hands up in the air.

Oh. Well, I guess he figured it out. And it doesn't matter. I stomp my foot again. "Screw it, Kai, go! I won't have killed a second person!" Tears spring to my eyes. "I've killed him already, and that's bad enough! Granted, my mom was responsible for it, but still! I did it! And I won't have you—"

"It's not your fault I'm here!"

"But it is!" I throw my arms up, just like he did.

"If you're ready, I'll turn the ventilators off."

"Tom! Kai!" Darn it, don't be so stubborn, all of you!

"Gwen, I'm not leaving you—"

I dart forward, my hands cupping Kai's face. "Please, Kai. *Please.* It's now or never. Go. You have less than a minute left. Go. You have all your life left to live, Kai."

"So do you—"

Dammit, he doesn't get it! "Kai! My life is over. If I went back, I'd have to live with the fact I killed *him*—and I couldn't live with the fact I also killed you." My thumbs brush over his cheek bones. "You need to go back, Kai. For me and—" I close my eyes and take a deep breath. Not what I wanted to say the last time I see him, but I'm working all angles here. "And remember, you talked about your long-term crush? Well, you're never going to see her again if you don't leave, dammit!" Tears spring to my eyes and spill over. If he won't do it for me, he might do it for her. I dig my fingers into his hair. "Go!"

Kai blinks hard. "Gwen, that… that's not really helping."

I groan. "Leave!"

"No—"

Dr. Isaacs looks back into the room. "If anybody would like to leave…"

My dad grimaces. "Uhh, yes. Of course. I apologize we interrupted. I apologize for my daughter. We'll leave—"

"Actually, we're not." Grampie lays a gentle hand on Dora's forearm.

Dad's eyes widen. "Dad!"

"Excuse me?" Dave asks, flabbergasted.

Kai rolls his eyes. "Geez, Gwen, I won't leave Cole and you!"

Gosh, why is everybody so idiotic today! "Tom is letting you go, Kai. Just get out of here, please. Find that girl, live your life, be awesome—"

Cole shakes his head. "Yeah, Gwen, you're not getting it. *You're* his long-term crush. You're the frog-bathing suit."

Silence.

Wait, wha—

The frog bathing suit?

That awful, wonderful frog bathing suit?

My hands shake. "Me?"

The frog on Kai's shelf. On his bed. The brothers' hallelujah-insider. The way he made me feel like I was it for him when we were making out in the truck—

A shy smile moves the corners of Kai's lips up. "Yeah. You. Not my fault you only show up once a year in the summer."

"But—"

Tom groans. "Yuck, get a room. Or better, get out of here. I released him. He can leave. Get it over with." He makes a dismissive motion with his hand.

I'm Kai's long-term crush.

Me.

In this moment, I curse fate. I curse her for bringing us together and ripping us apart in the cruelest way.

I'm Kai's long-term crush.

And yet it changes nothing. I'm done being selfish. For one short moment in time I had a glimpse of what could've been. Those days with Kai, they'll forever stay framed and embellished in my memory. They'll make the Realm bearable. But there's no chance I change my mind.

A tear drops from my eye. "Go. *Please*. If you truly care for me, you won't make me responsible. *Please*."

Kai shakes his head. "Gwen, I—" Moisture shines in his eyes as he looks from Cole to me and back. "Cole—"

Cole shoves at him. "*Go*, Butthead. If you don't, I'm going to find a way to make it hell for you here." He pulls off a fake smile and shows him the middle finger, then takes Claire into a big hug. "Claire? I want to go back with him. Please."

Claire sobs into Cole's shoulder. "I… I can't. You hate me, Cole. You'll tell my parents what a despicable being I am—"

Cole sighs. "I don't hate you, Claire. I never could."

Well, he's being much nicer about it than I would've been, that's for sure.

Hope colors Claire's voice. "You don't hate me?"

Dr. Isaacs clears his throat. "I'd like to continue with the procedure, please. The Neurologist is only in for one more hour."

Grampie scoffs. "Give the twins a minute, I'm optimistic they're going to come around—"

"Owen!" My mom gasps, horrified. "This isn't a joke, for Heaven's sake!"

Cole pulls Claire in tighter. "I don't hate you. I understand what you did. Why you did it. Heck, I can't even say I wouldn't have done the same thing if the situation were reversed. And we had us. But there's Kai…" He lets the sentence trail off, and Claire gets it.

She nods and sniffles. "I love you, Cole."

"I love you, too. I won't forget you, I promise. I understand." He throws one more look at his twin. "See you soon, Butthead." Then, he squeezes his eyes shut tight—

And fades out of the Realm.

Claire wails out once.

Kai rests his forehead against mine. "I wish I could be there for you."

I squeeze my eyes shut, but it does nothing against the burn behind my lids. "I know. Now leave, Kai."

A weird, strangulated sound comes from Tom that he turns into a fake gagging sound.

Kai pulls away and gives me one last look full of everything that should've been, but never will: Times together, adventures explored, kisses shared, and maybe even something more.

"Go," I whisper again.

One more look at his body in the bed, one more at me.

He closes his eyes—

Chapter Thirty-Three

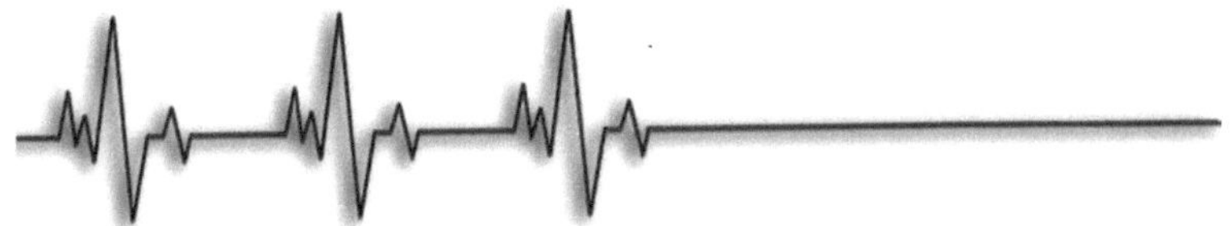

Death Taketh

*B*eep.
    Beep.
Beep.
Beep.

A strangulated gasp, a wild scream: "Stop!" Anna jumps out of her chair, yanking Dr. Isaacs away from Kai's ventilator. "The EEG! There's something—"

The doctor gently pries her finger off his sleeve. "Ms. Harrison, that's impossible. We've checked—"

His gaze falls onto the monitor. "Holy—!" With one quick step he's next to Kai, shining a flashlight into his eyes. "Unbelievable. Unbe—" He presses a button in the wall. "Code

Green in room 212. Code Green, speed it up!"

A weight drops off my shoulders as tears spring to my eyes. Kai made it. Kai is back. One down, one to go.

Grampie gives Dora's hand a slight squeeze, his fingers shaking. "Told you it would work out, Dora."

"Kai!" Dave is up and next to his son. "Kai!"

In the bed, Kai gags on his breathing tube.

"We've got to take it out." The doc begins to remove the sticky tape.

Where is Cole? Why isn't he back?

Grampie sways. "Now that things are looking a bit brighter, I would like to make an announcement."

I look at Claire. My trust in her is very much limited. "Why isn't Cole waking up?" What is she doing to him? I ball my fists at my side.

Her eyes are wide and tear-filled. "I don't know! I'm not doing anything, I swear—"

Grampie says, "…about that night when Gwendolyn was kidnapped."

Dad glares at Grampie. "Dad!" He looks at everybody. "I'm so sorry, we're going to leave now. My father is not the youngest—"

The door gets pushed open so forcefully, it rams into the wall. A medical team of six people storm in, taking positions around Kai's bed and beginning with whatever you do when somebody wakes up from a coma.

Where the heck is Cole? "Tom…?"

Grampie returns that angry glare at his son. "I might not be the youngest, but I'm not the stupidest either, Rob! I would like to say—"

Tom shrugs. "I dunno. It's not like I'm doing this every day, you know?"

Grampie carries on, unperturbed. "… is why I track my daughter-in-law's cell phone. And guess at which location I found her phone at when I went back to check a few days prior to Gwen's kidnapping?" He pauses for a sec and, a smug grin on his pale face. "Her location traced to the same shack Gwen was found in a couple of days later. Coincidence? I don't think so."

"Owen!" My mom stumbles a step back, as if the mere words have stolen her balance.

I suck in a sharp breath. "Whoa!" Grampie! He tracked her? I mean, I knew that since he gave me the heads-up of my parents' arrival, but he tracked her to the shack? That must have been when she took Tom to show—

Beep.

Beep.

Beep.

Beep.

"Oh my god!" Anna cries out once. "Cole! Cole! His EEG! His EEG!" She darts over to Cole, both hands on his chest shaking him as if to wake him. "Cole!"

I let go of a breath I didn't know I held. *Finally.* Maybe it took longer because he was stuck in the Realm longer?

The doctor curses once. "What the—?"

Claire falls over Cole in the bed, bawling, as I take another deep, long breath in.

Peace.

This is what peace feels like. The twins are back. I did my job. I paid my dues.

I fixed it.

Grampie's cold stare penetrates my mom. "… so I'm very much sure my daughter-in-law orchestrated Gwendolyn's kidnapping."

My dad, mom and everybody in the room are torn between the medical team taking care of Kai and Cole, and Grampie's accusations.

"Ridiculous." My mom shakes her head. "I apologize, Owen is borderline dement—"

"As demented as you are, my dear. And to clarify, I have handed the evidence over to the police. Judge Cortez was thrilled to have some movement brought into this case. In fact, I don't expect it to be much longer before they arrest you, Michelle." He glares at my mom.

"No," Tom whispers, "the money. Edan. If she's in jail, she can't—"

Dad, pale as a ghost, gawks. "Michelle?"

My mom presses her lips together. "One of my patients stole my cell—"

"Sure they did, Michelle. You were probably looking for it at the gas station they filmed you at."

Whoa. I'm stunned. Like, for reals. "Grampie!" Where's all that coming from?

Grampie straightens up, but only barely. He's white, pasty, and short of breath. The pulse in his neck hammers at an unhealthy pace, and yet his eyes spit fire. "I haven't trusted you in a while, my dear. Not since you tried to make Gwen look guilty."

"Look guil—"

"Hiding her away, making sure she doesn't remember. Talking about her being suicidal. And those pills you gave her, they weren't going to help her, were they?"

Dad supports Grampie, or he'd fall. He takes another stumbling step forward, not as threatening as he intended it to be. "They made her forget things instead of helping her."

My stomach plummets. What? No, I… They helped. Right? I didn't dream. I didn't—

The pieces fall into place. I didn't dream, but I also didn't remember anything. "The flashbacks," I whisper. They started when I didn't take my meds anymore. They were a sign of me getting better, not of me getting worse.

Mom puts her hands on her hips. "You don't know what you're talking about. It's sad to see you degrade so fast, Owen. Really sad. We should get you institutionalized—"

"Not necessary, my dear. Remember those pills you wanted Gwen to take? The newest of the new? Well, she didn't take them. But you left the container, and I did."

Pause.

"And I assume that's why I'm feeling like crap." He falters, and Dad barely catches him before his knees hit the floor.

"Hey! I need some help here. My dad—"

"Grampie!" I call out, covering my mouth with one palm. That crazy old man!

Two people from the medical team glance over and stop their work on Cole to help Grampie.

"Sir, we've got you."

"What did you say you took?"

Grampie's eyes bore into my mother's. "I don't know. What did I take, Michelle? It's supposed to be for mental health, but is it—" He grimaces. "—going to kill me? Boy, will the prosecution have a party with that one. Good thing—" Another grimace as he doubles over. "Good thing I gave Judge Cortez the remaining pills and my statement as well."

"What if she remembers me? After, I mean?"

The doc buckles up and drives us away from the gas station. "She won't, Tom."

Easy to say for her. "And if she does?"

She sighs. "I've got enough meds to suppress her memories. I'm her mom. Whatever I give her, she'll take. I know that's hard for you to believe, but we have the kind of relationship parents and their kids should have. The trusting kind, you know?"

Part of me feels envious, the other shocked. At least with my dad I know what I'm up against. With the doc, it seems that this Gwendolyn got more than she bargained for. Trusting kind, my butt.

I spin around to face a pale Tom. "That was part of the plan too?" Giving me meds under the pretense of helping me, but in reality making me forget? What the—

Grampie chokes and gags on his next breath and Dad falls down to his knees in front of him. "Dad! What did you do? Don't you dare die on me!"

Grampie smiles, barely. "Rob. It's okay. It's about damn time."

Dad twists on his knees without losing contact with Grampie. "Michelle! What was that pill? What the hell did you—?"

I fall on my knees next to Grampie's feet, a mirror image of my dad, my heart being ripped in two. No, no, no! "Grampie! You stupid, pigheaded old man! Why did you do that! Grampie!" I reach for him as Dad pulls Grampie up half-way onto his lap, supporting him.

My dad's voice breaks as he chokes on his next words. "Dad, no—"

"Take it from the mouth of a dying man—" Grampie sinks into my dad's arms. "There's more… to death… Calista was right."

"Do something!" Dad yells into the room. "For heaven's sake, do something!"

"Rob… it's okay… it's—"

"Grampie! Grampie, no!"

A strangulated gasp from Grampie, a gagging cough from Cole, a curse from my mother, a choked sound from Tom—and at the exact same moment when Kai and Cole open their eyes, Grampie closes his.

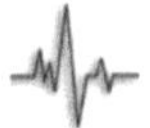

"Grampie." No. Please, no. I didn't even get to say good-bye, I—

Somebody hauls a medkit through my translucent form. "CPR? Or is he DNR?" Somebody feels for a pulse in Grampie's neck, finding none.

Dad cradles Grampie's head in his lap. Every breath comes out labored and heavy. "DNR," he chokes out. "Let him be. He doesn't want to be resuscitated."

Grampie's eyes pop open. "Hell no, I don't!"

For a moment I think it's happened. He acted all this out to get back at my mom, Grampie-style.

But Dad doesn't react. Neither does the medical personnel around them. They only nod solemnly and move away to give him space. "Sorry for your loss, sir."

"Why, thank you," Grampie replies and lifts out of his dead body. His eyes fall on me. "Gwennie."

My throat goes dry. "Grampie."

Grampie floats up and over to me, ignoring the others in the room. "This is real, right? I mean, not." He looks back at himself, lying in my dad's arms. Sorrow crosses his face. "I guess it is. Tell Rob and Doug I'm sorry I didn't give them more time, but I was long overdue."

I blink. Again. Again. "You died, Grampie." The room around me melts into nothingness. I don't hear Anna and Dave's crying next to their revived sons, I don't hear Cole's hoarse voice speaking for the first time in months, I don't see my mother trying to sneak out of the room.

My world focuses on Grampie, my one real and forever-friend in life, the one person who's always on my side. "You died."

A small smile lifts the corners of his mouth. "That I did." He helps me up to standing, wraps his arms around me and pulls me into a big hug. "But you shouldn't be here, Gwennie.

You need to leave."

"I can't, Grampie." I return the hug. It feels… normal. Like it used to. He even smells the same.

"Yes, you can." He pulls away and holds me at an arm's length. "And you must. This is no place for you yet. Go home, Gwennie."

"No, I can't. My soul released Kai's, and for mine—"

"Mine entered." Grampie turns all serious.

"What?" Hold on a second. "You planned this?" Hope extends a tiny tendril and wraps it around my heart. "How—?"

He gives me a sheepish shrug. "*Planned* implies too much foresight, but I would say I acted spontaneously with a certain outcome in mind after Calista called me."

"Calista." Called. And Grampie picked up. Eighth wonder of the world, right there.

"Correct, Calista. Let's just say my point of view has been adjusted over the last few days, and rightfully so, it appears. Anyway." He squeezes my shoulders once. "I'd like you to go back now, Gwen."

"Nu-uh." Tom shoulders past me next to Grampie. "We kind of have a deal here. Ain't happening."

That tiny tendril of hope withers away and dies.

Grampie doesn't seem impressed. "You must be Tom. The unfortunate soul who got caught in my daughter-in-law's scheming."

Tom raises a surprised eyebrow. "That's one way of putting it."

Grampie lets go of me. "You have every right be angry, but you should be angry at Michelle, not Gwen. She is a victim, just like you."

For the longest time Tom doesn't reply. The apple in his throat moves up and down with a hard swallow. "I… I see where you're coming from."

"Then you wouldn't mind letting my granddaughter go, I assume?"

Tom scratches his head and steps from one foot onto the other. "Actually, I would. She's still the one who killed me."

"And you planned to drug and scare her. You killed her friend. Can you really say you blame her for defending herself?"

Tom drops his gaze to the floor. "I…" He swallows once. "I didn't want to kill Sarah. I didn't want to hurt Gwen either. I… it… the drugs—"

Grampie's gaze softens. "I know. You didn't stand a chance. Michelle wanted you to take those pills, because she knew they'd get you high and out of control. Nothing worked better for her than an untrustworthy druggie to blame. You dying played right into her hands. One less witness, one less deal to uphold. Only it would've been better for her had Gwendolyn died as well. She might've even bargained for both of your deaths from the very start, who knows."

He lets go of me and lays a hand on Tom's shoulder. "I'll make you a suggestion, Tom. Let Gwen go. And Gwen, when you're back, help Edan. You know nobody else will."

Tom's eyes pop wide. "How do you know—"

"Pays to have a sister who's a medium."

And pays to know your granddaughter. Grampie winks at me. "I think you'd feel bad if Edan was the next person on your mother's list of victims, albeit by omission."

I nod so fast, dizziness swamps me. "I wouldn't want that." At this point I'm pretty sure my mother wouldn't have cared about Edan. Maybe she never intended to uphold her part of the deal, like Grampie said. But even if she initially planned to, it would bring up questions if she sent a lump of money to the little brother of her daughter's kidnapper and Sarah's murderer.

Yeah. She wouldn't have taken care of Edan.

Tom whips his head around at me. "You wouldn't?" He sounds surprised and… maybe a bit hopeful. The tiniest bit.

Whatever itsy bitsy bit of hope survived inside myself flexes its muscles like a pro-wrestler. "No, I wouldn't. Tom—"

"Will the doc go into prison?" His voice is soft. Low.

"For a very long time. Made sure of that." Grampie nods.

Tom closes his eyes, and when he opens them, something new shines from them, and it mirrors my own: hope. "Would you… would you do that? Help Edan? After what I did—"

"Yes." My answer comes without a second thought and it feels good, especially after using Tom's love for his brother as leverage to get me into the Realm. I wonder if Grampie knew about that as well. It would be so like him, Mayor-style, meddling in things until they're right, or at least somewhat right. And it would be total Grampie-style to cross *all* of my mom's evil schemes, because let's be honest: She never cared about Edan. Or Tom. Or, well, me.

Unbelievable what a deranged personality was hidden behind the façade of the woman I love like a real mom. *Loved.* Past tense, I guess, because she really is to blame for all this mess.

Without her, Tom and I never would've met. Without her giving him the drugs and tempting him he never would've taken them. He never would've killed Sarah, and I never would've killed him. The way it is, we both have sinned, and we both have to pay for that. But, his brother hasn't, and he shouldn't be the one to suffer from our actions. "I promise, Tom."

A heartbeat passes as our gazes lock, and for that heartbeat, the hardness in his expression softens, giving way to the boy who danced across the living room to me. "Then it's a deal," he whispers, nodding once.

A cold draft of air—and he's gone.

Grampie's smile widens. "Go home, Gwennie. Go and live life. Don't come back here until it's time, promise me."

Tears fill my eyes. "I promise, Grampie. I love you." I love this stupid, pigheaded old man who gave his life to save mine. "Thank you."

"I love you too, and anytime, Gwennie-girl. Grandfathers are supposed to die before their grandkids." One more hug. "Now get out of here, I've gotta find Grammie." He winks at me, and I swipe a tear from my eye.

"Bye, Grampie."

"Bye, Gwennie-girl."

Here's hoping my body is still alive in the real world. I close my eyes and think of Kai, of being with him, of holding his hand, of being alive, of being inside my body, of—

A cold draft of air, the short sensation of falling—

Then, everything turns black.

Chapter Thirty-Four

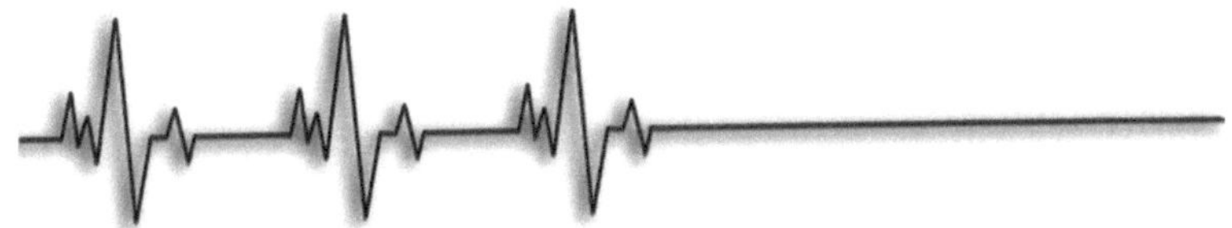

Funeral

The weather is surprisingly nice, considering it's a cold winter day in Kampton, Oregon.

Northern Oregon.

The sun's peeking out from behind the clouds just in time to warm up our little congregation assembled around the freshly dug grave in front of us. And when I say little congregation, I mean crowd. Besides Mrs. Matthews and our family, including Calista, the Harrisons and Dora, I know nobody. The whole town is here to pay their respects to their former mayor.

"… and may the Lord accept him in good grace and grant him eternal life." The pallbearers lower Grampie's coffin down into the grave.

Next to me, my dad sniffles. He's been taking it hard. Very hard. Seeing his father die in front of him from a medication his soon-to-be-divorced wife wanted to kill his daughter with—that's going to be years of psychotherapy. Years.

Could be worse though, because as it is, Calista has helped quite a bit. It's been three weeks since Grampie's death, and Calista has been talking to one or the other O'Karran-family members on any given day since then. Plus, the occasional Harrison-twin. I guess we all have things to process, and Calista understands. Maybe better than any of us. After all, she was the one who stuck her head into the Realm and found out about Claire and Tom's plan. She was the one to find out my mom was in it to win it. And she was the one telling Grampie all about it.

From there on, things developed a life of their own. Grampie, after hearing about Tom's involvement with my mom, had an epiphany and checked the tracking program on Mom's cell, which led to his discovery of her whereabouts a couple of days prior to Sarah's and my kidnapping. Then, having been Kampton's well-respected mayor for decades, Grampie contacted his friend Carl, who happens to own a chain of gas stations along the West Coast, from Canada to Mexico. He asked for video surveillance for that specific date, and lo and behold, Carl pulled something from the cloud—my mom and Tom. For once fate and coincidence were on our side.

So yeah, all Grampie needed was the ear of another good old friend, Judge Cortez. Once he'd had a good look at the evidence the judge put his ducks in a row to get my mom arrested.

Grampie could've let things be at that point, but no, he had to test his theory about Mom wanting to kill me and get himself killed in the process.

Thickheaded old man.

But hey, his plan worked. Mom is going to be behind bars for a very, very long time. And, on yet another positive note, all charges against me have been dropped. I would like to think my mom gave a full confession because she wanted to exonerate me, but I'm pretty sure it was at the recommendation of her lawyer and in an attempt to reduce her sentence.

Somebody sneaks their hand into mine and squeezes it. Kai. "I'm going to miss your Grampie," he whispers for only me to hear.

"Me, too." Although I'm much more at peace at this funeral than at Grammie's a couple of years ago, thanks to my newly acquired intimate knowledge about the afterlife's functioning.

A cold draft, the temperature dropping, the cemetery losing all color—

Kai's hand tightens around mine as Cole sucks in a sharp breath. He's not quite as used to this as Kai and me at this point, although he's also gotten the benefit of my grandparents' visits here and there over the last weeks.

Materializing next to the grave, Grampie looks down at his coffin. "Bye, frail old shell. Thanks for the ride."

Grammie elbows him in the side. "Behave, Owen. It's a funeral."

"What? It's my funeral." Grampie protests with his hands on his hips, and right he is. He gives Grammie a kiss on the cheek and comes over to me while the pastor drones on about eternal life, etc. etc. "Shh, kiddo. I checked in on Edan. He is doing well."

I know that. First thing I did after waking up in some intensive care unit—thanks, Officer Kleinman for that one—and getting cleared of my charges—thank you, Grampie, for that one—was talk to my associate at the bank, then to child protective services. They found Edan a nice foster family the next county over, and the money I transferred into his bank account will make sure he can go to college. And he will go to college, I'll keep an eye on that.

Grampie turns and points to the far right. "And this one is also doing much better."

I throw a careful glance over to the trees, where Tom leans against a big, old oak.

Tom, and— "Is that Claire?" I whisper. Cole twitches the slightest when he hears her name.

"Correct." Grampie beams. "They're helping each other. Nice kid, by the way. Every day a bit more."

Every day, my mom's influence on him wanes, he means. With my mom in prison for most likely the next couple of decades, he has tons of time to haunt her if he wanted to, although I doubt he wants to see her again. Not that I'm a psychiatrist, but I did have many a session on PTSD and working through emotional trauma, and I'd say for Tom, Claire could be a better help than getting revenge. I'm pretty sure Tom's a good guy at baseline who got crappy cards dealt to him. We were all pawns in a game played around us, with Tom and Sarah paying the highest price.

Speaking of. "How's Sarah?"

"Getting better at making a connection. You might see her soon." Grammie pats my forearm. Apparently, it's like Calista said and not quite so easy for a spirit to connect with a soul still alive, especially when you're not related. But Sarah has been practicing, and Grammie and Calista are optimistic she's going to have it nailed in no time thanks to that tiny piece of me that stayed in the realm when I entered. Makes for a good anchor.

The funeral progresses at the usual slow pace. When it's our time, Kai and I walk forward and throw a handful of rose petals onto Grampie's coffin down in the grave.

"One more please," Grampie grumps next to me. "I rather like that color down there."

I suppress a grin—because, let's be honest, grinning at your grandfather's funeral could invoke another round of psychotherapy I neither want nor need—and add a second handful.

"Thank you, dear."

"Now let Gwennie be in peace, Owen." Grammie winks at me. "Don't worry, honey, he won't be by all the time. Once in a while though, now that we know the connection is there." She smooths over my hair.

"That would be nice," I whisper under my breath and let Kai lead me away from the grave. Before we leave the cemetery, we stop and look back.

My dad and Uncle Doug are still at the grave, heads bent, lost in thought. Grampie and Grammie stand right next to them, and I could swear, the moment Grammie wraps her fingers around my dad's, Dad lifts his head and looks around, a confused look on his face.

"Did you see that?" Kai whispers.

I nod. "Yeah. I guess… I guess they're never truly gone."

"We would know, wouldn't we?" He squeezes my hand and gives me a smile, one of those that make me lose my sanity.

"We're kind of the experts." I lift his hand to my mouth and drop a kiss on his knuckles.

"But I don't mind waiting for another death until it's time for real." Kai shudders. "Been there, done that."

I throw another glance into the direction of the forest, and this time, Tom catches it. For a moment, our eyes connect. Eventually he nods once, lifts a hand in greeting, and disappears together with Claire.

Seven months after my mother got him into a mess that would make him a murderer and take his life, he looks like he could have a chance at peace.

I take a deep breath of cool, fresh air.

Same here.

Peace.

I pull on Kai's hand. "Come on. Hot chocolate. You, too." I yank Cole by the sleeve.

"Actually…" He gives us a sheepish smile. "Actually, I'm going to meet with Claire's parents."

"Oh?" Kai tilts his head.

Cole scratches his head. "I mean, I haven't seen them since her funeral, me being in… a coma, and all. I think we'd all like to talk about Claire."

"Good things?" Kai sounds skeptical.

"Yes, good things."

"Despite… everything? And *him*?" He jerks his chin to the forest. Tom. He means Tom.

Cole sighs. "Yes. What am I supposed to do? Let's be realistic. Neither of us are going to stay alone until the next time we meet." When Cole is hopefully like a hundred years old. Huh. That'll be weird when they meet—teenage-Claire and Grandpa Cole.

Kai salutes. "Brother, I've got to give it to you. You're way more understanding than I could ever—hey!" Kai ducks as Cole slaps him across the head.

"Shut up, Butthead. You got the short end of the stick with this whole deal, I know. For me… yes, I was sad I was gone. I missed everybody. You, too, weirdly enough. But I had Claire."

"Who should've let you go—"

Cole holds up a hand. "Yes, she should've. And I can mourn half a year of my life as lost, or I can take the knowledge of the afterlife I have *thanks to her* and live my life more at peace. And honestly, I chose the latter, which is why I need to get going. Claire's mom baked cake." He gives Kai another slap over the head. "Don't be so narrow-minded. All's well."

As he walks away from us toward the parking area and a couple in their early fifties, Kai sighs. "He really is the more reasonable of the two of us." He looks after his brother with a look of disbelief—loving disbelief, but still.

I cuddle closer to him. "He might be the more reasonable of you two, but if you weren't the butt-headed one, Cole would still be in the Realm." If Kai hadn't tried to quote-unquote kill himself, I wouldn't have saved him, and we'd never have gotten this whole thing started.

"Huh. True." Kai rubs his knuckles over my head. "Bull's eye, Gwen. Smart deduction. There's a reason I lo—I like you." His cheeks take on a pinkish hue, while my heart skips a beat.

"Did you just say what I think you said?" I bite my lower lip.

"What? Me? Naah." Kai waves off my comment, but his red cheeks say it all.

I throw my arms around his neck. "Well then. Same here, butt-head." I rub my nose against his.

Kai grasps the back of my neck and lowers his mouth to mine in a soft kiss. There's something so infinitely sweet and warm in his kiss, it lights me up on the inside and shines into every broken part of my soul, stitching it back together. He coaxes my lips apart with his tongue, and the light turns into fire—soul-burning fire.

Me likey.

Maybe we shouldn't be kissing at a funeral, but what's more life-affirming than—

"Gwen?"

My dad's voice is soft enough we don't quite jump away from each other, but it still brings the kiss to a screeching halt. We pull apart, although Kai never lets go of my hand. He pulls himself to his full height, shoulders straight and everything.

I clear my voice. "Yes, Dad?"

My dad looks at the hat he's holding in his hands. "I was wondering… I mean, I'd like to sit down and talk with you. Or, maybe, a cup of tea and some cake? Marble cake? Since Grampie, you know, that was his favorite…?"

Is this my dad asking to spend time with me? We haven't

really talked since that day, and mainly because he was busy. Not that I expected anything else, but to be fair, it was all related to either the murder investigation, divorce, or funeral. On the other hand, if it hadn't been for that, I bet he'd have spent most days at the Kampton branch of MSC, let's be honest.

"Or, I don't know, maybe later, Gwennie?" Dad plays with the rim of his hat between his fingers.

Kai and I exchange a look, and he gives me the slightest nod. Oh, whatever. Why not. We've all made mistakes. My dad's was focusing on his work and turning me into the prodigy I didn't want to be. Mine was jumping to conclusions and letting him get away with his actions. Guess we do have lots to talk about. I give him a smile. "Sure, Dad. That'd be nice."

His face lights up like it used to, when I was younger and he skipped a day of work and let me play hooky, so we could spend it together. "Wonderful. Why don't we take my car—" His phone rings and it takes all the self-control I have to not roll my eyes. His father's funeral—and he didn't even turn off his cell.

Dad takes the cell from his coat's pocket, thumb hovering over the screen.

My fingers squish Kai's so hard, he winces. Of course, work would call. Of course, Dad would prioritize work over family. Nothing has changed, and maybe it never will.

Who. Cares.

"Come on, let's go." This is pointless. As always.

I turn and pull on Kai's hand, but he won't budge. "What?" I give him an annoyed look.

Kai nods his chin at my dad—my dad, staring onto the

screen with an intense expression on his face. For a moment he seems frozen in time, unmoving, like a still frame.

And then he rejects the call with a push of his thumb.

"Where was I?" He slides the phone back into his pocket. "Right, marble cake." He wraps one arm around my shoulders and squeezes them as he guides me toward the parking area. "Kai, I hope you like it, too. I can't have my daughter's boyfriend not like our family cake." He chuckles, and Kai's eyes pop as wide as mine. I stumble over a small root, because I'm not watching where I'm going. Did that just happen? Did Dad… did he actually choose me over work?

Kai catches himself faster than me. "Yes, sir. I'm pretty optimistic I'm going to like it." He swipes his thumb across the back of my hand.

Dad chatters on and on, but I only half listen. I'm busy digesting this new, foreign sensation. I think it's called happiness. Hey, there. Long time no see.

A small chuckle breaks free, and in response, Dad squeezes my shoulder once more, and Kai my hand. My heart turns into mush.

Whoa.

This really is happiness. Welcome back, old friend.

Over by my dad's car, Grampie and Grammie wait for us. Grammie gives Dad a loving look, while Grampie gives me two thumbs up. Right he is.

Kai catches the gesture and winks at my Grampie, the only move he can make without my dad wondering what's wrong with his daughter's boyfriend.

Before I get into the car, I pause and look back to

Grampie's grave under a mountain of flowers, then to my dad and Kai opening their doors and sliding into their seats.

Fate is an odd teacher, sometimes. For the last seven months I stood with one foot in the grave. Fate has shown me what happens when you step in completely, and while the experience has taught me death isn't worth fearing, it has also taught me that life is worth living.

I let my gaze drift over to Sarah's mom talking to Calista.

I regret every moment, every decision that led to her death. The guilt is still there, not as strong as before I found out about Mom's scheming, but it's there. Will be for the rest of my life, I assume. What has changed though is my commitment to life. I've taken a big step away from the grave I had one foot in for the longest time. That's the lesson I'm proudest to have learned: Death is not worth living for.

A smile crosses my face as I open my door and slide into the seat next to Kai.

He reaches for my hand and weaves his fingers between mine.

My heart skips a happy beat ahead and my smile widens to epic proportions.

Yeah.

I'm ready to be living.

About the Author

Micky O'Brady is a pediatrician-turned-writer living in beautiful, dry Southern California with her husband and two critters (one son, one dog). Micky loves to write YA thrillers and sci-fi with a romantic twist, mainly because she wishes her life had been such an awesome mix of action and cute guys when she was a teen.

When she isn't up at around 3 a.m. (with a cup of tea, Earl Grey, hot) drafting stories she can't get out of her head, she can be found at a martial arts dojo, though maybe not at 3 a.m. She holds a first degree black belt in Krav Maga and a second degree black belt in Judo, and is convinced every girl should know how to kick some butt.

Micky also is a firm believer in the healing powers of Nutella eaten straight from the glass and in the magic that can happen on a rainy day, as long as there are fuzzy socks and a cup of hot tea involved.

Her previous publications include a doctoral thesis and several medical articles as well as a medical book about emergency communication. None of them are as fun to read as her YA novels though. Her first YA-novel, THE PRESIDENT'S DAUGHTER, and its sequel TRIAL BY ICE, are published by Curiosity Quills and available through all major retailers, such as Amazon, B&N, Kobo, and Smashwords.

Through Snowy Wings Publishing Micky is the author of the YA-sci-fi romance BETWEEN WORLDS, a super-cool contemporary romance-slash-pro-wrestling-story PLAYING WITH #FIRE, as well as another sci-fi romance, TIME WARPED, and its sequel TIME BOUND.